THE WINGED MAN

THE WINGED MAN

Moyra Caldecott

HEADLINE

First published in 1993
by HEADLINE BOOK PUBLISHING PLC

Reprinted in this edition in 1993
by HEADLINE BOOK PUBLISHING PLC

10 9 8 7 6 5 4 3 2 1

British Library Cataloguing in Publication Data

Caldecott, Moyra
Winged Man
I.   Title
823.914 [F]

ISBN 0–7472–0612–0

Printed and bound in Great Britain by
Clays Ltd, St Ives PLC

HEADLINE BOOK PUBLISHING PLC
Headline House
79 Great Titchfield Street
London W1P 7FN

For my brother who loved flying
and died winged
and for my family and friends,
visible and invisible . . .

Contents

THE WINGED MAN

Introduction

There is a tradition that there was a king in ancient Britain called Bladud, son of King Hudibras and father of King Lear, who lived some time between 800 and 500 BC. His story even today is honoured in the Somerset area of Bath, where many of the dramatic events of his life were said to have taken place.

It is said he was descended from Brutus who, in turn, was descended from Aeneas, the Dardanian prince who fled to Italy after the Trojans were defeated by the Greeks in the war Homer describes in *The Iliad*. Brutus came to Britain (the Pretanic Isles) with his wife, who was a Greek princess, and together they founded the impressive dynasty to which, after several generations, Bladud belonged. As High King, ruling from his capital Trinovantum, New Troy, now known as London, he inherited the traditions his ancestors had brought from Troy, Italy and Greece, but he was living among and ruling a people who were a mixture of the ancient peoples of the land and Celtic immigrants.

It is unknown when exactly the first Celts from continental Europe came to Britain, bringing with them what has come to be known as the Iron Age – but it is usually assumed it was in the eighth to the seventh centuries BC. Artifacts have been found in Britain, from this time, attributable to the Celts which may have come in by trade or by immigration. But artifacts alone cannot give us a full picture of a period in prehistory. It is often necessary to look at the living myths and legends of a people handed down by word of mouth through generations to supplement the fragments found in

ix

the soil by archaeologists. The author of this book has looked
closely at such myths and legends.

1

The Game of Fidchell

The night was drawing closer. The birds winging home in flocks alerted the prince to the danger. Soon the western sky would be fired with glowing gold as the sun left the Lands of the Living and, in a blaze of regal magnificence, visited the Lands of the Dead. Left behind would be a cold, dark world where only malevolent beings, murderers, robbers, wolves and owls – the scavengers of the night – dared move about. All others would gather close against the hearth, with wooden doors made fast against unknown terrors.

Prince Bladud urged his tired steed forward, anxious to reach the hill-fort before nightfall and before the gates were locked and barred. He could see the hill now, rising high above the plain and topped with steep, smooth, man-made ramparts. The forests had been cleared in the immediate vicinity so that the watchman on the ramparts had a long, clear view of any enemies approaching. Bladud had no doubt that at this very moment he himself was being observed, the summer dust from his horse's hooves drawing interested attention.

The shadows of the trees on the plain were stretched dark and long across fields unnaturally bright by contrast. He could hear the herdboys shouting to the cattle as they drove them in to shelter for the night. The first hearth fires were being lit, and thin plumes of smoke rose from one or two of the clustered homesteads on the plain. The lord of the fort, Keron son of Mel, was obviously not anticipating any attack or the alarm would have been sounded and these homesteads

1

would have been deserted, their inhabitants already clustered in makeshift tents within the safe confines of the hilltop fort, their animals lowing uneasily in unfamiliar pens.

The strangely intense light of the evening seemed to isolate every blade of grass, every flower, every rock and bush. There was a splendour and a glory about more precious than the gold so coveted by kings and so laboriously won from the earth. At this moment of transformation from day to night, it was as though all things had paused – poised – breath-holding in awe at the delicate, fragile balance of mystery on which our lives depended. In this light small men were giants, birds were harbingers, and all were suddenly uncertain of their own role in the universe. Bladud wondered at himself. What was he doing so far from home? What was he seeking? Who, indeed, *was* he? A man awakened – or a man dreaming?

The watchman called to him from the tower beside the great wooden gate. Bladud felt it all unreal – and unreal his reply.

'Bladud, Prince of Trinovantum, son of Hudibras the High King,' he called back. But who was he really – and why did he feel that the name he gave was that of a stranger?

He was now on the steep incline rising up to the gate, and armed men were coming out to meet him. He was surrounded, challenged, greeted and accepted. Bladud of Trinovantum, son of Hudibras, rode in to the hilltop fort of Keron son of Mel. The huge gates of oak crashed closed behind him. The bolts were drawn against the night.

The prince noted the jumble of little hovels of twigs and straw that lined the streets winding up to the great house, the sullen people who drew aside and flattened themselves against walls to avoid his horse's hooves. The place had none of the grandeur of his father's rath. There seemed no order to it. Smoke rose through ragged and rotting thatch and hung in the air unwholesomely. The smell was foul. Goats and pigs and children ran in and out of the huts – occasionally pursued by an adult wielding a stick. *What kind of master is this who allows such filth and disorder in his realm?* Bladud could not help wondering, comparing it with his father's fortified town where every house was in good repair and there was separate fenced space for the animals. The children back home would

2

greet any strangers with bright and curious eyes, and the smoke rose in neat columns from well constructed hearths to dissipate far above the town.

Leading his horse by the bridle, the young man plodded on, looking neither to left nor right. A woman leaning in the doorway of a hovel shouted something to him, and Bladud glanced with disgust at the creature, her hair a dirty tangle, her clothes stiff with muck. She made a rude gesture after his retreating back. Three children, so thin they looked ready to die of starvation, emerged from the darkness behind her and clung to her skirt, staring after him with hollow eyes. He began to wish he had not made such haste to reach this fort, but had instead spent the night in the fields or the forest. Wolves and night hawks would seem preferable companions, and one would as likely risk attack by robbers here as there.

Rounding a corner of the mean street, he found himself for the first time in an open space – and before him stood the house of Keron. What a contrast to the rest! Its walls were solid oak like the main gate, and it rose high above the untidy, sprawling village at its feet. Guards stood at the door and torches were already lit on either side, though the darkness of the night had not yet fallen. *This place feels as though it would be dark – even on the sunniest day*, Bladud thought, and glanced up at the sky. It was the colour of blood.

The guards exchanged words with his guide as he dismounted. He looked anxiously over his shoulder as his steed was led away, wondering if these men knew how to care for such a noble horse. But before he could intervene, a tall, thickset man appeared – the lord Keron himself. Clad in fine linen and well decked with gold and jewels, he extended his hand in greeting. Bladud had met him before at his father's court, for he was one of the many vassal lords who came to the High King's castle to deliver tribute. Was that torc of slender yellow gold around his thick red neck the same one given to him only last year by King Hudibras? Bladud had not paid him much attention then – he was only one of the many who pitched their tents around his father's rath at festival.

Prince Bladud was weary and longed to retire to bed, but the

Lord Keron was delighted with such distinguished company and was determined to make much of him. He insisted a feast must be prepared, which was not ready before midnight, and during all that time, growing hungrier and more exhausted by the moment, Bladud was forced to listen to endless anecdotes of Keron's prowess in battle or in single combat; Keron's cunning in dealing with his rivals.

Bladud soon learned a great deal about this petty ruler, and the more he learned the more he distrusted him; but, bound by the strict rules of accepting hospitality, he could not break away or speak his mind.

Casting around in desperation for something to distract him from the boredom that was beginning to smother him, his eyes fell on a young girl, Keron's daughter Rheinid, whose duty it was to serve the honoured guest with mead. Her hair was as black as a raven's wing, loosely bound away from her face but tumbling in a thick cascade down her back. She never spoke a word to him, but her dark and flashing eyes left him in no doubt that she found him desirable. He began to watch her every move, fascinated by the way she advanced and retreated – one moment boldly challenging him, the next, with long lashes lowered, playing demure and untouchable. She was dressed in fine russet-coloured cloth, with jewels on her arms and around her neck. Even her hair was clasped with gold. She moved with the grace of a cat and as the evening wore on, and as Bladud consumed more mead than he intended, he contrived to touch her arm and then her thigh as she leant over him to pour the heavy liquid. He did not notice the satisfied curl on Keron's lips as he talked on and on, watching every move and every changing expression on the young man's face.

At last the feast was ready, and servants entered the hall with plates and bowls and huge quantities of food. Bladud found the sudden smell of roasts and herbs almost unbearable; he had eaten little all day and was ravenous. As though Keron was deliberately torturing him he strung out the formalities of seating the various members of his household as long as possible, changing his mind several times as to where the honoured guest should sit. Eventually he decided that Bladud should take his own great carved chair at the head of the table, because, as son of the High King, he should take precedence over his humble self.

Bladud protested politely, but with no conviction – desperate to get the matter settled, and some food in his stomach. But Keron pretended to take his protest seriously, and once again the seating arrangements were changed.

Bladud bit his lip and moved his position once more. As he sat down, anger was forming a hard knot inside him and it would not take much more for him to forget the rules governing guest and host.

Suddenly he felt the cool and soothing touch of a hand on his neck, and turned his head to find Rheinid close behind him.

'My lord,' she whispered, 'forgive him. He entertains few such honoured guests.' *I wonder that he has any guests*, Bladud thought bitterly, determined never to set foot again in this miserable place. But the girl's full lips were now close to his face as she leaned over him, her breast pressing against his shoulder . . .

'Rheinid,' Keron said smoothly, 'sit now and enjoy the feast with us.' He gestured her to sit at the prince's left hand, the position usually occupied by a man's wife. The look in his eye left no doubt in Bladud's mind that Keron was throwing them together deliberately and he flushed. He felt tired, he was hungry, but he was also young and virile, and, at this moment, torn by conflicting emotions.

First light was already creeping over the hills and the first birds were stirring in their nests before Keron at last let Bladud leave the feasting hall. All stood up around the long table, eyes on the youth and the young girl, as their liege lord ordered her to show the High King's son to his bed. Dazed with exhaustion though he was, Bladud did not miss the ripple of lecherous amusement that passed around those present. Was he expected, after all he'd been through, to bed this woman?

Rheinid raised a lamp above her head and turned towards him, smiling. She looked beautiful and seductive, but he felt only a desperate urge to sleep. He followed her, staggering slightly with weariness and too much mead, and had to

5

steady himself more than once against the walls. Later he could not be sure whether in reality he was led deeper and deeper into some labyrinth or whether he was dreaming. The sun's golden light might be unchaining the world from darkness outside and a million living creatures might be freely on the move, but inside Keron's castle no beam penetrated. The lamplight flickered in the stale, thick air while grotesque shadowy shapes clustered at his back. It seemed to Bladud that they walked and walked, twisting and turning down corridor after corridor, their footsteps covering an area that must surely be ten times the size of the whole hill-fort, let alone the castle. Staggering, he sank to his knees, determined not to move another step but to sleep where he was on the cold flagstones, greasy with dirt. He was vaguely aware of the girl kneeling beside him urging him to rise. He felt her arms around him, attempting to pull him to his feet. His eyes seemed to close under lead weights, and he felt as though he was falling into a deep and bottomless pit. Her voice came to him from far away – hollow and echoing. Then he was aware of nothing more.

He awoke to find himself naked on a bed in a windowless room, two lamps providing the only light. Beside him, curled against his side, lay Rheinid, also naked. He raised himself on one elbow to look down at her, struggling from sleep like a swimmer who had almost drowned.

Had they . . . ? He could not remember. Her cheek was flushed from sleep, her hair soft against his chest. Almost without meaning to he ran his hand lightly over the curve of her hip – his own body instantly fired by the touch. She stirred and turned and, half asleep, they made love.

Bladud had never experienced such ecstasy, but it was short-lived. When it was over he felt fully awake and sober, remembering the details of the night before. What kind of father would offer his daughter so blatantly to a stranger? *A scheming father*, he thought; one who wanted some advantage from the High King. Bladud felt sickened to think how easily he had fallen into this trap.

Had Rheinid knowingly played her part? Was the smile on her lips one of sexual satisfaction, or something more

6

sinister? He could not read her expression. They had been as intimate as only man and woman could be, but now they were strangers.

He drew away roughly and stood up, turning his back on her as he pulled on his clothes. Now he could not wait to leave this place! The exquisite pleasure of a few moments earlier was gone, and in its place was all the unease and disgust he had felt the night before.

'My lord . . . ?'

But he could not bring himself to look at her. This liaison had not been of his making, and he was angered by his own weakness. If he looked at her now he would see her beauty and would feel unsure again. He would be once more vulnerable – out of control.

He felt a surge of anger, bitterness and, perhaps, fear. He had to get away from here. Far away.

He lifted one of the lamps from its stand and left the room without a backward glance. It was a very different young man who strode through the corridors now, demanding imperiously of the first servant he met that he be taken at once to his horse. When the man hesitated, Bladud drew his dagger.

Bladud had intended to leave without a word to his host, but Keron appeared as he reached the great front door, and saw the unwilling servant still held at knife-point.

'My lord prince, what is this? Stealing out like a thief?' Keron's voice was suddenly cold, his eyes narrowed dangerously as he looked from the dagger in Bladud's hand to the youth's embarrassed face. Bladud sheathed his knife, but responded sternly.

'My lord, I had a dream that I was held prisoner in this place – that I was forced to play a role I had no stomach for.'

'And you would insult me and abuse my servants because of a dream?'

'The dream was most convincing, my lord.'

'But nevertheless only a dream,' Keron said.

Bladud lowered his eyes beneath the dark and penetrating gaze of the older man. Perhaps he had indeed imagined the sinister aspects of what had occurred in this place. It was natural for a host to feast an honoured guest until the small hours of the morning, so perhaps there had been no plot to force Rheinid upon him. Had he misinterpreted all the hints and looks that had so disquieted him?

Perhaps he himself had dragged the girl to his bed in a drunken stupor. After all it was he who had instigated the love-making on waking. He was suddenly ashamed – and Keron was quick to exploit his youth and inexperience.

'Prince Bladud,' he said quickly, the icy menace of his voice now overlaid by smiling obsequiousness, 'your dream insults me, but I will not take offence. Come. A meal is prepared. Let us go in.'

'I . . . I am not hungry, my lord,' Bladud stammered. 'I thank you for your generosity, but I need to be on my way.'

'What! So late in the day?'

Bladud looked puzzled. Was it not morning?

'The sun is already setting,' Keron said. 'You have slept the whole day.'

Another night in this place! Bladud thought in despair. Every instinct told him to flee, but the web encircling him was so subtle he could not even be sure that it was there.

'I would prefer to go, my lord,' he repeated, making an effort to be decisive. But Keron had already taken him by the arm and was leading him back into the great hall.

That night Keron challenged the prince to a board game. At first Bladud wondered if this vassal king was regretting the previous night and trying to make amends in some way, for a man who played so ineptly should surely not wager such generous stakes. The young prince won game after game, and each time he was rewarded with gold and jewels, weapons and horses. At first there were only a few members of the household watching, but, as the evening wore on, more and more gathered round the table until a hedge of faces seemed to isolate them from the rest of the world.

Halfway through the evening Rheinid slipped in to take the place of the servant pouring the wine. Time and again he covered his goblet with a hand to indicate that he wanted no more wine – but no matter how often he sipped at it, his vessel was always full.

8

'I am at a loss, my lord, to suggest what stake would be appropriate now, since you have all but ruined me,' Keron said, at last.

'Only on your insistence, sir, for I had no intention of doing so. I suggest we quit now. I am weary and I must make an early start in the morning.'

'One more game, I beg of you, my lord. Just one more, and then we will all go to bed.'

There was a drunken murmur of assent from the men who were pressing close around them. Eyes red with wine and ale, Keron's entourage had watched every move in silence. Bladud felt their hostility towards him growing palpably.

Perhaps one more game, he thought. The concession might pacify them.

'One more game,' he agreed aloud. 'You choose the stake.'

Bladud fancied that a sigh passed through the watching crowd.

'Will you abide by whatever stake I choose?' Keron asked very quietly, and Bladud, if he had not drunk so much or felt so confident, would have been warned by something in that voice.

'Of course,' he said, anxious only to finish the game.

Keron stared at him closely.

'If you win, a year from today you can come to me and demand anything it is in my power to give you. But if you lose, a year from today you will grant *me* what I ask of you.'

Bladud was already setting up the board.

'I agree,' he said wearily. 'Your move first, this time.'

Up until now Keron had made foolish mistakes in the game, but this time – this time with such a dangerously open-ended stake – he moved decisively and with consummate skill. Within a very short time indeed, Bladud knew that he was in trouble and, struggling against the fog induced in his mind by too much wine, he fought to regain the ground he was so rapidly losing.

'My game, I think,' Keron said triumphantly, his voice barely disguising his feelings at having executed the plot so well.

As Bladud looked at the board in disbelief, he barely heard

9

the wild and discordant cheering of the crowd behind him. What had he promised? He had hardly paid attention to the stake proposed by Keron, so sure he was that he would continue to win. But perhaps it would not turn out so ill: the man would doubtless demand gold and jewels, and although his father would chide him for his carelessness, Bladud did not anticipate his refusing to honour his son's debt.

'I see you are a better player than at first appeared,' Bladud said ruefully. 'I will gladly give you back here and now all that you have lost to me, and more, rather than have you wait a year for your prize.'

'I am in no hurry,' said Keron with a smile. 'A year will suit me very well.' And he rose and stretched as a cat does after a satisfying sleep, raising one fist on high to indicate his victory. As a roar of delight shook the hall, Bladud turned to go – and found Rheinid waiting at his shoulder.

Not again! he thought, but nevertheless he went along with her. And this night he made love to her knowingly before he went to sleep. She was passionate, and it was good, but he still could not shake off the feeling that somehow she, and not he, was in control . . .

When he thought it must be near morning, he rose, and, with determination, left the castle.

This time no one tried to stop him. The guards drew back the bolts without his having to instruct them. His horse was ready and waiting. It was so easy.

As he rode through the great oaken gates and into the golden, singing countryside, he felt uneasily that something had gone from him – that something of himself had been left behind as hostage . . .

2

Journey Between the Worlds

Bladud soon found himself in a landscape of gently rolling
chalk hills – of soft, feminine curves, where the forests had
been almost completely cleared to make way for hamlets and
villages nestling beside fertile fields of barley, wheat and rye.
Many of the hills were crowned with grass-covered mounds –
burials from the ancient days, and reputed to be haunted.
Such was the superstitious awe they evoked that no one
would build a house or grow their crops close to them, and so
they remained for generation after generation, isolated and
mysterious. As Bladud moved through the valley he could
see them like a regiment of warriors keeping guard on an
ancient secret. He was intrigued. He was fascinated. Yet as
he had left the last village after rest and refreshment he had
been warned not to approach them, and instead was directed
round to the south, that would take him many miles out of his
way. Watched by the villagers, he had set off as instructed,
but once out of their sight he had doubled back so that his
route took him close to an area where there was a particularly
impressive group of these mounds.

For a while he kept to the valley, looking up at them from a
distance, curious and wondering. Then he could bear it no
longer: he had to know more about them. He left his horse
cropping happily below, and started to climb the hill towards
a cluster of three mounds. The long grass, uncropped by
grazing animals, swished against his legs. Yellow, white and
blue flowers shook out their scent as he brushed against
them. There was no sinister darkening of the natural world
around these burial places; all was light and bright and

11

burgeoning. But under the trees that topped the first mound he reached, the shade lay thick and black in contrast. At its summit he sat down to rest, propping his back against the trunk of an oak, and gazing out through the other tall trees towards the dazzling landscape he had left behind. He felt alert, but not afraid. He was prepared for any adventure.

To his disappointment nothing happened at first. He sighed – so many stories, so little substance. Drowsily he began to drift into reverie. And then it seemed to him that he was sinking back into the tree. That he was becoming the tree. He could almost feel what it was like to be a branch high in the air, bending to the wind. He could sense how it must be to live for centuries watching generation after generation of men and women live and die. He could feel how it must be to be rooted in the earth, forcing a path through soil and solid rock, holding the mighty empire of trunk and branch and leaf steady against storm and tempest. All this now seemed natural to him. Suddenly his probing roots met no hindrance and dangled freely in a hollow space before finding purchase again between the square slabs of man-carved stones. At the centre of this empty space he became aware of the skeleton of a man – his legs entangled in the roots, his eye sockets filled with dust. In his mind's eye Bladud could envisage the burial quite clearly. There was an elaborate dagger at the dead man's side, its hilt studded with tiny golden pins. There was a great gold brooch at the shoulder which no doubt had once fastened a cloak long since disintegrated with damp and time. In the bony fingers of the right hand was still clutched a golden cup, curiously ridged, and ringed with jewels.

Startled at the vividness of this vision Bladud jerked upright from where he had slumped against the tree. His heart was beating fast. Was this a dream? It did not feel like one. He felt suddenly desperately thirsty, as though he had been asleep for a very long time.

He saw, or rather felt, a movement to his left. He glanced round quickly to see a huge man standing beside him. As Bladud looked up at him, the figure seemed as tall as the trees, but when he sprang to his feet in alarm, he found the man not much taller than his own father. Bladud's first thought was that he was seeing a ghost, but he then dismissed this, as the stranger seemed solid enough. Swallowing his initial panic, the young prince tried to sound unperturbed.

'I hope, sir, I am not trespassing on your land. I intended no discourtesy . . .'

The stranger was dark-haired and bearded, and clad like a warrior king, though in clothes that would have been deemed eccentric in any court that Bladud had ever visited.

'No offence has been committed, lad,' replied a deep and pleasant voice.

The man appeared so suddenly and so silently that Bladud felt awkward. Had he been observing him for some time? And if no one ever came to these mounds, as the villagers claimed, why was he here?

'My name is Bladud of Trinovantum,' he said at last, trying to speak with the authority which his noble lineage entitled him to. 'I am son of the High King Hudibras.'

Bladud expected the stranger to identify himself in turn, but was disappointed. Instead the man continued to look deep into his eyes.

Bladud cleared his throat. 'May I have *your* name and lineage sir?' he prompted, feeling uncomfortable under the shrewd and steady gaze.

'You have come a long way to this place. Yet you have no fear?'

'Should I fear?' Bladud asked.

The man did not reply.

'I have waited a long time for you to come. You are welcome.'

'How did you know I was coming, when I did not know it myself?'

'Do you know everything about yourself?' The question seemed gently mocking.

'I thought I did,' answered Bladud uncertainly.

The stranger threw back his head and laughed aloud. Bladud flushed and began to resent the feeling that he was being treated like a green boy instead of a man. For a boy on the threshold of manhood this could seem intolerable.

As though he understood Bladud's hurt feelings, and now regretted his amusement, the man held out his right hand.

'Drink. You must be thirsty after your long journey.'

13

Bladud was about to refuse sulkily, but then he saw what the man held out. It was a cup of beaten gold, ridged and ringed with jewels exactly as he had seen in his vision of the burial inside the mound. He gasped and stared. His first instinct was to run away as fast as he could, and he indeed took a few steps backward. Yet something stopped him. Curiosity? For a long time Bladud stared at the cup, unmoving. Then he reached forward and took it, draining the clear golden liquid in a few quick gulps. It was strange and tangy to the taste, but quenched his thirst instantly. He handed back the cup, and the man took it, smiling into Bladud's eyes.

Suddenly Bladud seemed to be high above the mound and looking down. The landscape lay below him in every shade of green, huge trees appeared as small as puffballs, and a river he had just had difficulty in fording, no more than the silver slime-track of a snail. Strange. He turned and the whole earth seemed to wheel with him. *I am flying*, he thought. And then, with growing excitement, *I am flying!* The air held him. The air flowed around him like silk. Now the clouds were beneath him and the green forests above.

'I am flying!' he cried out loud – but from his throat came only a harsh and wordless sound. It frightened him. He had longed to be a bird when he had seen them winging so freely across the sky. But in reality to be a bird . . .

I don't want this, he thought. *I want to fly, but* . . .

He was suddenly no longer flying.

He was standing on the mound where he had drunk from the mysterious golden cup. And he was alone. There was no sign of the man who had offered it to him. He rushed in turn to each side of the mound, peering out across the landscape in every direction.

Now Bladud felt *truly* afraid. He had drunk from the golden cup: a magic potion strong enough to transform him from man to bird. What else had the stranger in mind for him? He felt weird, as though he were drifting between two worlds, belonging to neither.

In a panic he ran, stumbling, to where his horse was grazing at the foot of the hill. He leaped on and rode away from that place as fast as he could.

14

He had not gone far in his blind dash to get away from the mysteries of the mound when he found himself galloping down an avenue of standing stones. Alarmed after his recent experience he tried to rein in his steed, but the beast pursued his headlong course as though directed by a master greater than the human on his back. On either side the grey shapes stood tall and sinister and, though they were spaced generously apart, it seemed to Bladud they formed a continuous wall of invisible force to hold him in and propel him onwards.

Suddenly the stallion came to a stop, and Bladud all but catapulted off his back. Ahead stood two huge stones much larger than any in the avenue, and on either side of them, curving away into the distance, loomed a defensive ridge crowned by yet more gigantic upright slabs of rock. He had heard of such places from his father's High Priest, the Druid Fergal. Great circles of standing stones erected by giants who lived so long ago that even the local races who had inhabited this land before his own people arrived did not claim lineage from them. Some of the mighty slabs were fallen down, and the whole place gave an impression of disuse and dereliction. Overgrown as it was with tall grasses, brambles and trees, it was not easy to see how far the great circle extended.

'They are gateways,' Fergal had told him. 'But don't be tempted to pass through!' Entrusted by Hudibras with his son's education, his mentor had recognised only too well Bladud's insatiable curiosity – particularly about aspects of knowledge that were forbidden.

'Gateways to what?' Bladud had insisted.

'Some say the Otherworld.'

'What do *you* say?'

'I say we do not know, so we should leave them well alone. There are stories of young men who have dared to cross the threshold of the Otherworld while still in the flesh of this world, and they have never been seen again, or they have emerged a few days later, bent and old, white-haired and rheumy-eyed, so dazed and crazed that they were unable to remember a thing of what had happened to them. There are stories too of young men found wandering this world in search of their lost homes and families, which they claimed to have left only a few days before – but which proved to have been long since laid waste and perished.'

Bladud's eyes grew big with excitement. To enter such a place – and come back knowing . . . !

But now his steed would not go forward.

'One moment you won't stop,' the prince muttered angrily, 'and the next you won't start! Well, you can stay here. But I am going through.'

He swung off the animal's back decisively. Gripping his spear and checking the dagger at his belt, he strode purposefully forward between the two great silent stones – the mighty gateposts of the gods.

He expected something dramatic as soon as he entered, and braced himself, but nothing happened. The grass within the circle felt just as springy, just as feathery and prickly as the grass outside. The buttercups and clover, plantain and lacy saxifrage were just as prolific. Alder and rowan and hawthorn trees grew peacefully. The only slightly unnerving sight was one of the mighty stones fallen on its side, riven in half by an oak whose roots were so closely entwined with the rock that it looked as though living stone was being strangled by a vast serpent. He could see other stones standing nearby, almost totally covered with bramble, but clearly not forming part of the main circle. He wondered about the old tales. Could the spirit lands be entered through these ancient sites? Why were there no trees hung with crystal, golden men and women, music so unearthly and so beautiful that, once heard, a person was spoiled forever for the things of this earth? Part of him was glad that none of this was evident, yet part of him was bitterly disappointed. He decided to retrace his steps, to find his steed, and continue on his way. He had already suffered too many delays.

Returning the way he had come, he soon reached the stone which had been felled by the oak. But after walking some way beyond, he stopped and puzzled why he had not yet come upon the two gigantic portal stones, or the deep ditch and the ridge. There was no sign of them. Instead, in front of him, rose a much smaller stone. Glancing to his left and right, and then behind, he found he was standing within a lesser circle contained within the greater one. He did not remember seeing this before, and decided that he must have veered off his course without realising it. This circle was clear of undergrowth and bramble, as though it had been recently tended, and the stones shone silvery grey in the sunlight.

Beautiful, he thought, and went up to touch one, marvelling at the intricacy of light that sprang, sparkling, from a million minute crystals on the rock's surface. Suddenly he was not in such a hurry to leave, and began to experience a sense of peace such as he had never known before. Restlessness and impatience had always been a feature of his young life. He was often bored with the continual daily round and priorities of his father's court. True he enjoyed the bardic tales, but not when they were no more than chronicles of bloody battles and cruel massacres of enemies. Many a time he had thought that there must be more than this to life: the giving of gifts to secure the loyalty of vassals, the killing of enemies, and the vengeance, jealousy and greed of those around the High King. He admired his father for the strength and order of his reign, but he could not talk to him about the strange stirrings of his heart – the yearning for some meaning to his life beyond birth, procreation and death, beyond the displays of gold and the gathering of tribute and tithes.

Nor could he talk to his mother, for she was dead. It was perhaps her death that had first alerted him to these feelings of dissatisfaction. He often had the impression his life was speeding by, and yet it felt as though it were somebody else's life and not his own. He did not know exactly what he hoped to learn from the oracle he was now on his way to consult, but, if nothing else, he hoped she would explain who he was, and why he was here, and where he was going. *Nothing else matters*, he thought as he leaned his head against the stone. *Nothing else.*

'It is beginning,' Bladud whispered, and his heart skipped a beat. Something was different. He could not define it but it was as though he was becoming aware of things he would not normally notice: the tiny creakings and chitterings in the grass of busy insects, the sound of wings in flight from birds

17

so far away they were no more than faint specks in the sky. Similarly his sight grew more and more acute, till he believed he could see individual grass stems and the leaves of plants not only trembling in the breeze but actually growing. He watched a flower with intense concentration and saw it shake out its petals from the tight knot of its bud until it formed a blazing circle of yellow light and then – within moments – fade and droop and die. At first he felt elated by this strange sharpening of his senses, but then, as they became each moment more and more finely developed, he found the experience frightening and overwhelming. The faintest single sound became so loud that altogether the whole cacophony became no longer bearable. He covered his ears with his hands to shut it out. His eyes were dazzled by a blazing brilliance that, even with eyes closed, flickered through the lids. He crouched on the ground, his arms over his head, trying desperately to shut it all out: the sounds, the sights, the scents, the feelings . . .

And when he could bear it no longer, he lost consciousness, falling into silence and merciful darkness.

When Bladud woke again he was thankful to find that his senses seemed to have returned to normal, though now, for the first time, he realised how primitive and inadequate that normality really was.

He found himself lying on a couch in a light and airy chamber. As his eyes adjusted to waking, he noticed a young woman standing beside him. Her hair was loose, falling to below her waist in shining golden waves. Her eyes were the blue of the summer sky, her dress fern green. She was looking at him with close attention.

He was startled. Was it after all true what he had heard about the Shining Realms – the Otherworld that mirrored our earthly wishes and desires? She looked all that he had ever dreamed of or wished for . . .

Trying to sit up, he found his limbs so heavy he could scarcely move them. The woman smiled and leaned over him, putting her fine white hands under his shoulders and raising him to a sitting position as easily as she would a child. He wanted to speak to her but his tongue was too heavy. He

18

found he could not move it to form words, but uttered only a kind of croak when he opened his mouth. He was shamed that he seemed such an ugly lump of clay against her ethereal beauty.

Drawing back she poured liquid from a tall crystal flask into a silver cup and offered it to him. When he could not lift his hand to grasp it, she raised the cup to his lips. He could feel the liquid enter his mouth and run down his chin. And then he felt that it was bitter and burning, and he tried to cry out and push it away.

Another touch of a cool hand and the burning ceased. He looked up to find another young woman at his side, identical in every way to the first. Unhurriedly she poured some liquid from the same crystal flask, and held it to his lips. This time he tried to pull his head away in order to avoid drinking, but she persisted and he could feel it trickle down his throat. He braced himself, but this time there was no discomfort – and suddenly he found he could move his mouth more easily. Tentatively he flexed the muscles in his hand and found to his relief that they responded.

He looked from one woman to the other, marvelling at their likeness, puzzling that the liquid poured from the same flask should have such very different effects on him. Which of these two had given him the burning liquid, and which the cool? He could not tell. They were both watching him with amusement.

Suddenly he felt angry. Why was he, a strong and agile young man, being subjected to this humiliation? What did they want of him?

Then both young women offered him their cups together. No words were spoken but he felt he must choose between them, and that if he chose wrongly it would go ill for him. He looked from one woman to the other and could discern no difference.

'I am no longer thirsty,' he said coldly. 'I want no more to drink.'

The women continued to watch him closely, and to his chagrin he found that he was thirsty after all: very thirsty, and growing thirstier by the moment. He also found that his limbs were again growing heavy and unmanageable.

19

He forced himself to speak once more, from lips that would now scarcely open.

'Why are you doing this to me? Why . . . ?'

They came even closer, each offering him a cup – one of which he believed would save him, the other destroy him. With a tremendous effort he lurched forward, knocking both vessels from their hands, and reaching out for the flask itself. He strained every muscle in his body to grasp it, but could not. At least he must have touched it, because he saw it drop as he himself fell to the floor. The liquid splashed into his face, some falling on to his lips and into his open mouth. He swallowed.

'Whatever happens,' he thought, 'I have made my choice.'

Two emotions were now in conflict: relief that he had outwitted his two beautiful tormentors, and fear of the consequences of his drinking directly from the flask. He closed his eyes.

After a moment, as nothing seemed to happen, he gazed around and found himself no longer in the chamber with the couch, but lying on grass in the open. Around him he could see the tall stones ranged as they had been before the strange incident. The sky above was blue, with drifting summer clouds. Buttercups and clover clustered close against his face. Cautiously he raised himself, finding with relief that his limbs moved easily. He stood up slowly and peered around in every direction. There could be no doubt that this inner circle had received recent attention, whereas the rest of the huge enclosure had not. Here the grass was shorter, and all brambles and nettles had been cleared away. But now he did not feel the eeriness of before, and he wondered if he had merely fallen asleep and dreamed the whole incident. But surely it had seemed too vivid for a dream? He realised that it had some purpose, a meaning of importance for him – though at this time he could not think what. But, dream or not, this place had a power that could affect him against his will, and he would be wise to leave it. He strode out of the inner circle without further incident, and almost immediately located the two great portal stones he had experienced such difficulty in finding earlier. Outside his horse was waiting for him patiently.

Riding away through the tall, shimmering grasses, the seductive beauty of the two young women haunted him. He could not shake off a feeling that he had not seen the last of them.

3

The Oracle of Sul

In the region he entered next, the hills were high and the forests thick. To guard its secrets the very earth itself seemed to place obstacles in the way of the casual traveller. Only those who were serious seekers it seemed might penetrate to the deepest mysteries, and the directions given to him at Trinovantum were too vague to be reliable at this stage. Bladud reflected on the noise and bustle of his father's court, the endless comings and goings, the pressure on him to conform to his father's ideal of the heir to the High Kingship. He knew that his younger brother, Liel, passionately wanted the throne, and with his prodigious warrior skills he would no doubt be the people's choice. But Bladud remained his father's choice and, being the elder son, would have this advantage when the councils met throughout the land to elect a new High King at the death of Hudibras. How much time had he spent in his short life learning to kill? How often had he balked at the days and nights spent with the warrior bands listening to their boasting of conquests past and to come, while stirring up conflicts for the present as though they knew of nothing better to do with their lives than butt their heads against a fellow man or drive a dagger into his heart? Sometimes he wondered if there was something wrong with him that he lacked enthusiasm for the heroic pursuits of his fellows. He was never happy riding into battle, though the eyes of others glowed with excitement at such a challenge. He preferred galloping alone on the hills with only the sun and wind as companions, and nothing at the end of the ride but a pleasant weariness and a memory of joy. He preferred the

23

songs and stories that told of magical journeys and exploits, of mysterious and shining beings, of monsters defeated by cunning, and beautiful women won by love.

On this journey, he had felt happier than he had ever been, cherishing the solitariness of his days, exhilarated by the challenges of his quest. Many tales had been told of the Oracle of Sul – but not many men had ever encountered her. Was she indeed as frightening as they said? Did she curse as readily as she blessed? Did she truly know the future and foretell the minutest detail of one's life? Could she read the thoughts buried deep in one's heart, even those one refused to acknowledge to oneself? Would she be able to cure him of his restlessness – that inner itch of dissatisfaction that bedevilled him? He knew he was seeking something, but he did not know what. The constant fear that haunted him was that he would die an old man looking back on a life that he had wasted.

He was near his destination now. He knew it. But not wanting to arrive weary and in the shadows of evening, he chose to spend one more night in the open.

He left the tangled forest in the river valley and climbed one of the many hills that guarded the entrance to the oracle's domain. He reached the top just as the sun set: the whole sky was suffused with a pale glow ranging from delicate pearl green to gold and ultimately, nearest the sun itself, to red. In the valley below, the curve of the river he had left behind blazed like a polished copper sickle among the darkening foliage. Wild geese flew above him: black ciphers on the tablet of the sky – black sparks in a dying conflagration. Ah, to be able to wing it like the birds! Bladud watched them longingly as they covered in moments wide distances that would take him a day of exhausting effort to traverse. For a moment they were silhouetted against the vast red-gold ball of the sun, and then they were gone. Soon the sun, too, was gone, sinking into the blue distance on its mysterious journey into the Otherworld, leaving the earth without light – life barely tolerable in the dark.

Bladud stood on the top of the hill and watched the great drama that never ceased to amaze him, no matter how often he saw it.

'Sul,' he prayed. 'Mighty goddess! Guide me. Help me. Protect me.'

He had known of her long before he set out on this journey, but had never experienced her presence before – as now he did. In the cool breeze of evening he felt her breath; in the blue and gathering dark he saw the drawing of her cloak over the land; in the hush of all nature preparing to sleep he thought he heard her whisper his name. He knew now it had been his destiny to come to this place. He had thought it was his own decision to leave home and embark on this journey, but he had been wrong. She was drawing him to her. She was calling to him. She was guiding him, preparing the way for him, preparing him to meet her.

He watched until the daylight was gone, and then he lay down. But above him the mighty procession of the stars was in progress, and that night – the night before he reached her oracle – he could not sleep.

He had seen stars before but never so brilliant, so intense. They seemed much closer as he lay flat on his back and he had the distinct impression that he was moving, wheeling with them; that he was amongst them, no longer separate, no longer apart. He was on a journey passing through them, as easily as a boat passes through water-flowers on a still pond. He stared in amazement as the ground dissolved beneath him, as he hovered bodiless in an immense space – as filaments of light floated past him, from darkness . . . going into darkness. Strange how on earth one lamp can illuminate a huge chamber, but here in the night the powerful light of the stars made no impression on the blackness of the spaces between them. He had never been so aware of the contrast between dark and light – nor so little afraid.

What *was* he as he moved through the stars as freely as a bird moves through the air? For he could not believe that he was still the man he had once been. He remembered how, as a small child, he had leaped off a high rock, shouting to his companions that he was flying. He could still see their faces looking up at him in that long moment before he crashed to the ground – some with awe, some with hope, some with scepticism, but all with close attention. For the brief moment when he was not attached to the earth or anything on it, he really believed that he was flying. He strained every muscle in his small body to lift himself up. In his dreams it was so easy, and often he dreamed he was flying over hills, over forests.

He had dreamed once that he soared above his father's rath in the city of Trinovantum, looking down on the great White Mound in which his ancestors were buried and at the High King's great house from which his father controlled the lives of thousands upon thousands. They had seemed small and insignificant from that vantage, his father's formidable warriors no more dangerous than ants. But what was so easy in a dream was not so easy in reality. His child's body, light as it was, was too heavy for the air. He could feel himself falling. He could feel his bones crack against the rocky earth, and he screamed and screamed with pain and frustration. The other children laughed and mocked, all the more so because for one moment he had led them to believe that they too were not bound to the earth but *could* fly like the birds if they so willed it.

Bladud remembered, clearly as yesterday, the face of Fergal, his father's Druid priest, who had been watching the whole humiliating incident. The man looked down into the tear-stained face of the hurt and disappointed child, and there was something in his expression that came vividly back to Bladud at this moment. At the time he could only wonder why the priest did not pick him up and comfort him, as grown-ups usually did. Now it seemed to him the Druid had been in trance, as he had often seen him since, and was seeing not the weeping child but something else, something extraordinary.

Suddenly Bladud felt afraid. Was it some memory of the pain he had suffered as a child that day – the shock of falling? Or was it rather the Druid's strange expression that made him feel he faced a destiny that was too difficult for him – a task for which he was not yet ready?

He found he was no longer moving through the stars. He was back on earth, where the rough grass of the hilltop pricked his skin and made it itch. But was it the cold night breeze alone that made him shiver?

26

Above him, immensely far away, the stars were again minute points of light in a solid black dome, as remote and unattainable as they had always been.

With a start he turned his head at hearing a movement near him on the bare hilltop. As though to mock him, a huge owl flapped over his head and winged away into the dark – a hunting owl seeking earth-bound prey.

Dawn came at last – the sky at first a pale translucent grey. He watched the stars disappear one by one until only one was left, and that seemed loth to go. It shone like a shoulder brooch on a cloak of fine grey silk, focusing the eye and holding all together. It still remained like a faint flush of gold as the east prepared the world for the return of the sun. Stiff from the long hours on his back, Bladud hauled himself to his feet. His clothes were damp from the dew and he shook and rubbed off the stray grasses clinging to him before he looked around. It seemed the world had disappeared behind a white mist, and he alone was there to celebrate the first rays of sunlight. He was awed by the magnificence of what he had been shown.

'I will be worthy,' he whispered.

He could now feel the sun's warmth loosening his stiff limbs and bringing him comfort. He watched the world gradually reappearing: the trees at first like faint smudges – and then like delicate black filigree – until at last they blazed in every shade of living green. Birds were on the move high in the sky, pulling the luminous curtain of day across the earth.

As hill after hill appeared he counted. He had been told the oracle was guarded by seven hills. This was the place.

When the whole emerging landscape lay bathed in full sunlight, he left the hilltop and made his way down into the valley which lay to the west. He thought about Fergal, and wondered why the Druid priest had been so hostile to this pilgrimage, doing everything short of casting spells to prevent the young prince setting off. He could picture him now standing tall and lean and disapproving beside the gate, to deliver his last dire warning.

27

'Your destiny is to be High King of this mighty and civilised land. Meddle with the superstitions of savages at your peril!'

But Bladud was not prepared to listen. He had learned about this oracle from his friend Yaruk who was one of those very 'savages', one of the race who had inhabited this land long before Fergal's Celtic people had arrived – even before Brutus, descendant of that great Trojan Prince Aeneas, forefather of his own royal line, had come ashore on this island with his stolen Greek princess, to seek sanctuary. How many times had he been told that his ancient and noble family was far superior to all the local races – even superior to the powerful warrior Celts who imposed their will upon the indigenous population with such arrogant ease. He did not know what skilful and cunning manoeuvre his father's people had used to achieve this liaison with the Celts, so that Hudibras, with blood from Troy and Greece and Rome in his veins, held the most coveted throne in all the land.

But, growing up in the town founded by the Trojan Brutus and called at first New Troy, then Trinovantum, Bladud was not unaware of the tensions that often threatened that royal position. On the whole the Druids served his father's dynasty loyally, and over the generations any differences between the two so-called 'civilised' races had become minimal through intermarriage since both united in despising the 'savages'. Occasionally however one of the despised race *was* given a place at court to help keep the peace, and Yaruk was such a one. The boy had caught the eye of the High King on one of his regular royal progresses, because of his skill in carving.

There was scarce a place to put one's hand in the palace that did not boast a carving. The pillars holding the high roof were alive with images of animals and birds emerging from foliage. The roof beams were carved with heads and faces of every type and every expression, staring, leering and glowering from every angle. The throne itself was a masterpiece of wood-carving and Yaruk could make from the trunk of a dead tree a world of living creatures so cleverly executed that what one saw at first was only a fraction of what would emerge on closer inspection.

Bladud had been drawn to Yaruk, not only because they

were the same age, but because Yaruk shared interests unconnected with warrior skills. Bladud had been trained as hunter and warrior; it was essential that the eventual leader of his people should not only master these skills, but excel. He was fit and agile, and did what was expected of him, but whenever possible he would escape to where Yaruk squatted in a pool of silence, exercising his craft. At one time he had pleaded with Yaruk to teach him how to carve, but although he learned some skill he found that the genius for making the carvings rival life itself was beyond him.

Nevertheless the two became firm friends, and it was only to Yaruk that Bladud dared confide his inner restlessness – his feeling that there was something special waiting for him, though he did not know what. It was Yaruk who told him about the goddess Sul and her oracle, and it was not long before Bladud decided that only she could answer the questions that troubled him.

Himself a seer and a prophet, Fergal was angry when he heard about the boy's intention, no doubt resentful that Bladud preferred to consult an alien oracle rather than himself. He had been given charge of Bladud's education since birth and had high hopes for the boy under his own influence. Fergal had made it his mission in life to ensure Bladud's skills on the battlefield were matched by his scholarship. If he had noticed the restlessness in Bladud he had thought it but the pains of a youth growing faster than his peers. He had prophesied to Hudibras that the boy would make a great and extraordinary king and that the land would have many golden years during his reign. But he had not warned the king about the shadows he also foresaw hovering over his son's life.

What would this shaman tell him? And how would what she said affect him? Fergal realised he could not keep Bladud forever at his side, preventing the influences of the rest of the world from reaching him, but the moment of parting had come sooner than he had expected. It was with only the greatest effort that he had prevented himself setting out to follow the youth. Instead he recognised Bladud's right to independent decision, and accepted unwillingly that the time had come for the fledgling to leave the nest. This would be

29

the first of many tests Bladud could only face alone. Fergal had made his protests – but let the youth go on his way.

Bladud made his way down into the valley, where the river wound peacefully among the reeds. In many places trees leant over the water as though to peer at their own reflections. He was dusty and dirty from his long journey, and decided to bathe. Leaving his clothes on the bank, he waded through the water-weed and plunged into the coolth.

Returning to the bank refreshed, he looked up into a willow that overhung the river just before climbing on to the land. He was bemused by the play of light as every ripple on the water danced a mirror counterpoint in its leafy branches, transforming the substance of trunk and canopy into spirit-stuff as insubstantial as a dream. In the dazzling, glancing, dancing light he thought he saw the long, lithe body of a woman half turned from him. He stood still, up to his knees in the water, scarce daring to breathe lest she become aware of him and take flight. The curve of her breast and thigh followed the lines of the tree and he could not be sure whether she was a separate being or part of the wood itself. At last his urge to know if what he saw was real or not impelled him to wade further towards the bank. In the flurry of reflected light that shimmered through the tree as he disturbed the water, she vanished, and he was left with uncertainty: had she been there or not? If so, of what realm was she – spirit or flesh?

On the mossy bank beneath the willow he found no marks to indicate a physical presence. The grey roots twined and twisted like sinuous serpents, then disappeared underground to hold the gigantic tree firmly to the earth. He touched the bark and it was solid. He reached up to a fan of leaves, and they felt firm and leathery to his touch. A bird took wing from an upper branch with a screech and a whirr. He heard it flapping away above the forest, calling in agitation to its mate.

He shivered, aware that he was naked and cold. He reached for his clothes, drawing them on like another skin. Now with his breeches on, he paused to look over his shoulder, having the feeling that he was being watched. Yet he could see no one, though he stood still a long time, staring into the deep green depths and shades around him, turning his head slowly so as to miss nothing.

'If you are here, goddess,' he said at last, aloud, his voice sounding harsh and out of harmony with the natural music of wind-hush, insect buzz and water-lap, 'show yourself.'

And if I am not here? The thought in his own mind seemed to have a voice, low and amused and mocking. *And if I am not the goddess you seek . . . ?*

Impatiently he pulled on the rest of his clothes, anxious now to leave the place. Had he not been warned that in these wild regions of the west, in these forested hills, dark and secret places hid all manner of beings inimical to man? Had he not as a child listened, fascinated and terrified, to the story-tellers of his father's court in the dark of the winter, the hearth fires throwing great shadows on to the walls so that he seemed to hear the wolves howling in these very distant forests, as though the beasts were circling close around him in the shadows just beyond the circle of light the fires threw? Wolves he could face now that he was grown, with his dagger at his side, his spear in his hand. But there had been other things hinted at by the story-teller as he lowered his voice to speak in a whisper that made one's blood run cold. These other things could not be fought off with bronze or iron. These other things would not answer to a human challenge, no matter how heroic, but picked their own time and their own place . . .

Prince Bladud gripped his spear and checked that his dagger was safe at his belt. Squaring his shoulders, he set off alongside the river. At every scuttling sound his head turned until he felt ashamed of himself. What kind of warrior prince was startled at water rat or vole?

At last, some distance further on, he began to relax. It seemed that he was alone again.

It was noon when Bladud heard the sound of rushing water and knew that he must be approaching the oracle's sanctuary. An overgrown path, roughly marked out with stones carved with mystical and magical signs and symbols, led him further.

31

Bladud shivered. He had been a long time reaching this point and now he was not sure that he wanted to go on. Fergal had tried to dissuade him, and even Yaruk, one of the so-called 'savages', who revered this oracle, had warned him to be careful.

Yaruk had told him to leave his horse behind as he drew near the sanctuary. 'You must go alone and on foot,' he had urged.

The first two carved stones he did not touch. But when he reached the third, he ran his fingers over its surface, tracing the curves of a spiral. Subsequently he touched each new stone with similar interest, noting how his fingers tingled.

The path began to twist and turn and he had the impression that he was passing the same landmarks several times over, but each time was seeing them from a different angle. It seemed, too, that he was somehow gradually losing all sense of his past. Thoughts, memories, the busy images that normally crowd the mind and interfere with spiritual vision, were being left behind. He was now aware only of the moment he was currently experiencing.

The forest thickened. The path climbed. The noise of rushing water grew louder, and suddenly he faced a low cliff almost hidden by the heavy boughs of trees leaning over it and the ferns and creepers growing from it. Halfway up was a gash from which issued the waters of the stream he had been following – leaping from darkness into light. A cloud of steamy mist swirled around the entrance to the cave. Bladud had never seen anything like it: the stone alongside where the water issued was stained rust red. He recalled that Yaruk had mentioned 'blood' and 'smoke that thunders' and 'a hole in the earth which leads to perpetual fire'.

What now? There was no sign of any temple or shrine. A huge boulder rose from the cauldron of water swirling at the base of the cliff and it was carved even more carefully than all the rest: three perfect interrelated spirals. By using rocks and the protruding roots of a huge tree he was just able to reach the cave. He climbed carefully, his feet sending slivers of loose stone and twig skittering down below.

Close at last to the issue of water, he reached out gingerly and touched the flow. He drew back, startled. It was hot! He

32

wiped the sweat from his face with one arm, and looked around for a way into the cave. At one side he found just enough room to squeeze through without having to pass beneath the scalding water. He took one step forward, and nearly lost his balance. The rock underfoot was as slippery as the outcrop he grabbed to steady himself. For a moment he could go neither backwards nor forwards. Ahead lay darkness. But then his desire to know became stronger than his fear. Carefully he took another step on the slippery surface, feeling the hot spray on his face, its steam almost blistering his skin. A few feet into the cavern itself he suddenly reached a ledge behind the fall and found he could stand more safely.

He peered into the murky darkness. Beyond the dense cloud of sulphurous steam, he sensed that there was an open space. He eased forward and the swirling mist clouds almost suffocated him. Yet he persisted, and he was rewarded. For suddenly there was light in front of him. Only a blur at first, but with every step it grew brighter.

Clinging to the cave wall, he edged his way alongside the mysterious rushing stream, and came out at last, his lungs almost bursting, into clearer air. Above him could be seen the sky through a jagged hole. Scrambling up the rocks until he reached the lip, he then hauled himself over it. Thankfully he found himself standing upright on firm ground. Below him the steaming water disappeared into the depths of the earth. Ferns grew thickly around the edge of the hole, luxuriating in the warm steamy atmosphere. Bladud flung himself down on the springy turf, shaking with relief and wiping pouring sweat from his face and neck. His skin was red from the steam and, in contrast to the heat underground, he was now shivering with cold.

After a few moments of recovery, he gazed around, noticing that the forest grew as thickly here as down below the falls.

Suddenly he realised he was not alone; he was being watched from the shadows. For a moment he thought it might be the same young girl he had fancied watching while he bathed, but this time it turned out to be an old, old woman, gnarled and bent, her skin seasoned so brown by the

33

sun that it looked almost indistinguishable from the tree bark. Her head was practically bald, but what hair remained fell in white wisps and untidy strands over her bony shoulders. Her eyes, however, were large and bright.

For a seemingly long time they stared at each other. Bladud felt ridiculously like a deer caught in the beam of some predator's eye, poised and ready for flight, but unable to make a move.

At last the old woman broke the spell. She turned very slowly and began to hobble away.

'Wait!' Bladud cried out. He had not come this far and endured so much to return without achieving his objective.

But the old hag did not turn back.

'Wait!' he called again louder. Still she paid no attention, so he set off after her. She had not seemed very far away but, as fast as he moved on his young limbs, she seemed always to be ahead and out of reach. He was soon more annoyed than afraid, and pursued her with grim determination, impatiently dodging overhanging branches and tangles of thorn bushes, amazed that she could negotiate the forest's obstacles with such agility.

At last, almost out of breath and in despair of ever catching up with her, he stopped his pursuit and stood still, looking after the retreating figure with deep disappointment. 'I need you,' he whispered. 'Why do you reject me?'

She could not possibly have heard him, yet at last she stopped and turned to face him. Now she beckoned him to follow her, and this time he found himself keeping pace with her quite easily.

After a while they came upon a round construction of wood and thatch deep in the forest. She disappeared between portals carved with signs like those he had encountered on the way, the device of three interrelated spirals most prominent. She had indicated that he should follow, and after only a momentary hesitation, he did so.

Inside he found a dark interior filled with the same sulphurous steam as in the cavern. There was a small hole at the centre of the floor, where normally the hearth would be, and it was from this the steam was issuing. Directly above it was a round hole in the ceiling, from which the steam could

34

escape. All around the walls were ranged the paraphernalia of a shaman: feathers and furs and masks. Bundles of dried herbs hung from the rafters, while every nook and cranny was piled high with bones and skulls both human and animal.

Something moved in the shadows at the far side of the chamber and Bladud struggled to adjust his eyes to the dim interior. He then met the gaze of a pair of eyes low down, as though a man were crouching there. But these were not the eyes of a man. They were the eyes of a wolf. Involuntarily Bladud took a backward step.

The old woman saw his fear and signalled the wolf to her side. As obedient as a dog the creature moved to her, but its eyes never left Bladud's and Bladud's never left the wolf's.

She indicated that Bladud should sit. Reluctantly he sat down cross-legged on the floor. She reached up and took down a cloak of wolf's skin from the wall and wrapped it around her. Then she took a wolf mask and placed it over her face.

She began to move in a slow and rhythmic fashion, forming the steps of a ritual dance on the other side of the steam-hole. The wolf never took his eyes off Bladud for an instant, though the body of his mistress often came between them. As she danced, she began to hum, and the humming grew louder and more unearthly as the steps of the dance became faster and wilder.

Bladud could hear the rushing of water under the earth providing a kind of counterpoint to the sound she made. Just as the humming reached a climax, the wolf moved at last, lifting its head to howl as only a wolf can howl, recalling to Bladud all the night fears of generations of humans who have lived on the edge of dark forests and dreaded the wild denizens that stalk at night.

He clenched his fists, determined not to give way to overwhelming instinct and flee the place, giving up any chance of learning what the oracle might have to say. He had no idea if she knew who he was or why he had come. He could only hope that this frenzy of hers would lead on to something meaningful.

Suddenly the humming and movement stopped. Not gradually, as it had started, but so suddenly that Bladud was left with a deafening silence, though the sounds he had heard seemed to continue in his head.

Two sets of eyes were staring at him now – the woman's as inhuman as the beast's.

Bladud waited, longing to speak, to explain himself and his presence in this place. But the atmosphere was so charged with tension, he did not dare.

Suddenly there came a sound from above, and through the hole in the roof flew an eagle. Bladud stared with terror as it swooped around the room. He ducked, covering his face with his arms as it passed close. For a moment it paused to perch on the bony shoulder of the wolf-woman, and then it lifted off again, flying straight as an arrow out through the open doorway. Its mighty wing brushed against Bladud as it did so. He was astonished by the accuracy of its passage.

The wolf-woman lifted an arm to point a long finger at Bladud.

'You are the eagle's kin,' she said, 'and he has claimed you.' She paused, and in the room the silence was broken only by the rumbling of water under the earth. 'Like the eagle you will fly. Like the eagle you will see things that others who walk on this earth cannot see. You will be a great king. Your story will be told thousands of years from now.'

As she lowered her arm, the energy seemed to drain out of her so that now she looked no longer the formidable wolf-priestess, but more like an ancient totem stick with a moth-eaten cloak of wolf-skin hanging and sagging from it. The wolf turned and slunk back to its place in the shadows, dropping its head on its paws, ready to sleep.

Bladud felt as though released from some spell. That magnificent experience when the space all around him was filled with eagle wings and wolf magic was over. Instead he was a tired and hungry youth squatting on an earth floor in a smelly hut, with only a tame beast and an old crone. There was nothing more for him here.

At the door he paused and pulled from his neck the golden torc he wore as sign of his princely status. He tossed it at her feet.

36

'You will come back,' she rasped, not even glancing down at the priceless treasure he had given her.

'Never!' he muttered under his breath. And he meant it.

4

The White Mound and the
Island of Thorns

During the Festival of Lughnasa, Keron arrived with his
daughter Rheinid. It was a year since Prince Bladud had
spent those two nights in their rath on his way to consult the
oracle.

Trinovantum was crowded with visitors. Those who could
not find shelter for the night in the houses of friends and
relatives were encamped in makeshift tents around the
outskirts. Nearly every piece of land between the river Tain
and the fortified hill where the great castle of Hudibras stood
was occupied. The weather was at its hottest and the smell of
so many families and animals gathered together was
overpowering.

Bladud stood on the watchtower rising above the ramparts
to witness the travellers winding towards the town. He
enjoyed the excitement, the change in routine, but it was
fortunate that only a select few would actually come through
the gates into the hill-fort itself. If he wished, he could go
down on to the plain and mingle with his father's subjects,
clad in peasant clothes, his priceless rings, armbands and
torcs left safely behind. Thus unrecognised he could
participate in just as much as he wished of the bustle
and excitement. Equally at any point he chose, he could
leave them and once again enjoy the privileges of a wealthy
prince.

The crowds were gathering for a celebration of the god
Lugh, the Shining One, the Many-skilled, the god of Light
and Knowledge, the god who had come over the seas from
lands so distant that most men there that day had not even

heard of them. During the time of the festival the ancient tales of the god's prowess were told by many a skilful wordsmith. Even the young bloods of the court paused sometimes in their drinking and carousing to listen to the poems and songs that told of the 'Bright Phantom', Lugh of the Shining Shield, who came from his mysterious realm in the east guarded by a golden tree, to defend this very land against the giant Balor and all the dark forces that beset them.

This year Bladud chose not to mingle with the crowds, but concentrated on practice for the games to be held in the great god's honour. His brother Liel was favoured to win the longest footrace, but Bladud was determined to beat him. The oracle had said he would be a great king and to be that he had to excel at everything.

He left the tower and headed towards the higher ground, where the White Mound crowned the hill on which the fort itself was built. He turned his gaze to the river, the broad Tain which carried the big ships from faraway places to the safety of his father's harbour, now in full salt tide and flooding the marshlands to the south. One day he would sail away in one of them. One day he would explore other lands, other cultures. If he was to be a true king, he owed it to his people to see the whole shape of the world and all its potential. For how could he lead them wisely if he could see no further than his own nose? When he became king he would not want to perpetuate only what had gone before. He felt sure there were other ways of doing things. He wanted to bring his people forward into a better world; a wider, more satisfactory state of being.

As he stood beside the White Mound, the burial place of ancient kings, he reflected that here his ancestors, the Trojan Brutus and his Greek wife Imogene, had lain while generations of their descendants had allowed their cultural heritage to disappear, mingling their blood with the fierce Celtic warrior tribes that had overrun the country. There was Celtic blood in his veins too, for his Trojan ancestors had not wed their own race exclusively, but in his dreams he always harked back to that Greek princess, torn from her home and all that was familiar, to sail the wild and stormy seas with her exiled husband and land at last upon this shore and live out her life among alien people. She must have stood where he was now standing, looking over the broad sheet of silver water, longing to take ship and sail to her family and hear her own language spoken again, her own songs sung. *One day*, he thought, *I'll go back to her land and seek out the burial places of her family and tell the ghosts that linger there that I, one of their own flesh and blood, have cared for her and have brought her spirit home.*

He reached out and touched some of the white crystals that covered the great mound. They were cold and sharp, transported on that very river from far afield, and so white the mound shone in the sunlight that travellers could see it gleaming and glinting from a very great distance.

Tradition had it that this was not only the burial mound of early kings and queens of his dynasty, but contained the head of Bendigeid Vran, Bran the Blessed – the head that had been severed in Ireland centuries before but which still gazed out towards the east from its burial place in the White Mound, giving protection to all the land, and wisdom to whoever had the courage to consult with it. The White Mound was an extremely sacred place, and for any man to touch it who was not a priest of the very highest order was taboo.

Bladud could hear the distant hubbub of the preparations in the fort and in the town below, but up here he was alone. Looking around himself cautiously to make sure he was not observed, he carefully prised a piece of crystal from the mound's surface. *I will take this and lay it upon the graves of Imogene's kinsfolk*, he told himself, but his heart beat faster at the sacrilege it would appear he was committing. The crystal fragment was small and fitted easily into the palm of his hand. Suddenly he looked up to witness three huge ravens coming to land on top of the mound, and his mouth went dry. The raven was always associated with Bran.

As they shifted about to find a comfortable perch on the rocky knoll, their wings spread out like great black shadows over the white stone. He could swear that their yellow eyes bored accusingly into his. He thought of putting the crystal back, but decided against that. Instead he lifted his chin and stared defiantly into the eyes of the raven closest to him.

41

'If you come from Bran the Blessed, you will know why I have taken this,' he said, holding it up for the bird to see. 'I swear on oath by Lugh the Light that I will surrender my life if I do not take this crystal to Queen Imogene's family tomb in the land of her birth.'

One of the ravens gave a raucous cry and lifted off the mound, its great wings flapping like unsecured sails in a storm. It rose high and circled three times before flying away.

Bladud turned to face the other two, which were still staring at him.

'And I swear an oath by the goddess Sul that I will give my life if I do not bring joy to the heart of the great Queen Imogene by doing thus.'

The second raven shrieked and left the mound, flying low along the river course towards the sea.

For a long time Bladud and the third raven stared at each other in silence. The young man could feel the crystal clutched in his hand grow warm with his body heat.

'I cannot put it back now,' he whispered hoarsely. 'I have sworn, and must honour my oaths.' But what had he done? Why had he sworn such fearsome oaths? What if he could not carry out what he had vowed?

The raven moved down the side of the mound towards him, walking awkwardly, clumsily, nevertheless menacingly. It reached out its beak and pecked at a ring on the hand that held the crystal. It tugged and jerked at it as though trying to pull a worm from the ground. Its sharp beak cut into the prince's finger and drew blood. Terrified, Bladud pulled the ring off and offered it to the bird. The raven seized it and flew off at once, rising high, high into the air until it seemed to dissolve into the blue.

Bladud sank on to the grass trembling and sweating. The mound beside him no longer looked merely a heap of earth studded with chunks of white crystalline rock. It had become a place of power, of mystery, of terror. The long-dead eyes of Bran could see.

But if Bran could see what Bladud had done, surely Queen Imogene could see it too? Surely she could feel the reverence

42

he held for her, and the purity of his motives in taking this piece of crystal? Surely she would protect him from any harm that might befall him due to his sacrilege?

He bent his head and shut his eyes and prayed for her help and her forgiveness. In his mind's eye she stood beside him, her hair bound in long, thick golden plaits falling from beneath a golden circlet studded with gems. Her white hand reached out to him, and on her wrist shone a bracelet of gold with a pearl shaped like a swan. Her eyes were like the sea, and she gazed at him as she would at a lover.

Bladud caught his breath, his heart missing a beat.

But as he opened his eyes and reached out to her, she was gone, and he was alone again beside the ancient mound, and the sounds from below, of shouting and clattering, of bustling human life, had returned in force to dispel all magic.

Early on the morning of the day of the great race the runners, both men and women, gathered. Around the perimeter of the field in which the race was to take place an unruly crowd jostled, shouting for their favourites, whistling and chanting.

It was with surprise that Bladud recognised Rheinid standing in the line-up. He had almost forgotten her. But now, remembering, he stared at her. She looked across at him and met his eyes. It was clear from her expression that she had not forgotten any detail of the time they had spent together.

He studied her body: her bare feet and limbs were more sun-bronzed than when he had seen them last. She must have been training for this race. She was certainly beautiful: raven black hair plaited and bound, limbs supple and strong but not over-muscular like some of the women, back straight, head held high. As one of her neighbours joked with her, she laughed and he could just catch the melodious sound and see the flash of her white teeth.

The marshals were beginning to order the competitors into place. Bladud took one last look at Rheinid, then decided that he must have no distractions, and shut her out of his mind.

Liel yelled something to him and he knew their personal challenge was on. For either of them to win the race would

43

not be easy. For months young warriors in training had competed amongst themselves for the privilege of running at the Lughnasa, so those that were gathered on the field were fit and ready and raring to go. All knew that if they could beat the two princes of the royal house, they would win more than just the race.

For a moment, Bladud caught sight of Yaruk waving and shouting before he was pushed roughly back into the crowd by the marshals. The prince waved to him and grinned. It was well known that Yaruk's people wanted Prince Bladud to win this race, for they realised Prince Liel had no love for the 'savages', and it was only Bladud's continuing patronage that allowed a few of them any kind of honourable position within the privileged society of their conquerors. He hoped he would not let them down. His succession to the throne did not directly ride on this one performance, for it was an accumulation of victories over the years that raised the prospects of the crown, and every individual contest was important. Inevitably the people would judge their leaders by their ability to win, their physical strength and fitness. They believed the land itself would bear healthy crops and support healthy livestock only if its king was strong in wind and limb.

Bladud looked towards his father who stood on the wooden dais, his sword raised above his head. When that sword was lowered the race would be on. Hudibras remained tall, muscular, powerful, with no unwanted flesh on him. His hair was greying, yet no youngster could challenge him to battle and hope to win. His rule was firm and respected, and in his time the land had been relatively peaceful. If the sub-kings grew restless and ambitious, Hudibras would know of it almost before they did themselves. And if gold could not settle them down, the sword soon would. Hudibras was undisputed High King of a mighty land and any heir of his would have a hard task to follow him. Nor would the people tolerate a weakling in his place.

Suddenly the sword flashed down, and the whole field was on the move!

Bladud paced himself well, as did Liel. Neither sought the forefront at the beginning. The course was long and the contest was rough. In the jostling for position many were hurt and forced to leave the field. Seen from above it would have appeared more a battle than a race, and not even princes of the royal household were immune to injury.

Bladud saw a promising youngster tripped up; it being his first Lughnasa, he had not yet learned to concentrate on survival first and speed later. But as the numbers thinned out, the race started in earnest, and it was then the survivors concentrated all their efforts on speed. Knowing he was flanked by formidable rivals, Bladud was far from complacent. He wondered briefly if Rheinid had survived the initial challenge, but dared not spare a moment to look around.

As he stretched himself to the limit, the roar of the crowds was almost indistinguishable from the pounding of blood in his head.

At the very moment when he believed he would die if relief did not come, he found himself lying prostrate in the dust at the feet of his father. Hands were pulling at him, lifting him, raising him up on shoulders. Eager faces were thrust into his, voices shouting. He was the victor!

But over the heads of those who carried him in triumph he saw his brother Liel similarly borne aloft. It was clear the two had won the race together, and the watching crowd was mad with excitement. For a brief moment he looked into his father's eyes, and he saw there the trace of a shadow: the realisation that on the king's death the succession might be disputed and his people divided in their loyalty. But the moment of insight was over almost as soon as it was born, while Bladud and Liel were jostled and back-slapped and almost drowned in ale.

Long into the night these celebrations continued, and many a fight broke out between the rival factions supporting one prince against the other. Bladud endured it all as though in a dream, his head swimming in the ale and the great hall revolving sickeningly. Grinning faces came and went. Ribald songs rose in a crescendo. Occasionally he remembered Rheinid and once he thought he saw her across the hall, but almost instantly she disappeared behind another group of lurching revellers.

* * *

The following day saw the climax of the festival, when the winners of the great race were presented to Lugh. There would also be the offering of sacrifices, the presentation of gifts, the granting of petitions, the settlement of debts.

Bladud slept late and was woken roughly.

'Prince!' Yaruk urged him. 'Wake up! Wake up!' He was clearly afraid that Liel would have the advantage if Bladud missed any of the big events of the day. Bladud opened his eyes gingerly, then shut them at once as the light cut into them like a knife. As Yaruk shook his arm, his head thumped with a dull but persistent ache, his mouth feeling full of sand.

A cup was held to his lips.

'Prince . . . my lord,' Yaruk whispered 'it is noon. The sacrifices are due to start. The King and Prince Liel are already in place. They are waiting for you . . . but they might not delay much longer.'

Bladud struggled back to full consciousness, pulled on his clothes and drank the foul-tasting liquid he was presented with. Then he left his room and with Yaruk at his back urging him on, hurried through the narrow streets to the open space which lay in front of the White Mound. Here the main ceremony was traditionally held, and he could see the King and Prince Liel and Fergal the Druid all in full regalia. As rowdy and undisciplined as the race had been, so this event would be stately and orderly. Lesser priests and nobility were carefully ranged in hierarchical ranks, and as Bladud passed the rulers from outlying sub-kingdoms he spotted Keron with his daughter Rheinid. She was now dressed from head to toe in yellow, with gold in her sloe-black hair and wound about her tanned arms. He caught the flash of her dark eyes as he passed.

King Hudibras had reserved the place to his right for Bladud, as an indication to the people that Bladud was his chosen heir. Liel stood on his left.

One by one the pure white animals were sacrificed and the smoke of their burning rose to Lugh's shining orb. Using the language which his dynasty had brought from Troy, through Rome and Greece, to this grey island, Hudibras spoke a prayer of dedication, of praise, of hope for help and guidance

46

and protection in the future. Very few of the spectators could understand the words, but Bladud could, for he had made a point of learning the ancient tongue of his forefathers. When it came his turn to present himself to Lugh, to vow service and ask for protection, help and guidance, he spoke it clearly and with conviction. Looking up into the infinity of blue above, he knew that Lugh heard him, and believed that the light pouring from the sun at this moment was only a shadow of the light that would sustain him in his long and dangerous journey through the many realms of life.

But when Liel's turn came to dedicate himself to Lugh, he stumbled over the words as though he had learned them by rote and understood nothing of their meaning. He blurted them out so fast it was clear the whole ritual seemed nothing to him but a waste of time.

A special day was set aside for the settlement of debts, the payment of blood-money, the exchange of contract vows, and it was then that Keron made his move.

Hudibras was seated in the great hall on his throne, a huge chair elaborately carved by Yaruk from an oak tree felled by lightning. His two sons were seated on either side of him on lesser chairs, and Fergal the Druid stood slightly behind him, his hand resting on the back of the king's throne in symbolic gesture.

Bladud had been watching and listening intently to everything that occurred, his mind actively participating in every word, every judgement, but now he had begun to tire, and the last two cases that had come before the king he had barely noted. But suddenly he was all attention, for Keron, leading his daughter by the hand, was now standing before them. Liel, too, straightened in his seat and looked at the beautiful girl with lively interest. Her hair was combed down around her like a fine black cloak, falling from a crown of red flowers in her hair. Her arms were bare and her dress the colour of ripe corn, but she wore no jewellery. Her father, on the other hand, was clearly wearing every piece he possessed, taking no chances that anyone might overlook the fact that he was a man of substance. As Bladud remembered the poverty and degradation of Keron's subjects, his lip curled.

47

Keron bowed low before the dais. Rheinid, too, inclined her head and bent her knee. Hudibras noted her pride, her confidence, her grace, and wondered how such a daughter could belong to such a father.

In the silence the herald announced that the lord Keron son of Mel had come for settlement of a debt incurred in the game of fidchell.

Bladud started. Until this moment he had forgotten the stake he had foolishly agreed with Keron. The intervening year had been eventful enough to drive the details of that unpleasant night from his mind. So here he had come to claim his stake! What treasures would he demand? He wished he had had time to warn his father.

The memories came crowding back. As he looked at Rheinid, his blood stirred in memory of what they had done together in her bed. But with those erotic memories resurfaced his anger at having been tricked and manipulated.

Keron spoke for some time before Bladud began to listen properly. The first part of his speech consisted of boasting about his own prowess and that of his ancestors, which proved an exhaustive inventory.

'Yes, yes, enough!' Hudibras at last said impatiently. 'Why does your private game of fidchell concern the crown? Has someone dishonoured his pledge? Get to the point. Name the pledge. Name the debtor.'

'Your son Prince Bladud is the debtor, my lord,' Keron now declared in loud and ringing terms that no one in the whole court could fail to hear. 'And my daughter here is the pledge.'

Hudibras stared, as did everyone, at the young woman standing beside Keron.

Bladud was shocked.

To the furthest corners of the great hall a buzz of voices spread until the noise was almost deafening. What was this? What had he said? Was Prince Bladud refusing to pay some debt? Who was the girl? Had anyone ever heard of this Keron?

The King glared at his favourite son.

'What is this?' he demanded.

Bladud flushed.

48

'I – I am not sure, my lord . . .' he stammered.

Keron seemed unperturbed by the commotion he had caused.

He was smiling smugly at various acquaintances in the crowd now pressing closer to the dais.

Bladud looked at Rheinid and thought he saw in her eyes a certain satisfaction and triumph. It did not look as though she had been forced into this against her will.

Hudibras fixed Bladud with a questioning glare.

'I – I did indeed play fidchell with this man, father, a year ago. But there was no mention of the girl as stake.'

Hudibras turned to Keron.

'My lord, our agreed stake was that whoever won could ask of the other what he wished a year from that day.'

A gasp went around the assembled throng, and then there was silence, no one wanting to miss a word.

'Is this true?' Hudibras asked his son.

Bladud nodded dumbly.

'Did the lord Keron win?'

'Yes, my lord.'

Hudibras turned back to Keron, his face an iron mask.

'What do you ask for, sir?'

'That the Prince Bladud should marry my daughter Rheinid.'

The silence in the crowded hall was palpable. It was as though every man and woman in the place was holding breath. All eyes were fixed on the face of Hudibras.

For a long, long moment he stared at Keron's mean, smug face.

'Then my son is honour bound to marry your daughter,' the great king said coldly but firmly.

The hall exploded into sound once more. Everyone was shouting, everyone trying to be heard above the hubbub. Who was this unknown girl? Who this upstart, petty lord? Why should their favourite, their loved and honoured prince, heir to the throne of the High King – why should he marry this nobody, this trickster's daughter? Why had their prince laid himself open to such a situation? But he was young. Surely the king could . . . ?

But the High King's expression was implacable. His son

had given his word, and now there was no way out of it – as well Keron knew.

Bladud felt he was falling into some deep quagmire. Surely his father would extricate him? It was not that Rheinid was undesirable – it was just that he had been tricked. It was just that he was not ready for marriage . . . it was just that marriage was the last thing on earth he wanted at this time. He wanted travel, adventure – he wanted choice! At this moment he hated Rheinid. She was no innocent counter in this cunning game. She was a willing player, and she was dangerous. He looked into her dark eyes, and what he saw there chilled him.

He leapt from his chair.

'My lord . . .' he began passionately, determined to plead for his release from the pledge.

'You have given your word and you must honour it,' Hudibras said icily.

Bladud turned to Keron. 'Ask anything else: any jewel, any amount of gold, horses, cattle, land . . . Name it and it is yours.'

'I have named the stake,' Keron said, well knowing that, through his daughter's marriage to the crown prince, jewels, gold, horses, cattle, land would become his anyway.

'What kind of man are you that you give your daughter away on a game of fidchell?' Bladud shouted furiously. 'What kind of woman allows herself to be treated thus!'

The crowds murmured angrily in agreement.

Suddenly Liel spoke, rising to his feet beside Bladud.

'What kind of man are you to insult a woman so?' he demanded, gazing at Rheinid with deep admiration. 'You are a lucky man indeed to be offered such a prize, and gladly would any man here take your place!'

'Would *you* take my place, brother Liel?' Bladud asked bitterly.

'Gladly!' he repeated.

Keron stepped forward hastily, afraid to lose the advantage of the situation. Everyone believed Bladud would be king after the death of his father, for Hudibras made it no secret that he intended Bladud for the crown. Keron wanted his daughter to be queen.

50

'It was Prince Bladud who gave his word, my lord.'

Bladud looked desperately at Rheinid.

'My lady. It is not that you lack beauty in my eyes, but it is not my wish to be married at this time. I am a restless man, so you would be better off with my brother Liel. Take him in lieu of me.'

'You insult me, my lord,' she said smoothly, 'if you think I am so desperate for a husband that anyone will do. I have no doubt Prince Liel is a worthy man, and I am grateful for his courtesy' – she threw him a glance as appreciative as the one he had given her – 'but it is you whom I hold in my heart, and have done so since you came so passionately to my bed a year ago.'

'Enough!' Hudibras said sharply. 'The pledge is sealed. The marriage will take place. Sir, take your daughter away and prepare her for the wedding feast. This assembly is concluded. Any further matters must wait for another day.' He stood up irritably and strode out of the hall, the crowds falling back on either side before him.

Bladud sank back on his seat, stunned.

Liel stepped down and took Rheinid's arm, and ushered her and her father protectively through the hostile crowds.

Bladud could not persuade his father to release him from his pledge, no matter how hard he tried. For, as Hudibras said, how could the people trust a king who broke his word and would not honour his debts? That Keron had made his announcement in front of the maximum number of people was not an accident. He knew very well that no matter how the king and the prince might feel about the proposed marriage, there was no way they could wriggle out of it when their claim was witnessed by the whole court and all the sub-kings of the country. Whatever hostility was now aimed towards himself and his daughter – for marriage to Prince Bladud was a prize coveted by any young woman and there were many noble families vying for the honour – he would risk it. Keron took the precaution of not appearing in public from then on without armed guards. Within days the Festival of Lughnasa would be over, and Bladud managed at least to persuade his father to delay the marriage.

'Everyone is tired of feasting, father,' he said. 'It is time for them to return home and attend to their own affairs. Why not plan the wedding for the spring? The feast of Beltain would be appropriate for a wedding.'

Hudibras looked at him thoughtfully. 'Is this some ruse to escape this marriage?'

'No, my lord father. I will not go back on my word, though I bitterly regret having given it. But the delay will give our people time to get used to the idea, and for the feast to be prepared properly. It is surely not meet that the son of the High King should be married in haste, or his guests fed on the scraps and dregs from a previous feast?'

At last Hudibras grunted his assent. He himself would dearly like his son to find a way out of his commitment without sacrificing honour. Time might well give them an opportunity. If not, at least his people might settle down to the idea. He had observed the resentment clear on the faces of many of his nobles, and if the wedding was held now, it might well end in bloodshed. Besides, much as he despised Keron for pulling this trick, the girl seemed fair enough. She was in fact, he learned, the daughter of a distant kinswoman of his own dead wife.

So it was announced that the wedding of Prince Bladud and Rheinid daughter of Keron would take place during the Beltain festival of the following year.

Keron was not pleased with the unexpected delay, but could do nothing about it.

Finding his father adamant on the question of his marriage to Rheinid, the young Prince Bladud turned to Fergal the Druid for help. He was a thin, spare, sallow-skinned man with eyes that seemed much larger than they were because of the dark smudges that habitually ringed them, for Fergal rarely slept. Bladud knew that the best time to consult him on any private matter would be late at night.

'This girl. This Rheinid. What are your feelings about her?' Fergal asked severely as they settled down beside a little flickering lamp in Fergal's chamber.

Bladud was at a loss what to say. What *did* he feel about her? He was not sure.

52

'You hate her?'

'Y-yes.'

'Does she repel you?'

'No.'

The thin line of Fergal's mouth lifted in a half-smile. 'Then do you desire her?'

There came no reply, so the question was repeated.

'Yes,' admitted Bladud unwillingly.

'You hate her, yet desire her?'

'N-no. Not exactly.'

'What then?'

'She has been forced on me . . . She has forced herself on me.'

'And if you had met in some other way, you might have wanted her as your wife?'

'I don't know. I don't think so.'

'You must confront your feelings, boy. I cannot help you if you don't know yourself what it is you do want.'

'I want to be rid of her.'

'You are sure?'

'Yes.'

Fergal looked at him hard.

'Yes,' he repeated defiantly, and at that moment he was sure that was what he wanted.

'So be it,' said Fergal, and stood up.

Bladud stared at him in some surprise.

'Do you never sleep?' Fergal asked brusquely. 'Go to your bed, boy, and sleep.'

'But . . .'

'The matter need no longer concern you. Go sleep. Leave everything to me.'

Gratitude flooded Bladud's heart. He almost wanted to hug the old man, but Fergal was not a man you hugged no matter how grateful you felt. The prince left the room with a lighter step. His troubles were over. Fergal would deal with everything.

Curled among the luxurious furs of her bed in the great house of the High King, Rheinid stirred uneasily. As she opened her eyes, above her a great shadow seemed to be forming. She

53

called out to the guard her father had posted at her door on this last night before they set off for home. But he clearly did not hear her.

Bladud slept long and deeply, and was woken at last, when the summer sun was high in the sky, by a louder than usual hubbub in the courtyard. He could hear voices raised in anger.

'What now?' he muttered impatiently, dragging himself sleepily out of bed and into his clothes. He had been in the middle of a beautiful dream, a recurrent one in which he travelled on a ship sailing between deep red cliffs and up a shining river. A woman stood at his side; he could feel her thigh against his, her hand in his. He could see the wind blowing out her golden hair. He could feel the eagerness with which she gazed on the green, richly forested hills either side. He could sense her relief after so many stormy days at sea – after all the uncertainty as to when they would ever make landfall. He tightened his other hand on the hilt of his sword. Who would they have to contend with for this beautiful land? Who might they have to kill? A giant of stone had guarded the river mouth, and it had taken all his skill at persuasion to urge his men past it.

But then he woke. He always woke.

Muttering a curse he flung the door open and strode out into the blazing sunlight of the yard. The guards had Keron firmly in their grasp, and when he saw Bladud his shouting grew louder, his struggles to escape more desperate.

'What is this, my lord Keron?' Bladud snapped. 'Have you not caused enough trouble here already?'

'Where is she?' screamed Keron. 'What have you done with her?'

Bladud stared at him in surprise. This man, whom Bladud had come to see as a master of cool and calculating cunning, was now passionate with rage, hatred and sorrow. This was no act or pretence.

'Release him,' he commanded the guards. As they hesitated, he repeated the command. Keron shook himself free and stormed towards Bladud. The guards watched him closely, ready to move.

Perhaps it was because Bladud looked genuinely puzzled

54

that Keron stopped a few paces from him.

'I don't know where she is. I swear it. Did you not have guards?'

'Yes, I had guards,' shouted Keron, 'but who knows what sorcery was used! I've had them tortured but they swear they heard and saw nothing. Rheinid would not have gone anywhere against her will. She could defend herself against any man – except perhaps one she loved and trusted.'

'I swear I know nothing about this! But if anyone has harmed her I will see that they are punished in a way that will satisfy even you.' Bladud spoke with such conviction that Keron began to believe him.

Fergal! Bladud was thinking. *Fergal, what have you done? Lugh, great god of light, show me where she is. Let her not be harmed!*

But Fergal was nowhere to be found. His chamber was empty and his servants insisted they had not seen him leave it. When the distraught prince sought out his fellow Druids, they too had no idea where the High Priest had gone.

The court was soon in a furore. Luckily perhaps for Bladud, the High King had ridden out of the rath early in the morning and could not be immediately recalled.

It was not long before Liel came storming after Bladud demanding to be told what he had done with the girl. He clearly believed his brother responsible and found Bladud's protestations unconvincing.

If this could be proved against him, Liel thought with bitter satisfaction, Bladud would be finished as the golden boy, the natural heir, the favourite of the people! He secretly rejoiced at the turn of events, and determined to establish his brother's guilt.

Bladud refused to be drawn into a quarrel and strode tight-lipped away. It seemed to him that already those who had previously been on his side over Keron's trick were now turning against him. He did not know where to begin to look for Fergal or Rheinid.

Giving Liel and the others the slip he found his way up through the narrow streets to the White Mound where at least he would have a chance to think. There, as a child, he would communicate with the spirits of his ancestors, and

55

particularly with the beautiful queen of Brutus, Imogene the Greek. She had seemed more real to him than his own dead mother. Part mother, part lover, part goddess, she would comfort him when he was truly in trouble. As he grew older and busier, perhaps more rational, he had turned to her less and less – but this day he knew that he needed her again. There was nowhere else he could go.

The river below was full of boats riding on a silver tide, and beside them, swimming with quiet elegance, were five and twenty pure white swans. As he whispered his prayer to Imogene, the swans lifted simultaneously off the water, making a thunderous noise as their feet beat against the surface in the effort to lift their bodies into the air. At last, necks stretched to their limit, they broke free and, resembling a graceful flight of arrows, headed towards the Island of Thorns.

Thorn Island. Bladud remembered the times he had spent with the priest Fergal on Thorn Island. It was a place of extraordinary sanctity since the very ancient days. On the high ground stood a circle of tall standing stones that must have existed since the beginning of time. Even Yaruk's people had no memory of its building, though they had used it for their secret and sacred rites until the new rulers of the land forbade them access, fearing that it gave the rebellious population uncanny powers.

Below the hill, to the west, spread a grove of oak trees, sacred to the Druids, to which Fergal and his fellow priests would frequently retire in order to commune with their gods.

On an area of flat ground to the east had been built a labyrinth of dry-stone walls, barely higher than a tall man. This was the work of Bladud's Trojan ancestors, who in turn had descended from the Minoans of Crete. So in this place, not far from the city of the White Mound, and embraced by the two streams flowing into the Tain, the three mystical centres of three different races stood side by side.

Imogene had often come to Bladud in visions and dreams associated with white swans. In one recurrent dream of great clarity both he and she, as swans linked by a golden chain, had flown together over a still and silver lake, and he could yet remember his joy and exhilaration as they winged it high

56

in the air. He could still recall their reflection in the mirror surface of the lake below, the thrill of recognition as he realised it was he and she reflected there. He longed to fly again as he had flown that night, and he could never see a swan without thinking of Imogene.

Now he had asked her for help in finding Rheinid and, as if on cue, the swans on the river had taken off in flight towards Thorn Island.

Kissing his hand in gratitude to the invisible Lady of the Mound, Bladud turned and ran down the hill. Dodging and darting, he retraced his steps to his home, where he pulled a grey cloak over his shoulders and a hood over his head. He did not want to be followed, and the Golden Prince could not pass unnoticed through the town gates. He confided only in Yaruk, who hired him a mangy horse belonging to a merchant. His own stallion, Lightning, would be swifter but too easily recognised.

With Yaruk seated behind him, together they made what progress they could. But when they reached the island, Yaruk was left behind with the horse and the cloak. Since the tide was in, Bladud was forced to swim across the shallow river. If Fergal and Rheinid were indeed there, they must have crossed at low tide, when the ancient stepping stones rose above the mud flats.

Bladud could never suppress a shiver of apprehension when he set foot on this island. The tales of ancient magical battles involving beings from other worlds, which excited him in the safety of his own hearth, now came to terrify him. There was an atmosphere about the place which he could not define, but he sensed he was standing on the threshold of other and unfamiliar realms. For a moment he felt like turning away.

'How stupid to assume a flight of swans could be a message from the dead,' he chided himself, swinging, as he often did, between belief and doubt.

Nevertheless he would look for Fergal in the grove, the sacred place of his people.

He entered the leafy shade under wide-spreading trees, moving respectfully as if aware that he was trespassing. At first he encountered occasional pools of sunlight between the trees, but as the grove grew denser, sunlight merely flickered and flashed until, deep within, it almost disappeared. These inner regions were dim and difficult to penetrate. He had started by following a broad path which soon divided and sub-divided until he was walking on a track he could barely discern. Following instinct, pushing aside undergrowth, he searched for the clearing where the rites and rituals took place, but although he could not have gone far astray, it was nowhere to be seen.

He stopped. What now? If Fergal and the girl were on the island, it was clear they had not come this way. No sign of broken twigs, or of bramble branches or bracken fronds thrust aside.

Peering up into the branches of a huge beech tree, he was startled to meet the gaze of a horned god. But looking more closely, he found it was no more than the distorted shape of knots and branches in the bark, creating the illusion of Cernunnos.

He shrugged and walked on a pace or two, then heard a twig snap somewhere to his left. A mature and antlered stag was there, its head lifted, sniffing the air. For a long moment they stared at each other; Bladud had an uneasy feeling that there was something unnatural in the animal's gaze.

At that moment the stag moved off, and Bladud followed him.

The stag led him deeper and deeper into the forest, always keeping just out of reach. It showed no fear, and frequently looked over its shoulder as if to ascertain that the two-legged creature was following. Bladud became surprised at the size of the forest. He knew the size of Thorn Island, and this grove was only part of it, yet they walked and walked and never seemed to reach the end of it.

Just when Bladud had decided he would follow the stag no further, they came upon the sacred clearing of the Druids, where stood the stone altar used for sacrifices. There he saw Fergal in front of the altar, both arms raised above his head. One hand held a sprig of mistletoe, the holy plant of the gods, fallen from heaven and grown on the sacred oak without contact with the earth, the other a golden knife with an obsidian cutting edge. On the altar he could make out the figure of a young woman, her long black hair falling like a curtain over the cold stone.

'Fergal!' he screamed, but to his horror no sound came from his throat. He tried to rush forward, but his limbs seemed rooted to the ground. As helpless as a tree, he knew he was about to witness something he could not prevent. His rage almost choked him. He had always hated the Druid propensity to blood sacrifices, but this was murder.

In the old days stories were told of prisoners piled high in wicker baskets and burned alive as sacrifices to the gods. Sometimes, even today, when disasters threatened, it was said a human being was offered to the gods, but in Bladud's lifetime the only sacrifices he knew of had involved animals. The prince could still remember once two white bulls bound by golden chains and crowned with mistletoe. As a child, then, he had been sickened by the gush of blood as the axe fell – the sudden contrast between the powerful living beast and the ugly, lifeless carcass. Far from filling him with religious fervour, the sight left him feeling disgusted and depressed.

'No! No! No!' he screamed now, but still no sound came from him.

The stag had disappeared, but as he cast his eyes about in desperation to find some help in his predicament, he noticed that the grove all around the clearing was crowded with shadowy figures.

The gods themselves are gathering to watch this ghoulish act! he thought bitterly. *How could they allow this young and vibrant girl to meet such a death!* He remembered her breast against his shoulder as she stooped to pour his wine in her father's house. He remembered her bronzed limbs ready for the race. Passion at last broke him free of his invisible bonds and, with a shout of fury, he raced into the clearing to seize the upraised arm which held the knife.

But there was nothing . . . there was no one there! He stood alone in the Druid's clearing, in the sacred grove beside an empty altar. No Fergal. No Rheinid. No shadowy figures among the trees.

He was astonished and bewildered. It had all seemed so real. On the cold stone of the altar lay a single red flower.

Wearily he turned to go, but then swung back to the altar

59

again. Surely this flower was one from the crown Rheinid had worn in her hair on the day she had been brought before his father at the great assembly.

He reached out slowly with a shaking hand. Would this too disappear? But it was real. He held it up – soft and cool, though a little limp. So she *had* been here.

Fearfully he examined the altar stone and the ground all around it. No sign of blood. No sign of struggle. But there on the grass, where a path led out of the clearing, another red flower. It was crushed as though trodden underfoot.

Without further hesitation he set off along the same path, studying the ground for more flowers. He was now in a mood of dull, aching anxiety. What game could Fergal be playing?

This time as he followed the path, he was very soon out of the grove, and with great relief he suddenly came into bright daylight. The darkness of the wood, the feeling of being perpetually watched and followed, had oppressed him. Now the sunshine lifted his heart, and left him feeling he could again face anything. He looked gratefully up into the blue sky. The afternoon was well advanced.

He was now near the hill crowned by the ancient ring of tall monoliths. It reminded him of the one where he had encountered the two spirit-women and their magical flask, so he had every intention of leaving it well alone. But somewhere in the back of his mind a memory was stirring.

He had questioned Yaruk about these stone circles that appeared in such numbers across the land, since his own people were loth to approach them. Yaruk had told him stories of how wisdom had befallen this one and that one who had entered a circle, how people had acquired unnatural strength and knowledge. While some had encountered spirit-beings yet lived to tell the tale, others had disappeared and never been seen again. He noticed that the hawthorn bushes, from which Thorn Island took its name, grew thickly around the perimeter, but not within the circle itself. Inside the grass and flowers grew wild and tall, the sunshine bathing them in a most inviting radiance. Perhaps within the circle everything would become clear to him. After all, he had ventured into one of these forbidden places before and come out alive.

From this vantage point he would be able to survey most of the island. From the circle he might gain knowledge and strength to outwit the wily Druid. He hesitated on the threshold for a moment nevertheless.

The tall stones were rich in white crystal, of the same kind that covered the burial mound of Imogene – of the same kind as the fragment he had stolen. But it was only visible when one was as close as he was. From a distance the stones looked grey even in the sunlight, though they might be seen to sparkle once or twice when the sun caught them at a certain angle. Under cloud the stones looked dark and ominous, and at night they could inspire real fear in the heart of anyone who chanced upon them.

Taking a deep breath, he plunged inside the charmed ring and waded through long grass towards the centre. There he stopped, uncertain. He wondered what to do. Should he pray? But to whom?

Since these ancient people had built their temples in circular form, this was surely a sign that they worshipped the sun – that great circle in the sky, the symbol of wholeness, of eternity that has no beginning and no end.

He felt a strange compulsion to turn. And he began to turn and turn and turn . . . a circle within a circle . . . within a circle . . . The sun seemed to turn with him . . . the earth under his feet was turning . . . the tall and towering stones blurred as he moved faster and faster, until it seemed they formed a shining and a continuous wall all around him. He felt as though he was confined within a crystal, looking out – and what he saw made him gasp. Filmy figures, half transparent, surrounded him – not dark and menacing and watching, like the ones he had seen before in the sunless grove, but shimmering with light. Moving in a continuous dance of which he became part. No longer a stranger in an alien land, but an integral part of a time and place that felt like 'home'.

The beauty of it was exquisite, and his feelings were wonderfully extended – but soon the intensity became too much and he fell on the ground in a faint.

As he regained consciousness, he found himself back in the

61

steaming sanctuary of the Oracle of Sul. He saw no surprise in the old woman's eyes: it was as though the year since he had consulted her had never happened, and he stood in exactly the same position, even wearing the same clothes as then. His heart missed a beat. Did this mean that time could be manipulated so that Keron's claim and Rheinid's abduction had never happened? Momentarily he felt as relieved as if he had woken from a nightmare – but then, strangely, he experienced a sense of loss.

Was he actually sorry that Rheinid had not re-entered his life?

The oracle smiled, her bead-black eyes shining with amusement. Bladud stared, confused. It seemed to him that the ancient, wrinkled, toothless hag was growing younger before his eyes, the years, the decades sloughing off like the skin of a snake. She stood before him at last as a young and beautiful woman: a woman with long raven black hair, with firm bronzed limbs . . . Bladud stepped back astonished. Rheinid herself?

A huge bird that had been sitting quietly on its perch at the rear of the sanctuary now lunged forward. But not the eagle he had seen here before. This was a raven, he could tell from its harsh and raucous cry. He put up his arm to protect his eyes and stumbled from the hut, tripping and falling. He expected the raven to attack him. He could hear it screeching and beating its wings close above his head. And then it seemed the creature must have flown off. Cautiously he raised his head. He no longer lay in the sanctuary of the oracle, but once more in the stone circle on Thorn Island. He sat up and looked around in wonderment. There was no sign of mystical beings. No oracle. No Rheinid. He was all alone on the grass of a derelict and deserted temple.

But no – not completely alone. On nearly every one of the tall stones that ringed him was perched a raven, silently watching him.

He stood up slowly, keeping a wary eye out for the huge black birds. He felt weak and exhausted and confused by these powerful and magical places. There and then he decided to head straight back to the fort and accept whatever punishment his father thought fit to mete out to him for the disappearance of Rheinid. He would abandon his attempt to pursue. Halfway down the hill he looked back. They were still there, watching him. He walked on with gritted teeth, pretending a confidence he did not feel.

But then, as he came in sight of the stone-built labyrinth which lay between the hill and the river, he saw two figures enter it. Unmistakably those of Fergal and Rheinid.

He stopped in his tracks, longing to get back to the fort, among familiar faces where everything was predictable. Yet if he could take Rheinid safely back with him, how much easier his life would be!

The decision was made. Without further hesitation he sped the intervening distance to the labyrinth and reached the entrance within moments. But they were already out of sight amid the narrow corridors twisting and turning torturously between the stone walls.

He called out, but the sound of his voice merely came back to him as blurred and incomprehensible echoes.

'Fergal, I must see you! I must speak with you!' he shouted again.

He paused. He listened. But no other voice joined the reverberating echoes of his own.

He hurried forward, cursing the structure. This labyrinth had been designed specifically to cause confusion. His people had long since forgotten its purpose, but they knew it harked back to the early history of his race before they began their migrations from their distant homeland in the east.

Bladud took one turn – and then another. Faced by an endless choice of corridors, he decided to always pick the right-hand one, for someone had once told him that in this way he could eventually reach the centre. But turn right then right again as he might, he never seemed any nearer to the centre, and he had long since lost track of the exit. Thoroughly out of breath he leant against a wall and thought bitterly about Fergal.

You have done it to me again, old man! he muttered. *You and she probably never entered this place at all. I'm sick of your illusions! I'm sick of playing games!* How would he ever find his way out again? The sun must be near to setting, for its light was much dimmer than when he had entered. The sky above the unroofed labyrinth glowed a uniform orange, as though the outside world had gone up in a giant conflagration and he alone was left, trapped in this accursed place – the doomed victim of tricks and deception.

He sank down on his haunches and buried his head in his arms, too tired and discouraged to go on. What if he never did become king? Did it really matter?

I'll get on a ship and sail away, he thought. *I have places to see . . . I have things to learn . . .*

There he stayed until the sunlight was almost gone, and the first star of evening hung above his head in a sky of pale aquamarine.

Then he stood up, and decisively took a turn to the left. Immediately before him lay the open space which formed the centre of the labyrinth. And there, seated on a stone bench, was Rheinid. Of Fergal himself there was no sign.

Her shoulders hunched, in that first moment she seemed as disconsolate as he. But when she noticed him, a light flooded her face, and her whole body straightened up, as a drooping plant revives under life-giving water.

Calling out his name, she rushed at him and flung herself into his arms. Just as eagerly he clasped her to him, and they were laughing, kissing, talking all at once.

As they pulled apart at last, Fergal was standing beside them.

'I see,' he said with amusement, 'you know now what it is you want.'

Bladud stared at him, speechless. So all this anxiety and fear had been merely to teach him, to make him face and accept his own feelings.

'Damn you!' he burst out indignantly.

Fergal raised an eyebrow, still smiling. 'If you want to get out of here before dark, you had better follow me.'

They had not gone far towards the town when they heard a commotion from the hill, and looking up they saw a group of guards attacking someone on the slope just below the stone circle. Bladud left Rheinid's side and sprinted to the victim's aid.

'Stop!' he yelled, and the guards drew back unwillingly, one of them administering a vicious last kick to the man's ribs.

'My lord.' Their leader bowed.

Bladud stared at the crushed and bleeding figure on the ground.

'Yaruk!' he cried, and knelt at his side to raise him in his arms. Yaruk, barely conscious, managed a rueful smile with swollen lips.

'What is this?' Bladud shouted angrily to the guards.

Torna, the leader, looked down at the prince holding his victim.

'My lord, Prince Liel sent us out to find the lady Rheinid, and we found this man skulking out here. Then we saw him try to enter this forbidden place.' He indicated the circle with an expression of disgust. Such a place was not only taboo but associated in the minds of Torna and his like with vague and dark and loathsome practices.

'This man is a friend of mine,' Bladud said haughtily. 'And, as you can see,' he waved an arm to where Fergal and Rheinid waited beneath the hill, 'the lady Rheinid is unharmed under my protection.'

Torna looked annoyed, and his men drew back embarrassed.

'My lord, we thought . . .'

'You did not think, man,' Bladud said bitterly. This kind of incident was all too common. Bladud swiftly commanded two of the guards to lift Yaruk up and carry him.

'If he dies, you die!' He glared into the sullen and resentful eyes of Torna, then he turned back to Yaruk with pity and affection.

'I'm sorry, my friend. You must have been concerned that I was away so long.' Bladud put his hand on his shoulder. 'The lady is found. All is well. But there are many strange tales to tell about the chase!'

Yaruk smiled painfully.

'Take him – fast but carefully. See that my father's physician attends him.'

The captain saluted with bad grace, and the group set off.

Once Bladud and Rheinid had returned to court, they were

65

inseparable. Their eyes were interlocked even when their arms were not. It was clear that a great deal had changed between them. Though he detested Keron, Hudibras himself could see that for Bladud to marry Rheinid now would be no punishment, but a reward. Yet when Bladud asked that they might be wed immediately, and not wait for the feast of Beltain, Hudibras refused.

'No, the girl must return home with her father,' he insisted. 'We need time for proper arrangements for a wedding worthy of my son. If I bowed to every changing whim of a youth who blows cold one day and hot the next, what do you think would happen to my kingdom?'

Bladud was silent. His body burned to be close to Rheinid, so how could he wait through the long winter? But he realised his father was in no mood to alter his decision.

Rheinid departed with her father in some haste. Keron was shrewd enough to know he had pushed the king's patience to the limit, so would be well advised to put as much distance between them as he could for a while. His plan was working out better than he had hoped, and it was a bonus that Rheinid and Bladud were now so much in love. Listening to their protestations of undying devotion, and seeing the desire in Bladud's eyes, he felt confident there would be no backing out of the marriage arrangement. He could not have wished for it to turn out better, Keron thought smugly, as he rode out through the great gate of the High King's castle.

But Hudibras had refused to let Bladud accompany them even part of the way, and it was Prince Liel who rode at Rheinid's side as she left her lover behind.

5

The Cauldron and the Wheel

As the night of Samhain approached, in every rath in the land, every hut, every cottage, every house, they locked and barred the windows and doors, for this was the night when the graves gave up their dead and beings from other realms walked the earth. Most people chose to pass the night awake, noisily carousing with friends to keep fear and ghosts at bay. Bladud was visiting his uncle Urien. Four oxen were roasting to feed the multitude who crowded in for safety behind the wooden walls of his stockade. The whole place was so well lit with fires and torches it could almost have been day. It would be a bold and persistent ghost indeed that would venture into such a place.

On the night of the great feast Bladud was in a detached mood, as though he was merely an observer rather than a participant in this event.

He drank the wine that was copiously poured into the silver goblet he held, but no matter how much he drank, it seemed this night to have no effect on him. All around him servants and slaves kept passing around joints of meat. He became half aware of an argument starting up. Two huge fellows were each demanding the largest cut of the roast. The servant had offered it to one of them, but the other claimed he was the braver warrior and so the champion's portion was rightfully his. Bladud glanced over at his uncle, but the king seemed merely amused, continuing to eat and drink without concern.

Bladud watched as the argument turned to physical blows. Within moments the convivial mood of the whole hall had

67

changed. Men leapt up, overturning benches, and rushed to the walls where their weapons were hung. As though nothing was happening, the king continued feasting, while all around him his guests took sides and attacked their neighbours, while the two who had started the fracas lunged and lurched up and down on the very table where the king was seated. Dishes scattered across the rocking wood, chairs flew through the air.

And then, through the mist of this mêlée, Bladud noticed a man walking towards him, calmly untouched by the chaos and violence around him. He thought he recognised him. But from where?

He remembered suddenly, when the man halted right before him, lifting a golden cup, ridged and ringed with jewels, from which he invited the prince to drink.

Bladud stared around at the blood and sweat, at the fires already started by the overturning of the lamps. He stared at his uncle's grease-stained face, his eyes glazed with wine as he surveyed his subjects with drunken satisfaction. And then Bladud took the cup from the hand of the stranger and drank from it.

All at once he was no longer confined inside the hall, but stood outside on a huge grey plain, with mist swirling around his ankles. It was daylight, but there was no sign of the sun.

Suddenly a battle-axe descended towards his head, and instinctively he raised his sword arm to protect himself. Now he was in the middle of some fearsome battle, no longer an observer but a participant. These were no shadowy figures, and as his sword bit into solid flesh, he knew he was fighting for his life. He had fought at his father's side ever since he was old enough to wield his sword, but had hated every skirmish, and he hated this. Yet his mysterious enemies kept coming, and he needed all his strength and skill to survive. What he had first assumed to be mist was actually smoke issuing from fire beneath a huge cauldron. Continually lines of men approached it, dragging their dead. As they drew near they mounted some steps and flung the corpses into the boiling cauldron. On the other side of it the revived and healed bodies of the dead warriors climbed out to return to the battle. On and on it went, this deadly cycle. Massacre following massacre.

Wearily he fought on, and still his assailants came at him, till he was in despair. Was there no end to this? Generation after generation . . . army following army . . . war upon war . . . Blindly men gave themselves over to mutilation and death.

He felt an overwhelming urge to tip over that cauldron and smash it to pieces. He had heard tales of magical cauldrons that promised immortality, but this endless cycle of life was pointless. Those that emerged from it merely went on killing. What kind of life was this? What point was there to immortality if there was no point to life in the first place or possibility of progress in the new life when it was restored? Then all began to fade – the grey plain disappearing . . .

He found himself back in the hall of his uncle.

The next morning Bladud took leave of the wreckage of his uncle's hall, the men asleep among the broken seats, and the spilled wine. He set off for home. The last time he had travelled this way it was in summer, with every shade of green to delight his eyes. But now the year was on the turn and the colours of gold and flame were everywhere.

Though a curl of mist followed the curve of the river, the hills were clear and shining in the sunlight. Autumn sunlight always seemed more fragile, more transparent than the blaze of summer. He sucked in deep breaths of the clean air, trying to forget the bloody images of the night before. And, such is the resilience of the human spirit, the dark gloom of his nocturnal thoughts dispersed as swiftly as the river mist.

Birds sang graciously from every tree. Spider webs decorated with tiny gleaming crystals of dew were strung from many a tall grass. Hares were out fearlessly seeking their breakfast on the fields.

Bladud felt like singing. In the woods his horse's hooves scarcely made a sound on the thick carpet of fallen leaves and damp moss. He looked up and rejoiced at the shafts of light driving through gaps in the high canopy above. Golden leaves sifted down slowly and silently, some landing on his shoulders, richer and more beautiful than any golden brooch fashioned by craftsman's fire.

If there were spirits abroad this day, they were not the dumb, warring spirits of the night before, but spirits of joy that sang in the silver streams, whispered in the shining leaves, floated like gossamer in the glimmering air . . .

This pleasant mood lasted a good part of the day, but towards the evening he witnessed an event that brought back the horror of his vision of the grey fields of battle.

He was in the shelter of a copse, when he heard men shouting, cattle lowing and hooves pounding. In a position to see without being seen he witnessed Keron and his followers driving cattle before them in feverish haste. Behind them, other men were in hot pursuit.

Suddenly a group of men from Keron's party, led by Keron himself, wheeled around to ride straight for their pursuers, while the rest continued shouting and hollering and cracking whips, to drive the cattle forwards in a cloud of dust.

Bladud watched as pursuers and pursued then joined in battle. A shower of spears, their iron tips plunging into screaming men and beasts alike. He saw the flash of swords, the hauling of riders off their mounts, the punching and wrenching and stabbing.

At first Keron's men took the advantage, and their pursuers were forced into retreat. But then a further band of men came galloping up from the east to join the fray. For a moment he thought these were reinforcements for Keron, but the pursuers seemed to take sudden heart and turn back to the fight.

Bladud watched as Keron and his men were trapped and squeezed between these two opposing forces. He was too far away to reach them in time and go to their aid. He saw Keron hauled off his horse and hacked to pieces, most of his followers sharing the same fate.

Bladud was horrified to witness such savagery. Cattle raiding between the sub-kings was not uncommon, for it was in his cattle that a man displayed his wealth. After such a raid it was normal for months of sporadic feuding to sour the relations between the raiders and the raided, until his father,

70

the High King, was called in to adjudicate, to extract compensation or demand the return, with interest, of the stolen cattle. Bladud would not have expected such indiscriminate slaughter and dismemberment.

Bladud rode out as fast as he could but by the time he arrived at the scene of the massacre the victors had galloped off. Sickened, he stared down at the gruesome sight. It was only the blood-soaked clothes that identified Keron, for his head had been carried off as a trophy by his enemies.

Bladud wanted to turn and ride away, to get as far as he could from this hideous place. But he must go to Keron's rath and tell them what had happened. These bodies must be identified and honourably buried.

As he approached Keron's hill-fort, he realised that the horror was not yet over. A party of the men who had so ignobly slaughtered Keron were now attacking his rath itself. Its gates were tight closed, but it was by no means impregnable. Better planned hill-forts had entrances set safely behind a series of twisting and turning paths, so that no enemy could ride directly up to the gate. Others had also more than one encircling defensive earthen ring surmounted by its rampart, and some ramparts had spikes leaning outwards to prevent an enemy scaling them. But Keron's defences were simple, and his best fighters now lay dead on the open plain below.

Rheinid! Bladud thought, and a cold hand seemed to grip his heart. What would these men do to her?

This time he did not stop to consider what possible good he might do against so many. He set off riding harder than he had ever ridden before. Already as he reached the foot of the slope, his sword was out and his face distorted with battle rage.

The gate lay open and the attackers were swarming around a town already burning. He rode among black smoke and through screaming women and children, scarcely concerned if the hooves of his horse trampled anyone in the way. He could think of nothing but of finding Rheinid before the others did.

In the chaos he managed to reach the great house without challenge. Its door was severely battered; fire balls were

71

thrown on the thatched roof. Riding to one side and standing on his saddle he leapt to a gap in the walls high under the eaves. Slithering through, he scrambled down and ran through the corridors and chambers of Keron's house. Terrified servants scattered before him.

He found her in her own chamber. She was standing watching the door, a dagger in one hand, as if daring any who entered to molest her at their peril. Her face did not lighten when she saw him, but her grip on the dagger tightened.

'Rheinid!' he cried.

But suddenly there were men at his back and more violent men pushing forward. Turning to them, thinking to assert his authority as the High King's son, he did not see her lunge forward. But he felt her dagger pierce his flesh.

'My lord!' Torna, one of his father's guards, leapt forward, sword raised to drive it into her heart.

'No!' Bladud shouted. 'No!' And he flung himself between them.

Torna hesitated, then drew back. Behind him other men crowded into the room but, recognising the prince, they retreated.

'My father shall hear what shameful things you have done this day!' he shouted.

But then it seemed that all around him a dark cloud was forming. For a moment he saw Rheinid's face come close to his, and then it vanished.

She reached out to catch him as he fell forward.

For Bladud the next few days passed in a haze of weird and disturbing dreams. The wound Rheinid had given him was deep. Sometimes he saw her leaning over him solicitously; and sometimes he saw her, raven-winged, flying above his bed. Sometimes she lifted a cup of cool water to his lips, and sometimes he was pursuing her through a forest that became deeper and darker with every step. He saw her face in waterfalls, in rocks, in trees. He heard her voice in the wind, in the whine of a spear seeking its mark, in the shriek of a bird of prey. And all these visions seemed equally real.

On the third day her face above him was joined by that of his own father.

72

Bladud studied the High King's face carefully, wondering if he was really there. The man was grey-bearded, grave, stern; but the eyes that gazed into those of his son were full of affection and concern.

Why is he here? Bladud thought, but then the face was dissolving. *Not real*, Bladud thought. *Nothing holds. Nothing stays . . .*

As Hudibras straightened up, his presence seemed to fill the room. Beside the door Rheinid waited, wondering what he would do next. If Bladud died, she knew her own life might soon be over. But if he lived – what then?

The great king walked from the room without a backward glance at his son, and without acknowledging Rheinid's presence. For him she might as well not have existed.

Biting her lip she stepped forward to look down at the wounded prince. His eyes were still closed, but it seemed to her he was sleeping more peacefully than before. She was still there at midnight when he opened his eyes and spoke her name.

As Bladud slowly recovered and prepared to return home, he suggested that Rheinid should accompany him, but she refused. She was convinced that his father had somehow been involved in the murder of her father. Though Bladud protested it was impossible, he was sufficiently haunted by Torna's unexpected presence at Keron's rath to have serious misgivings.

But meanwhile, night after night, she lay with him as his strength returned, and when the time came to part it was a difficult wrench for both of them.

As the winter deepened Bladud suspected Hudibras did not want his son's marriage to take place.

One late afternoon, as the prince stood with his back to a huge log fire, while the wind howled outside and the snow piled up on the burial mound of his ancestors, he pleaded for the wedding feast to be moved forward, seeing that Rheinid was now all alone in the world. He looked anxiously at his father, sunk in deep furs, his elbows resting on the arms of the royal chair.

'That girl was forced on you. So why would you want to go through with this?'

'I love her.'

'She has bad blood. Her father was a trickster and a cattle rustler.'

'Her mother was a descendant of the same royal line as my own mother.'

Both Rheinid's mother and Bladud's were indeed from the same ancient and respected Celtic family. Both had died when their children were very young. Rheinid was Keron's only acknowledged offspring. Bladud was the sole child of his father's first and only happy marriage. Liel was the son of his second wife, later divorced in favour of a third, but equally unsatisfactory marriage.

'She took a dagger to you.'

'But only when she mistook me for an enemy. What was she to think when the rath was under attack by our own people?'

'She might have killed you.'

'But she didn't. And her spirit in defending herself surely shows of what mettle she is made?'

'We will wait until Beltain, as we had planned, and then we shall see.'

'And what guarantee have I that she will still be alive by Beltain?' Bladud said with rash bitterness.

The face of Hudibras suddenly clouded. He stood up and glared at his son.

'What are you suggesting?'

'Torna is your man, my lord.'

'Torna was sent to attack cattle raiders. He exceeded his duty. He has been punished and dismissed from my service.'

Hudibras would say no more, and Bladud was wise enough not to press the matter further.

One day in the gloomiest and darkest month of the year, the watchman sent word to the High King, alerting him to the arrival of a considerable entourage of carts and horsemen, followed at some distance by a motley crowd on foot, carrying what appeared to be their worldly possessions.

Warriors and scouts were at once sent out to investigate.

Bladud and Yaruk stood on the ramparts, watching the grey columns of figures bent against the icy and driving rain, as they struggled through the thick mud. It was not the time of year for travelling or visiting. Soon people were gathering all along the ramparts to observe. No one feared attack in this weather, so children were lifted up on shoulders to get a better view.

Bladud could see the captain of his father's warriors meet up with the leading horseman, his followers positioning themselves around the two while they talked. The weary columns of travellers bunched up behind them increasingly as those out of earshot did not realise they were meant to halt. To Bladud it was obvious they had travelled a considerable way in this inclement weather. The sight of the city of Trinovantum, promising shelter and warmth, food and rest, must have seemed very enticing to them.

The crowd was on the move again, the captain of the High King's warriors now leading them. Beside him rode a figure in a billowing cloak, but from this distance it was not possible for Bladud and Yaruk to identify who it was. 'Some king, driven out of his rath and seeking sanctuary, no doubt,' Yaruk said. This was not an uncommon occurrence, though most such skirmishes were fought in the summer months.

'Their leader doesn't ride like someone who has suffered defeat,' Bladud argued, for even from this distance he noticed the proud bearing.

In victory Celtic kings were arrogant and boastful; but in defeat they were abject with shame and self-pity.

Three huge black ravens flew down to share Bladud's vantage point on the ramparts. He looked at them uneasily: what did they presage? They strutted up and down for a while with clumsy, ungainly steps, and then took off, heading towards the approaching travellers. As the birds circled, Bladud could see the High King's captain flailing at them with his sword to drive them away. But the leader of the travellers raised an arm as though to greet them, and one landed on a shoulder, the others flying off towards the raw, red sun setting over the marshes.

'He who is a friend to the raven,' Yaruk said darkly, 'has black fire in his belly.'

75

'But Bran employs ravens to guard his burial mound, and Bran's other name is Bendigeid Vran – the Blessed,' said Bladud. And then: 'I'm going down to meet them!' And he was away at once, running and leaping like a deer to the stables where his stallion was housed.

On a signal from the captain the gates were opened wide. Bladud rode out in a certain thrill of excitement. He was bored and weary with confinement in the town, restless for the spring, and now here was something that promised some interest. On his approach, the raven lifted off the cloaked shoulder and flew away.

As Bladud reined up before the stranger, the hood was flung back and at last he could see who it was. He gasped. Rheinid's cheeks were red from the cold, her dark eyes sparkling like polished jet, her thick hair plaited up with gold and woven around her head like a crown. There was gold at her throat and on her wrists. A huge brooch of gold pinned the cloak to her shoulder. She looked magnificent in spite of the mud splashed on the hem of her garments and the rain pouring on her head.

And so she entered the city triumphantly with Prince Bladud at her side, and the people falling back from her path, bowing but gazing admiringly at her stunning beauty. If any of them remembered how it was she had come into their prince's life, they did not think of that now. Everyone loves a romance, and the prince looked very much in love as he rode that day beside her into the ancient city of his Trojan ancestors. The Celts who were present were pleased that one of their own would reign beside the Trojan, and those who knew her mother had been kinswoman to their own much mourned queen were pleased for that as well. To the original native people both Celts and Trojans signified oppression, and some turned away from the procession thinking only of the extra work in feeding and housing so many intruders. Others, however, were seduced by the grandeur of the lady and followed behind, trying to catch a glimpse and enduring all kinds of indignities as they were pushed aside. There was a saying that if you jostled a Celt you provoked an instant conflagration, but if you shoved one of the locals they moved aside like water flowing into an alternative channel.

Rheinid would have liked time to rest before she met the High King, but messengers had already arrived to escort her directly to the great hall.

The room fell silent as she confronted him at last. She stood straight and proud, her mud-soaked cloak held close around her, the hood let down to reveal her head with its striking crown of black and gold.

'Lady Rheinid,' Hudibras said coldly. 'What brings you here before the appointed time?'

'I come, my lord, to claim the marriage you contracted with my father.'

'Are you so much on heat, my girl, that you cannot wait until Beltain?'

'If your son could have waited too, my lord, no doubt I would have been happy to do so.'

Saying this, she flung back her cloak so that everyone in the great hall could see she was pregnant.

The brow of Hudibras darkened.

'Another trick, my lady?'

Rheinid turned towards Bladud who stood dumbfounded, at her side.

'A trick, my lord?' she asked.

Bladud flushed.

'No,' he muttered, turning helplessly to his father, not knowing what to say.

It was clear to all that Bladud was very much in love. When Rheinid was in the room with him his eyes were on her every movement. When she was absent, he was restless and ill at ease. It seemed to the shrewd old eyes of Hudibras that Rheinid was not as tied to his son by love's sorcery as he was to her. But she had beauty, spirit and dignity, and her mother's blood ran in her veins as surely as did her father's, so she might make a good queen. The king therefore decided to allow the wedding to go ahead.

A compromise date was fixed halfway between Rheinid's unexpected arrival and the Beltain Feast.

The sun seemed to return earlier than usual to the icy land. Long before they expected them, the spring flowers were already blooming; the birds came back from their sojourn abroad in chattering strings. The temperature was mild; the fearsome gusts and gales that usually blew away the winter in preparation for the Spring Festival were missing this year.

'You see,' Bladud said to Yaruk. 'Your premonitions of disaster were unfounded. The goddess herself is smiling on this wedding.'

It certainly seemed so.

While the cattle were being led in for slaughter prematurely from their winter grazing, and the cooks searched feverishly for the necessary ingredients for the wedding feast, Bladud and Rheinid were hardly ever apart. In the background Liel watched their evident enjoyment of each other with bitter envy. Rheinid, who sensed his passion for her, avoided meeting his eyes, and when he spoke to her she answered with cool detachment.

In spite of the haste of the preparation and the difficulties for the cooks in assembling enough good things to eat at the tail-end of winter, the three days and three nights of festivity for the wedding of Bladud and Rheinid would be remembered for generations.

The two young lovers were seated at the high table in the place of honour. On either side of them were ranged the sub-kings. No one was seated opposite them for the long tables of the great hall had been rearranged to leave space in front of the bride and groom for the entertainments. Between courses of rich broths and roasts, of fruit and sweetmeats, while wine flowed and the guests laughed and talked, in this space dancers trod their measures, jugglers performed their amazing feats, musicians played their instruments. At Bladud's request Yaruk sat at the high table – the only member of the conquered people to be so honoured. The slaves and servants of his race served him nervously, either with too much deference as they put on him all their aspirations for the improvement of their own lot, or with insulting clumsiness to indicate that they thought he had somehow sold out to the conquerors by sitting with them at this feast.

It was on the third night, when some of the rowdiness was

dying down from sheer weariness and satiety, that the great south door was flung open and into the hall strode a huge man rolling an immense wheel before him. Those who were not yet too dazed with food and drink to register his presence stared with curiosity as he advanced – the iron rim of the wooden wheel thundering on the floor and drowning out all other sounds. The man himself was half naked, clad only in a few furs like a wildman of the woods, which contrasted dramatically with the finery of the wedding guests. Guards closed in on him at once, but Bladud raised his hand to stop them rough-handling the intruder out of the place.

'All are welcome on this day of all days,' he said cheerfully. 'Let him come forward. Give him food and drink.'

'I have not come for food or drink,' said the man in a voice so deep it reverberated in the rafters.

'For what then have you come?'

'I bring a challenge to the people of Hudibras the king,' he declared, and scanned the line of honoured guests at the high table with a penetrating gaze. As the beam of his attention touched each man, that one would shift in his seat and look uneasy, and as soon as the gaze moved on to his neighbour he would mutter angrily that the intruder should be flung out.

'This is a wedding feast, and not the proper time for challenge,' Hudibras said coldly.

'What better time?' the man replied.

Hudibras turned to Bladud. 'This is your feast, my son. What do you say?'

Bladud was staring at the stranger fascinated, his face flushed with wine and happiness. He felt he could take on the world if need be, but so far the stranger had not looked once into his eyes.

When he did so, Bladud felt a current of energy run through his body that almost stopped his breath.

'What is your challenge, sir?' he asked, knowing that whatever it was he would have to take it on.

Rheinid touched his arm.

'This is not wise, my love. Send him away,' she whispered anxiously.

Liel leapt up. 'Let there be a challenge, and I'll be the one to meet it!'

79

No, Bladud thought. *It has to be me.* But Rheinid held him back, and the wine had slowed his ability to respond.

Liel jumped on to the table among the greasy dishes, knocking over a flagon of wine so the red liquid flowed like blood into the laps of the distinguished guests.

'What is your challenge, sir?' he shouted to the stranger. 'I, Liel, son of the High King, will take you on whatever you demand.'

'It is a simple challenge, sir,' the rough man said. 'You must roll this wheel from one side of the hall to the other.'

'What?' Liel's jaw dropped, as loud laughter rocked the hall. 'You insult me, sir. Any child could do that!'

'If a child could do it, sir, you will have no difficulty in doing what I ask.'

With a shout of rage Liel leapt down from the table. 'Clear the way! Let us get this nonsense over with.'

Those nearest jumped up and pushed the tables and benches back to form a clear path from side to side of the great hall.

'What forfeit will there be?' Liel demanded, sure that he would manage it easily and have the chance to punish this man for making a fool of him. He could hear the laughter and the jeering shouts all around.

'No forfeit shall be set. The deed carries its own logic.'

'When this is done,' Liel snarled furiously, 'I'll have a challenge for you that will not be so easily met!'

The man bowed his head in mock humility.

'Any man who wins this challenge may set his own terms for me.'

Impatient to get it over with, Liel seized the rim of the huge wheel – and in that instant his life almost ended. He uttered a scream that brought silence to the hall. All were frozen in astonishment as they watched their warrior prince hopping about in front of them, gripping one hand in the other and screaming with pain.

The stranger watched impassively, still holding the wheel's rim, waiting for the commotion to subside.

Hudibras was on his feet immediately.

'What is it, son? What has happened?'

80

The guards closed in on the stranger again, but when they came to touch him, they too drew back in agony.

'You son of slime!' shouted Liel. 'What trick is this?'

'No trick. You said yourself, the task is simple.'

'That wheel is burning hot!' Liel held up his hand so that all could see the flesh of his palm had been burned away where it had touched the wheel.

'Yet *I* can hold it,' the man replied mildly. 'Is there no one in this great gathering capable of doing so too?'

'I will try,' Bladud said.

'No!' Hudibras snapped. 'This is no fair challenge.'

'Yet it is a challenge and has been accepted,' the man said. 'Let your champion warriors try, all those who are used to bearing the pain of battle with fortitude.' Again that touch of mockery.

Various men rushed forward, knowing that if they succeeded where even Prince Liel had failed, their reputations would be immediately enhanced.

One by one the warriors took hold of the wheel, each time in a different place, hoping to find a spot that would not burn, but one by one they reeled back in agony.

At last Bladud could bear it no longer and, breaking from Rheinid's restraining arms, went forward to confront the stranger.

'I'll take up the challenge where these others have failed,' he said firmly. 'In which direction shall it be rolled?'

Smiling, the stranger indicated that it should be rolled from east to west.

There was dead silence as Bladud prepared to take hold of it. Seeing what had befallen the others, he knew what to expect and believed this challenge was about bearing pain with fortitude. He did not know how much pain he himself could bear, but he did know that the whole court of Hudibras would suffer dishonour if no one could prevail.

Tentatively he reached out his hand, but held back just before his flesh made contact. All were watching him closely – scarce a breath stirring in the great hall. He looked into the man's eyes but could not read them. It was as if all living things, the whole world, waited to see what he would now do.

He closed his eyes and the after-image of the wheel stayed

81

with him – now a blazing disc of burning gold, its centre a whirling mass of livid flame, its spokes hardly distinguishable in the conflagration. He would not plunge his flesh into that inferno; it was not the way.

To the watching crowd it seemed their future king stood helpless and irresolute before the stranger and his accursed wheel, his eyes tight shut. For the first time in his life Hudibras felt the beginnings of a sense of shame for his first-born, favourite son.

Suddenly the stranger withdrew his own hand from the wheel, and for a moment it stood poised, motionless, balanced on its rim. The man's eyes never left Bladud. He could see what the crowd in the great hall could not see: the immense effort Bladud was making to draw on secret reserves of strength and wisdom to meet the challenge. Only he witnessed the moment when Bladud realised this was not a test of physical strength or courage, but of understanding. It was clear the wheel was not just an ordinary wheel. The wheel was a symbol for the sun. The sun, a blazing wheel of fire was, in its turn, a symbol for that which is unknowable – yet itself all-knowing. It was a symbol for the vortex of energy that empowers the universe. But it was not the symbol, but what lay behind the symbol, that he had to grasp.

He reached out his hand and with a prayer in his heart to that which is symbolised by the sun, he touched the wheel – rolling it lightly and easily from one side of the hall to the other – from east to west.

It was the noise of stamping and clapping, cheering and whistling that brought him back to the ordinary world. The crowd went crazy with delight that their favourite prince had beaten the challenge. They rushed forward and lifted him high on their shoulders, to carry him round the vast room, tossing him up in the air in their exuberance.

Over their heads he looked for the stranger, but saw no sign of him or his wheel. Afterwards, when he made enquiries, it seemed that no one had seen him leave.

6

Confrontation

The child was born, a boy they named Lear. At this time, in the eyes of the people, Bladud could do no wrong. No hero ever stood so high in their estimation as he had done since the mysterious incident of the wheel. Only Liel nursed a festering grudge, convinced that Bladud had somehow set up a trick to make himself look good and Liel to look bad. Bladud himself tried to remember exactly how it had happened, but could not; the moment had passed, and with it its magic. He even sent men out to look for the wildman and his wheel, but no trace of him could be found.

Late in that summer Hudibras and Liel set off on a campaign to the north, where several princes were on the move, hungry for land and power. Bladud was left to manage the kingdom, and Rheinid acquired a taste for playing queen.

Though the nights were full of fire and passion in their bedchamber, Bladud increasingly found that Rheinid's concept of ruling was very different from his own. When miscreants were brought before them, her recommended punishments were often disproportionately severe. At first he gently chided her, believing that it was perhaps no strange thing for her to be so callous of human life, having been raised by such a father. But when a group of slaves tried to escape, and were recaptured and dragged before Rheinid during his absence, he was shocked to find they had been tortured to death most horribly on her orders.

'What would you have me do?' she demanded. 'If I let just

one of them get away with it, we would lose all control of them.'

'There are other ways of keeping control,' he replied. 'Did you examine their reasons for wanting so desperately to escape?'

'What would you have done?' She confronted him, unrepentant, her cheeks flushed, her eyes blazing. *How weak the man is!* she was thinking.

'I would have tried to put right what they believed to be wrong, and if I did not I would expect the whole thing to happen again and again.'

'These people need to be disciplined. My father always said . . .'

It was now his turn to flush with anger. 'Don't talk to me about your father!' he snapped.

'Oh no!' she cried. 'I'm not surprised you don't care to talk about him, remembering the manner of his death.'

Bladud was shocked at the fierceness of her reaction – the sudden hate he saw blazing in her eyes. Did she truly believe that *he* had something to do with her father's killing? Why could he not talk to this woman? Why could he not make her see that the course of her vindictive actions was terribly wrong and would lead to yet more trouble than she hoped to avoid? Already he had sensed resentment in the faces of the local people. Many, sullen and unfriendly, were turning away from him now when before they would have greeted him with smiles. Would he ever be able to undo the harm she had caused?

'You had no right to take matters into your own hands.'

'No right?' she said haughtily. 'Am I your concubine that I have no rights? No, I am your wife! When you are king, I will be queen – and *my* son will be king after you!'

'But I am not king yet. Hudibras trusted me to act with good sense.'

'And I was protecting that trust! *He* knows that only a strong arm keeps order. May the gods help this land when *you* become king!'

Bladud was silent, staring at the woman whose body he knew so intimately, yet whose heart and mind he now knew

84

he had never reached. It was in sorrow, more than anger, that he turned and walked away.

He paced up and down, up and down, beside the great white mound, at first muttering under his breath, but then talking out loud – pouring out his worries and dissatisfaction.

'I love her,' he murmured. 'When I touch her it seems there is no more beautiful experience on earth. When I am away from her I long to be with her again. But sometimes . . .'

The white mound lay silent in the sunlight, as though his ancestors were listening to every word.

'Sometimes I feel such anger. Sometimes I feel I don't know her at all. Sometimes I fear . . .'

What do you fear? the grey dust of Imogene whispered from the hollow hill.

'Sometimes I fear I do not love her at all.'

There! He had said it. He had given voice to that nagging doubt he had felt deep inside him even at the most intimate moments of their relationship. And had he seen her looking at him sometimes, had he caught a cold glance when she was not expecting him to turn his head? Was it possible that she, too, did not really love him, despite her passionate protestations? Yet those unsettling moments would slink away like snakes into their deep holes, so quickly that he could not be sure they had happened at all.

Love is never what you expect, he seemed to hear Imogene say quietly as though she were walking at his side. *Sometimes moments of resentment are nothing more than the sticks and leaves that float upon the surface of a deeply flowing stream.*

Bladud could not grasp the full implications of what Imogene had just said, for he was still too young, too restless, too immature.

From the river below came the sound of a voice, a ship's captain shouting commands to his men. Rows of oars bit into the water in such perfect harmony that they looked as though activated by one single man, creating a regular pattern quickly fading where the oars stirred up the surface of the river. Bladud could hear the creak of the heavy rigging which held the furled sails, amid the rhythmic chant of the oar master. He felt once again that old yearning to travel far away, strengthened by his desire to escape from present problems and confusions.

Without waiting for the king's return Bladud took it on himself to summon all of the slaves that had been assigned to him into the great hall. These were men and women who had been captured in past wars, some of them scarcely remembering the time when they had once been free, many with children of their own born into slavery. They came with trepidation, much alarmed by the recent punishments administered on the command of Bladud's wife. Could it be that their beloved prince intended some similar harm to them?

But when he had them all assembled he spoke to them quietly, promising that the severity inflicted in his name would never be repeated. In his ears rang the stirring speech delivered by his ancestor Brutus to King Pandrasus, pleading for the freedom of his Trojan slaves. Bladud told the people gathered before him that all of them were now free men and women. If they wished to stay and serve him as previously, he would be glad of it; but if they wished to leave the town and seek out their long-lost ancestral homes, he would not hold them. No one would harass them; no one would haul them back to servitude.

For a moment a stunned silence filled the hall, and then all began whispering at once, scarce believing what they had heard – questioning their neighbours, reassuring their friends.

Bladud held up his hand, and instantly there was silence again.

'Go now, and think about it. And then one by one, come back and tell me your decision.'

A man stepped forward, one who had been close to Bladud all his life.

'Forgive me, lord, but is this in your power? Surely your father . . .'

'I understand your hesitation for my father, at one time or another, has given you all to me. But you are my personal slaves, to do with as I wish. I cannot free my father's slaves or my brother's – but you I can. And I will. I want you to know that the severe punishments meted out in these past few days were done without my knowledge or my authority, and will never happen again. This freedom I now give to you is my pledge on that.'

Now there was an outburst of rejoicing, cheering, kissing and hugging – smiling and laughing, excited chattering . . .

Bladud watched the scene with tears in his eyes.

When Hudibras and Liel eventually returned triumphant from their conquest of the rebellious princes, the king was in a mood to be magnaminous about Bladud's seemingly reckless gesture.

'Send Rheinid to me,' he commanded impatiently, when the reason had been explained.

She arrived before her father-in-law dressed in her finest, most flattering garments. Some of her hair was caught up on the top of her head with a gold pin; the rest flowed around her shoulders, only slightly dishevelled, as though she had dropped everything and come in haste as soon as he had called. In fact she had spent a long time preparing for this meeting, knowing that it was inevitable.

She was still furious with Bladud, taking as a personal insult his pointed gesture in freeing his slaves, and relations had remained about as bad as they could be between them. Determined not to admit she had been wrong, she would not talk or bed with him and her bitterness soured everything at court.

Now she came before Hudibras flushed and breathless like a contrite young girl, sensing that he would support his favourite son in condemning her severity.

'My lord,' she said, scarce above a whisper, her eyes misty with tears. 'My lord, forgive me! I did only what my father would have done.'

'Your father is dead, lady, and his ways are dead too. You will find I do not rule my kingdom as Keron governed his.'

At that she burst into heart-rending sobs.

'Forgive me, lord,' she murmured. 'But I loved my father. I had no mother, no brother, no sister – no one but my father to guide me.'

Bladud was astonished to see the woman who had previously been so hard and harsh, so cold and bitter and strong, now look so gentle and soft and weak. Had he perhaps wronged her? Had she really no conception that her wanton cruelty was an evil? She looked so vulnerable, as she fell on to her knees before his father, pleading forgiveness, that he could not help but rush forward and lift her in his arms. She clung to him as though he alone could make up for all the family she did not have.

Hudibras was embarrassed, not knowing what to make of this scene. His instincts had told him frequently that she was not to be trusted, yet looking at her now he could not recall exactly what he had seen in her before to make him think that.

He uttered no more than a stern warning that she must never again make decisions of life and death while at his court. 'Such matters are for the crown alone,' he thundered.

'I'm sorry, my lord . . . I'm sorry.' She sobbed, and buried her head deeper in Bladud's shoulder.

'Enough!' Hudibras said gruffly. 'No more will be said. Take her away, son. Take her away.'

Bladud led her out of the great hall and to their private chambers. There, still weeping, she made love to him as though to dispel his doubts, and to make up for all the bad feelings that had lately come between them.

No more was said about the dead slaves, and it seemed as though the earth had closed over the pit into which their poor bodies had been thrown.

7

The Talking Heads

It was the time for the cutting of the mistletoe. All around the
country, the Druids were preparing for the most important
ceremony of the year in their sacred groves.

For the first time since Bladud had gone seeking Rheinid
there, he was required to re-enter the forest on Thorn Island.
Hudibras had encouraged his eldest son to learn as much as
he could of the ancient Druid rituals. He was not a fully
fledged initiate, for the training was long and arduous, and
Bladud had many other commitments and duties as prince
and royal heir, but he was far enough advanced to play, on
this occasion for the first time, a small part in the most secret
of the ceremonies.

When Fergal led the small group of seven towards the
sacred grove, it was late in the afternoon, for they were
required to spend the night in the forest before the day
of the ritual. As they crossed the main river flanking
the island, the winter sun was staining the water red,
as though they passed across blood to reach the place of
dedication.

The great river already exuded a fine white mist as the
evening chill touched the water, and long threads of it were
winding along the lesser channels that surrounded Thorn
Island, coiling around their feet as they walked towards the
grove.

Each man carried two objects carefully wrapped in
deerskin: one the skull of a man or a woman, the other a stone
head representing a god or a goddess. Bladud held his
burdens against his chest as he gingerly picked his way

through the swirling mist, the ground at his feet now becoming invisible.

As they entered the domain of trees, the vapour was already snaking up trunks and slithering around bare branches.

The last rays of the blood-red sun barely picked out the beginning of the path before them. Fergal carried a flickering torch which had been lit from sacred fire, from the sun itself, its light caught and concentrated through a crystal lens.

Once arrived at the clearing devoted to the ceremony this torch was used to light a fire before the altar. On seven wooden plinths encircling it, now clearly illuminated by the rising flames, each man placed his precious burden. On each a skull and a stone head, side by side.

Fergal carefully set down the pouch he carried, containing the sacred instruments, and then he raised his arms to the fire and uttered the invocation, starting low but ending with a shout that rang across the island.

In the silence that followed he began to strip off his clothes one by one, the cloak, the jacket, the tunic, the belt, the breeches, the boots – even the golden collar that was the mark of his druidical rank. When this was done he stood as naked as the trees before the sacred fire. Bladud watched closely. This was the part of the ceremony he most feared. Scarcely breathing the six men watched the seventh. His eyes were shut. Fergal was an old man, but at this moment his lean body was as firm and straight as that of any young warrior.

The only sound was the crackle of the twigs as the flames devoured them hungrily.

Fergal opened his eyes and stepped forward. With bare feet he stepped into the fire. He stood for a brief moment, then walked calmly through. He did not flinch or cry out. On the other side he raised his arms to the sky and sang a paen of praise to the great god of fire and light, the Shining One.

And then silence fell again and the second man stripped and stepped forward.

Bladud watched one after the other walk the fire.

The one just before him, a young student like himself, was trembling as he pulled his clothes off and Bladud watched

90

him with misgiving. His face was ashen, and as he stood naked at last he was shivering uncontrollably. The prince wanted to call out to the Druids to tell them it was not fair to make this one go through the fire for he was not ready. But to his shame he said nothing, but stood there as though spellbound by the charged atmosphere of the ritual, watching.

The young man at last put his foot forward into the flame and his scream was one of the most terrible Bladud had ever heard.

Swiftly two of the Druids stepped forward and hauled him out of the fire. He was sobbing and jabbering and shaking, desperately conscious that he had failed to pass one of the crucial tests he had worked so many years towards. Fergal bound some leaves on his burned flesh and helped him into his clothes and sent him off limping into the dark forest. He was no longer, nor now ever would be, part of their secret and sacred ceremonials.

It was Bladud's turn.

As the silence returned, he stood, as the young man had stood, looking into the flames curling around the flowing logs. He tried to compose himself. He tried to remember that he himself was not just flesh that could be burned, but an eternal being capable of existing in many different ways, some unimaginable to him at this stage.

He whispered the prayer he had been taught, but this time he noted the meaning of every word and clung to it as a drowning man clings to a raft.

He stepped forward.

Strangely he felt no burning. The ancient sacred words roared through his mind like a wind storm. His body became pure sound, and filled the universe. High above the visible sky, thundering orbs of fire picked up the same reverberations, and under his feet, deep in the unseen, unknown fastness of the earth, crystals began to form.

Ah, that he could stay here forever – in this place of power! In this state of potency. On this threshold of endless potential.

But suddenly he was through to the other side, and could see the three Druids standing before him holding out his clothes. Speaking their mystic words over him as he re-clad himself. The fire ceremony complete, the next stage was about to begin. But what of the missing man's plinth? Would it go unattended – and how would this affect the efficacy of the ritual? The procedure demanded the sacred number seven and now there were only six. But when Bladud glanced over at the plinth where the failed novitiate should have stood, he was startled to see there another tall, hooded figure.

During the night the fire gradually died down, and at the nadir, when Bladud felt he could scarce endure the cold and dark a moment longer, the full moon sailed into view over their heads, illuminating everything with its pale and eerie light. Above him the trees became a delicate fretwork of jet and crystal while, below, rivers of silver flowed around islands of absolute blackness.

It was as though the moon had awakened the forest and he could hear minute creakings and stirrings and whirrings just above the threshold of silence. And then he heard a wolf howling, the long, sad note of its call chilling his blood. He saw its eyes, polished by moonlight, across the clearing, under the trees – watching him. He looked around at the others to see if they had seen the beast, but there was no indication that they had. As still and silent as they had stood through the night, they still stood there, their faces hidden under their hooded cloaks.

He looked back at the wolf: it had turned and was about to leave. Behind it, in the shadows, he sensed the presence of the rest of its pack silently padding through the trees, pacing the forest . . . He felt an overwhelming longing to go with them and, before he realised what he was doing, he had crossed the clearing and was plunging into the shadows after them, tracing their route at first by their moving shadows, and later by their distinctive smell.

After a while, afraid he was losing them, he called out. He did not notice that his voice was no longer human: it was a wolf-howl that came from his throat as he lifted his head to the moon. And it was a wolf-howl that answered him.

They came for him and he ran with them, loping through

92

the forest into the open ground beyond, feeling the moon-silver air rippling through his fur, thinking thoughts without words . . .

Once again Thorn Island became a vast arena for magical reality, and the plains which the wolf pack traversed seemed endless to Bladud.

First they spotted a badger, and the hunt was on. But the gentle creature could not outrun them, and it was easy to prevent it from reaching its set where it might find safety. Its life-blood soon flowed into the earth. The fox gave them more trouble – darting and dodging, fleet of foot, but at last it too was cornered and torn apart. Then, grunting from the forest, tusks down in an aggressive charge, came the wild boar.

Two of the wolves were dead before the others succeeded, by circling and pouncing, in wounding their prey. Bladud came close enough to hear its rasping breath: the boar was in pain and its bloodshot eyes bulged with rage. Bladud felt the frenzy of his peers to end the brute – their insatiable hunger for flesh – and himself, at this moment, sharing in it. Snarling, he sunk he teeth into the tough bristles that covered the powerful creature and then lost his footing as the boar swung round and shook its body violently. At last Bladud was flung clear, and for a moment lay panting on the ground. But the boar was intent on revenge and within moments had returned for the attack. The wolf pack had withdrawn to a safe distance, snarling and snapping but keeping well clear of the fearsome tusks. Bladud tried to get up but the enemy, cumbersome though it appeared, was too quick for him. It was Bladud who now felt the terror of being the quarry, the agony of flesh being torn from his body . . .

When he became conscious again he was back in the clearing, standing in front of his plinth.

In a daze, he looked across at the other figures. None of them appeared to have moved at all from their original positions. Nothing had changed. He shivered in memory of how real his experience had felt.

For a moment he thought it was dawn. A glow of light stronger than moonlight – stronger even than sunlight –

suffused the clearing. Bladud blinked, then shaded his eyes with one hand the better to see what was happening. And then he gasped. Two huge white bulls, their horns bound with golden bells, knelt docilely on their forelegs before the altar, while Fergal, flanked by the Druid priests, raised a mighty axe above their necks. All the figures in this bizarre tableau blazed with an unearthly light. All their movements were slow, stylised, dreamlike . . .

He watched as the blade moved slowly down. He watched as the blood fountained slowly from the snowy necks. He watched as the Druids on either side raised golden bowls to catch the potent liquid. He watched as the two strong beasts slowly sagged and fell limply into death. He watched as the bowls were passed around among the three priests for them to drink.

And then the two lesser Druids approached the four figures who still stood frozen beside their plinths, offering them the bowls of blood. For a moment Bladud hesitated, sick to his stomach, but so powerful was the momentum of the ritual that he found himself clasping the golden bowl with both hands and lifting it to his lips.

After all had drunk, Fergal poured the contents over the heads on the plinths. Turning to face them, Bladud was astonished to see they were no longer skull and lifeless stone, but living heads with eyes that stared into his own.

Bladud knew that the skull he was given to carry was that of Locrine, the son of Brutus.

He now bowed low before his ancestor, awed in the presence of such a man.

'Prince of the Royal House of Brutus.' The head spoke with a strange and hollow voice. 'Why have you neglected your heritage?'

Bladud was puzzled. 'How have I neglected my heritage, lord?' he whispered, hoarse with nervousness.

'Prince of the Royal House of Aeneas,' the head declaimed. 'Why have you neglected your heritage?'

Bladud stared at the talking head, bewildered. 'Lord, I . . .'

But the head did not seem to hear him. It spoke a third time.

94

'Prince of the Royal House of Imogene, you will fail your people if you do not look to your heritage.'

And then, before Bladud could question further, the flesh on the head seemed to turn grey before his eyes. It became that of a rotting corpse . . . then a dry and dusty skull.

Desperately Bladud turned his gaze to the stone head beside it.

There he saw before him the beautiful face of Lugh, the Shining One – with golden locks, eyes of fire, lips of burnished bronze.

'Lord . . .' The words stuck in his throat. 'Lord . . .' he tried again, bowing to the ground before him. He could not find a way to express the questions that boiled and bubbled in his heart.

'Royal prince . . .' Bladud heard the words as though from a great distance. 'Look to your ancient heritage and your future destiny. Let not the present become a weight around your neck.'

'Lord . . .'

But the face of Lugh had disappeared and Bladud faced only a stone head.

Despairingly he turned away, hoping that Fergal would interpret for him. But Fergal was already busy with the next part of this elaborate ceremony: the cutting of the mistletoe, the All-Heal, the semen with which the earth would conceive the spring.

There was no longer any sign of the carcases, nor any indication of the bulls' spilt blood. Had this too been illusion?

The little group left the clearing in procession. The dawn was fairly under way, and at every moment daylight increased. They found the sacred plant, illuminated by blazing sunlight, in the high branches of an oak.

Old man as he was, Fergal himself climbed the tree and, high above them, raised his golden sickle. As he brought it down, the mysterious plant that had never touched the earth fell . . . fell . . . fell to the ground.

After many sacred words spoken over it, they each took turns to crush it into the soil – its white juice fertilising the winter barrenness, giving promise of new life, new growth, new abundance.

Sure now that indeed the winter would give way to the spring, and death give way to life, the little group turned for home.

Unable any longer to contain his curiosity as to who had taken the place of the failed student, Bladud engineered a stumble so that he could pull off the stranger's hood. Eagerly he looked into the face, and saw nothing. The cloak was empty – if total darkness could be called emptiness!

Horrified, he let go and stepped back. The cloak floated to the ground. And Bladud felt the brushing of a wind on his flesh so cold, so icy that, for a moment, his breath stopped and he knew what it must feel like to come upon death face to face.

The winter seemed to take an extra long time to pass that year and the darkness oppressed Bladud's spirits more than it had ever done before. His relationship with Rheinid seemed more confused and ambiguous by the day. Without question they satisfied each other's sexual needs, but more and more their radical differences of opinion provoked quarrels. For one thing, Rheinid could not accept Yaruk as friend. Her coldness and haughtiness towards him offended Bladud, though Yaruk himself never complained.

'Let it be,' Yaruk said. 'You cannot expect her to give up the prejudices of a lifetime so easily. Change that comes gradually goes deeper and lasts longer.'

Rheinid however complained to Liel that her husband expected her to consort with savages, and never seemed to approve of anything she did or said. Liel taunted Bladud with not being able to satisfy his wife, and offered to take her off his hands. The two princes almost came to blows and were only prevented by the intervention of Fergal. When the Druid heard that the quarrel had started over Rheinid his face turned grim.

'The gods put this woman in your path,' he said sternly. 'And you chose to accept her into your life. It's up to you now to find out the gods' intention and fulfil it.'

Liel snorted. 'The gods!' he sneered. 'They should have

looked twice at this boy before they committed Rheinid to his care. *I* would have been a better choice!'

'But you were not,' Fergal said coldly.

Bladud remained silent. He was beginning to feel Rheinid a burden. She wanted to be with him all the time, yet he could not relax with her. Their life together had become a series of confrontations. He loved her, he felt sure, but . . .

Then one day, curious as to where he disappeared to so often after an argument, Rheinid followed him to the White Mound.

For some time she watched him pace to and fro, head down, beside the burial mound and then she saw him come to a standstill, looking up with a smile of recognition, as though someone had suddenly appeared. Rheinid crept forward, peering closer. She could see no one, yet her husband was speaking. She heard very little of what he said, but enough to know he believed it was a woman. Trying to move closer to hear more, she must have made a sound, for he turned and spotted her. He looked as shocked as a sleepwalker suddenly awakened.

Rheinid stepped forward boldly. 'So,' she said, 'I find you, my husband, communing with the dead.'

'Did you see her?' he asked eagerly.

'Indeed,' she replied. 'Who is she?'

'Queen Imogene.'

'Imogene?'

'The princess the Trojan Brutus brought from Greece. Is she not beautiful?' he added with shining eyes.

'Beautiful,' Rheinid agreed, but with so little expression in her voice, he began to doubt that in fact she had seen her.

'You saw her? You really saw?'

'Husband – what makes you talk to ghosts?'

Bladud's face clouded. 'Rheinid, what makes you spy on me?'

She laughed bitterly. 'When a wife is left so often in the night she begins to suspect her husband has another lover. Is flesh and blood too much for you, Bladud, that you leave me for a bodiless wraith?'

Bladud turned away from her and strode down the hillside in silent anger.

She watched him go: as silent and as angry.

That night in the great hall when all were gathered for the evening meal, Liel accosted him, grinning.

'I hear you have a secret lover, boy,' he said, and his friends around him laughed uproariously. Bladud went white. Surely she had not told him? 'A lover that doesn't need a real man to satisfy her!'

Bladud looked across at Rheinid. She was laughing with the rest. Without a word Bladud rose and strode out of the room.

Next day he asked for an audience with his father to suggest that he should leave the city for a time, going across the sea to visit the lands of his ancestors. To Rome and Greece and Troy.

Hudibras was not at first pleased to hear this but Bladud persisted.

'It is time these links are strengthened,' he said, 'or we will lose them altogether.'

Hudibras looked at him thoughtfully. The Celtic element in the country was increasing all the time as more and more immigrants came across from Gaul. It would do no harm to re-affirm the ruling dynasty's links with mighty Troy and Greece. Besides, he had not missed the tensions between Rheinid and Bladud, nor the restlessness of his son.

He agreed that Bladud could go, but for no more than a year.

'If you stay away too long, who knows how things may be when you return?'

Hudibras had also noticed Liel's hunger for the throne.

Once he had made up his mind Bladud went down to the river and spent time there with the sea captains who had brought in their big ships from across the ocean. The Phoenicians boasted of the fearsome storms they had weathered, and the monsters of the deep they had outwitted, but some, who were not Phoenicians, persuaded Bladud that it would be safer to cross the narrow channel between Britain and Gaul, and then, using a combination of land and river travel, make his way south to Massallia, and only there risk the danger of the open ocean.

As the ship slipped away on the tide in the grey dawn, Bladud's emotions were not what he might have expected. He had longed for this moment for as long as he could remember, and in all the days of preparation, and of farewell to his father, his son and all he had ever known, he had not heard one whisper of regret from his own heart until this moment. He had never in his life been as sure that he was doing the right thing, as he was about this journey. That last night Rheinid had chosen to make love to him with a passion she had not shown for months, and yet when the time came for him to leave his last sight of her was of a woman raised on one elbow in the bed, hair damp and tousled, cheeks flushed, looking after him with blazing hatred in her eyes.

When they reached the open sea and he looked back at the land, all he could remember was the woman whose scent still lingered in his nostrils and the feel of whose flesh was still on his limbs. He almost demanded that the captain should turn the ship around.

But the pull of his personal odyssey was in the end too strong, and he turned his back on the White Island and the woman who disturbed him so much, and searched the horizon for the first sight of Gaul, a country he had never seen before.

8

Leaving Home

The journey across Gaul proved as hazardous as Bladud expected. As they entered the territory of each different tribe, they were inevitably accosted in a less than friendly manner, sometimes threatened until they parted with valuables. Occasionally they had to battle their way free. The river routes were well used and the Gaulish captain had been plying his trade up and down for more than twenty years, so seemed to know exactly what reception to expect from each tribe, and exactly how to handle them all. Before ever they had set off, he obtained from all his passengers, most of whom were merchants, sufficient stock of booty to satisfy the demands of even the most rapacious he expected to encounter. Iron daggers were particularly welcomed by the rough and violent men who regularly boarded them. Yaruk had given good advice when suggesting Bladud should look as poor and humble as he could.

Day after day they worked their way south, the creak of the oars still echoing in the prince's head even when he was asleep. Day after day, thick dark forests hemmed them in, with only occasional villages, well fortified, near the water's edge. Sometimes the river broadened out, and sometimes they encountered a similar boat passing the other way. Then the captains of each boat would exchange information by shouting in their incomprehensible burring tongue across the water. The crew would join in, and for a while their noise was almost deafening after the previous long silent stretches of the journey.

To begin with they travelled only by day, but Bladud's

captain receiving news from a passing boat gave orders that that night, for the first time, they would travel in the dark. All on board were sworn to vigilance and silence. Bladud could feel the tension all around him, and no one slept. Each man kept watch on the dark banks on either side. Not for the first time was he glad that the captain was so experienced on this lawless river.

They were almost through the dangerous stretch they had been warned about, and were beginning to relax, when suddenly, rounding a bend, they found themselves amidst a fleet of little boats, manned not by local tribesmen but by bandits. With these it would not be a matter of barter or bargain. These would not leave off until they had stripped the merchant boat bare and killed all on board.

The enemy had been lying in wait under cover of darkness, but as the long, cumbersome, flat-bottomed boat drove into their midst, torches were lit on every side and suddenly, almost blinded by fire after the previous long darkness of the night journey, Bladud and all on board were fighting for their lives. Luckily, because of the warning received, weapons were to hand.

Bladud found himself defending himself on a surface that rocked sickeningly and seemed more often than not to slide away from under him. One great brute seemed to have singled him out and no matter how he dodged and ducked, nor how many other battling figures came between them, still single-mindedly pursued him. Lighter in build, but evidently not more agile, the young prince was cornered at last against a stack of bales. He thought his last moment had come when he saw the man's battle axe raised above him, his own sword, knocked from his hand, scuttering across the deck. He shut his eyes and waited for the end. But in that long, strange moment of complete darkness a fireball of light seemed to explode in his head and he sprang forward, kicking his attacker in the groin with a force he did not know he possessed. The axe grazed his shoulder as the man doubled up in agony. And then the captain was beside him dragging him clear. Blood poured down his arm, but the tide had turned for the bandits and they were at last driven into retreat.

As dawn approached and they limped on, the oarsmen almost too weary to raise their oars, Bladud found he had lost some good men and the Gaulish captain had similarly lost several of his. Part of the hold was blazing and bales of valuable woven cloth were destroyed before they could be doused.

There came a time when the river became too shallow, too rough, too narrow for their boat, and all of them had to disembark. Those wanting to go further south were obliged to travel overland for some distance, until they reached another great river which would carry them all the way to the Phoenician sea port of Massallia.

The land travel came as a relief. The wound on Bladud's shoulder was not healing well and he was glad to be taken in by some friendly villagers and nursed back to health. The language created no difficulty as the people encountered were Celts – though some confusion was occasionally caused by the differences in the local dialects.

When he was well enough he was taken into the forested mountains to hunt, and he gradually regained his strength. One day he became separated from his companions and found himself alone. He called and called, but no one answered. After a while he began to realise that no matter how desperately he shouted, no one was going to come to his aid. There was only himself to rely upon and the forests stretched for hundreds of miles. If he set off walking in the wrong direction he might never find his way out again.

Wearily he sat down, his back against a giant tree. His shoulder was aching again with the exertions of the day, and he was hungry. He sat thus for a long while, staring into the shadows until darkness fell. Then he must have fallen asleep, for he found himself in a palatial room with a long table loaded with every type of food he had ever known. Guests in rich attire were seated at the board, drinking and eating, laughing and talking. As he walked towards them they all stopped short and stared at him, some with joints of meat halfway to their mouths. He looked at the food and his mouth watered. He could hardly restrain himself from rushing at the table and seizing what he could. He looked around to see if he could spot the host.

'Welcome, stranger,' at last a quiet voice said. Bladud looked for the speaker and met the eyes of an old and venerable king. 'What brings you here?'

'I am lost and I am hungry, sir,' Bladud found himself replying.

'Let the stranger amuse us for his supper!' another voice called out.

Suddenly there was an uproar of voices shouting for entertainment from the newcomer. Mugs were beaten on the table, boots on the floor.

Bladud stared around in astonishment. Every eye was upon him, every mouth was open demanding something of him. He looked appealingly at the king who had spoken to him with such kindliness, but he was now sitting back watching impassively. The prince could see that if he wanted to eat, he must work for it. But he was no entertainer. What should he do?

'Let him answer a riddle!' someone shouted.

'Yes. Yes. Let him answer a riddle!' Others took up the refrain.

'What riddle shall I answer?' he asked anxiously, wondering if he would be refused food if he could not give the correct answer.

'Who is three in three in three in one?' the king suddenly said. Everyone laughed.

'I am three,' Bladud found himself answering with scarcely a pause for thought. 'Body, soul and spirit. I live in three realms: the physical, the spiritual, and the sacred. The three realms are created by the three powers: the divine father, mother and child. The source is the one from which all these emerge.'

As he finished speaking the banquet and all the delicious food disappeared, as did all the elegant lords and ladies, the tall silver torches, the great panoply of the king's house . . .

He was once again in the forest – but he was no longer alone. He blinked up into the light of a blazing torch and dimly behind it he could see the figures of the companions he had lost.

Not long after this Bladud left his new-found friends, impatient to continue with his journey. He was guided through the mountains until he came upon a broad and shining expanse of water, the mighty river he had been told would flow down to the sea and carry him to the south. He found one of the big cargo boats that was going the whole way to Massallia and bartered some gold for his passage. Their progress was slower than Bladud would have liked, but it proved more peaceful than before. The captain had arguments with crew and customers, but they were left alone by bandits.

'Probably because he pays them to stay away,' one of the other passengers remarked darkly.

Day after day Bladud watched the forest slide past until at last the river broadened out so much he could scarcely see the banks. They had arrived at the port of Massallia on the edge of the great ocean and nosed their way into a huge concourse of ships. Bladud had thought Trinovantum a big city, but it was a village to this. Ramshackle houses spread as far as the eye could see, many built one on top of the other so that families lived above one another, out of contact with the earth. Streets were narrow, dirty and crowded. The smell of fish, the noise, the heat were almost unbearable.

Bladud negotiated with a sea captain for the first boat out of there. Its destination was a Greek colony on the Italian coast.

They were not more than a day or two out of the harbour when they experienced one of the storms he had been warned about. It hit suddenly while Bladud was sleeping, and he woke with a jolt to find his small world in turmoil. Every plank on the ship strained and creaked in the howling wind. Merchant goods were hurled from side to side, as the vessel plunged and rose and lurched and spun. It might as well have been a toy shaken in a giant's hand, and Bladud was made aware in that one terrible moment just how precarious this life is – how thin the thread that holds us over the chasm of the unknown. How easily it is snapped.

In terror he battled to get himself out of the dark coffin of the tiny cabin on to the open deck. They seemed to be poised, timelessly, in a cage of white lightning, thunder cracking like a mighty whip overhead. He was not sure if the frail confining walls of his cabin were not preferable to the wall of dark water now towering above him. But by now he had been flung far away from the cabin door, and could not retreat there. The captain shouted something to him but he could not distinguish the words. He saw men bailing water over the sides as fast as it flooded in, so he seized a bucket and joined them. But suddenly the mast snapped, and several screamed in agony as the great wooden beam crashed down on them.

We'll never get out of this alive! he thought and wondered what demon had lured him away from his comfortable home. The illusion of safety and permanence which helps us to function in a mysterious and dangerous world had deserted him now, and he felt himself utterly alone and unsupported. He felt himself falling into a bottomless pit of despair, and indeed might have surrendered all effort to survive, if he had not at that moment caught sight of two figures walking on the water, illuminated by a flash of lightning. Almost instantly they vanished in the darkness that followed, but he was no longer concerned with the storm raging around him. He no longer feared death. He only had to be certain he had really seen those figures. He had to be sure . . .

His eyes strained into the swirling, murky maelstrom of wind and water, eagerly waiting for the next lightning flash. When illumination came again, he glimpsed them quite clearly.

And one of the figures was himself.

As the tempest died down and dawn approached the battered ship was still miraculously afloat. They made straight for the nearest port to repair the damage the storm had wrought.

Bladud remained very quiet and withdrawn, thinking of what he had seen. As he stood on the shore, gazing out at the smooth, silvery shimmer of the sea in sunlight, the events of the night before already seemed unreal . . .

9

The Sibyl of Cumae

As chance or destiny would have it Bladud's ship was bound
for Cumae, a thriving Greek colony on the Italian coast. They
approached it on a clear and golden day at the Winter
Solstice. This was where Aeneas, the grandfather of Brutus,
had once landed many centuries before; led to this place by
the messengers of the gods. Bladud thrilled to his story for he
himself felt his destiny lay in a land very distant and different
from his own country.

The sailors raised a cheer when they caught sight of the
blue mountains of the island of Ischia, and they rowed with
good heart the final calm and silver leagues to the port of
Cumae on the mainland. Since not only the captain but
several of his crew hailed from this town, there was quite a
welcoming party when they landed.

Bladud had learned a little of the language of the Greeks
through practising some of the ancient rituals of his family,
but over centuries of being handed down from generation to
generation the Greek he used was almost incomprehensible
to the modern inhabitants of that country. On the journey he
had therefore worked hard to learn what he could from
captain and crew, and now, with a certain amount of goodwill
and patience all round, he could just about make himself
understood.

He would spend several days at Cumae before having to
make the choice of continuing his journey by land or by sea. He
could cross the central mountains and embark on the last stage
of his journey from the eastern coast of Italy, or he could sail
south from Cumae on a trading ship bound for Athens.

His first inclination was to take the overland route, thus putting off even more days of being cooped up in a rocking vessel at the mercy of every wind and storm. But before he made his decision he was determined to consult the famous sibyl, as his ancestor Aeneas had done.

While the crew was busy securing and unloading the ship, the captain invited Bladud to stay at his home and the prince accepted the invitation gladly. He was bustled away into the town and was almost overwhelmed by the hospitality of a houseful of women: the captain's wife, his mother-in-law and two sisters-in-law, all of whom spoke far too fast in an unfamiliar dialect.

Most of the sprawling town itself was divided from the sea by a sacred hill which was crowned impressively by the Temple of Apollo and the Temple of Zeus, and at the foot of this hill the caverns of the sibyl had been hollowed out. The marble of these Cumaean temples, gleaming white in the sun, astonished and delighted Bladud. 'When I get home . . .' he murmured, and this became an almost constant refrain throughout his travels . . .

Apollo the sun god seemed the nearest Greek equivalent to Lugh, and, even as he walked about the crowded streets of the Greek colony, he began planning an edifice to impress and astonish his countrymen back home – a temple to the Divine Light worthy of both Apollo and Lugh.

The captain luckily knew the protocol for obtaining admission to the sibyl's cave: what dues to pay and to whom. He took Bladud first to the market to purchase two goats, one pure black and one pure white, in exchange for a length of finely woven cloth the prince had brought with him from Britain. Though their own weaving was far superior to that of his countrywomen, the locals were nevertheless impressed by the distinctive chequered pattern in different colours.

To his disappointment Bladud heard he would have to wait several days to see the sibyl. Since the time of Aeneas her reputation had grown considerably, and there were many others who had travelled for weeks, even months, for the privilege of consulting her. The townspeople were now used to the streams of foreigners and lost no time in milking them of everything they could. Luckily the friendly sea-captain was at hand to save the prince from the worst of their depradations.

While waiting his turn to visit the sibyl, he climbed the steep hill to the Temple of Apollo. The captain had introduced him to a young priest who agreed to take him into the sacred precincts. The processional way had several gates guarded by keepers and at each one they stopped while a certain ritual of question and answer was performed.

'What do you seek?'

'I seek the Light.'

'Whom do you seek?'

'The Light Bearer.'

'What is his name?'

'Apollo.'

And so on until they reached the entrance.

The way was lined with white marble statues and columns, through which Bladud could glimpse the shining sea and the distant darker blue of the magical island of Ischia. During this time of year, his homeland would be torn by gales and blizzards. His countrymen would be gathered close around their hearth fires, logs crackling in the flame, shadows flickering, the story-tellers spinning their tales . . . Here the sun was warm on the skin, though the breeze carried a slight chill from the high, snow-covered mountains of the interior.

Bladud felt delighted with everything he saw: the tall, dark cypresses and the clumps of more familiar oak trees that had turned autumn gold. *I'll always remember Cumae*, he told himself, *for the sound of the sea, the crunching of acorns underfoot and the blazing gold of the oak leaves*.

As they entered the temple itself, gliding reverently over the polished marble floors, and climbing the steps to the varying levels, Bladud's attention was caught by a series of carved bas-reliefs. He stopped before the long frieze and stared, ignoring his guide's light touch on his elbow, trying to move him on.

'That is Daedalus,' the young priest said softly, pointing to the winged man. 'He landed here at Cumae, and built this temple in gratitude for his safe flight.'

'And the boy?'

109

'His son. But he did not fly so far. He fell from the sky and died.'

'They *flew*?'

'Yes,' the young man confirmed. It was a well known story in these parts. Back in the town that evening, Bladud learned more of it.

There had been a savage war between Athens and Crete, and when the latter triumphed the tribute exacted by King Minos consisted of seven young men and seven young maidens to be sent each year to feed the minotaur, the monstrous offspring of the unnatural mating of Queen Pasiphae with a bull. Bladud was told that Daedalus was a brilliant architect of Athenian origin who had fled to Crete after committing some crime, and who was there employed by King Minos to design and construct a building safe enough to confine the monster. So Daedalus constructed the famous labyrinth, a maze so confusing that no one who entered it would ever find the way out. But then Daedalus had suggested to the lovely princess Ariadne that her Athenian lover, Theseus, be given a ball of thread so that he might retrace his steps out of the labyrinth once he had slain the minotaur. For this treachery Daedalus and his young son, Icarus, were imprisoned in the dark tunnels of the labyrinth themselves, and its exit sealed up. While there, the ever ingenious man had constructed wings for the two of them.

'But Icarus flew too high in his excitement,' the captain continued, 'and the wax that held his wings melted, so he fell into the sea and drowned. But Daedalus managed to get as far as Cumae.'

Bladud was astonished. This must surely be no more than a fable. No man could possibly fly across the sea such a long way. Yet the story rang in his heart in a way that would not let him rest. There was something there: something that felt real, something that felt possible. He must find out more about this Daedalus.

Bladud gazed up at a great bird that coasted, wings spread, above them. Then it turned to the open sea and, within moments, was no more than a speck in the distant blue. Bladud felt a strange premonition, as though everything

110

close around him was suddenly far away – as though he was adrift in a vast space coasting on the air. In his mind he was flying above the silver sea . . .

It was still dark when the young priest came for him the next day. Together they led the two goats towards the entrance of the sibyl's underground lair.

First there was to be the sacrifice: the spurting blood, the burnt flesh, the attendant priests chanting their incomprehensible prayers and invocations, the smoke rising through a canopy of oak leaves. Then came the ritual washing, as the acolytes poured water over Bladud's naked body from vessels decorated with sacred motifs. The dawn air was chill and he shivered. After that he was clothed again in purest white.

Alone he entered the long tunnel carved into the living rock. The passage was strangely but precisely carved, with openings to let in light set at intervals along its length, so that he found himself walking through darkness and light alternately, each time experiencing a deepening sense of mystery – a detachment from all he had left behind.

He had been warned that the sibyl's chamber lay at the extreme end where there was no sign of light ahead – only a profound and impenetrable blackness.

His heart began beating so loudly he fancied he could hear it echoing against the stone walls. It was as though its drumming came from within the rock, the earth itself . . .

His overpowering instinct was to turn and flee, but he had come too far for this.

What would she look like? Some said she was a thousand years old. The story was that the god Apollo had fallen in love with this mortal girl and had offered her anything she wished. She had lifted up a handful of sand and asked for as many birthdays as there were grains of sand in her hand. He had readily granted this wish, but when she refused to lie with him, he withheld the youth she would have desired to accompany those years, and now, though crumpled and fading with age, she was doomed to live, and live, until the sands she had held in her hand were spent.

It was reported that there were nine books in her cell, in

which all the past, present and future history of the world was written. Bladud could imagine some yellowing old crone, with a hand like a crow's foot scratching away with a stylus on goatskin that was almost turned to dust, watching with eyes that never saw the outside world – writing, writing, writing until everything that had ever happened was recorded . . .

Suddenly there was a blaze of light ahead, issuing from the left. He could now see clearly the blank wall where the tunnel ended ahead of him. On either side of him ran a ledge crowded with offerings – statues, pots, jewels, amulets, faded flowers . . . Kings had come here to leave their gold. Peasants had come to leave ears of corn. Bladud hesitated for a moment, then slipped a golden bracelet off his arm and laid it at the very entrance to the sibyl's chamber.

When he looked up, he saw her. She was seated in the centre of fire, yet she did not burn.

He had thought the Oracle of Sul looked old, but she was young in comparison to this one. The sibyl resembled a skeleton with only a thin veil of papery flesh drawn tightly over it. Her eyes were huge and luminous in the sunken face, staring directly into his.

How should he begin? He had rehearsed a dozen speeches. He had been advised by the captain, by the young priest who had been his escort, by the other, older priests who had performed the ritual at the entrance. Up to this moment he had felt confident of knowing what to say.

But now? Now it was as though she sucked the soul up out of his body through his eyes! He felt total panic and a desire to flee, now, before it was too late!

He tried desperately to speak, but his throat and mouth remained dry. Only a meaningless croak came out.

The flames were now dying down, and he could see that she was not seated within the fire but behind it. On a table behind her was a stack of books.

In her hand she held a branch still covered with leaves. Even as she stared at him she was cutting little signs and symbols into them with her long, yellow, claw-like fingernails.

He tried again to speak, but another croak was all that he could manage.

112

Her eyes never left his.

Did he really need to speak? If she was so all-knowing surely she would know what he had come to ask?

He stared back into her eyes. She smiled suddenly, but her smile had no warmth and no mirth in it.

Then she reached up, clutching a handful of the leaves she had just inscribed. She held them up towards him for a moment, then flung them forward. As they hit the flame they flared up and he instinctively put his hands up to shield his eyes from the dazzling brilliance. When he opened them a crack he could just make out a figure beside the sibyl. He knew without any shadow of a doubt that it was Daedalus, though how he knew he could not tell. Bladud's eyes were watering and smarting with the heat and the glare, but he strained to keep them open, terrified he would miss the significance of the vision. Daedalus was half man, half bird, his wings growing directly out of his arms, and, even as the young prince watched, he lifted off the earth and flew powerfully towards the sun.

The image was brief but intense, ending in a light too bright to look upon. Bladud's eyes closed again and when he opened them the figure was gone, and the leaves, some not yet consumed, were still drifting down. With a gasp he leapt forward and scrabbled for them in the flames. What kind of answer was this? What did it mean? Would he, Bladud, fly or would he not?

His fingers burned as he desperately tried to retrieve the leaves, but he could not even reach them. Then one drifted towards the front of the fire, already blackened. He reached for it, but hesitated to take hold because he realised it would fall into fine ash at the slightest touch. And then he noticed a white figure against the black, where she had scratched it. He stared at it – crouched on the floor, sweat pouring down his face, his fingers in agony. He saw quite clearly, for a brief second, the symbol of a death's head.

He reached forward. He touched it. And instantly it disintegrated and there was nothing left of the sibyl's message but a dusty black mark on the floor.

He stood up, ignoring the pain in his hands, angry enough to challenge her to be more specific.

113

But she was there no longer. The chamber was empty. Even the books had gone. He stood for a long time, his hands pressed under his armpits to try to dull the pain of the burns.

But the fire died completely down and she did not return, nor was there any sign of any of the other leaves she had inscribed.

He stumbled back along the corridor and emerged half-blinded into the light, his face streaked and blackened with soot and sweat, his hands badly burned, his pure white robes no longer so pure, so white . . .

'Where does she go when she is not in her cave?' Bladud asked the captain and the young priest, when he had recovered somewhat.

'No one knows where the sibyl goes,' the captain replied. 'No one has ever known.'

'But surely she must live somewhere. She must shelter from the wind and rain? Someone must have seen her!'

'She is not like other women. She need not even eat to live, because she cannot die until the count of sands is done.'

Bladud paced impatiently. He longed for another chance! But next time he would be prepared. He would stand upright, like the prince he was, and demand . . .

'Some say she lives among the fumeroles . . . the boiling lake,' the young priest added suddenly.

Bladud stopped his pacing. 'What fumeroles? What boiling lake? Where?'

'No one ever goes there,' the captain warned. 'It is where the fires of Hades are closest to the surface of our world.'

'*I* must go!'

'It is not even certain you will find her there, and it *is* certain you would take great risk.'

'I would risk anything to learn what I must learn from her!'

'Even falling into the clutches of the Dark Lord of the Underworld?'

Bladud hesitated. He dreaded such a fate – what man would not? But the old snake of curiosity was on the move, creeping from its lair under his heart in search of satisfaction.

'Just show me this place, and I will go.'

'Not I,' the captain said firmly.

114

Bladud looked at the young priest. He shook his head.

'I will find it either with your help or without,' he pressed on. 'But with your help I might more easily survive.'

The young priest looked thoughtful. 'I will show you how to get there, but I will not enter the infernal regions with you.'

After passing several villages, they finally entered a forest of dark pines that barely admitted the sun's rays. Bladud heard no birdsong; everything around him was silent and still. The ground was so thickly carpeted with pine needles that not even the tread of their feet could be heard. The young priest kept looking nervously over his shoulder, and between them conversation instinctively ceased.

At last Bladud's companion came to a halt.

'I can accompany you no further,' he whispered, as though the forest was filled with listening ears. 'You are not far from the place now, and must go on alone.'

Bladud looked around him. In every direction the forest stretched apparently without end.

The priest pointed. 'Your way lies there. Walk straight until you find what you are looking for.'

'Straight?' Bladud thought. That was impossible. No labyrinth could be as tortuous as the way through those dark and sombre trees.

'I will wait a while here to ensure you are on the right track,' the priest whispered. Bladud was grateful for that, and set off at once, but when he next looked back, the young priest had already disappeared. A cold hand clutched at his heart again. He was afraid. But to go back would prove as difficult as going forward. His footprints had vanished as the soft needles sprang back into place once he had passed.

Suddenly the trees thinned out, and ahead of him he saw an eerie, yellowish daylight filtering through mist. Astonished, he faced a landscape of steaming rock and sulphurous smoke. There, cradled between hillocks of bare rock which were twisted and knotted like rope, lay a dark lake of mud which bubbled and boiled.

As he stepped forward, he could feel the warmth of the earth through the leather of his shoes.

115

'Sibyl of Cumae!' he called out in a clear voice. 'We have unfinished business. I come in the name of my ancestor Aeneas – the same who entered the World of the Dead and yet returned to tell the tale. Appear to me and you will not regret it.'

'Why will I not regret it, mortal?' A cracked but mocking voice spoke at his shoulder. He spun round to see her standing close behind him.

'Because I will plead with Apollo for your release,' he said.

'And why would Apollo listen to you, mortal, when he has been deaf to my pleas these many centuries?'

'Because I will speak his name and build his temple in a mighty country that as yet knows nothing of him.'

The woman stared at him silently.

'Take me where you took Aeneas,' he said, 'to the World of the Dead. Let me speak with Daedalus, the winged man.'

'You are the son of Aeneas?' the sibyl asked.

'I am of the line of Aeneas,' he replied. 'His blood runs in my veins.'

'The son of Aeneas,' she repeated softly as though she had not grasped what he had just said. She seemed to be looking back in time and what she saw there was a sweet memory.

She was in love with Aeneas! Bladud thought suddenly. That is why, of all the people who must have asked, he was the only one she ever granted the privilege of the journey into the Underworld.

'Come, son of Aeneas,' she said – and in that dried-up shell of a body the river of life flowed again. 'Come,' she said softly, and took him by the sleeve and led him forward over the burning land . . .

As they walked, the ground grew hotter, the fumeroles of sulphurous smoke became closer together until he was running with sweat and he could see nothing through the thick yellow fog. *Is she leading me to my death?* he asked himself. But he did not want to turn back. Whatever awaited him he would face.

Shapes began to emerge from the fog – dark, twisted, tormented shapes – the skeletons of trees blasted dry by the

116

heat. The ground became cooler. They were climbing. He could now see faint glimpses of blue sky through the cloud. They reached a place at last clear of the scorching and noisome fumes, and faced a thick forest of spruce and ash and oak.

'Son of Aeneas.' The sibyl spoke for the first time. 'Consider carefully. You ask to enter where no living man should enter. You ask to see what no living man should see. Can your mind bear the burden of it? Remember – it is not only death you risk here.'

'I have considered,' insisted Bladud impatiently, though in fact he had not. 'I will walk in the footsteps of Aeneas!'

'Be it so,' the woman said darkly. She turned to the forest and raised her bony hand. 'No one may enter the kingdom of the Dark Lord alive without the Wand of Destiny,' she said.

He waited. What was this Wand of Destiny? How could he obtain it?

'Go into the forest,' she said. 'Seek it out.'

'But what does it look like? How will I know when I have found it?'

'You will know.'

'And if I don't find it?'

She did not reply, but turned from him and walked away down the hill, soon disappearing into the thick sulphurous fog below. He opened his mouth to call after her, but she was already gone. He was alone.

Everything seemed to depend on his finding this mysterious wand.

Taking a deep breath he stepped forward and entered the forest of Avernus. He waded through the undergrowth. He stared up into the branches. He walked and walked, but he saw nothing that looked like a Wand of Destiny. Exhausted and near to despair he stopped at last.

She has no intention of taking me to the World of the Dead, he thought bitterly. *This is just a ruse to distract me and get rid of me.* He did not look forward to making his way back over the burning fields without a guide. He was in the deepest, darkest part of the forest and for some time he had heard no birdsong, no high-pitched buzz of cicada, no rustle or murmur of life.

117

I will lie down and rest, he decided, *before I try to find my way back*. With difficulty he cleared a comfortable space on the forest floor and lay down wearily on his back, gazing upwards. Gradually he began to feel calmer. He did not drift off to sleep. He stared at the dark branches, the lattice of leaves, the tiny everchanging patterns of light as the air moved, the sun moved. Suddenly his eyes were dazzled by a blaze of light. At first he thought it was the sun shining through a gap in the leaves. But when he looked again he realised it was not. One of the highest branches was itself giving off light. It was as though it was made of gold, its leaves sparkling and shimmering.

He leapt to his feet. The wand! This must surely be what he was seeking. He rushed to the foot of the gigantic holm-oak on which he had spotted the golden bough, but from this angle he could no longer see it. Had he been mistaken? He searched the tree for footholds, but there seemed to be none. He returned to where he had rested and lay down, his body fitting exactly into the mould its weight had left in the fallen leaves. He stared and stared but could not distinguish the shining leaves.

Disappointed, he rose to his feet, determined to leave the place and abandon the whole idea of seeking Daedalus in the Underworld.

But he had taken no more than a few steps when the longing to finish what he had started grew strong again. *I'll climb the tree*, he thought. *I'll make sure*.

He returned to the oak and worked his way around it carefully until he could see a possible way up. It took him three attempts before at last he gripped the lowest branch. He climbed with difficulty, pausing from time to time to catch his breath and plan his next move. He soon lost sight of the ground. Halfway up the difficulty of progressing further was so discouraging and the conviction that he had been mistaken in thinking he had seen the magical wand so great, he almost turned back. *Just one more branch*, he decided. *And then if there is nothing* . . .

The next branch brought him in full view of the golden bough. He gasped. It was just within reach if he stretched to his limit. Never had he seen such beauty. Every red-gold leaf was exquisitely veined with white gold. Every twig bore at least a score of such leaves.

He reached out. He almost touched it and then drew his hand back. Such beauty! What right had he to despoil such a wonder?

But his hesitation was short-lived. His desire to enter the World of the Dead was too intense. He reached up again. He grasped. He tugged. The bough would not break off the tree. He took a greater risk and manoeuvred himself a little nearer. He grasped it once again more firmly. He prayed, and tugged. This time it snapped and the sound was like a clap of thunder from a cloudless sky. He fell back into the branches with the precious object in his left hand, trying to grab for safety with his right. He fell, twigs scratching and tearing at him. But the stronger branches held and he was able to climb down at last with the magical bough intact.

Safe on the ground he paused to control his trembling. He stared at the branch in his hand. The leaves shivered and shimmered, making faint, beautiful sounds – delicate music – music from realms less gross than this.

When he was sufficiently recovered he thought to find his way out of the forest and back through the burning land to the sibyl. But he did not need to, for she appeared before him at that moment.

'Come, son of Aeneas,' she said simply, and started to walk away.

Nothing more? No sign of appreciation for what he had been through, for what he had endured, for what he had achieved?

He followed her.

They emerged from the forest of Avernus at nightfall. He was surprised that they had not in fact returned to the smoke-filled valley, but were in another region, equally inhospitable. The rocks were bare and black and a dark lake lay below them, one last streak of blood-red fire on its surface, a legacy of the setting sun.

They climbed down from the heights and came to a standstill on the shore.

'Here we will spend the night,' the sibyl said, breaking her silence at last.

The youth looked around himself uneasily. This was an oppressive place. He held the bough up high like a torch but though it was a brilliant source of light, for some reason it made little impression on this fell spot.

The first part of the night seemed endless. The sibyl spent most of it praying and chanting incomprehensible words to incomprehensible gods. At one point a huge hunting-owl hovered over them, its wings caught in the light of the golden bough, its huge eyes reflecting Bladud's image as though in mirrors. It did not stay long and the prince was glad to see it go.

He had been told he must 'purify his mind', and spent fruitless hours trying to achieve something he did not understand. Eventually he decided to gaze at each leaf of the branch individually, trying to focus on the essence of light and beauty it seemed to represent for him. This way the clammy darkness of the night, the terror of the bottomless lake before them, and the journey into the unknown ahead of them, retreated into insignificance. The last hours before the dawn passed swiftly and pleasantly.

As the sky began to take on the faintest tinge of grey and it seemed there were fewer stars in the east, the sibyl's voice rose in a crescendo. She lifted her arms in a dramatic gesture to the heavens and called on Apollo to see them safely through their ordeal.

Bladud raised his right arm across his breast in a salute to Lugh, adding Apollo's name in a whisper, just in case . . .

As the sibyl's voice died down, he heard the beginning of a distant rumble as though rocks were falling off a mountain some distance away, the sound carrying unnaturally far in the silent dawn air. And then it seemed to him the sound was nearer, and there was a vibration of the earth underfoot. The rumble grew to a roar – a grinding and a tearing and a thundering – and before his very eyes the earth split asunder and a huge gaping cavern was revealed.

'Hurry!' The sibyl took his arm and dragged him towards it.

'No!' he cried. But with extraordinary strength she persisted.

The darkness inside seemed impenetrable. Nevertheless they entered. After a time their eyes adjusted somewhat and she hurried him over rocks that were still moving apart, leaping over the gaps like a young doe. Terrified to be left alone, he followed her closely, dreading that the earth that had so precipitously parted might close over again as suddenly, trapping them inside forever. He clung to the golden bough, trusting that somehow its magic would see him through.

As they went deeper and deeper it was strangely easier to see, but this brought no comfort for the place was full of monsters – weird and horrifying creatures, hybrids of animal and man, of animal and animal, of bird and animal and man. Clawed, beaked, furred and fanged they rushed towards Bladud crying out in voices as human as his own, pleading that he should take them with him, uttering curses when the sibyl made it clear he could not. Some pawed him, and some reached out with deadly claws to tear his flesh. He drew the knife from his belt and lunged at one that had come too close. The blade passed right through the creature as though through smoke.

'Do not waste your strength,' his companion warned. 'They cannot harm us. They are dwellers between the worlds and have no power anywhere but in the minds of those who invite them in.'

Bladud shuddered and sheathed his knife, drawing back as they circled around him screaming hideously and malevolently.

At last he and his guide emerged from the cavern into a gloomy landscape, through which flowed a broad, dark river. At the narrowest point there was a ferryboat manned by a wild and ragged figure with hard, tough muscles like knotted rope, eyes like burning coals. Harassing him at the landing-place was a crowd of people, all demanding to be taken across. The ferryman was refusing some and beckoning others on to his boat.

'What is happening?' Bladud asked, bewildered.

'The ferryman is Charon, conveyor of the dead.'

'Why does he refuse some and yet take others?'

'Some have died in disbelief. Some are not ready to accept

121

the meaning of their death. But hurry,' she urged. 'He will not wait.'

They ran to the place and Bladud hung back as the sibyl spoke to Charon. He was uncomfortably aware of the crowds at his back whose places they were intending to usurp. He saw Charon shake his surly head.

'Show him the Wand of Destiny,' the sibyl cried, turning to Bladud.

He held it out and in that dim place it flashed and flamed like a beacon. Charon's eyes were dazzled as his own had been when he first saw it. The ferryman withdrew his restraining arm and let them on to the boat. There were cries from the shore as they pulled away and Bladud was ashamed to leave so many behind.

The sibyl, sensing his distress, comforted him by saying: 'They are dead. Time does not press at their back. But we – we have only until the sun sets in the upper world to make our visit.'

He wondered how they would know what the sun was doing in the upper world, for in this place there seemed to be no sun.

The boat slid slowly through the thick and sluggish water, losing them precious time. Charon did not speak again or look back at them.

On the other side they disembarked in a marsh of grey mud and had to wade ashore through dense reeds. Ahead of them was the mouth of a cave, which the sybil said would take them through the mountain. They heard a fearsome barking and howling, and when they drew nearer Bladud was horrified to see a gigantic hound with three heads – one barking, one howling, one whining. As they approached all three barked and the beast advanced on them menacingly, baring teeth that could have torn a lion apart, each fearsome jaw slavering in anticipation. Bladud could see that what at first appeared to be a hairy mane around each neck consisted in each case of a nest of serpents. As the three-headed hound became more and more agitated, the snakes began to uncoil, hissing and waving in the air.

'Cerberus, the guardian,' whispered the sibyl. She put her hand into a pouch she wore at her side and withdrew something which she threw in front of him.

The monster paused and to Bladud's delight took it into one of his enormous mouths and swallowed it. Within moments he seemed to become drowsy and, growling feebly, lay down to sleep.

'Quick!' the sibyl cried, and they hurried past the stupendous bulk, each head now resting on the ground. As Bladud cast a terrified backward glance, he could have sworn one eye was still open and a muscle twitched as though something in the beast was still awake and on guard.

But they were safely past and into the tunnel that led through the mountain. The path was narrow and in many places precipitous. From the shadowy regions just beyond sight they heard voices – some wailing, some moaning, some crying . . .

'Those who passed Cerberus, but became lost in the mountain,' whispered the sibyl. Bladud noticed there were many paths branching off the main one. He was thankful he had a guide.

They emerged from the mountain into what passed for light in these regions – a dim and sickly glow. They passed many people on the move, some apparently lost and wandering aimlessly, others pushing forward purposefully.

The road they followed passed beneath the battlements of the mighty castle of the Dark Lord of Death, the King of the Underworld, Hades himself, the brother of Zeus. The towering castle was protected by three gigantic ring walls and a river of white fire. Above the battlements rose an iron tower where the giant Tisiphone kept brooding and ceaseless watch. From within Bladud could hear howls and shrieks and the sibyl pointed out that those who had misspent their lives learned to regret it in that fell place.

Bladud shuddered and for the first time truly wished he had not come here. But she led him past the castle to where the road divided. There they found a gate of diamond.

She took his arm. 'Here you must lay your golden burden down,' she said, and drew a flask of pure water out of her pouch. She sprinkled both of them with cool clear drops, and

123

showed him where he should place the golden bough. He did so, and then, with beating heart, waited to see what would happen.

The mighty gate rolled back, lightning flashing from every facet of its surface. Caught in webs of light Bladud stood bemused and dazed until the sibyl pulled him forward once again and they entered a realm that was more beautiful than any he had ever heard the bards describe. Gentle fields and hills of flowering grasses, trees without blemish, happy people all young and fit, houses of silver with roofs of white feathers . . . waterfalls . . . birdsong and music . . .

Staring around him with relief at last to find a place that was not full of fear and pain, Bladud would have stopped where he was, had she not drawn him on again.

'Hurry,' she said. 'There is not much time and you have not yet earned your sojourn here.'

He hurried behind her, waving and smiling at those who waved and smiled at him. 'It seems so like earth,' he said. 'I had expected it to be different.'

'This realm is the one nearest to the earth realm,' she said. 'Memories of earth still influence the creation of images. We cannot go to the realms that lie beyond however many golden boughs we bring.'

'What are they like?'

'Not even I know that, son of Aeneas. And there are many tests even the dead have to pass before they may enter there.'

She spoke to one or two of the spirits they encountered and seemed to gain some information, for she called to him and started running. Not for the first time Bladud noticed that the ancient crone had taken on the form of a young and vigorous woman.

Ahead they saw a silver river, calmly flowing beside a flowered bank. There were people crowding towards it with glad cries, many leaping in and swimming to the other side, others cheerfully waving them goodbye. Bladud looked to see where the swimmers were heading but the other bank of the river was obscured in white mist and those who reached it instantly disappeared.

124

'Lethe,' the sibyl said. 'The river of forgetfulness.'

'Why would they want to forget this lovely place?'

'They are going to have new lives on earth. Old memories could hinder them.'

Suddenly it dawned on Bladud they might be too late. 'What if Daedalus has already crossed?' he cried in alarm.

The sibyl spoke urgently to some gathered on the bank. She passed from one to the other. At last they came to a man in middle years, hard and seasoned, with the eyes of an eagle and the strength of a bull.

'Daedalus?' Bladud cried out, scarcely daring to hope.

The man paused and looked round briefly, and then turned away.

'I have to talk to you!' Bladud had been through so much to find him, yet it seemed as though the spirit was about to pass out of his reach forever. He tried to take hold of his arm to pull him back, but there was nothing there to grip.

'Stay!' Bladud cried. 'I beg of you – stay.'

Daedalus looked at him in surprise. 'You are alive?'

'Yes. I am alive. I've dared the very depths of hell to reach you.'

'Why?'

'I must know about your flight. I must know!'

The sibyl was agitating at his side, telling him they must go soon or they would be trapped for all time. Daedalus was still moving towards the river.

'I want to fly. I know it can be done. You did it. Tell me!' urged Bladud almost incoherently. 'How did you construct the wings? What with? How did you attach them to yourself?'

Daedalus gazed at the living prince. For a moment it looked as though he would stay – he would speak with him – he would tell him what he wanted to know . . .

But at that moment the earth shook. Bladud turned round in alarm and saw a vast figure striding across the green and flowered fields, withering them with every step. The air had become dark and chill.

'Hades himself,' whispered the sibyl in alarm, and looked around hastily for a way to escape. 'You have angered him!'

Bladud could feel the heat from the fell figure as though from a furnace. The sibyl interposed her own body between his and the Lord of Shadows.

'I call on Persephone the queen!' she cried. 'Great lady, show us thy mercy!'

'Apollo's creature of a thousand years!' roared the Dark Lord. 'Have you learned nothing? To bring a living being to this land! To try to change the fate of one who has chosen to enter Lethe's stream!'

What would have happened to them Bladud later dreaded to think, had not the queen that moment appeared. Persephone, the lady of spring, pale from her winter palace, but with eyes that still saw in memory the golden world of the sun. She held in her hand the shining bough Bladud had brought to her diamond door. She held it up above their heads and a shower of light engulfed them. Hades glared, but did not touch them.

The sibyl bowed to her and then started to run along the river bank, dragging Bladud by the hand. Afraid as he was, he still looked back over his shoulder to see if there was any chance of establishing contact again with Daedalus. But Daedalus was gone, the river swirling, the current strong, the mist thick . . .

Ahead they saw two gates – one plain and stark, carved of horn, and one elaborately fashioned of ivory. Neither appeared to be attached to any building but stood isolated in an otherwise empty field. The sibyl was making for the further one – the one of ivory – but Bladud took the initiative this time and rushed to the nearer, the gate of horn. He heard her cry out that he should not go through, but he would not listen and flung it open.

As he stepped on to the threshold he found himself being drawn into a vortex. The images he had recently seen whirled before him in a violent and confusing blur, transforming, becoming other, taking on their true meaning.

Sounds and visions too powerful to endure overwhelmed him. It was as though he were about to fall into the first chaos – the Void – the matrix of the worlds before order was conceived and the wild and boundless passions of the first energies were tamed. Terrified, he clung to the door

126

post, until the sibyl reached for him and hauled him back.

'Not this one,' she cried, 'the other.' She drew him, staggering and bewildered, to the gate of ivory. Through this they entered the world as he had always known it – the nakedness of reality comfortably and safely clothed in illusion.

10

Imogene and Athene

If he had thought Cumae was impressive compared to Trinovantum, Athens made Cumae appear no more than a small provincial town – and Trinovantum just a sprawling, untidy village.

When Bladud arrived in the great city early in the spring, almost immediately his eyes were drawn upwards to the sacred hill where gleaming white temples clustered high against an ineffably blue sky. Spreading out below, on the plain, were endless streets of wooden houses, clustered close together in greater numbers than he had ever seen before in any one place, yet wide roads in between allowed carts and chariots to pass by easily.

Immediately below the sacred hill stood larger, public buildings of stone. Many were surrounded by shaded colonnades where people could walk and talk, away from the crowded streets where merchants noisily plied their trade, where townspeople jostled for vegetables and meat.

Bladud's guide was a young Athenian called Diomede, whom he had met on the voyage from Cumae. Returning home rich after seeking his fortune abroad, Diomede welcomed the young foreigner hospitably and without reservations into his own home.

The morning after Bladud arrived in Athens he woke to a loud hubbub in the streets. Puzzled, he dragged himself out of bed, and, blinking in the light, gazed sleepily out of a window on the second floor. In the narrow street below the crowds were flowing like a river in spate towards the town centre, and to the sacred hill of the Acropolis. Chattering, eager, purposeful: women with flowers and ribbons in their hair; men in crisp white tunics, their beards neatly trimmed, hair curled and shining; excited children laughing and singing and shouting to their friends. There was no sign of pushing or jostling or bad temper.

Behind him the door flew open and Diomede burst into the room. 'Damn!' he said. 'We'll be late.'

'Late for what? What is happening?'

'Athene's festival! I overslept. Come, get dressed. If we hurry we might still get near the front.' The young Athenian rushed out of the room.

Bladud dressed himself hastily, but when Diomede returned he looked askance at the prince's coarsely woven breeches and thick tunic and boots that were lashed up high on his calves. He himself wore a light, white cotton tunic and open sandals.

'What's the matter?' Bladud asked, seeing his expression.

'Nothing,' Diomede replied after a moment's hesitation. 'Just hurry. We'll never see a thing if we're stuck at the back.'

As they rushed out among the crowds now thinning in the street, Bladud realised that this was the day which honoured the great warrior goddess Athene, daughter of Zeus, who protected Athens itself and ensured its strength and prosperity. On this day all her subjects, many scattered across the world in the Athenian colonies, made a special effort to return to the mother city to show their gratitude.

As they drew nearer to the sacred Acropolis, it was almost impossible to make progress through the crowds, yet somehow the sale of bread and fruit continued and loaves were being passed cheerfully overhead as people at the rear shouted out their orders.

Diomede pulled at Bladud's arm. 'Come,' he said, and they pushed and squeezed themselves into a side alley less crowded than the main thoroughfares. 'I know someone who might let us have a place on his roof.'

Looking up, Bladud saw that every roof in sight was already covered with spectators and could not believe that there was any space left in the city from which they could see the procession. But he struggled after his friend nevertheless.

Diomede thumped on a door. No answer. More thumping – followed by shouting. At last a face looked down from an upstairs window, and recognised Diomede. Moments later the bolt was drawn and Bladud and his companion were let inside. The roof was already crowded, but it afforded a good view of the processional route, where garlands of flowers tied to posts held back the excited populace.

How orderly! thought Bladud. He could not believe his own people would be deterred by such fragile barriers.

Diomede introduced him to his friends and there was something of a stir when they heard that the young foreigner had come from the Pretanic Islands, which many of them had believed existed only in legend. While they waited for the procession he tried to describe something of his life there, but his descriptions were greeted with such hoots of merriment, as more and more wine was consumed, that he soon gave up.

He felt suddenly extraordinarily lonely – a stranger in a strange land.

Suddenly they heard a distant roar from the crowds and all looked down. The people were now straining close against the garlands, peering expectantly towards the left. They could hear a ripple of sound from that direction, growing louder and louder until it broke like a gigantic wave into the street below.

Young men on horseback came first in the procession. Then came men who led heifers lowing and scuffing up dust, followed by columns of people carrying standards, bowls of fruit, baskets of corn, flowers, branches heavily laden with olives. Young girls strewed petals from baskets. Others carried wine and water jugs on their shoulders. The procession seemed to continue forever, a moving frieze, clean and clear and brilliant in the sunlight.

Bladud found himself cheering with the rest until suddenly he noticed a young woman walking in the procession who made his heart almost stop beating. Her golden hair was bound with a ribbon from which several long curls had slipped. Her shapely body was slightly twisted to the left as she held a tall crystal rhyton on her shoulder. Her skin was as white as a swan's wing. It was Imogene! He leaned forward. All his life he had seen this same woman in his dreams . . . in his waking visions . . . in his heart. She was Imogene, the Greek princess, taken from her family by force to marry the Trojan prince Brutus. She was his ancestor . . . his obsession . . .

'Imogene!' he shouted, and scarcely felt the hands of Diomede on his shoulders, roughly pulling him back.

'What are you doing? You'll break your neck!' Diomede yelled, holding him tight. But Bladud fought him. He had to reach her. He could not let her pass out of his life.

Seeing the struggle, several of Diomede's friends joined in and Bladud was pulled back from the edge. When he wrenched free it was too late for she had gone, and there were only horsemen to be seen in the street below.

'I must find her!' he shouted frantically, and pushed his way back into the house. Though he heard Diomede calling him, he took no notice as he rushed through the cool rooms, dark in contrast to the blazing light in the street. Once out amongst the crowds he pushed and shoved and jostled, the good humour of the people soon turning sour as the foreigner shouldered his way roughly through them. To make better progress he ducked under the flowered ropes. Angry voices shouted at him. Angry faces glared. Hands grabbed at him to pull him back. But he could think of nothing but that somehow, by some miracle, Imogene was alive and *there* – within reach . . .

And then all went blank as one of the beautiful young men on horseback leant down and struck him hard on the head with his bronze staff. As Bladud fell he had a vivid impression of the owl's head with staring eyes carved on its tip.

When he became conscious again he was back in the house of Diomede's friends. The procession was long past and the crowds had dispersed.

'What were you thinking of? You could have been killed!' Diomede said accusingly as soon as he opened his eyes.

'I had to find her. I *have* to know who she is.'

'Who? Who do you *have* to find?'

He described the girl he had seen, but Diomede and his

friends just laughed, saying they each knew at least ten women who would fit that description. Clearly none had noticed her particularly as she walked by, though to Bladud it had seemed she had a special and extraordinary radiance.

His head already ached where the bronze owl had hit him, and it ached even more with the continuing banter of the young men.

'If it's a woman you want,' they said, nudging each other and laughing, 'we can introduce you to any number.'

'What sort do you want? Tall? Short? Fair? Dark? Thin? Fat? Athens is full of women who'd be delighted to spend the night with a foreign prince!'

Many a detail was then given of the local courtesans. It seemed to amuse Diomede's friends that he, from such a backward and barbaric country, should consider himself a prince. While Diomede was with his friends he ran with the pack, but when they left the house he told Bladud he might be able to identify the girl from her precise position in the procession.

'She must come from one of the top families,' he said, 'for only their daughters are allowed to approach the goddess.' It seemed the crystal rhyton played an important part in the presentation ceremony in the temple.

'The goddess Athene is a formidable warrior,' Diomede told him. 'It is said she sprang fully armed from the head of her father Zeus, and it was with her help the Greeks defeated the Trojans.' Diomede paused. 'You were lucky,' he added. 'You, a Trojan, interrupted her procession and yet you received nothing more than a blow on the head!'

Bladud rubbed his skull ruefully. 'I meant no disrespect . . . I just wanted . . .'

'To lust after one of the goddess's handmaidens while she is engaged in a sacred duty would certainly be considered disrespect.'

'It wasn't lust . . . I just wanted . . .'

Diomede laughed. 'Whatever you wanted . . . whatever you thought . . . you *did* disrupt her procession. I just hope the goddess will be satisfied with the punishment she has already meted out.'

'What could she do to me?' Bladud asked in alarm.

133

'Almost anything. Her powers are limitless. That owl now, the one that struck you, it can see in the dark. There is nowhere you can hide from it.'

'It was a bronze owl on a stick!' Bladud exclaimed.

'You really believe that?' asked Diomede darkly.

Bladud fell silent, remembering the malevolent glare in its eyes as it fell upon him.

During the next few days Diomede took Bladud around Athens. The young foreigner found the city fascinating. In the long colonnades surrounding the market Bladud met other, older men: scholars who impressed him much more than the young bloods to whom Diomede had first introduced him. They seemed to spend their time debating, morning, noon and night. Diomede, who did not enjoy mind-games, was impatient to draw his young friend away.

'I always thought our own Druid training was the best in the world,' Bladud said, his eyes sparkling after a long and heated debate with one old man, 'but these men could teach Fergal a thing or two!'

Yet at first he had been disconcerted by the Greek method of analysis and cross-questioning, and somehow felt that deeper meanings were being ignored or lost in such cold, bald probing. Among his own people he was used to the inspired use of myth, where truth was often caught in passing, from the flash of a particularly relevant symbol or verbal image.

Everywhere he went Bladud was obsessed by finding Imogene. By day he searched the streets for her, by night he dreamed of her. Sometimes he thought he saw her walking ahead of him in a crowd, but as soon as he tried to reach her the crowd closed in and she was lost. Sometimes he dreamed he saw her climbing a mountain, but though he called her name she neither looked back nor slowed her place, and he always awoke before he could catch up with her.

Then one late afternoon Diomede took Bladud to the theatre. And there she was.

Arriving early, they sat and watched the stone benches of the huge amphitheatre gradually fill up. Bladud could not believe that all those thousands of people, some at a

134

considerable distance from the stage, would be able to hear clearly, but Diomede assured him that they could. Bladud reflected on the story-tellers in his own country, where one man with nothing more than the fire of his words would inspire the small group gathered around him to see great battles, and feel the passions of love and hate. Here there would be actors, music, scenery; a chorus of men in masks would strut and proclaim. Here *thousands* would be transported out of their humdrum lives by the illusions of high drama.

Dressed in a white embroidered tunic like any Athenian, his arms and legs bare and bronzed, Bladud looked so handsome that Diomede teased him over the number of young girls who turned their heads to gaze at him. But suddenly their eyes were drawn to a group of latecomers who had become the focus of all attention. People bowed and drew back to let them pass. Officials guided them to the best seats in the theatre.

Bladud was about to ask who they were, noting the silver-haired elegance of the older couple, but then he saw the young girl moving sedately behind them. It was she! Imogene! Beside her, holding her arm, walked a tall young man with black curly hair and the physique of a god!

Diomede noticed his friend's expression. 'So that is her?' He gave a low whistle. 'You might as well aspire to Athene herself!'

'Why! Who is she?'

'That, my dear barbarian, is the princess of Boeotia!'

Bladud drew in his breath. 'And who is the man at her side?'

'Some Thessalian prince, I believe. There is talk of marriage.' Diomede looked at Bladud sharply. 'What are you thinking, friend?'

These days Bladud rarely thought about Rheinid or his son, for there had been too many adventures, too many new experiences to distract him. There had been times in the night when the memory of Rheinid set his body on fire . . . but she was very far from his thoughts now.

'I must talk to her,' he whispered to Diomede.

'That's not possible.'

135

'I am also a prince and I am to be a king one day.'

'Yes, but . . .' Diomede's unspoken words implied that a kingdom in the barbaric isles could hardly be compared to the realm of Boeotia.

Bladud flushed angrily and started to argue, when trumpets were sounded for the performance to begin.

'Ssh! Ssh!' people nearby whispered, and Bladud, with all the thousands gathered in that place, fell silent. Clearly the actors enunciated their words, and competently they made their moves, yet Bladud saw and heard nothing. His eyes never left the young woman who reminded him so much of Imogene. He watched her raise her hand to tuck an errant curl into the golden coronet around her head. He watched her laugh when the rest of the audience laughed. He saw her wipe a tear. And always at her side sat the Thessalian prince. More than once Bladud saw their heads lean together, whispering.

At the end of the performance, and before Diomede could stop him, Bladud leapt to his feet and pushed his way past the rows of people and down the aisle steps towards her. He felt desperate. At first his progress was unimpeded, but when he came nearer he was halted by the royal guards.

'I am Prince Bladud of Trinovantum,' he said to them with as much dignity as he could muster, though his heart pounded wildly. 'I would like to pay my respects to . . .' But the guards continued to edge him away.

'Lady! Princess!' he called out, hoping to catch her eye. She turned her head to look at him. For one moment those green-grey pools of light gazed straight into his own hazel eyes. For a moment he thought she would recognise him, as he recognised her, but instead she turned away, her expression cool and undisturbed. To her he was clearly no more than one of many young men who worshipped her beauty. The Thessalian prince then took her elbow and they moved gracefully away. The guards threatened Bladud. The king and queen did not even look round.

After this incident Bladud became gloomy and morose. He was deeply confused. His new-found friends, the philosophers, were forever trying to persuade him that nothing was real unless it could be proved by reason or the senses, yet his own experience told him that a large proportion of life remained mysterious and inexplicable. Though Diomede insisted that the young woman he had seen in the procession and at the theatre was the Princess Alcestis, only child of Lysander, king of Boeotia, his heart kept telling him she was, somehow, Imogene, his long-dead ancestor.

'Be sensible, man,' Diomede exclaimed in exasperation. 'How could she possibly be who you think she is?'

'I don't know how it can be,' Bladud said stubbornly. 'That's why I must find out more about her.'

Diomede suggested he would make no progress without first placating and then petitioning the goddess Athene.

'You had thoughts of violating her handmaiden,' he warned, 'so you will get no nearer the princess until you have won the goddess's forgiveness and trust.'

Bladud denied that his thoughts had ever been impure, but he decided that at any rate Diomede's advice was probably worth following.

But what offering should he take to Athene? He could buy a goat or a calf, as other supplicants did, but he felt somehow those would not be appropriate. He thought of the golden torc he had given to the Oracle of Sul, and the golden bracelet presented to the Sibyl of Cumae – but Athene already had more gold than Midas. It had to be something very special. Diomede might mock, half believing in the power and malice of Athene, and part disbelieving, but Bladud had endured yet another nightmare in which his eyes had been attacked by an owl, and when he had woken in the morning his lids were swollen and red and he could hardly see. The condition cleared in time, but he could not shake the feeling that some malevolent force was hounding him.

He approached the Temple of Athene on the Acropolis with no clear idea of what he intended to do. He bowed low before the statue. In one hand the figure held a spear, and in the other a shield. Several curls escaping from her helmet softened a face that was otherwise uncompromisingly stern. An owl sat on her shoulder. Bladud studied it closely, making sure it was truly cast in gold and not likely to fly at his face.

137

'Great goddess,' he whispered. 'I have come . . .' His voice trailed away. What was he doing addressing a statue of painted marble?

He had bribed the priest to leave him alone in the sanctuary, yet Bladud heard a movement behind him. He looked around quickly. As he entered he had noticed several polished silver screens placed about the chamber, but had not paid them much attention. He now saw the image of the goddess was reflected in them, and it seemed to him these reflections had the flush of living flesh. For a moment he fancied that the images moved. Quickly he looked back at the statue itself. Its position unaltered, it stared back at him with expressionless eyes.

Once more he glanced back over his shoulder. Disturbingly lifelike, a myriad images of the goddess surrounded him.

He stood up and turned around. Was there some priestess disguised as Athene in the chamber with him? He peered closely, but could see no sign of any other human.

'Why have you come to this place, mortal?' A female voice spoke suddenly, though the lips of the mirror images did not seem to move.

'Great goddess,' he muttered. 'I have come to . . .'

He turned from image to image desperately. Which one of them was the 'real' goddess? Which were merely reflections? The statue stood unchanged, unmoving – but the images were changing, moving, all the time.

Bladud stepped forward. Nothing dire befell him. He stepped again, and now saw his own reflections – many of them – whereas those of the goddess had disappeared. He took yet another step – and another. His own image vanished and he saw in its place the reflection of another.

'Imogene!' he cried out, reaching out his arms.

There was the sound of laughter from every side – the laughter of women.

In desperation he rushed hither and thither, trying to locate the figure reflected so clearly in the mirrors. Image after image mocked him until at last he fell back, defeated. There was now no reflection to be seen in any of the mirrors. Not even his own.

He turned slowly back towards the statue of Athene, and stood staring at it long and hard, his face as stern as her own. Then he took off his wedding ring and laid it at the feet of the cold and heartless statue. 'I swear by the gods of my people,' he said, 'she will become my wife. If you will not help me, I must find her by myself.'

He turned on his heel and, without a backward glance at either statue or mirrors, he left the Temple of Athene.

Diomede had made enquiries among his many rich and influential friends in Athens, but no one could provide access to the royal family of Boeotia.

'However,' he said, 'I have thought of one way you might get to meet her.' He then told Bladud about the Festival of Apollo at Delphi. 'The princess lives not far from there,' he added. 'She and her family are bound to attend the games. It is more than likely her father will present the laurels to the victors, and so if you compete and win, the princess will have to notice you.'

'And what if I don't win?' Bladud asked.

'You must win. You have three months in which to train.'

And so for three months, with many other young athletes, Bladud trained. At home religious festivals were marked by competitive games, too, but the young men and women who competed did not go to organised gymnasiums, or practise on well laid out stadiums. They ran, jumped and wrestled on the day as best they could on muddy fields among crowds who often spilled enthusiastically over on to the course. Bladud was young, strong and fit and he soon became confident enough to believe he had a good chance of winning.

'Will the princess herself be competing?' he asked Diomede, remembering Rheinid's bronzed and fleet form at the races during the festival of Lughnasa.

Diomede laughed. 'Women have their own races at the Festival of Artemis. But in Apollo's games only men will compete. At Olympia at the Festival of Zeus women are not even allowed to watch.'

'May women watch at Delphi?'

'From a distance.'

'But how am I to impress her from a distance?'

139

'That's why you must win. If you win you will be invited to a great banquet at the palace. You will be wined and fêted for days. You will become *someone*!'

'I *am* someone.'

'Not to her. Not to the Greeks. But if you win at the Delphic races you will be noticed. And then if you follow it up with a win at the Olympic Games next year, you will become the companion of princes and kings . . .'

'But in my own country I am the prince and others vie to be my companion.'

'No one knows anything about your country here. Here you have to win respect on your own merits.'

'Very well,' Bladud said firmly. 'I will show you what a prince of the Pretanic Isles can do and I will make you think again about my country.'

Day after day he ran, pushing himself almost beyond endurance. He practised discus-throwing, wrestling, javelin-hurling, chariot-racing – and every day he improved his performance until, among the athletes at least, he had won respect.

He saw little of Diomede these days, for Diomede was out drinking with his friends most nights while Bladud was making sure he was early to bed and up before the dawn to train. Bladud had never been so determined to win at anything in his life. Even his ambition to succeed over his brother Liel was nothing to the ambition he now had to show these arrogant Greeks what a so-called 'barbarian' could do – and to impress the Princess Alcestis.

The day came at last when it was time to set off for Delphi.

As they passed through the rich and wooded country of Boeotia, Bladud was aware the whole time that they were in *her* country. These were the hills she had grown to love. These were the forests that shaded her from the searing summer sun. Those olives ripening might one day supply her with oil. Those lilies might be picked to decorate her chamber. She had become a goal and an obsession for him as much for the fact that she resembled so closely a woman he had loved in his dreams for so long, as for his determination that he would make her acknowledge him, love him, marry

140

him – to show the world that a Pretanic prince was worthy to marry a Greek princess. He visualised taking her back to his country as Brutus had taken Imogene. His marriage to Rheinid had virtually been over before he left Trinovantum, and no one surely would dispute his right to take another wife.

As they approached Delphi, climbing further and further up the rocky, winding path, Bladud became more and more confident of success. This was Apollo's territory and Apollo had supported his ancestors against Athene. Let her try her tricks here, and see how far she would get!

The party came to a halt. They had arrived. Bladud leapt lightly and confidently off his horse. His ankle turned on a round stone, and he fell to the ground in agony.

11

Delphi

Diomede and Glaucon, another athlete, carried Bladud to their quarters in the long wooden building standing where the path to the shrines and the path to the stadium divided. A physician was called and to Bladud's relief pronounced that no bones were broken. A thick compress of herbs was bound around his ankle and he was warned to keep off it until further notice.

But the Games were due to start in just three days' time.

'Will I be able to run?' Bladud asked anxiously.

The physician pursed his lips. 'If you put no weight on your foot, and keep the compress on day and night, it is just possible. But I doubt it. I will come back and look at it in three days.'

'There is a sanctuary to Asclepius here,' Glaucon suggested. 'We could carry you there.' When Bladud looked puzzled he explained that Asclepius was the god of healing and medicine.

The doctor shrugged. 'Visit Asclepius by all means, but keep off that foot, and don't remove the compress.'

'You'd be better off making a sacrifice to Athene,' Diomede suggested darkly.

'I would rather go to Apollo,' Bladud said decisively. This was, after all, Apollo's mountain – his special place, the very heart and centre of his cult.

'You'll never get near the sanctuary of Apollo during his festival,' Diomede warned, 'unless you've already arranged it with the priests. People will have been queuing every day for the ceremonies!'

Bladud groaned. 'I feel in my bones that Apollo is the only one to help me out of this.'

'There is a small shrine to Apollo down by the shore,' Glaucon said suddenly. 'It is said that is where Apollo once took the form of a dolphin in order to guide a ship full of priests from Minoan Crete to these parts to become the first priests of his own cult here. But hardly anyone ever goes there these days because all the major events take place up on the sacred mountain itself.'

Bladud at once insisted that this was where he wanted to go, so Diomede and Glaucon rigged up a chair with a pole so that they could carry him between them on their shoulders.

They started off in great good humour, laughing and joking about his weight, and singing songs as they swung along the path. But soon the way grew more precipitous, and every step was more difficult than the last, with their awkward burden. The forest was thick around them and it was not easy to see how much further they had to go.

'I hope Apollo takes pity on you,' Diomede said irritably. 'For I'm not carrying you up again!'

Glaucon began to worry that the temple would still be where he remembered it. He had only seen it once when he was a child, and that from the sea, from his grandfather's fishing boat.

Diomede was furious when he heard this. 'You mean this whole thing might be a waste of effort?' he grumbled.

'It will not be a waste,' Bladud said hastily. 'Even if no shrine to Apollo remains there now, if it was once a sacred place, it will still be sacred.'

Diomede scowled as they took up the chair again.

But at last they saw the sea gleaming through the trees, and the path no longer seemed so steep.

When they burst out into the open their hearts lifted at the beauty of the scene. A bay of shining silver lay before them with hills curving in a delicate arc around it, gradually shading off in various exquisite shades of blue into the distance. A small circular temple of white marble stood on a promontory near a marble jetty with steps leading down into the water. Wild flowers and creepers clambered round the

144

base of the building and, in some cases, invaded it. One white column was hung with festoons of crimson flowers. There was no sign of anyone else – no priest or acolyte – no activity or habitation anywhere. It seemed indeed a deserted and forgotten place.

Diomede and Glaucon set Bladud down, and then they stripped off and leaped joyously into the water, shouting and laughing and splashing like two young boys. Bladud watched, smiling, longing to join them. He could feel that this was a good place to be, and was thankful he had left Delphi behind with its crowds, its stalls of souvenirs, its buildings crowded together and the air thick with the acrid smoke from innumerable burnt offerings. Here, in this peaceful and beautiful place, it would surely be possible to commune with a god.

He looked at the little shrine thoughtfully. It was no more than a paved marble circle, with steps leading up to it, and ringed with slender columns roofed with a dome of crystal rock so fine and transparent that the sunlight glowed through it. In the centre of the paved floor was a bronze tripod, green with age, in which presumably fires were lit when prayers were said. There was no place here for the slaughter of animals. No elaborate system of walls and screens to provide secrecy. The clean sea breezes blew through it. The sun shone into it. The sea lapped at its foundations. He wanted to be alone. He very much wanted to be alone.

When his two friends had bathed their fill, and they had eaten a meal together and rested, he insisted that they leave him and return to Delphi before nightfall. They protested that they would keep him company, but he was so insistent that at last they agreed. He suspected they would not be sorry to return to the buzz and excitement of the festival above. He was made comfortable and they left him with what remained of the food they had brought with them. Glaucon had carved him a crutch and he soon mastered the use of it.

They assured him they would come back in two days.

'If my ankle is not better when you come again, I'll stay down here until it is. I'll not leave this place except on my own two feet.'

145

Pretending reluctance they left him alone at last. He could hear their voices gradually fading as they climbed the forested slopes.

When he could no longer hear his friends he took a deep breath and looked around again. Far out the sea was mirror pale. The air was still and silent. Small waves whispered softly against the marble jetty just below his feet.

He had never felt so much at peace. He could not think why he had been straining so hard all his life to please others, to compete, to succeed, to win. The last few months of intensive physical training would have been for nothing if he could not run in the Delphic races, but suddenly he did not care. It was as though, at this moment, with the sun sinking beyond those distant blue mountains, he was totally content with himself and his life.

A flock of birds winged away from the mountain forest and skimmed low over the sea. Even that sight did not disturb him. One day he would fly . . . He would not need to strive and strain . . . It would come to him when the moment was right . . .

That night Bladud took a long time trying to find a comfortable place to sleep. He packed a natural hollow in the earth with soft plants and leaves, but he still lay hour after hour gazing up at the stars instead of sleeping.

Around midnight the stars seemed to go out one by one and he found himself in total darkness. The air was hot and sultry and very still. He found it increasingly difficult to breathe. He reached for his crutch, thinking to move into the shelter of the shrine, but the crutch must have slipped somehow, and he could not find it in the dark.

Suddenly a livid flash of lightning illuminated the edge of the forest before him, and he saw a huge figure silhouetted against the trees – watching him. But as soon as it appeared, it vanished, and total darkness fell once more. Thunder rumbled over the mountains and echoed through the hollow caves and against the precipitous gorges. Fearfully Bladud reached out and felt around him like a blind man. He crawled from his makeshift bed, but still could not find his crutch. He believed he would see it in the next lightning flash, and

146

determined to keep his eyes to the ground. But when it came he could not resist a glance at the place he had seen the strange figure, so missed his opportunity. This time he saw no one, but he could not shake off the feeling that he was not alone.

In the next flash he saw the figure again but in a different place. And in the next she had moved again. He was now sure it was a woman, and he immediately thought of Athene. No mortal woman could move so swiftly and in such absolute darkness. He had no idea how he might escape, but he pulled himself to his feet and stumbled and hopped towards Apollo's shrine. Diamond-tipped spears of white lightning pursued him, striking the ground just behind him, the thunder whip-cracking over his head.

Frantically he muttered prayers to Apollo, to Lugh, to every god of whom he had ever heard, praying for help, for forgiveness, for protection. His ankle was in agony as more than once he put weight upon it. He could no longer see the figure for he concentrated only on the little temple, straining every muscle to reach it, convinced that once there he would be safe. Suddenly he felt a blow on his head that sent him spinning across the ground, and knocked the breath from his body. In that moment it seemed to him there was a huge gathering of beings around him, crowding in, staring into his face, some malevolent, some benevolent, all watching to see what he would do.

I am dead, he thought. *I am dead!* But suddenly he was more angry than afraid. He had been shown visions. He had been given promises. He had dreams that needed to be given substance.

'I am not ready!' he shouted. 'I have things to do!' He thought of all the wonderful things he believed he could achieve if he were given another chance, and as the images of these took shape, the images of the watchers slipped back and merged with the shadows of the forest.

With one desperate effort he reached the shrine and hauled himself up the marble steps just as the rains came pouring down.

Exhausted he sank on to the cold marble floor, with his back to one of the pillars. Hour after hour the rain drummed

147

on the roof of the little temple, but at last he fell asleep and heard it no more.

When he woke an almost full moon hung like a silver lamp over the water, throwing a shimmering silken veil over everything. A gleaming path led directly from it to him.

Are the gods outside ourselves – or do we create them? he wondered. 'There are so many different kinds of reality,' he sighed. 'How is one ever supposed to find one's way?'

When the dawn came he heard a sound from the sea – a high-pitched musical call. He looked around and saw dolphins leaping out of golden water, drops of liquid fire falling from their flanks. Without a thought for the pain in his ankle, he slithered across the floor and down the steps, and joined them. For hours he swam with them, at first holding on to a fin so as to be drawn along through the water, then swimming by himself. With every moment the pain in his ankle seemed to decrease.

The second night he slept long and deeply, the stars dropping into the dark well of his mind to stimulate visions of extraordinary splendour. He was flying towards the sun, with flames falling from him like water in the wake of a boat.

When he woke the dolphins were calling him again, and again he answered their call. Green and cool the liquid ocean bathed his body with its healing balm – and when at last he climbed out on the jetty there was no pain in his ankle at all.

Diomede and Glaucon arrived expecting to see him still on his crutch. They put out hands to steady him as he came out of the sea, but he leapt lightly on to the step and greeted them laughingly.

'No need for that,' he said. 'It's completely healed.'

If Bladud had found Delphi crowded before, it was trebly so now. On the eve of the Games the whole place buzzed with activity. Most athletes were accompanied by families and friends or an entourage of admirers. The local priests were joined by others from far afield to help handle the sudden rush of supplicants. Bladud saw the queues for the oracle and was thankful he had decided not to consult her. Diomede suggested they attend the ceremonies at the Omphalus, the carved rock that the Greeks believed was the centre of the

148

world, but, seeing the crowds of people packed so tightly around it Bladud refused.

'This may be the centre of the world to you,' he said. 'But it is not to me.'

At the line-up for the first race there was still no sign of Princess Alcestis or her father, but beside him Bladud found the Thessalian prince. Though the young man did not recognise him from the incident at the theatre, Bladud instantly felt that Fate had put them together for some reason. He glanced at the other athletes and no one would have blamed him had he felt discouraged at the competition assembled there, but he hardly noticed the others. This race was between the Thessalian and himself – and the prize was to be Alcestis.

All through that day the heats continued and by the evening both the Thessalian and himself were still in competition.

That night Bladud slept fitfully, tossing and turning.

On the third day the finalists in all the races were set against each other for the much coveted laurel crown and all that went with it. And on that day the trumpeters ushered in the king of Boeotia and his entourage to the best seats above the stadium.

Bladud stood at the starting line and looked up at the princess. Since he had last seen her, at the theatre in Athens so many months before, he had begun to wonder if he was not mistaken about her. Surely he had exaggerated some slight resemblance to Imogene? But as he gazed at her now again, he did not believe that he had.

The king's sword flashed in the sun, and the race was on. But Bladud set off precious seconds behind the Thessalian. In all the previous races Bladud had paced himself perfectly, knowing just when to unleash a special burst of speed and when to hold back. But in this the most crucial race of all, when he was competing with the very best athletes from as far afield as Macedonia and Sparta, Colchis and Crete, when he was pitted against the winners from a great and far-flung empire, the sight of a woman had distracted him at the starting line. For the first few moments he was falling well

149

behind, so to catch up to the others he needed that special effort he usually reserved for the end of the race. But make up the lost time he did, his attention becoming fixed on the muscular figure of his rival directly ahead of him. He was scarcely aware of the screaming crowds who had risen to their feet, or even of the princess who now leaned forward the better to see the runners passing below her. He was aware only of his body straining almost beyond endurance, his heart pumping, his breath searing his throat, and always, just ahead of him, that damned Thessalian prince!

They were in the penultimate lap when it seemed to him the Thessalian had sandals of gleaming gold and was running more swiftly and with even greater ease than before. Bladud blinked the sweat out of his eyes and looked again. He had been mistaken about the sandals, but the man had undoubtedly gained distance and pace. *She is helping him to win*, Bladud thought bitterly, remembering how Athene herself possessed famous golden sandals that enabled her to cross great distances in no time at all. He thought of calling upon Apollo for help: did he not possess a golden arrow on which a man might fly? Or Hermes, the messenger, with his winged sandals. But something in him scorned to use such tricks to win this race. Stubbornly he shut his mind to temptation, and he prayed only that the winner might win the race by his own efforts alone. At that precise moment the Thessalian stumbled and almost fell, and those few moments of uncertainty gave Bladud a chance to draw level with him. In the final lap they were running neck and neck, and when they reached the garland marking the end of the race, with one last desperate effort Bladud plunged forward and took the laurel by inches.

In a daze he saw faces whirl around him. Mouths open, shouting, cheering . . . congratulatory blows were raining down on his back, knocking out of him what little breath he had left. Desperately he sought the one face that meant something to him in this host of strangers and at last she emerged out of the haze of confusion – cool, calm, exquisite above him on the dais, her eyes looking directly down into his. And then he was helped to his feet and urged to climb the steps to receive the victor's laurel. Afterwards he could remember stumbling. He could remember mumbling his thanks as the king of Boeotia placed Apollo's laurel wreath upon his head. He could remember becoming aware of the sweat running down his naked body – the dust and the dirt. He could remember wanting to turn his head to look at her now that she was so close, but finding he could not. He could remember the face of the Thessalian as the man congratulated him, giving him a hero's hug but with eyes resentful and unsmiling.

Glaucon had been eliminated from the heats early on. When he and Diomede managed at last to extract their friend from the admiring crowd, they led him away and oiled him and scraped him and fussed about him until he pleaded to be left alone.

'Are you mad?' Diomede cried. 'This is celebration time.'

'I want to sleep. Can we not celebrate tomorrow?'

'Tomorrow? Who knows if tomorrow will ever come!'

'There's a good chance it won't come if I don't get some sleep tonight!'

But Diomede would not listen. Everyone wanted to greet the new hero, and Diomede wanted to be at his side when they did so.

The whole mood of the straggling temporary village on the side of Mount Parnassus had changed. The shrines were now deserted, the gods forgotten. The loud, discordant songs of drunken revellers took the place of the solemn prayers for victory. Torches flared everywhere, making day of night. Total strangers greeted Bladud as their closest friend. Diomede kept a firm grip on his arm, trying to protect him, but nevertheless he was pushed and pulled, slapped and shaken and hugged by so many drunken and maudlin admirers that he soon felt he had participated in a battle and not in a race.

'When will this banquet be that you promised me?' Bladud asked Diomede at last.

'It will be tomorrow. Tonight you belong to the people.'

Would this night never end? In truth he felt no elation at his victory, for the prize he longed for was still eluding him.

At last, at dawn, he was permitted to drop into bed. And,

only as he fell asleep did he take some satisfaction in what he had achieved. He smiled, thinking how the despised 'barbarian' had won over all the elegant athletes of the 'civilised' world.

When it was time for the victory feast in the palace of Lysander, king of Boeotia, he did not dress as a Greek would, but clad himself in the clothes he had brought from his own country: tight leather trousers and leather tunic, with elaborate embroidered sword belt and embossed scabbard. There was gold at his throat, on his arms and on his fingers, and a gold-hilted dagger tucked into the calf straps of his boots. A crimson cloak was held on his shoulder by a huge golden brooch inlaid with garnet and jet.

He strode proudly into the great hall – a handsome and vigorous young prince of a distant and powerful land. Golden lights glinted in his chestnut hair and across his bronzed skin. More than one young woman gasped and gazed longingly at him as he passed.

The moment had come! Though very much aware of Alcestis standing beside her father, he forced himself not to glance at her. He paid attention first to her mother, the queen, a silver-haired, elegant, gentle and unobtrusive woman. The king, in contrast to his own hard, muscular, warrior father Hudibras, was almost effete. He was tall and slender and seemed overdressed in fine embroidered clothes.

Only after the formal greetings were delivered did he permit himself at last to look at the princess.

She was everything he had dreamed – hair as gold as sunshine, eyes as blue-green as the ocean. Her clothes flowed over her limbs in soft and graceful folds, revealing curves that set his heart racing. But even at such close range she seemed somehow shadowy and elusive, as though a dream woman scarcely committed to flesh and blood. A sudden memory of Rheinid disturbed him – vivid and vibrant and flushed with life – and then the princess held out her hands to him. He felt the cool, light touch for a second before she withdrew. He heard her soft melodious voice.

Impatiently he reached forward and seized her hands in his. As he stared into her eyes, there was no mistaking his intent. He felt a small, ineffectual tug as she tried to withdraw her hands from his grasp, and, for a moment, she looked disconcerted. But then, as he pressed her fingers, a slight flush came to her marble cheeks and she lowered her lids. He felt a certain triumph that he had caught her attention at last, even if her response was not all that he would have wished.

'Prince Bladud,' the king said pleasantly, reaching over and taking his daughter's hands from the young man's grip. 'You must do me the honour of sitting here on my right. My daughter will make way for you.'

As though nothing unusual had happened – yet Bladud felt that it had – the royal family and their guests proceeded to their seats and prepared themselves for the banquet that would last throughout the night. Princess Alcestis moved away from him and took her place beside Dolius, the Thessalian prince.

That was only the beginning. The celebrations continued for many days and Bladud, who had gone unnoticed before, in spite of his royal lineage, was now of great importance, and the highest in the land vied to do him favours. His Trojan ancestry was on every lip, and even Diomede stopped teasing 'the barbarian'.

Alcestis, meanwhile, avoided ever being alone with Bladud. Sometimes he fancied he caught her looking at him intently as he talked to someone else, but as soon as he turned towards her, she dropped her eyes, or looked away.

While he was lodged at the court of Lysander, Bladud took the opportunity to enquire about the kinsmen of Imogene. He was introduced to an old scholar, Hermias, who knew the history of her family, and could direct him westward along the coast to a region where the story was still told of how Aeneas's grandson Brutus had freed the Trojan slaves and carried off the princess.

He even questioned Hermias about Alcestis's ancestry, convinced of some family connection between her and the original Imogene she so strikingly resembled. Yet there seemed to be no evident link. Bladud then persuaded the old scholar to accompany him on his pilgrimage to the burial mound of Imogene's forefathers once the celebrations were over.

At their formal parting Alcestis appeared calm and composed, but when Bladud took her hand he found it trembling. He gazed intently into her face, trying to meet her eyes.

'One day, Princess, I will tell you what this meeting has meant to me,' he said.

'I hope indeed you will return to visit us,' her mother said hastily, seeing that her daughter did not intend to speak. She had taken to the young foreigner and had even occasionally wondered if he would make her daughter happier than the Thessalian chosen as her future husband for purely expedient and political reasons.

'Will you return for my wedding, Prince?' Alcestis said suddenly. 'It will be celebrated on the second full moon from this day.'

'I hope to return before then,' he replied, 'if indeed I will be welcome.'

'You will be a welcome guest at my daughter's wedding,' the king said quietly.

Bladud bowed to Lysander.

Alcestis turned her head and he could no longer see her expression, but he believed he saw in the droop of her shoulders and her head some evidence that she was not altogether happy.

12

The Tomb

As Bladud and Hermias travelled a road that wound through steep wooded hills, they spoke of many things, not least the mystery of the flight of Daedalus.

'He must have been a great necromancer,' Bladud mused, 'that he could achieve such a flight.'

'Maybe it was not by magic that he flew, but by science,' Hermias suggested.

'If that is so, why now cannot all men fly?'

Hermias agreed this was a puzzle.

'It may be that he held back his secret from others.' He reminded Bladud that though Daedalus might have been a genius, he was also a ruthless and unscrupulous man. 'He fled first from Athens to Crete with the shadow of a murder on his conscience. Then he fled from Crete to Cumae because he had betrayed his benefactor, King Minos, by helping Theseus escape from the labyrinth. When King Minos tracked him down to Sicily, Daedalus was party to his treacherous murder by the Sicilian king. It may well be he wanted to remain the only man in the world who could fly. Maybe, if he had lived longer, he might eventually have passed on his secret. For no one knows what happened to him at the end. Perhaps he died before he expected to.'

'If I ever fly,' Bladud vowed, 'all men will fly!'

Hermias smiled. *He is marked by the gods for great things*, he thought. *That is why Athene will not leave him alone.*

They rounded a bend and suddenly Imogene's homeland was laid out before them. A broad plain lying between the sea

155

and a great arc of inland hills. A city had grown up around the estuary, and the travellers could see the gleam of white houses at sea level and the towering walls of the royal palace rising above them on an outcrop of rock.

As victor of the Delphic Games, Bladud was welcomed as an honoured guest, but he soon learned that the current royal line had no connection with the earlier dynasty of Pandrasus and Imogene. His defeat by Brutus had left Pandrasus weakened, and shortly afterwards, a rival family had seized power in the country. However, the king's archivist was able to inform them where they might find the burial mounds of the Pandrasus family.

Following the river into the hills, they found the ancient necropolis so overgrown it was almost inaccessible. The elderly Hermias sat down to rest on a rock on the outskirts, while Bladud hacked a path for him through the thorny scrub. He came upon several dilapidated mounds, and was just wondering how he could identify the one containing the remains of Imogene's parents when he spotted three huge black ravens watching him from the summit of the largest mound of all.

He appeared so shocked, Hermias assumed he had never seen such birds before in his own country and hastened to assure him that there was nothing to fear from them. But Bladud was remembering the three ravens that had observed him take the sacred crystal from Imogene's burial mound in Trinovantum.

He stared at them, and they stared back at him.

At last he regained his composure and stepped forward. He reached into the pouch he carried at his side, and drew out the little chip of white quartz he had removed from the White Mound. It did not look particularly special now as he held it up in the bright Greek sunlight, for the earth around them was full of such pieces. But to him it was charged with significance.

Suddenly Hermias called out to him and, looking up, Bladud saw him pointing excitedly to something out of sight on the mound's other side. After a moment of hesitation, he went round to join the old man, and what he saw made him

156

gasp. The back of the burial mound had been broken open, and a dark tunnel led into the interior. Over the deep scar of this forced entrance plants trailed and creeper hung thickly.

Dare he go inside?

He peered up at the ravens to find all three were still watching him closely. Bladud gripped the crystal tightly and made his decision. To enter a tomb is to desecrate it: but this was already desecrated – probably by grave robbers hundreds of years before. He felt sure he had been led to this place for some purpose, and he would not leave without finding out what it was.

The entrance was halfway up the side of the mound and he began to climb, scattering small pebbles and crushing flowers as he did so. At the mouth itself he parted the curtain of creeper and peered in. The darkness was absolute.

'What can you see?' Hermias called out eagerly from below.

Bladud shook his head. 'Nothing. I need light.'

'We could make a torch,' Hermias suggested at once.

He climbed back down and helped Hermias construct a makeshift torch, binding wood with strips torn from their clothes and green creeper, and lighting it with some difficulty by rubbing dry sticks together. Then, squeezing himself through the hole and wriggling down the narrow passage the grave robbers had excavated, he dropped down into the tomb and held the torch high above his head. He found himself in a chamber not unlike a beehive, under a domed ceiling fashioned skilfully by huge overlapping blocks of stone. Around the walls, on low stone benches, lay the mouldering skeletons of the ancient kings and queens, princes and princesses of Imogene's royal line. Some of the bodies had been roughly pulled about, no doubt to remove the jewellery they had worn even in death. Dismembered bones lay here and there in disorderly and dusty heaps. Shards of pottery littered the floor, and pieces of wood that had once been carved ornately but were now full of worm holes, crumbling to dust at a touch.

Something glinted briefly in the light of his torch. He bent down to feel around for it and found a ring. When he lifted it up and held it to the light, his heart missed a beat. This was his own ring! The one the raven had snatched from his finger on the White Mound of Trinovantum. He stood gazing down at it in disbelief. He heard a sound behind him and turned quickly, thinking it was Hermias whose curiosity had finally got the better of him.

But this was not Hermias.

Out of the shadows at the limit of the torchlight loomed a huge disembodied head. It shimmered in the air – not quite solid and yet not quite transparent.

Bladud stared in terror.

The eyes stared back into his, but not with malice.

'Bran?' he whispered.

Was there an acknowledgement in the expression of the eyes?

'But why are you here? Your place is in the White Mound at Trinovantum!'

Bran smiled. *Would you imprison me in where and when, my friend?* A deep voice seemed to reverberate in the tomb chamber.

Bladud bit his lip, feeling foolish suddenly. And then he held up the crystal.

'I have brought the crystal,' he said.

I see it.

Bladud stood irresolute. Questions were crowding into his mind. 'My lord,' he stammered at last. 'There is something . . .'

Do what you have vowed to do, Bladud, son of Hudibras, of the line of Brutus and Imogene.

It seemed to Bladud that Bran's head was beginning to fade. The prince took an urgent step forward and cried: 'Stay! My lord. Please stay!'

But the mysterious head had already vanished. Bladud felt ice cold standing alone in the stone burial chamber. For a moment he hesitated, not knowing what to do. Then he slipped the raven's ring back on to his own finger, and placed the piece of crystal at the very centre of the round chamber.

'Let King Pandrasus and his queen know,' he declaimed loudly, 'that their daughter, though abducted against her will, lived to be a great queen much loved and honoured. I, her descendant, have brought a crystal from her burial mound in New Troy to lie here with the bones of her family in pledge of that.'

He felt a tremendous sense of relief as he finished speaking, as though some heavy weight had been pressing on his soul and the burden of it had finally been lifted. Was it the guilt of Brutus who had abducted her, or was it the longing of Imogene herself to return to her homeland?

Bladud suddenly realised he had in a sense been a prisoner all these years – a prisoner of the dead – held in thrall until he carried out their will.

He turned to leave, but paused at the entrance to look back. The tomb chamber looked exactly as he had seen it when he first entered: dust and darkness, broken bones and pottery sherds, benches and skeletons. He could just discern the white quartz crystal he had carefully placed at the centre. There was nothing else that had physically changed. And yet everything had changed.

Hermias was patiently waiting for him, sitting under an oak tree in the shade. His expression was questioning as Bladud approached.

'I'm not going back to Boeotia,' the young man announced firmly. 'The princess can marry her Thessalian for all I care!'

Hermias looked surprised, but said nothing. He could sense that Bladud was disturbed, but not ready to talk. He would wait.

But if Bladud wanted now to break free from Imogene, she herself did not seem willing to let him go. On the way back they stopped overnight with a priest who was a friend of Hermias's, and found the talk in the household was all about the impending wedding in Boeotia. The joining of two such important kingdoms would affect a lot of lives, and the splendours of the occasion were designed to be remembered in song and story for many, many years to come. Though Bladud tried to divert the conversation to other topics, no other could compete. It seemed that Princess Alcestis had been the most sought-after princess of any of the city states

159

for years. Not only was she beautiful, clever and kind, but her country, positioned so near to Thessaly, Delphi and Thebes, was strategically powerful.

'And to think that she herself may not even be of royal blood,' remarked one of the group gathered for a convivial evening in the house of Hermias's friend.

'What do you mean by that?' Bladud turned to him instantly.

'The king and queen had no children, and the oracle at Delphi told them they never would. His advisors insisted he should put away the queen and marry another woman, but he refused. And just when the controversy was at its height a baby girl was found in a basket at the foot of their bed. None of the guards or servants had seen or heard the child arrive.'

'Someone was lying,' Hermias said.

'Of course.'

Bladud seemed struck dumb by what he had heard.

'No one in all these years has dropped a hint that they knew anything and everyone who was in the palace that night has been questioned again and again.'

'And this "foundling" is now the Princess Alcestis?' Bladud asked suddenly.

'Yes. Though the queen at first hesitated, the king at once insisted on keeping her.'

'Was there any indication whether she came of high or of low birth?' Hermias asked.

'She lay naked in the basket wrapped in a white fleece, but round her neck was a golden chain with a gold and pearl pendant shaped like a swan. Princess Alcestis still wears that chain now as a bracelet. The child was so beautiful that some even suggested she was not just an ordinary child but the daughter of some god or goddess. You remember the story of Zeus seducing Leda in the guise of a swan?'

'The princess seems pretty solid flesh and blood to me,' laughed someone.

Hermias looked at Bladud, wondering what effect this new information would have on the young Pretanic prince.

'Come, Hermias,' Bladud said decisively. 'We must get some sleep. Tomorrow we start early. We have a wedding to attend.'

160

The scholar raised his eyebrows, but said nothing. They stood up and took their leave in spite of protests that the night was young.

In silence the two walked to their quarters. In silence they retired to bed. All night long Bladud tossed and turned. But in the morning he was up before first light, shaking Hermias by the shoulder, insisting that they be on their way.

The crowds were so dense on the roads they had great difficulty in making progress. But Bladud was determined and, luckily, his fame as a hero of the recent Games was so great that people made way for him. Even the harassed captain of the palace guards allowed him into the courtyard, where only the closest guests of the family were allowed. The first ritual of the wedding ceremony was about to take place.

Hermias had already explained to Bladud that the father of the bride must offer a sacrifice to his ancestors, and the gods who protected his household, asking their permission for his daughter to leave the family. After this ceremony she could travel, veiled, to her bridegroom's house where she would be carried over the threshold. The final act would be performed at his hearth where she would be introduced to his ancestors and his own family gods. She would there touch sacred fire and be sprinkled with holy water. Prayers would be said for them, and the young couple would share their first meal of bread, cake and fruit.

Bladud had no clear notion as to what he was intending to do. He only knew that he must get there before it was too late. Too late for what? For *him* – or for *her*?

Hermias studied his set face anxiously. 'My friend,' he whispered, seizing his arm and trying to pull him back.

Bladud shook himself free and strode forward.

Alcestis was standing beside her father, dressed in filmy white, a fine veil like a mist drawn back over her golden hair, though not obscuring her face. He could see her exquisite profile, but she had not yet seen him.

Statues of the household gods had been brought from the house, and were set up before a small open-air altar. A pure white kid was held in the arms of the High Priest, while other

161

priests chanted as they tended a fire of laurel twigs and corn stalks.

Bladud stood transfixed as the scene unfolded before him. The flames crackled, the priests and the king intoned the ritual words, the blood spurted on the white fur and white marble, some drops even spattering the pure white of the wedding dress . . . Bladud heard the words of severance: the princess being released from her own household so that she might join the household of her bridegroom.

As the last words were spoken he stumbled forward, calling out her name. All turned towards the unexpected interruption. Her expression was dazed, as though she had been woken suddenly from sleep.

'What is this?' demanded the king angrily.

'My lord,' Bladud blurted out, 'the princess must not marry this man!'

There was a shocked murmur from the other guests. At the back Hermias strained to see what was happening.

'And why is that?' the king asked, in a voice dark with anger.

'Because her destiny lies with me.'

For the first time Hermias noticed Prince Dolius. As was the custom he had been standing in the background for this part of the ceremony, but now he strode forward furiously with drawn sword.

The queen stepped out quickly and placed herself between the two young men, her slender hand raised imperiously.

'I will have no violence here,' she said sharply. Though a quiet and dignified woman, who very rarely spoke in public, her voice now stopped the Thessalian in his tracks.

Suddenly a noise above them made all look up. With a powerful thundering of wings three white swans with necks outstretched pounded across the square of sky above the courtyard, flying so low that their heavy bodies almost grazed the rooftop. As they flew they emitted a strange, almost human, cry. Not one present but was shaken by their sudden and timely appearance, for all knew that the foundling girl child had worn a swan pendant around her neck. As though the wind from their passing had blown them to the ground the crowd fell to its knees, many pressing their foreheads to the earth. Only the immediate protagonists in the drama remained standing. Bladud looking upwards with a face openly astonished, a chill running down his spine as he realised that he was still being manipulated by forces he did not understand.

Prince Dolius held his sword still raised, but his mouth was wide open in surprise and alarm.

The king, dumbfounded, took a step backwards. The queen and the princess Alcestis drew together, daughter's hand in mother's. Hermias at the back, still standing, saw all as though it were a play enacted on a stage.

As suddenly as they had come the swans were gone, but the effect of their passing did not fade as quickly. The silence lasted a long moment, and then everyone began talking at once. Everyone believed it was a sign. The gods had sent a sign!

Prince Dolius dropped his sword, and now seemed irresolute. Something had gone out of him – some confidence – some power.

Bladud stared at Alcestis. Surprisingly she seemed to have gained assurance. There was a glow about her, an almost unearthly beauty. Ever since she had first learned that she was a foundling she had wondered who she really was. Though she loved her adopted parents, she had always been haunted by a feeling that she was just passing through – that this was not where she was meant to be. She had accepted the Thessalian obediently because her father had arranged the marriage, not because she loved him, but because she could see that this would be a way of showing her gratitude to the king who treated her so generously.

She now looked across at Bladud, and their eyes met. She had felt her heart leap when he had stood so close to her while receiving the laurel wreath at the Games. She had been aware of his every move, his every word, at the celebration feast, though her father had sat between them. Even on the night before her wedding day she had lain awake dreaming of him, imagining what it would be like to lie with him, to travel to his strange and distant land . . .

Bladud could not believe what he seemed to be reading in the eyes of Alcestis. Was it possible . . . ?

The king must have read it too, for he suddenly made a move to resume control of the situation.

'Guards,' he commanded, 'escort Prince Bladud out of the palace. He is no longer welcome in my house.'

Two men moved forward, but hesitated before they laid hands on him. As the victor of the Games, he was under Apollo's personal protection.

The king repeated his command angrily. But Prince Dolius suddenly intervened.

'My lord,' he said. 'I cannot proceed with this marriage if it is against the will of the gods.'

'You surely don't believe that!' the king cried. 'Prince Bladud spoke as a rival for my daughter's hand, not as a messenger of the gods!'

'Nevertheless,' the Thessalian insisted, 'I think this matter should be looked into further.'

The guards moved away from Bladud. The crowds murmured. After what had happened most thought Dolius was right to be cautious.

'My lord,' the queen spoke now, 'I feel it would be dangerous to ignore the signs we have been so clearly given.'

Others, close to the king, nodded.

The next few days passed in a kind of haze for both Bladud and Alcestis. It was as though their lives had been taken out of their hands, and others were making all the decisions for them.

The king was still trying to keep safe the alliance with Thessaly, but Prince Dolius was afraid to defy the gods and refused now to marry Alcestis. The queen was torn between her desire to give her beloved daughter everything she wanted, and her sorrow at the thought of losing her to Bladud's distant country. By now it was clear Alcestis herself had fallen in love with Bladud, and she totally believed that the gods had intervened to grant her the marriage that was truly meant for her.

'How can you ever tell,' Bladud asked Hermias, 'whether what you do is of your own free will or determined by forces beyond your control?'

Hermias had no satisfactory answer to give him.

While Alcestis and Bladud were delicately stepping around each other trying to get to know each other better, the king and Prince Dolius were doing business.

Careful diplomacy was necessary so that neither kingdom would bear a grudge against the other, and later seek revenge. The marriage had originally been proposed because each country knew it would benefit from an alliance with the other. And although this alliance was no longer to be cemented by blood, agreements beneficial to both parties could still be worked out.

Once the Thessalian had departed, the king called Bladud to him.

'My daughter is now estranged from our household gods and cut off from her ancestors by the ceremony that has already been conducted. But your own ancestors and your own household gods are far away over the sea. She cannot undertake that journey unprotected.'

Bladud assured him he had no intention of putting the princess in such jeopardy. 'I had not thought, my lord,' he said 'to return to my own kingdom so soon. My father is without doubt still in good health, and not about to give up his life or his throne. He was content to let me come here, and he would be content to let me stay a while.'

The queen's face lightened at the thought that she would not lose her daughter so soon.

'Which household gods do your family worship, Prince?' Lysander asked.

'We do not have household gods in the same way as you do, my lord. But ancestors I have here in this very land. Brutus, grandson of Aeneas, from whom I am descended, married Imogene, the daughter of King Pandrasus. I have just recently visited her family tomb.'

'The marriage ceremony must take place then at that same place,' the king said decisively. 'My daughter must be accepted into your ancestral line at once.'

'My lord!' The queen looked horrified. 'A tomb!'

'It is not what I would have wished. But as this man has no hearth, no kinsmen in this country, no shelter for her here . . .'

Bladud had no inclination to return to that place. There was something about it that disturbed him deeply. 'Pandrasus's line no longer rules that land, my lord,' he protested.

'We will speak with its present ruler, who will make no difficulty, I am sure. I cannot leave my daughter unprotected. It is bad enough that foreign gods . . .'

'No gods are foreign, my lord,' Bladud said respectfully. 'They are not of this earth, and therefore cannot be confined by boundaries.'

'My lord.' Hermias, who up to now had been standing quietly nearby, stepped forward. 'Is not Prince Bladud the victor of Apollo's Games and thus under Apollo's protection?'

Lysander pursed his lips. 'Is Apollo known in your country, Prince?'

'Apollo is not known there by that name, lord, but when I return home I intend to build a temple to him.'

The king grunted.

The royal procession that set off for the tomb of Bladud's ancestors would be talked about for many years to come.

Runners had gone ahead, and the royal household now in the country once ruled by Pandrasus sent messages back that the visitors would be welcome. When they arrived, colourful tents had been pitched for the overflow, while Lysander's immediate family and closest friends were given accommodation within the palace precincts.

A magnificent feast was provided.

Alcestis and her mother retired to their chambers, and nothing more was seen of them during the first evening. The bridegroom should not see the bride's face again before she passed into his family. In a sense she was naked – stripped of her family gods and her own ancestors.

Hermias watched Bladud with some anxiety as he sat morosely among the convivial and increasingly rowdy throng. He was drinking more than usual yet the wine seemed to have no effect on him. From time to time the king would look hard at him, no doubt summing up his prospective son-in-law – perhaps even impressed that he kept his dignity and held his drink so well.

In the morning a small group set off up the river valley to the foothills where the ancient burial mounds were situated. Though the ceremony of the ancestors was to be held near the tomb of Pandrasus, the wedding feast would be celebrated at the royal palace. Many of the guests, having drunk so much the night before, preferred to sleep late and join the festivities later. Bladud rode silently beside the palanquin which carried the veiled Alcestis. He had not yet told her that he was already married, though on several occasions he had started to do so. Everything had moved so fast and now it seemed too late. Alcestis had lost the protection of Prince Dolius and his family because of his interference, and would be disgraced if he too rejected her. Everything that was happening seemed inevitable. Everything seemed intended, planned by a power greater than themselves.

At the tomb an arch of flowers had been set up for the bride to pass through, as a substitute for the door to his house.

Bladud was relieved to realise that there was no question of them entering the burial mound itself. The ceremony would be held outside. He looked around to see if the three ravens were anywhere in sight, but there was no sign of them.

The sun shone brilliantly. Birds sang. Flowers bloomed. There was no sense at all of menace – nor of underlying, brooding mystery. Bladud's spirits began to lift. He had found the woman he had been seeking all his life – beautiful, gracious, loving. How unlike the violent and headstrong Rheinid! Perhaps if there was a spirit-force here at work it was a benevolent one.

The ceremony itself began with unfamiliar prayers to unfamiliar gods, and then Bladud was requested to step forward. As the king placed the hand of Alcestis in his, Bladud called on the names of his own ancestors to accept her into their line. Then he prayed for the help, guidance and protection of Lugh, and of all the gods of his people, and asked that they take his new wife, the Princess Alcestis, into their care. Finally, he called upon Apollo.

'Spirit-force beyond our comprehension, mysterious traveller of light, let us not come to harm nor bring harm to others.

Let us be your light-bearers in this world and in the next . . .'

He felt good – as though someone beyond this world was listening. With eyes closed, he thought of flying – of soaring into the deep, dark blue of the Grecian skies. He felt immortal, magnificent, unlimited . . .

But when he opened his eyes again, it was to find himself still on the earth – mortal, ordinary, limited. All eyes were fixed on him: they had felt his inspiration. They had felt the presence of a god. There was a moment of silence as each and everyone adjusted from that moment to the next . . .

Bladud picked up his veiled bride in his arms and carried her through the arch of flowers.

A small makeshift hearth of stone had been built beside the burial mound. To the right stood a priest with sacred fire lit direct from the sun through a lens of glass. To the left stood another priest with a crystal vial of holy water from a spring on Mount Olympus. Bladud lowered his bride to the ground and stood beside her as she passed her right hand unflinchingly through the sacred flame and bowed her head to be sprinkled with the sacred water.

As he lifted her veil there was cheering, singing and rejoicing all around.

Suddenly behind her he could see another woman – a shadowy figure with eyes which were wise with the knowledge of centuries. The eyes of the long-dead Imogene. The eyes he had seen so often before in vision and dream.

Bladud took a step back. And then behind Imogene, he saw Athene, as insubstantial as a reflection in rippling water. Her sword seemed to be raised over his head.

Bladud looked around. It was clear that no one else could see the figures standing behind his bride. He stepped forward to take Alcestis in his arms, to put his lips to her lips. He closed his eyes. She wound her arms around him and melted into his kiss. He felt her warmth, her passion, her desire. Yet his own feelings were confused. As a young boy on the threshold of manhood he had experienced strong feelings for Imogene, the beautiful woman of his dreams, and now he could not be sure it was not her, rather than Alcestis, he still desired.

The crowd laughed and cheered to see how long the lovers kissed. They saw nothing of the conflict in his heart.

13

The Olympic Games

'What is going on?' Bladud asked. It seemed everyone in the palace was running towards the gate, cheering and waving.

'The Truce Bearers have come! The Truce Bearers!' someone yelled.

Curious, the Pretanic prince hurried to the terrace where he would have a better view of what was happening. The great gates had been flung wide open and three men wearing olive wreaths and bearing standards, were bursting through them. Crowds of youths and children followed them in, running and jumping and leaping with excitement.

Bladud felt a touch on his arm and found that Alcestis had joined him. She slipped her arm through his and, nestling her cheek against his chin, smiled at the evident pleasure of the crowds.

'Who are the Truce Bearers? I didn't know we were at war.'

She laughed. 'Not us. But others maybe. These are the heralds for the games at Olympia,' she said. 'Every four years there is a truce for the duration of the games. All enmity must be laid to rest for three full moons at least.'

'You will be competing, of course,' remarked a voice behind them. Lysander had joined them.

'I?' Bladud had indeed heard of these, the most famous games of all, dedicated to Zeus, the king of the gods. But he had not thought to participate. He had joined the contest at Delphi to meet Alcestis, not particularly to win the laurel.

'If you could win at Olympia,' Lysander continued, 'if you

171

are crowned with the sacred olive, the honour of Boeotia would be second to none.'

Bladud looked at him sharply. The honour of Boeotia? Lysander seemed to be involving him more and more in the daily business of government, frequently seeking his judgement on disputes within the kingdom. It was almost as though he had forgotten this was a visitor from a distant country, and was grooming him as his heir. Bladud himself had drifted along thoughtlessly, enjoying a pleasant life among these beautiful hills with an affectionate and gentle wife, and more luxury than he had ever dreamed existed. But these last words of Lysander startled him. When was the last time he had even thought about his home? When was the last time he had thought about Hudibras, his father? Hermias and Lysander were his closest friends now. But what of Yaruk? What of Fergal? What of his pride in his own vigorous land, the land Brutus had won for his descendants? What of the honour he would win for that? He had not spoken to Alcestis about leaving Boeotia, because he had avoided thinking about it himself. But how long could he postpone the decision? He had already been away from home much longer than he had intended, yet there was so much more here he wanted to experience before he turned his back on it.

As the Truce Bearers came to a halt in front of them, they raised their standards high and declaimed the words they had been trained to deliver.

As soon as they had finished, Lysander spoke up to pledge the champion of the Delphic Games to represent Boeotia. Bladud opened his mouth to protest, but such a cheer went up from the crowd gathered around the heralds, that he would not have been heard. Alcestis kissed him, her eyes dewy with pride and joy at the honour her father had bestowed on him. Realising it would be damaging and churlish to refuse, he raised his right arm to accept the challenge. *It may be that Boeotia bears home the olive crown*, he thought, *but I will not let them forget it was a prince of the Pretanic Isles who won it for them.*

There followed a time of strict preparation. Lysander would

accompany him to Olympia, but the queen and Alcestis would remain at home since these games were strictly for males. If Bladud had thought the Delphic Games drew a crowd, he was warned that he would be astonished at Olympia.

This was the first time since their marriage that Alcestis and Bladud had to be parted, and he rode away with strangely mixed feelings. Not a moment passed but he rejoiced in her beauty and the warmth of her gentle affection, but even so there were times when he believed she fell short of the woman he wanted her to be. Alcestis had lived a very safe and sheltered life, and though she was not much younger than himself, she seemed in many ways still a child. She wanted only to please him, and in love-making it was always he who must take the initiative, and it was always he whose satisfaction was the issue.

Many times Alcestis looked at him with troubled sea-blue eyes, wondering at his sudden impatience, and he, noticing this, wondered in turn why nothing could ever be clear and simple. Though in Boeotia he apparently had everything a young man could want, still he was restless.

Now, as he and Lysander rode away from the palace, his heart sang. He was on the move again. Each day would be different. Each day would be unexpected.

Their journey took them through Athens, and here Bladud felt compelled to revisit the Temple of Athene. Though time and again he turned away from the building and tried to shut his mind to it, as insistent as a recurring dream, some inner voice commanded him to go there. At last he submitted, angry with himself.

A priest friend of Hermias allowed him access to the inner sanctuary, and once again Bladud stepped through that imposing door.

This time, as he entered the great hall of Athene, he found no mirrors placed strategically, but hanging from the ceiling were several large silver balls, each many faceted, each so highly polished that as the light from the high windows hit them they generated a spectacular network of beams of vivid light criss-crossing the dim interior. Should he step forward,

173

he feared he would become enmeshed and trapped in these light beams.

He tried to withdraw, but the door had been shut behind him, and it would not open. A flash of anger gave him a moment of courage. What could not be avoided had to be faced, his father had taught him, and so he would now face this great force that appeared to be playing cat and mouse with him. He squared his shoulders and stepped forward.

Something, high in the shadows, darted across the open space. He could not see it clearly, but he knew it must be the owl. There was a flutter as a beam of light touched the shoulder of the goddess, and for a moment he fancied he saw the golden bird settle its wings. But the next moment only sightless golden eyes were staring into his.

He walked with a boldness he did not feel to the centre of the chamber, coming to a standstill in front of the gigantic statue of the goddess.

At first he stared at her defiantly, as a warrior confronts his enemy, but then he fell to his knees, pressing his forehead to the ice cold marble floor. It seemed to him that only she held the key to who or what was Imogene. Why was he so constantly haunted? This day he determined not to leave her sanctuary without an explanation.

There was total silence all around, though it seemed to him the hall should be loud with the cries from his heart.

At last he could bear it no longer and looked up. There in front of him stood Imogene herself. He rose to his feet. Beams of light converged on her from every direction. Shafts of sunlight shining through the slit windows bounced dazzlingly off the facets of the silver balls.

'Imogene!' he whispered.

She did not reply – but opened her arms to him like a lover.

His heart beat hard. There was a mistiness about her, an insubstantiality. He resisted the urge to step forward into her embrace.

'My lady,' he whispered. 'Why will you not let me be? Have I not done everything you wanted? Have I not brought you home?'

She smiled but still did not reply.

174

'Answer me! Talk to me!'

'Come,' she said softly at last. 'Come with me and I will show you . . .'

Old, old feelings stirred. He was an infant again, at the White Mound – lonely, lost, seeking a mother who would understand him. He was a youth, bored by all the girls he knew, seeking instead a lover who would give him mystery and excitement. He was an adult seeking a mentor to explain the universe to him . . .

'Come!' she said again. Her voice was so seductive, so compelling, that Bladud took a step forward. And then he halted as everything in him rebelled against being manipulated in this way. He desired his independence, his sovereignty over himself. He himself wanted to choose, to decide, to be responsible . . .

'No!' he shouted and drew his sword to strike out at her. He knew he could not kill her, for she was not living, but he wanted to show her, dramatically, that he was breaking free of her, that to him she now meant nothing, no matter what she had been to him in the past.

The sword blade passed through her figure from head to toe. His gesture could not have been more violent or more decisive. But in front of him he now saw two images of Imogene, complete in every detail. They were both smiling, both beckoning . . .

He struck out again: twice.

Before him stood four complete images of Imogene, unscathed.

In a frenzy he struck again and again, and every time he struck, the images of the woman multiplied. He shouted and whirled and struck until the huge hall was filled with figures. Sweat and tears almost blinded him, but he continued striking . . .

At last, exhausted, he stopped to rest on the hilt of his sword, shaking . . . panting . . . He looked around in defeat. He was still surrounded by a throng of images – but the images were no longer of Imogene . . .

They were images of himself.

Stunned and bewildered, he turned towards Athene, who rose so powerfully and majestically above them.

He opened his mouth to speak, but no words would come.

Behind him the priest who had led him there was waiting to escort him out. Bladud's eyes fell from the calm face of the goddess. All the figures, the images, were suddenly gone, and he stood at the centre of an empty hall. The sun must have gone behind a cloud, for all the beams of light were extinguished.

Once they had crossed the narrow land bridge near Corinth and began to near their goal, the road became more and more crowded, and what had seemed a trickle in the mountains near Boeotia, a stream from Athens, now became a river flowing with inexorable force towards Olympia. Oxen in herds scuffed up the dust, lowing plaintively in response to the whistling and whips of the herders anxious to reach their destination and prepare their beasts for the multiple sacrifice to Zeus and for the subsequent feasting. Cartloads of fruit and vegetables rumbled past, young bloods on horseback, rich old men in carriages, poor men on foot, stall holders pushing their wares on ramshackle barrows . . . all united in one purpose, all going in one direction.

At Elis where a month was to be spent in final and supervised training, Bladud began to wish he had not agreed to compete. As day followed day, the training was so painful and rigorous that there was not a night but he went groaning to bed, thinking fondly of the games held in his home country, where men and women were tested for their normal human abilities and not forced to conform to some extreme idea of perfection. The trainers were merciless, and Lysander and the other sponsors watched their protégés day and night, to make sure they did not lag behind the others.

At last came the day for them to travel the sacred way to Olympia itself. Bladud had the strangest feeling as he looked down on the road ahead, that the crowd did not consist only of mortals of flesh and blood, but that a shadowy throng of disembodied beings, long-dead contestants, their families, their friends, officials, judges – and even the ghosts of the sacrificial victims – were travelling with them.

A loud voice suddenly called his name, and he turned to find Diomede and Glaucon pushing their way through

176

towards him. Glaucon had not been chosen to compete, but had decided to join Diomede as a spectator.

'Watch out for Pholos of Athens,' Glaucon called out, as the crowd pushed them further apart again. The Athenians within earshot gave a loud cheer, which was instantly taken up in chanting the names of other athletes of other city states. Bladud heard men named from as far afield as Cumae.

Every possible vantage point, including the hill overlooking the stadium, was already packed with a solid mass of bodies the day before the official start of the Games. Bladud had never seen so many people all together and felt that if he did not get away by himself somehow, even for just a few moments, he would go crazy. But Glaucon came to his rescue once more; he knew of a sacred grove nearby, and somehow they managed to elude the crowds and slip away.

Downstream from the noisy temporary city that had grown up to honour Zeus at Olympia, they came upon a peaceful wooded area where the voices of cicadas were the only ones to be heard. After Glaucon pointed out the sacred grove, he left him to go back and join in the excitement surrounding the Games.

There was no visible impediment to entering the grove, and Bladud wondered why it should be declared off-limits when it appeared no different from its surroundings. But as he entered he began to sense the difference. There was something about the place that seemed to slow down his heartbeat, even his breathing. As he wandered slowly among the trees, he noticed with pleasure a small tortoise making its way laboriously across his path. Soon he realised the whole place was full of tortoises, little gentle animals munching leaves, dozing in patches of sunlight, or slowly pacing the ground. The whole, desperate issue of who would be victor at Olympia suddenly seemed ridiculous. Bladud sat down with his back against a tree, and watched the tortoises. Perhaps he would not go back to compete. What would happen to Boeotia after all if he did not win?

A shadow fell on him, and he looked up. A tall and beautiful woman stood before him. Was the pine scent stronger suddenly? Were those jewels glistening in her golden hair, or raindrops? She may have been watching him

177

for some time because she seemed amused at his startled expression. A youth stood a pace or two behind her, equally amused.

Bladud rose awkwardly.

'Lady . . .' he began. But surely this was no mortal woman. Her skin shone like silver, her garment seemed of such fine weave that no loom known to him could possibly have fashioned it. Yet this was certainly not Athene. She was altogether softer, gentler, more seductive. The goddess Aphrodite came to mind.

'You are the son of Aeneas?' she said quietly.

He found himself nodding.

She laughed. 'Then you are my grandson – like Hermes here.' She indicated the youth, who then stepped forward. Bladud saw his sandals had wings at the heels, and his heart skipped a beat.

'I am not the son of Aeneas,' he muttered in embarrassment, 'but I am descended from his line.'

She leant forward and kissed his forehead. With that kiss a fine web of silver threads seemed to float down upon him, confining his body and making it impossible for him to move. He looked at her in alarm, remembering, for the first time since he had entered, that this grove was a forbidden place. He had heard an old tale that the goddess Aphrodite had fallen in love with the Trojan Anchises and seduced him. Their offspring had been Aeneas, half human, half god. He had never thought of it before, but if the story were true, he himself, as a descendant of Aeneas, must have something of the Otherworld in his own veins!

She walked round him, eyeing him up and down as someone might view a sculpted work of art. Hermes sat on a nearby rock and watched them both.

'You seek to win the olive crown at Olympia?' she asked at last.

He did not know what to answer. Since he had entered the grove, the contest had become a matter of less importance to him.

'Hermes will run it for you,' she said. 'You will win.'

'But would that not be cheating?'

The strangers both laughed. 'Do you think Athene will

178

play fair? Her favourite Pholos is even now being prepared to win.'

'I don't care to win that way,' Bladud said. 'I'd rather lose the race.'

'If you do not win, your father-in-law Lysander will turn against you. If you do not win, you will lose Alcestis.'

Bladud was startled. Surely not? But this was a being from another realm. And no doubt she could see what mortals could not see. Suddenly he desired to win more than anything else on earth – but he wanted to win by himself. He wanted Bladud to be the one to win, not Hermes on his behalf.

'Thank you,' he said, his voice strengthening. 'But I'm confident I can win without your help. I have worked hard. On the training grounds there is no one who can run faster than I. Not even Pholos.'

Aphrodite looked at him intently. Half expecting her anger, he braced himself for it. But it did not come.

'Run your race yourself then, mortal,' she said mildly. 'And we will see. Come, Hermes!'

They both turned to walk away.

Bladud wanted to call after them. He wanted to un-say what he had said. But he could not, because at heart he still desired to win without supernatural help.

They were gone and he was alone with the tortoises again. He looked down at the threads that still bound him; they were melting and running off him like water.

As soon as he was free again he ran back to Olympia as fast as he could.

Later he looked closely at Pholos, to see if he could detect the influence of Athene upon him, but nothing seemed to have changed in his rival's appearance.

When the runners were lined up for the great race at the line scratched in the sand of the stadium, Bladud glanced across at his rival, but he still could see nothing unusual. He looked around at the crowds pressing in to get a better view, and at the long dusty distance ahead of him. There was no sign of Aphrodite or of Hermes. He even looked at his own feet, half hoping, half dreading, at this tense moment, that they might sprout wings. But nothing had altered. He was alone. He had sought to run this race himself, and he was now committed to doing so.

What if he had made a terrible mistake?

But there was no more time for thoughts or regrets. The trumpeters had raised their gleaming instruments – and within seconds the starting note rang out.

They were off. Very soon, the two favourites, Bladud and Pholos, were in front. For a while they ran neck and neck, the crowds screaming out their names. Then Pholos began to draw ahead and Bladud sensed another figure coming up beside him, ready to overtake. That was too much. Was the goddess dragging him back because he would not accept her help? Was he to be humiliated? He increased his effort, and managed to sprint ahead of this second challenger. But the man soon came up beside him again, and in order to shake him off Bladud was forced to run harder than he had ever run before. Soon he gained on Pholos, anger and determination driving him on. Who was this third man? There had been no one else so swift in the training bouts. Yet another burst of speed brought him level with Pholos – and at last, with lungs aching, he flung himself forward to win the most prestigious race in the world.

After the ceremony of crowning the victor, he turned to Glaucon to enquire about the mysterious third man.

'What third man?' Glaucon asked.

'The one who kept pace with us the whole way. The one who nearly beat me.'

Glaucon and Diomede shook their heads.

'There was no third man,' they insisted. 'You and Pholos were alone out in front the whole time.'

14

Return to Trinovantum

For several years Bladud continued to enjoy a peaceful life in Greece, loved by his wife, honoured for his victories at Delphi and Olympia, respected by Lysander and his people.

The only thing that threatened to spoil his contentment was that Alcestis conceived no child.

While discussing this one day, Bladud suggested she should visit the Temple of Demeter and enlist the help of the great earth goddess whose power pulled the mighty trees from dry and dusty seeds, who clothed the barren earth with flowers and grass, and who poured her strength into the corn.

Alcestis agreed, but suggested that he, at the same time, should supplicate for his own fertility. It was at this point he let slip that he knew he must be fertile because he already had a son. The story of his marriage to Rheinid then emerged.

Alcestis went suddenly white and, seeing her shocked expression, the golden prince for the first time felt not so golden. He had not kept this knowledge from her deliberately. At the beginning things had happened so quickly and strangely that the matter had not arisen; and later it became more and more difficult to tell her, for the very reason that he had not already done so.

'My love, it is no big thing,' he said hastily. 'I was tricked into marriage and there was little love between us. In my country it is not uncommon for a man to have more than one wife.'

'And was I not tricked into marrying you?' asked Alcestis

181

with uncharacteristic bitterness. 'In my country it is unheard of to have more than one wife!'

'I will divorce her. There will be no problem.'

'There is already a problem,' she said coldly.

'Divorce is possible in your country.'

Alcestis did not reply, but walked away from him and closed the door between them. Day after day, night after night, he tried to talk to her, to be close to her, but she would have nothing to do with him.

At last, after many days apart, she called Bladud to her chamber.

'You must go back to your own country,' she said sternly. 'You must divorce this woman, or else live with her, but you cannot return to me a married man. I will be no secondary wife to any one.'

Bladud looked at her. She was so beautiful. And her life had become intertwined with his. He had loved her initially because he had identified her with his spirit-guide Imogene. But since then he had grown to love her for herself, and the very differences that had troubled him at first he now cherished most. He did not want to go back to Rheinid, and she could see it in his face.

'If you do not do this for me,' she said gently, 'you will never see me again.'

Something in the way she said it chilled his heart. This was not some threat against him, but against herself. He sensed that if she could not live as his wife, she would choose not to live at all.

'Alcestis . . .'

'Leave me,' she said with extraordinary control. 'And do not return until we can have an honest and honourable marriage between us.'

Why, why had he been guided towards her? Why given all this, if it was not meant to be?

'Go,' she said, and it was the pain in her voice, rather than the anger, that made him go.

'I'll return,' he vowed, 'when I can make up to you for what I've done.'

She bowed her head and his last image was of her sitting on

the couch in her chamber, sunlight shining through the window on to her bowed and golden head. Her hands were in her lap, the left one fingering the fine chain of the gold and pearl swan she wore always round her right wrist.

Was she wondering at this moment – as he was – who she really was?

It was not easy to uproot himself. There was a coolness about the queen that suggested Alcestis had confided in her, but the king was clearly shocked that his 'son' was deserting him. Alcestis had chosen not to tell him the reason for Bladud's going lest he felt obliged to seek vengeance and destroy with the one bloody act both the men she loved.

When Bladud first announced his intention to leave, the king refused to permit it.

'If you have had some quarrel with my daughter, these things pass. Why give up so much for such a small cause?'

'My lord, you always knew that there would come a time when I had to return to my father and my own country.'

'Surely *I* am your father now, and this is your country?'

'Yes, indeed, my lord, you have been as good to me as any father. Nevertheless . . .'

'The land you will one day rule here is of much more consequence than some small barbarian kingdom on a remote island.'

'Forgive me, lord, but my father's is no small barbarian kingdom on a remote island. He is High King over many kingdoms, and for those who live in the Pretanic Isles *that* seems the centre of the world, whilst Boeotia is remote and scarcely known.'

Though Bladud spoke with some vehemence, Lysander did not take offence at this. Having turned his thoughts to his homeland and the task he had to perform there for Alcestis's sake, Bladud was impatient to be gone.

The king laughed.

'Ah well, I can see that argument won't sway you. But surely your love for my daughter . . .'

'It is my love for Alcestis that is driving me to this, lord,' Bladud interrupted.

183

'How so? My daughter would be better queen of her own people and the land she knows, than ever ruler of a foreign place, no matter if it is not so small, nor full of barbarians.' The last he said with a twinkle in his eyes, and Bladud could see he still had not grasped the seriousness of his need to go. The guilt of what he was holding back was burning within him. What had seemed a fairly unimportant omission had now taken on monstrous proportions. Bladud was in a quandary. As an honourable man he should tell his surrogate father the truth. But if he did, it would put the king in a difficult position, as Alcestis had understood.

'My lord,' he said, taking a deep breath. 'I left a wife and child behind. There was no love between us, but I made the mistake of not divorcing her before I left my homeland. I am going back now to remedy that.'

Lysander looked stunned.

Bladud stood upright, facing him, waiting for the first blow. *I will not defend myself*, he was thinking. *If I am to meet the consequences of what I have done, it is only just. I will not give Alcestis more grief by resisting.*

As Alcestis had gone white at the news, the king went red. Veins stood out on his neck as he fought with the emotions that came crowding in. His first gesture was to put his hand upon his sword, but he did not draw it from its scabbard.

Slowly he turned away from Bladud and walked towards the window. For a long time he stood with his back to the young man he had grown to love, gazing sightlessly out over the palace gardens. Was he remembering a time when he himself had taken a mistress without his wife knowing of it? Was he remembering that by that same mistress had come a daughter . . .

At last he turned, his face stern and sombre, but composed.

'If that is the case,' he said quietly, 'the sooner you leave and attend to this matter, the sooner you will return.'

Bladud was too astonished to speak.

'One favour I will ask of you, however,' Lysander added.

'Anything, my lord.'

'Do not inform my wife or daughter that you have told me this. In honour I should kill you.'

184

'Do you want to kill me, lord?' Bladud asked humbly.

The king took time to reply. 'If I had found this out from someone else . . . If you yourself had not told me face to face . . .'

Bladud bowed his head. 'I honour and respect you, my lord. I swear that I will never do anything again that would cause you to raise your sword against me.'

'Will you return to Boeotia?'

'I hope to, my lord.'

'But *will* you?'

'I – I cannot swear to that, my lord, for I do not know how things stand now in my own country. But I *do* swear that I will divorce the Princess Rheinid and then I will either come back to live with Alcestis here, or send for her to be my High Queen, ruling over the kingdoms inherited from my ancestors. Indeed it would be appropriate that a Greek princess should again reign where Imogene once was queen.'

As he said the last words, a shiver went down his spine. Was not the reach of Destiny longer than time itself?

Bladud did not see his wife again before he departed. She kept to her quarters, feigning illness and refusing to see him. The servants, of course, gossiped and speculated, but none knew the truth. The official explanation was that Prince Bladud had been called back to his own country by his father the king, though he had promised to return. And the princess was understandably upset because he would not take her with him. There was much talk about the dangers of the journey, and many a tall tale about the barbaric regions of the Pretanic Isles where giants ate children and monsters breathed fire.

The king made a formal ceremony of Bladud's departure so that the people would not think he was leaving under a cloud, and there was much talk of his eventual return.

By the time the ship reached the port of Massallia, the captain, most of the crew, and several of the passengers were ill. Bladud himself had developed a fever, so was put ashore to lie tossing and turning in a stranger's bed, soaked in sweat and victim of lurid and disturbing dreams. One in particular kept recurring. He was walking along a narrow path which was fenced on either side. Behind the flimsy, open-slatted fence, and leaning over it, were crowds of shouting people who tried to grab him as he passed, their faces distorted with demonic frenzy. Terrified, he wanted to turn back, but he knew somehow he could not. He had to go forward. He walked as carefully as he could straight down the middle of the path, but it was narrow, and sometimes an arm longer than the others managed to claw at him and draw blood. Would that path never end? Where was it leading? He dared not speculate.

Some way along he felt the nature of the crowd begin to change, and he looked nervously from side to side. They seemed to have become supernatural beings now – gods and goddesses of every kind – huge, menacing and hostile.

'What have I done?' cried Bladud, as he cowered and crawled along, more terrified of their touch than he had been of the mortals. His head was in agony where a snatching hand here and there had ripped out clumps of his hair. Scarcely able to bear the pain, it seemed to him he could go no further. He was bleeding and broken and in total despair, when suddenly he could see the end ahead of him.

I must reach it, he thought desperately. He found himself confronted by two young women – each holding out to him a cup containing liquid. The one was silver, the other gold. Both were studded with priceless gems. Almost fainting with exhaustion and thirst he reached out – but suddenly remembered the two spirit ladies he had encountered in the ancient stone circle in his homeland. Each had offered him a cup – the liquid in one had almost destroyed him, while in the other it had revived him. He looked again at the two women now before him, and was startled to see that one appeared to be Rheinid, and the other Alcestis. Both were smiling.

He reached out his hand confidently to take the cup from Alcestis – and then hesitated. There were too many mysteries surrounding her, too many links with the supernatural. What if she had come into his life to bring him harm? At least Rheinid was easier to understand. He reached for her cup, but the hint of triumph in her eyes gave him pause.

186

His arms dropped to his side. Behind him he could hear the crowd still howling for his blood. Behind him too was the silence of the gods.

He shook his head. 'I am not thirsty,' he said, with great effort.

At that moment he woke up, his fever gone. A stranger was leaning over him.

'Drink. It will do you good,' the stranger said. Bladud looked up at the man suspiciously. He studied the cup. It was ordinary earthernware.

'What is it?' he whispered hoarsely.

'This? This is fresh spring water from the mountains,' said the man in some surprise.

Bladud raised his head from the bedrest painfully, and reached for the cup. Noticing his own hand as he took hold of it, he was surprised how thin it looked. The physician tried to help him, but Bladud insisted on taking it himself. He drank greedily, the water spilling over the rim on to his face and down his chest. Cool, cool water from the earth. Pure, life-giving water.

The strange, terrible dream was already fading, leaving only an aftertaste of ill-defined unease.

Gradually Bladud recovered his strength, but the year was out before he reached Trinovantum. Having been weakened by the fever, as he travelled north through Gaul he fell prey to many other illnesses. When at last he reached the shores of his own country he was no longer the golden youth who had set out with such eager recklessness so many years before – nor even the mature and athletic hero who had departed from Greece. He was now a man exhausted by hardship – gaunt and drawn of face. And beneath his garments, his skin had become a mass of sores.

Bladud found his father much aged, but still fit and in full control. Liel, at the king's side, was not at all pleased to see his brother. No doubt he had begun to hope that he would be the next High King. He greeted him, of course, with a show of outward affection, but Bladud could see the resentment and disappointment in his eyes.

187

Hudibras however seemed genuinely delighted to see him, and there was no mistaking the relief in his eyes as he hugged his favourite son.

After their emotional greeting was over, the king began to chide him for staying away so long. Yet when Bladud spoke glowingly of all that he had experienced and learned on his travels, the king soon put his anger aside. He was pleased with the new maturity he sensed in his son.

Rheinid was not present at this first meeting, and Bladud let the conversation run on for some time before he asked after his wife and his son. It was Liel who answered.

'So you have remembered them!' he said bitterly.

'Why would I have forgotten them?' countered Bladud.

'Your brother has taken good care of them for you, my son,' Hudibras interrupted pointedly.

Bladud looked hard at Liel. If he and Rheinid had grown so close in his absence, it would make the matter of divorce much easier to broach. Yet there was some dark beast stirring in the depths of his heart. Was it anger? Was it jealousy? He felt shocked at himself. He had not known what to expect of Rheinid on his return, but he had never imagined that she might have turned to his brother.

'Where is Rheinid?' he asked as casually as he could.

Bladud had sent messengers on ahead of his arrival, so that the court would be prepared for his return. Rheinid had chosen to show her disapproval at his long absence by not being present to greet him.

'She will be sent for,' Hudibras declared at once.

Later, on his way to his quarters, Bladud asked where his friend Yaruk was, and was told that he had left the court of Hudibras shortly after Bladud himself had departed.

'Why did he leave? Where did he go?'

But Bladud's informant either did not know or was not prepared to tell. There was something in his expression however that made Bladud suspicious.

Liel or Rheinid's work, I'm sure, he thought, and vowed that Yaruk's return to court would be a priority.

The clouds that had been sagging greyly over Trinovantum when he disembarked were now unloading their burden of rain. As Bladud plodded from one wooden building within the palace enclosure to another, his feet dragging through the mud, he thought again about the brilliant light of Greece, the days of seemingly endless sunshine, the skies of deep, deep blue. He thought of the orderly buildings, the courtyards paved with coloured marbles, the columns of white stone supporting high ceilings. He thought of trailing vines, of brilliant flowers . . . He thought of elegance and order.

In comparison everything around him looked chaotic, primitive, ugly. Even the carvings on the wooden columns seemed grotesque against his memories of Greek statuary. He was determined now to bring something of what he had learned in Greece to his own land. Either he would introduce some of that culture to this island – or he would leave home again and never return.

He found Rheinid waiting for him in their quarters. She was standing to face him as he entered the antechamber. Her cheeks were flushed in anger, her body as taut as a bowstring.

His heart skipped a beat. He had forgotten how beautiful she was. The cool elegance of Alcestis seemed unexciting beside the vigour and fire of the woman before him.

'Rheinid!' he breathed, feeling the years spent abroad already draining away. Nor did he clearly remember why he had left home in the first place. Rheinid's violent cruelty to her slaves. Rheinid's trickery and treachery . . . none of this came to mind at that moment.

'So, husband,' she said scornfully. 'You have come crawling back?'

'I do not crawl, lady,' Bladud kept his voice under control.

'No?' She raised an eyebrow.

He gazed at her steadily. 'I have come back . . .'

'To me – or to the crown?' she demanded, cutting in before he could finish his sentence.

'To my son.'

'Ah – your son!' she sneered. 'You mean Lear? Prince Lear who has given up even asking where his father is. Prince Lear who would not recognise you if he walked through the door at this very moment!'

'Yes, my son,' Bladud replied tersely – gathering strength against her bitterness. 'Where is he?'

'He is where he should be – with his foster parents, learning how to be a king.'

'With whom have you fostered him?'

'With King Urien, your uncle.'

Bladud bit his lip. He had little respect for the man. 'And did my father approve of this arrangement?'

'He did not object.'

'You must have known that I would not have approved of Urien.'

'You were not here. I made the best decision in the circumstances for my son.'

Bladud was silent. There was nothing unusual in sending one's son out for fostering. Many royal parents felt that an upbringing by trustworthy strangers was better for a child than to risk the indulgent dotage of his natural parents. Foster parents, if well chosen, would educate and protect a prince far from the dangers and intrigues that were inevitable in his father's court. But King Urien was definitely not the man Bladud would have chosen. He would have preferred the wisdom of Fergal and Hudibras to serve as the major influences on the boy, as they had been on himself.

Rheinid and Bladud looked at each other. The leaders of two warring tribes could not have faced each other with more animosity. Yet underneath there was a pull that neither welcomed – nor neither could deny.

He turned and strode out of the room.

She must have run across the chamber after him because he heard the door slam so hard behind him that the whole wooden structure of the house seemed to shake.

Within a few days of his arriving Bladud rode out of Trinovantum alone, intent on bringing his son home. In truth during the years of absence he had not thought much about Prince Lear. He had taken his leave when the boy was an infant and, as far as he was concerned, without personality. But he realised now that running beneath his preoccupation with all he had found in Greece had been the confident expectation that 'his son' existed. And that this son would one day continue his work, his dreams – particularly now that it seemed unlikely that Alcestis could bear children.

He had thought quite a lot about Lear on the long journey home and for the first time he had felt guilt for being away from him so long. But he had comforted himself with the belief that Fergal and Hudibras would attend to his education as they had attended to his own. Now his anger that this was not the case was proving all the more uncomfortable because he knew that, however vociferously he might blame the others, it was he, himself, who was ultimately responsible.

He had not seen his uncle since the time he had witnessed the murder of Rheinid's father while journeying from Urien's castle. Memories of those few days came flooding back, inextricably bound up with old memories of Rheinid, and the conception of the very son he was now riding to reclaim.

Urien was not bad, as Keron had been, but he was a rough and bombastic man, whose only interests were hunting and warring, neither of which he excelled in. His kingdom would have long since been lost to him if Hudibras had not assisted him in keeping it. Bladud was all the more surprised Hudibras should have been happy for such a man to provide the model for his grandson.

Bladud was forced to stop several times on the journey, for he was not feeling well. Sometimes the sores on his skin would irritate him beyond endurance, so there was nothing for it but to stop and bathe in a stream to cool their fiery agony. His head ached and his limbs tired easily. He longed to be back in the comfort of his palace in Greece, with respectful servants and a loving Alcestis attending to his every need. And although he could easily have reached Urien's castle before dusk on the second day, he chose to spend the night resting on a bed of leaves in a nearby forest.

Though exhausted, he could not sleep. What was to become of him? Since that strange illness in Massallia, his strength had been persistently undermined by ill health. The most pernicious symptom was this disgusting rotting of his flesh. He had managed to hide it so far from his father and friends, but if it became generally known, his chances of becoming king would be slim. It was believed that a king represented his land in an important and mystical way, so if

191

the king became diseased the land would likewise become diseased and its people would starve. To rule a kingdom a man had to be strong, perfect in wind and limb. The people were already beginning to murmur that his father was becoming too old and should now step down; and it was only the extraordinary and uncompromising strength of Hudibras, despite his age, that kept him on the throne. Liel was obviously eager to take his place and would not hesitate to publicise his brother's afflictions as an excuse for doing so. In Bladud's weary state he would not have minded this so much, had he trusted Liel to act as a good and noble king, or were it not for his son Lear. To allow Liel the throne would be to disinherit Lear, and that would mean a double guilt upon his shoulders regarding his neglected son.

Bladud groaned in despair.

The morning seemed a long time coming, but Bladud must have dozed off in the small hours, for he was woken by the sound of hounds baying.

At the noise of cracking twigs close by, he looked up to see a pregnant doe, panting with exhaustion and terror. He rose on his elbow slowly so as not to startle her and for a long, long moment the two creatures stared into each other's eyes. It was as though there arose a sympathy, a rapport – a communication. Even when he rose to his feet, she did not move away. And as he approached her, she held still. He took her in his arms and her head fell against his shoulder – weakly – wearily. She could run no further. Picking her up he carried her to a small cave he had noticed earlier when he was making camp for the night. He had decided not to sleep there himself, for he had wanted to lie in the fresh open air and to see the stars through the leafy canopy of the forest. He placed her tenderly inside the cave, and dragged branches across its entrance, scratching himself savagely with bramble thorns as he built a wall of protection.

Almost the moment he was finished, the hunters and the hounds came bursting into the clearing.

He could not hide what he had done, but he stood defiantly in front of the cave, with his sword drawn.

The hunters were no more than boys, one lad very young

192

indeed. But the hounds were on to the doe's scent, madly yelping and barking and leaping around him, trying to gain access to the cave.

'Call them off!' he commanded imperiously. 'Call them off at once!'

'On whose authority?' The oldest youth yelled insolently.

'On the authority of the High King Hudibras!' Bladud snapped. The youth, who appeared to be the leader, paused, staring at him. Bladud had the bearing of a royal prince and gold gleamed at throat and arm. Also – there was something familiar about him . . .

'Prince Bladud?' Urien's son, Daned, enquired tentatively.

Bladud nodded. 'Call them off,' he repeated tersely, 'or I'll run them through.'

Instantly Daned whistled and the hounds hesitated, though frantic to get at the quarry. He whistled again and called them to heel. The other boys were staring, astonished, at the scene. The hounds, though confused, were for the most part well trained, but one, younger than the rest, lunged forward through the barrier of branches and thorns. As Bladud ran his sword through the hound, it fell, twitching and yelping, then went limp.

The boys gasped. They could not believe what they had just witnessed.

The youngest boy leapt off his horse and ran towards the fallen beast, his face distorted with rage and sorrow. Sobbing, he cradled the hound's limp body in his arms. And then he rose and rushed at Bladud, beating at him with his small fists, shouting every imprecation and curse he could think of.

Bladud held him off at arm's length, shocked at the extremes of pain and hate in the young boy's face. Suddenly he noticed a likeness to Rheinid . . .

'Lear?' he whispered. 'Is this Prince Lear?'

Daned stepped forward and tugged the angry child away from him.

'It was his own hound – his first,' he said, looking resentfully up at Bladud. 'He loved him. It was his first hunt.'

Bladud fell silent. Horrified at how quickly everything had happened. To save one life he had destroyed another. His sympathy for the doe had probably cost him his own son's love.

'The doe is pregnant,' he muttered. 'Surely you could see that? Surely you knew she was not fair game?'

Daned refused to look ashamed. 'What are you doing here?' was his only reply.

'I was on my way to see your father – and my son.' He glanced at Lear, but the lad broke away from Daned's grip and, ignoring Bladud with dark and sullen bitterness, returned to the hound, lifting him in his arms. Tears streaked his dusty cheeks, dripping on to the pitiful carcase.

The hounds were beginning to lose patience and there was a restlessness among them that presaged no good for the cowering doe.

'Take those hounds back to the castle,' Bladud ordered sternly. 'Go – now – before there is another tragedy!' He brandished his sword at the animals. Hastily the boys called off the hounds and with a great flurry of turning horses and angry looks set off back to the castle.

Bladud knew that their side of the story would be well told before he himself reached his uncle's court, and probably no one would be in a mood to listen to what he himself had to say.

When they had gone at last he dragged the branches away from the cave mouth and examined the doe. She was now in labour and her cries were heart-rending. She died as her fawn slid from her in a pool of blood.

Bladud knelt down beside her and gently lifted the little new-born creature. Alive, but motherless.

When Bladud reached his uncle's rath, he entered the great hall carrying the newly born fawn in his arms. There he found Daned with his father, King Urien, but no sign of his own son, Lear.

'What is this I hear, nephew?' King Urien asked after preliminary greetings were completed.

'Just an hour ago the mother of this fawn was hunted to her death by a gang of unruly boys,' Bladud said, avoiding

Daned's eyes. 'His name will be Alun and I intend to keep him, and bring him up like a son.'

He called a servant to his side and handed over the trembling creature.

'Give him milk,' he commanded, 'and keep him safe from the hounds.'

Daned eyed Prince Bladud curiously. All his life he had been hearing about this great prince: this athlete, warrior, paragon. Yet here stood a thin, unhealthy looking man – sentimental about an orphaned fawn!

'Nephew, sit, eat with us,' Queen Olwen said now, mildly, sensing the tension in the air.

'I will eat, aunt, when I have seen my son. Where is Prince Lear? Why is he not here to greet his father?'

Urien snapped his fingers and despatched a retainer to fetch the young prince.

'He was greatly upset by what happened,' Olwen said. 'He would not be comforted.

'Has he not learned to take sorrow and hardship like a man in your care?' There was no mistaking the edge to Bladud's voice.

'At his age?' Olwen protested. She would like to have added: 'Where were you when these lessons needed to be learned?' But she did not. On returning from the hunt, Lear was silent and sullen, obviously fighting back tears. He would talk to no one but had retired to his room and barred his door. Hearing that Bladud was on the way Olwen had tried to entice him out, but he refused. When Daned explained what had happened, Olwen threw up her hands. Lear had proved difficult enough without this added aggravation. He was an intelligent boy, quick to learn, but with an unfortunate tendency to take offence and bear grudges. She had said to her husband on more than one occasion that it would go ill for anyone who crossed him when he became king.

The retainer returned without Lear, and spoke in a low voice to the king. Urien's face went red with anger and he snarled at the hapless man who ran out of the hall once more – no doubt returning to the task of trying to persuade the stubborn boy out of his retreat.

Olwen arose quietly and slipped out unnoticed. It was not long before she returned with Lear, holding him firmly by the upper arm. She placed him in front of Bladud without releasing her grip on him.

'Greet your father, Prince Lear. He has come a long way to see you.'

The boy would not meet his eyes. Bladud could see only the top of his dark curls, and the tensely rebellious body beneath. The lad was sturdy and well built.

'My son,' Bladud said quietly. 'Prince Lear, are you man enough to forgive me?'

The boy looked up suddenly, surprised. Hazel eyes met hazel eyes – the boy's angry and bewildered.

'I have come to take you home,' Bladud continued. 'I regret I have been away so long.'

'*This* is my home!' Lear said bitterly.

'Your home is with me.'

'And where is your home?' asked Olwen pointedly, still holding the boy's arm, but no longer so firmly.

Bladud hesitated. Where indeed?

Lear did return to Trinovantum with his father at that time, although Bladud found no pleasure in the company of his son. The boy sulked and spoke only in monosyllables, when there was no avoiding it. Try as he would Bladud could not win him over.

One night Bladud confronted Rheinid with his request for a divorce. Since his return they had not shared a bed and indeed had seen very little of each other in private. They were, in fact, so estranged, it did not enter his head that she would object if he suggested they go their separate ways.

But he underestimated her desire to be High Queen. Hudibras had made it clear, once again, that Bladud was his heir, and the reaction of the people to his return had left her in no doubt that he was also the people's choice.

She at once set about trying to mend the rift between them and it was on the night she had gone to much trouble to entice him back to her chamber that he told her he wanted to break from her completely.

Shocked, she turned away from him and pretended to be

busy adjusting the lamp. She should have expected this since she had thought often of leaving him for Liel. But only if Liel was to become High King.

Bladud waited for her reaction, growing more anxious as the silence extended. At last when she turned, he was surprised by a softness, a sorrowfulness he had never seen on her face before. She reached out her hands to him, tears welling up in her eyes.

'Husband, how can you do this to me?' she said, her voice breaking. 'After all the years I have wasted waiting for your return. Who will have me now – an old woman, cast off by the man she loves?'

'My brother Liel has made no secret of his feelings for you,' he said sharply.

She turned away from him again and flung herself face down on the bed, sobbing as though her heart were breaking.

Bladud stood awkwardly at her side. This was so out of character he could not but believe it was a trick.

He took a step forward.

'Rheinid,' he said softly. And again, 'Rheinid!'

Whether it was the unexpectedness of seeing her as vulnerable to the pain of rejection as any other woman, or whether it was because the spell she had once cast on him was still active, he could not later have said, but before he realised what he was doing, he was beside her, lifting her, holding her, kissing her.

They made love with the old passion and afterwards he lay beside her thinking about Alcestis and what he should do about the two women in his life – each of them important to him in her own way.

Rheinid raised herself on her elbow and surveyed the naked man beside her. In dawning horror she realised that he was covered with sores. She recoiled, in disgust.

Bladud did not notice her reaction. His mind was far away.

Carefully she disentangled her limbs from his, drew on a robe and crossed to the other side of the room.

'Bladud,' she said softly. 'Do you still ask me for a divorce?'

Bladud turned his head and looked at her – mane of blue-black hair to her waist – eyes like dark pools in a forest. How could he leave her? How could he walk away, never again to know that feeling she gave him – that feeling no other woman – not even Alcestis – had been able to stir in him?

'I cannot desert Alcestis,' he said. 'I have made a vow. Surely there is a way you both . . .'

But he did not finish his sentence for the old Rheinid was back and, with fury, she drove him from her chamber.

'Go to your foreign whore!' she shrieked.

Bladud ducked as a jar came flying at his head. Dragging his clothes on, and without his boots, he fled.

Not long after Bladud's return Hudibras called a meeting of the High Council. The messengers rode out, and in the lull before the counsellors arrived from every corner of the kingdom, Bladud climbed to the White Mound. Would the magic still work? Or would he find there merely a pile of earth and white rock covering a few mouldering bones?

The prince's first reaction after his travels was disappointment in his own country. The cluster of mean and smoky huts, the cattle hunched against the bleak, grey rain, made his heart sink. Not all Greek buildings were gleaming white marble – the houses of the ordinary people were also constructed of wood and thatch, but somehow they looked better in the bright sunlight. Their streets were straight and clean, often paved with flagstones, while in his own country they were no more than muddy tracks meandering between houses. His father's castle was indeed spacious – a group of large, well built wooden houses protected by a stockade – but he yearned for the stone-built palace in Boeotia set against a hillside with terraces of brilliantly coloured flowers, with its columned walkways to give shade, and windows looking out on a vista of distant mountains.

The river now below him faded away into the distance, a pale sun shining through the mist to touch it with silver.

He was standing where he had stood so many times before as a youth. Would Imogene come to him now – or had he left her behind in Greece? Did she really exist? Had she ever existed as she appeared to him? Had the vision he had seen so many times and assumed to be Imogene, the queen of ancient New Troy, been in fact rather some kind of premonition, a prophetic image, of the woman who would eventually be his queen?

No matter what feelings he had just experienced for Rheinid, he could not ignore the fact that Alcestis had been 'given' to him by the Fates in a most extraordinary way.

Now he could feel a presence – but he could see no one.

'Imogene!' he whispered, the skin prickling on the back of his neck. 'Imogene!' he repeated.

The mist deepened, extinguishing the light on the river. It swirled around the white stones of the mound . . .

Bladud stepped forward and reached out to touch the wall of crystal and felt the solid and dependable earth dissolving around him. His hand met nothing. He took another step. He stretched out his arms. Again nothing. He stumbled on the uneven ground – and found himself lurching through an open doorway, into the dark interior of the mound.

Shallow steps. Ice cold stone brushing his shoulder. As he proceeded further he struck his head on the ceiling and was forced to stoop. By the time he reached the burial chamber he was almost crawling. Inside was the darkness he would expect to find at the centre of a stone. Absolute darkness . . . He was crouched like a child in the womb of a dead mother . . . waiting . . . And then, whether because his eyes were growing used to the dark or because some light was seeping into the place he could not tell, gradually he found that he could see dim shapes, and then, clearer images.

He no longer seemed to be in the tomb but out in some open space, a green field, standing under a huge spreading oak tree. He looked up in wonderment and saw that one side of the tree was green and healthy and the other rotten and withered. Beneath the tree was a well, gnarled roots curling round it like fingers around a cup. But the water in the well was choked with weeds and debris.

He turned at a sound behind him. The warrior king – the one he had encountered before with the golden cup – loomed large before him.

'Drink,' he said, holding out the cup.

Bladud looked into it. It was empty. He was puzzled.

'Drink,' the warrior repeated in a deep and commanding voice.

Bladud decided he was meant to fill the cup from the well itself. But the water there was murky and stagnant and he did not relish putting it to his lips. Should he obey the spirit without question? Surely not! *I will fill the cup*, he thought, *but I will not drink*.

He dipped the golden cup into the sluggish liquid – and instantly staggered back from a flash of light that almost blinded him. When his sight returned, the tree was in full leaf with birds singing in its branches. The well was clear and bubbling with sweet water. The warrior and his magic cup were gone.

Bladud stood staring at this scene for a long time. What did it mean? But soon, as he looked around him at the pleasant landscape, the edges of his vision began to blur and a white mist came creeping across the green and golden fields. The topmost branches of the tree were fading from sight. He tried to will the mist to disperse, to no avail. He blinked and rubbed his eyes, desperately straining to see through it, but the vapour would not halt its advance, and he was soon totally enclosed in an impenetrable cloud. It felt cold, damp, suffocating – and before long he lost consciousness.

When he came to, he found himself back on the hillside beside the White Mound and saw the river mist curling away under the warmth of the sun. He could hear gulls shrieking and squawking. He could see the buildings of Trinovantum sprawling below.

It was a long time since such an august council had been convened. Vassal kings from far and wide were present. Urien was seated with Hudibras at the High Table. Lear, too young to take part, stood in the background with other royal princes to observe statecraft in action.

When all were gathered and settled – and it took some time for the noisy greetings and back slappings to subside – Hudibras announced that this council had been called to choose the next High King.

'I know it is usual to wait until after a High King's death before choosing his successor, but I have two able sons, and I do not want a conflict between them when I am no longer here.'

Most people present believed they had been called together to ratify an already foregone conclusion. There was no doubt in anyone's mind Hudibras intended Bladud for the throne, and very few had any objection to this. The few who did object had been carefully wooed and bribed by Liel over the years.

Hudibras made a rousing speech in praise of both his sons, but recommended to the council that they choose Bladud. There was some objection and argument from the supporters of Liel but when the council voted there was an overwhelming support for Bladud.

All seemed set fair until suddenly Rheinid caused a stir by coming dramatically in front of them and claiming that her husband was not fit to rule. The buzz and hubbub ceased instantly. All eyes were fixed on her. It was clear from Bladud's expression that his wife's words were as much of a surprise to him as to everyone else. Everyone else, that is except Liel, who now moved to the front.

'What game is this?' growled Hudibras. 'Take care, lady.'

'Your majesty, I do not make this claim lightly,' she said. 'Prince Bladud is a great and honourable prince – but cannot become High King. Come, my husband, stand before these people and contradict me if you can.'

Puzzled, Bladud moved to her side. Liel moved in at once to stand to his right, and slightly behind.

'Rheinid, what is this?' Bladud whispered.

'Is it not a law since ancient times, my lords,' she began in ringing tones, addressing the whole throng with such clear enunciation that even those at the back could hear her every word. 'Is it not an absolute law given us by the gods for our protection that no man may rule a kingdom who is diseased?'

Bladud gasped. He could see now what she intended.

'Rheinid.' He took her arm, but she shook herself free. Her cheeks were flaming, her eyes bright. She knew exactly what she was about, and would not be stopped.

'If a king is diseased, his kingdom will be diseased. True or false?'

'True,' the answer came.

Suddenly both Liel and Rheinid put their hands on Bladud's clothes and ripped his tunic off him.

201

There he stood, naked to the waist, his golden torc glinting magnificently around his neck. But the sores which he had so far kept well hidden were now revealed for everyone to see.

There was a gasp all round. Hudibras looked stunned.

'His whole body is rotten and stinking!' cried Rheinid.

If she could not be High Queen with him, she would be High Queen without him. Rheinid and Liel exchanged significant glances of triumph.

15

Swineherd

Bladud lay on the floor of the forest on a thick bed of dead leaves and stared up at the fretwork of sky he could see through the screen of living ones.

After Rheinid's dramatic revelation the scene had turned really ugly. There was an uproar in the hall largely orchestrated by Liel's followers. Those loyal to Bladud claimed that a few sores did not make him ineligible for the throne. He did not hear who first mentioned the dread word 'leprosy' – but the instant it was said those around him drew back, looking at the man they had been cheering a short while before with total and unmistakable horror. Bladud looked around him and his whole world had changed because the centre of it, himself, was now perceived in a completely different way. From being seen as an honoured, active, thinking human being, and a royal prince whose every pronouncement should be respected, he was now seen as a lump of rotten meat to be shunned for the disease he could bring upon others.

Even his father was looking at him differently, and his son Lear was vociferously shouting with Liel's supporters for his downfall – perhaps not quite understanding what was going on, but remembering only that this was the man who had killed his hunting-dog.

Bladud tried to insist that he did not have leprosy, but no one would listen. Some were yelling for his death. Others for his isolation and incarceration. He could not believe how quickly the mood of so many had changed. How quickly idols could be toppled and heroes disgraced! All that he had done in his life suddenly counted for nothing. He was unclean. He was diseased. And everyone wanted to be rid of him before he tainted them, too.

He peered across the shouting heads at his father. The eyes of Hudibras were full of pain. He loved his son, but he was shocked that he had not come to him privately and confessed his illness. If he had done so, perhaps something better than this could have been arranged. But revealed as it was in front of hundreds, there was nothing he could do to save his son. Rheinid had chosen her moment well.

Hudibras raised his sword arm imperiously and within moments the cacophony had died down. Bladud stood alone, while all the rest were bunched and crowded around the edges of the room, drawn back as though trying to avoid some dangerous animal.

'My people,' Hudibras began sternly, 'how quickly you lose your good sense. That my son is sick I can't deny. But that he has leprosy is not proved.'

'Let him be examined!' someone called out.

'If you yourself did not think it was the dread disease, brother,' Liel said accusingly, 'why did you try to hide it from us? Surely the Council should have been informed of your condition *before* they made their decision about the succession?'

Bladud tried to speak but was shouted down.

'Why did you not tell us before the vote!' the cry went up, and Hudibras was obliged to restore order once again.

'I confess I am disappointed, my son, that you were not more open and honest with us. This behaviour is very unlike you.'

'But father, it is not leprosy. I swear it! Must everyone confess to every blemish he may have?'

Fergal stepped forward.

'I have seen leprosy before, my lord,' he said, 'and I would say this does not look like it to me.'

'Let the Druid examine him!' Bladud's supporters cried.

'Let him be examined!' others yelled.

'But not by Fergal,' Liel said firmly. 'Fergal has been like a foster-father to him.'

Fergal's face darkened with anger.

'You doubt my honour, sir, if you suggest I cannot be trusted in this matter.'

There were shouts of: 'Let Fergal examine him!' And others: 'Not Fergal!'

Liel turned to his father. 'My lord,' he said. 'I do not mean to dishonour Fergal. *I* trust him completely.' Liel was no fool. He knew the old Druid would find many ways to avenge a slur on his honour. 'But I fear the people would always be in doubt if this decision is made by someone so close to the prince.'

'What do you propose then?' Hudibras asked coldly.

Liel pointed to another Druid, Bradon, a plump and comfortable man.

'The Druid Bradon has but recently arrived from the Holy Island of Anglesey,' Liel continued. 'He has not had time yet to meet my brother, so the impartiality of his judgement cannot be questioned – by the people,' he added with a swift conciliatory glance at Fergal.

Hudibras eyed Bradon distastefully. He would have much preferred Fergal to examine his son, but the statesman in him could see the advantage of seeking a judgement from a disinterested outsider.

'Let it be so,' he growled.

Bladud was examined by Bradon in private. That is, he stood naked before him while Bradon walked gingerly around him, careful not to come too close.

Then Bradon went to the Council and announced un-equivocally that it was leprosy.

From his isolated chamber Bladud heard the roar that greeted these words. It expressed the regret of the many who loved Bladud, and the triumph of those supporting Liel's claim to the throne and who now believed they would reap the benefits of their loyalty.

Hudibras, heavily, sadly, bowed to the decision, and announced to his people that Bladud would henceforth be confined so that he could not infect anyone else.

Only Liel and Rheinid, and Fergal, noticed that Hudibras

205

did not revoke the judgement of the Council by confirming Liel as his rightful heir. When Liel started to point this out, he was quickly silenced by the king. The hall was cleared as Hudibras retired to his quarters, morose and gloomy. He would see no one for the rest of the day, nor say one word more on the matter.

Bladud's prison was not unpleasant, but for a man who had roamed the world and had not yet satisfied his wanderlust, it proved a hateful place.

As the days and weeks in confinement went by, Bladud began to dream again of Daedalus – Daedalus who had also been incarcerated in a prison, but who invented a way to fly out of it.

At first Fergal visited Bladud every day, unafraid of contagion because he genuinely did not believe the prince was infected with leprosy. He brought with him various salves and herbs, and worked hard to heal him. But the sores persisted, and got worse through the unhealthy life the young man was forced to live. Bladud could barely sleep at night for pain and irritation.

He asked for special tools and wood and reeds to be brought to him, and Fergal arranged that he received them. But one day Fergal did not visit. Nor the following day . . . Day after day passed and Bladud saw nothing more of the Druid. He tried to send messages via the slave who nervously pushed his food through a hatch in the wall each day, but the slave was deaf and dumb and could not be made to understand. Bladud tried writing a message in ogham letters on a sliver of wood, but he could not be sure the slave understood that this should be delivered only to Fergal and no one else.

Fergal did not return, and Bladud sank deeper and deeper into despair – not realising that Liel had sent the priest away. He tried and tried to construct serviceable wings, but no matter how ingeniously he used the materials at his disposal, in that place he could not hope to succeed.

At last he could bear his situation no longer, and decided he'd rather die than spend the rest of his life caged, with his flesh a perpetual torment to him. He decided to take a gamble. If his plan worked he would survive and be free, if not, he would die but would find out once and for all if there were other worlds beyond or not.

He was kept in a small house isolated from the rest of the town, with windows just large enough to admit a small amount of light and air. The house was built of wood, with a steep thatched roof. Inside, the chamber was well appointed, with a comfortable feather mattress laid on a bed of wooden slats, also a single chair, one table, and some rush matting on the floor. Each night he was given a small earthenware oil-lamp.

One night Bladud piled everything that could easily burn against one of the walls. He scooped up the rush matting and crumpled it into a rough pyramid-shape beneath the mattress. Then he piled the cushions, the chair and the table on top, and finally tipped the contents of the lamp on to the rush matting. Within moments the whole pile was ablaze.

At first he crouched as far away as he could, but when he sensed the wall was sufficiently weakened by the flames, he took a running jump through the fire, landing with all his weight and force against the smouldering wall.

The structure gave way, and Bladud fell through it in an agony of singed flesh. But he was free!

He rolled on the ground until the flames caught in his clothes were extinguished, and then he staggered to his feet and stumbled off into the night. And so it was that he came to be lying on the forest floor, gazing up at the stars which gleamed and flickered through the gaps between the branches. And so it was that this bed of leaves seemed so sweet and comfortable.

When day came he still did not feel like rising. His first exhilaration at breaking free from his prison had passed into utter weariness, and forced him to stop and rest.

Where was he heading? Where *could* he go? Nearly all his father's vassals by now knew that he was a pariah, so none would be likely to take him in. No doubt hunting parties were already out to drag him back. Leprosy was not common in the land but it was known well enough to be feared.

He thought of sneaking aboard a ship and returning to Greece, for Rheinid had been quick to ensure that a brief divorce ceremony was performed, and therefore there was no longer a barrier to his happiness with Alcestis. But until he was whole and well again, he could not bear to face his wife. He did not want to risk what had happened here also happening in Greece. Then *every* door would surely be closed to him – every face set against him. Besides he was sure the disease tormenting him would eventually pass and he wanted above all to return to his father's court and stand naked before the whole Council, to show them how wrong they had been. Yes, he wanted to be High King. Anger had sustained him in his flight: but now, as he lay in the forest, its hidden face, fear began to show itself. All his life he had been able to count on horses or boats for transport. He had grooms, servants, slaves to wait on him. He had friends and relatives to support him. Wherever he went he had found a comfortable place to lay his head. Even as a stranger in a distant land, it was not long before he was living as a prince in a palace. Now here he was in rags, weak and covered with sores – an outcast who dare not reveal his name or lineage. The meanest peasant owned more than he did now. But worst of all he felt himself deserted by the invisible realms. In his prison none had come to him. Not Imogene . . . not the warrior king . . . not even the two ladies from the stone circle. He had felt no presences though he had longed for them. He had heard no answering voices though he had called and called with the desperate but silent voice of his heart. Where were the secret Beings that had always come to his aid before? Even stern Athene and her disconcerting owl would have been welcome.

He turned his face into the leaves. All the strange and inexplicable things that had happened in his past he now ascribed bitterly to hallucination. And Daedalus? How could he have believed such an impossible tale? Man had never flown, and would never fly. He would crawl about in the dust for his allotted years, and then be snuffed out like a candle. The smoke that rises for a few moments after the flame is gone, such was his memory in the minds of others. But soon even that would fade, and it would be as though he had never existed.

Yet somehow these bitter thoughts rang false. In the

depths of despair, though he believed he had shed everything, there was *something* left. Something he could not account for nor understand. He told himself he did not believe it because his rational mind could not explain – but he *did* believe!

Bladud opened his eyes and sat up. Grazing nearby on the fresh green shoots of a sapling was a very young fawn, with no adult deer in sight.

'Alun?' he whispered. The young creature pricked up its ears and stopped chewing, looking at him with large and trusting eyes. 'Alun,' Bladud repeated and held out his hand. The little animal stepped daintily towards him – and licked the hand that humans had rejected.

All summer long Bladud and his four-legged companion foraged for a living in the forests and the fields. Bladud avoided all contact with other humans, being afraid as much to cause offence in others as to receive it himself. The clothes that had been badly singed as he escaped his place of confinement turned to weathered rags. His skin turned brown in the sun, but still the sores raged. He began to look more and more like a wildman of the forest as he tied against his skin the leaves which Fergal had taught him contained healing properties. The fawn grew big and strong but never left his side. At night they slept close together in whatever shelter they could find.

Bladud had possessed no weapons when he escaped the prison, but he soon made himself a knife out of flint stone. Yaruk had once shown him how to do this by skilfully striking one flint stone against another, utilising the natural property of the stone to flake in a certain way. Yaruk's people had ancient roots in the land and long memories.

In summer food was plentiful, though Bladud, tired of a diet of leaves and berries, sometimes raided the fields of the farmers for more solid vegetables or fruit, and the cattle byres for milk. In the past, riding high on his horse, he had seen little of the tiny flowers hidden in the grass, the industrious insects building webs and nests and traps. He had been scarcely aware of nature's elaborate yet simple cycle of interdependence and regeneration. Fergal had taught him

209

many things in colourful myths and legends, but now he began to see their symbolic meaning, their subtle mirroring of the sacred dance of Nature. He particularly identified with the ancient Celtic story of the golden prince, Llew Llaw Gyffes, who was betrayed by his wife, and murdered, yet did not die. Transformed into a wounded eagle, sitting in the branches of a tree, his flesh rotting as Bladud's was now rotting, Llew waited with patience for the regeneration he knew must come.

Bladud began once again to believe in the unseen, mysterious and magnificent realms that surround and enclose us.

As the leaves began to fall and the cold winds blow in from the north, Bladud began to wonder if he should build a hut against the winter. He had not thought to do so before for he deemed it safer to keep continually on the move and thus leave no trace of his passing. All summer long he had been moving steadily westward, till he began to recognise some of the landmarks from the journey he had made as a youth when seeking the Oracle of Sul. On that occasion she had promised that he would one day be a great king. Was she just a trickster – of which there were many in this world both in and out of the body – or did she truly know?

Then one day he came face to face with a man, before he could take cover. He was burly and darkly bearded, and had the look of Yaruk's people. Bladud's first reaction was to scuttle back into the cover of the forest like a frightened animal, but he had run and hidden for too long, and suddenly he felt as though it was time for him to make a stand. It was time for him to rejoin the human race.

From the way the man was looking at him, Bladud could tell he had no idea who he was. So far from Trinovantum . . . so far from any royal court . . . this man had probably never heard of the prince on the run, the prince believed to be a leper.

The two stood still, eyeing each other warily. Alun, the deer, stepped back behind Bladud for safety, but peeped out at the stranger.

The bearded man looked from the ragged wildman to the deer and back again.

At last the silence was broken.

'It's a sight to see a man and deer so close,' the stranger said gruffly.

Bladud put his hand on the creature's head. 'We are companions,' he said quietly. 'Where I go, he goes.'

'And where do you go?'

Bladud shivered. A cold wind was bending the tops of the bare trees behind him. Soon there would be frost and snow. 'I seek work and a place to sleep out of the wind.'

The stranger stared at him. He was gaunt and ragged and weather-beaten, but he spoke gently. 'I have work for a swineherd,' he said at last.

Bladud hesitated. Was this appropriate work for a royal prince? Then he gave a wry smile. *What royal prince?* he thought.

'I would be glad of it,' he said. 'Does food and a roof go with it?'

'Food and a roof.'

'Will my companion be safe?'

'You may keep him with you.'

'Have you hounds?'

The man laughed, his face lighting up for the first time. 'I – with hounds!' he grinned.

Bladud felt embarrassed. He had forgotten what very different lives peasants lived from the great lords in their raths, and what a very different life he was about to live himself. Would he perhaps be better off in the forest with the beasts whose ways he had learned, than with unpredictable and treacherous mankind?

'My name is Yarr son of Morg,' the man informed him.

'Mine . . .' Bladud paused. 'Llew, son of Llaw Gyffes.' Would the man notice the reference to the old tale? But it seemed he did not, for he accepted the name without demur.

Bladud was then taken back to the peasant's smallholding and shown the black pigs that would be in his charge, and the tiny, rickety shed beside their pen that would be his shelter against the winter.

'I'll never sleep easy while he is out there,' Liel confided to Rheinid. 'He could return at any time and take everything

211

away from us.' They were now formally married and had good prospects of the crown. But to King Hudibras he said: 'My lord, while Bladud is out there loose, who knows how many of your subjects he is infecting with his disease?' It seemed to him that Hudibras was doing very little to bring Bladud back, while he himself was agitating to send hunters and hunting-dogs out to search for him.

'Son, surely you know your brother better than that?' Hudibras replied mildly. 'In time we will find him, but I will not hunt him down like a wild animal. And I am certain he will take good care not to bring his own misfortune to others.'

'If people were to learn his secret, father, they might take it upon themselves to kill him so as to protect themselves. Whereas if he were safe with us . . .'

'Enough!' Hudibras said gruffly. 'I will bring him back for his own safety, but I will not do it your way.'

Liel bit back the words he wanted to say. His hold on the crown was still precarious. He must be careful. Seeing he was getting nowhere with the stubborn old man, he bowed himself out of the royal presence.

Shortly afterwards Rheinid found him giving orders to a group of heavily armed warriors.

'You are sending them out, despite your father's wishes?' she asked.

Liel glanced at her irritably. 'It is in your interest as well as mine that we know where Bladud is at all times.'

She turned and walked away in silence, disturbed to have seen him speaking to Torna, the man she held responsible for her father's death. Where had he sprung from? She had not laid eyes on him since that hateful day, and now here he was at court, and he and her husband seemed as thick as thieves.

She suspected Torna was being employed as an assassin, not to bring Bladud back alive. Why else was he briefed so separately and secretly from the others? Why else did he slink away with such sinister purposefulness? She sensed Torna would take pleasure in his commission because she knew he had always hated Bladud. What was this twinge of pity she was feeling for Bladud – this wish that things could be otherwise? Did she not want to punish him for his rejection of her? She knew in her heart that Bladud was a man worth ten

212

of Liel, but he had spurned her one too many times, and she would not forgive him . . . She knew that if she told Hudibras now what Liel was plotting, it would not be too late to save Bladud's life. Yet she kept silent.

Mists rose from the river most mornings now, and occasionally Bladud woke to find the world transformed with frost crystals. His shed barely held off the cold, and he was tempted to accept when his master, Yarr, suggested he move into the cottage with himself and his wife. Yarr's wife, Nola, had at first been suspicious of this stranger who had appeared from nowhere and who would give no details of his family or his past. But in time she had grown to like him. He kept to himself and showed respect towards her husband. He worked well and hard. As she began to soften, she saw that the best of their food was put out for him. Then she suggested to her husband that the swineherd should be treated as part of their household and live with them. As the couple had no children, she began to think of Bladud as a son.

But Bladud refused. He thanked them politely, but claimed that he would rather stay in his shed. After their persuasion failed, Yarr helped him render the shed more weather-proof and comfortable.

'Your speech is not like ours,' Yarr commented one day, as he helped him to lash reed thatch to his roof. Indeed he had begun to suspect that his swineherd came from some noble house, but was somehow disgraced and on the run.

'I have lived in many places,' Bladud said, not untruthfully. 'A wanderer picks up many ways of speaking.'

'My wife would like you to come at least to our house for your meals.'

'Your wife is kind, but I must stay with my charges.'

Yarr knew this was not necessary, but he was shrewd enough to see that Bladud, for whatever reason, wanted to keep his privacy. Nola, his wife, was a non-stop talker, frustrated by the isolated life they lived on their smallholding, and he did not blame Bladud for wanting to avoid her. He had learned over the years how to shut off the sound and think his own thoughts while she rattled on. He was fond of her and regretted that they had not been blessed with

213

children. 'Children would have given her something to occupy herself with,' he reasoned. And so he would nod and smile and occasionally reply to her chatter – but mostly he just humoured her affectionately.

After the first difficult days of struggling to come to terms with his unexpected occupation, and to learn the idiosyncrasies of his swine, Bladud had settled down reasonably well. As soon as darkness fell – and it fell early in the winter – he thankfully went to sleep rolled up in the tattered fox furs and sheepskins Yarr had provided. Alun lay beside him, giving him some of his body heat. His health was still not good and he became easily tired. During the day he took his pigs out into the forests to forage for acorns and roots, sitting on boulders beside streams for hour after hour, thinking and dreaming, while the pigs snorted and guzzled. At first they had seemed all alike to him, but gradually he noticed how each had a different personality. He even gave them names. He began to worry when they strayed, and he searched for them most diligently and anxiously when he thought they were lost. But sometimes his mind was so far away from his task it was a wonder that at every sunset they were always all safely back in their pen.

Then one day in the forest he was deep in thought as usual when Alun alerted him to danger by pushing at his hand. The creature's brown eyes were wide and terrified, his body trembling. As soon as his beloved master had registered the danger Alun was off, springing and leaping to safety – soon to be out of sight. The pigs, who had been rooting and snuffling a moment before, now looked restless and uneasy, sniffing the air and turning their heads about. Bladud gazed around and soon spotted the cause of their uneasiness. Emerging from a thicket came a huge male boar, with vicious tusks and bristling pelt, its eyeballs red as fire. Bladud leapt up at once, touching the knife Yarr had given him to make sure it was easily to hand. The boar had obviously scented the female pigs, as Yarr had warned Bladud might happen. 'You mustn't let him get at them,' he had instructed.

The beast was bearing down on Beauty, one of Bladud's favourite sows. She was by no means a beauty, but somehow showed a gentler, more affectionate disposition than the others, and she often came at Bladud's call to receive titbits from his hand. Now she looked very small and vulnerable as the great, fearsome brute approached her. She did not turn tail and run, as Alun had, but stared fascinated at his wild magnificence. Had she memories, Bladud wondered, of when her ancestors roamed the forests as free and fearsome as this boar – just as Bladud himself held memories of his very different life before? Did she yearn, as he did, for old haunts and old ways?

He shouted suddenly to divert the boar's attention. Several of the male pigs were also rallying to the defence, but none possessed the deadly armament of the wild animal, or stood a chance against him.

The boar glanced disdainfully at the man and continued to advance on the female of his choice.

Bladud leapt forward, grabbing up a broken branch, and began to beat at the beast. This turned the animal, who stopped in his tracks and glared at his attacker.

As Bladud continued to beat at his hide, the boar became angry. Suddenly he charged, but Bladud leapt aside. Though the creature just missed him, he turned at once and charged again. This time he came so close that Bladud could smell his foul breath. If only he possessed a spear or a sword! The small knife and the branch were useless. The branch snapped as he brought it down again on the animal's muscular back, and its next charge was dangerously close, one tusk grazing Bladud's thigh. He was inadequately armed against one of the most dangerous animals in the forest. Bladud tried to plunge his knife into his opponent, but failed, and almost lost an arm in the attempt. He began to think about running, but knew the boar would probably outpace him. Nervously he passed his knife from hand to hand, feeling its weight, preparing to strike. His only chance now was to throw it. And his aim had to be accurate, for he would not get a second chance.

'Help me,' he whispered, visualising the warrior of the burial mound, remembering his bulk, his sword and dagger, the spear strapped to his broad back.

No sooner the thought than the figure himself appeared. Huge – three times the size he had been seen before – towering above the boar, with spear raised and aimed. The animal paused, for a moment seemed to look straight at the spirit-being, and then resumed its attack on Bladud. But that moment had given Bladud time to pull himself together. That brief pause assured Bladud that he was not alone. He flung his knife with confidence, and it hit its mark. The boar screamed and writhed, rolling on the ground to try to shake itself free from the agony of the knife wound in its eye.

Bladud glanced back to where he had seen the figure of the warrior – but there was now no one there. The pigs were squealing and running in every direction, tumbling over themselves to get away from the wounded animal.

Having no means to finish the beast off and release him from his suffering. Bladud set off in pursuit of his charges, trying to round them up and herd them back to their pen. His thigh and arm were bleeding and painful, but he had work to do before he could attend to himself.

The wounds inflicted by the boar's tusks soon became infected. At night Bladud tossed and turned, his body again racked with fever. Disturbing dreams and hallucinations haunted him. In many Alun took on the form of a delicately featured young man, a loving son, who tended and nursed him through his illness. In others Bladud stood unarmed on a rocky hillside, being pursued upwards by a boar with only one eye. Cornered at last, he faced death by either leaping off the cliff or being gored by those deadly tusks. This sequence always ended with his taking the leap. Sometimes he felt the terrors of the long descent and the agony of breaking bones as he hit the rocks below. Sometimes he woke feverishly just before he reached the bottom. But the last time he experienced this recurring nightmare, he took the leap again – and instead of falling he began to soar into the air. Looking down, he could see the boar glaring up at him from the rocky summit, growing smaller and smaller as he flew higher, until the fearsome beast looked no more than an insignificant dot. Beneath him, from horizon to horizon, the landscape unfolded like a green embroidered cloak of silk . . . billowing and floating over the full and fertile body of the Earth Goddess. Bladud no longer felt pain, and his heart sang.

When he woke this time, the fever had gone.

216

Soon after Bladud had departed for Greece, his friend Yaruk had been abruptly dismissed from court. Rheinid had found some trumped-up reason for this, because she had long found it intolerable that Bladud would confide in this local savage in a way he would not confide in her. She knew Bladud had spoken with him about her brutal treatment of her slaves, and since then it seemed to her his eyes never ceased to accuse her. Whether this was really just a figment of her guilty conscience was beside the point. She wanted Yaruk out of her sight – so Yaruk had to leave.

Remembering the close friendship Yaruk and Bladud had enjoyed, and not knowing how else to start looking for the vanished prince, Torna the assassin set off in search of Yaruk.

Torna was a ruthless soldier with a history of harsh treatment towards the indigenous people, so when he came among them to ask about Yaruk, he found it difficult to tell whether they really did not know his whereabouts, or whether they were deliberately keeping information from him. No one seemed to have heard of Yaruk, let alone know where he was living, yet Torna knew that a native who had been accepted at the court of the High King and had become a close friend of the royal prince must surely have been spoken about in his own community. The more stone walls he came up against, the more wild goose chases he was sent on, the more convinced Torna became that Yaruk would be in contact with Bladud. He resorted to methods he had used before when extracting information from those not willing to give it, yet most of his victims still resisted, though their bones were broken and their flesh was burned. At last one gave in, and Torna learned that Yaruk had last been seen heading into the mountains of the far west where many wild tribes lived. An ideal place for Bladud to hide.

Torna set off there at once, full of confidence that at last he had received useful information. If the Trojans and Greeks thought the Celts were uncouth, and the Celts thought the local people were savages, the mountain tribes living in this distant region were regarded by all three races as partly animals, partly ghosts. They alone had remained unaffected

217

by the waves of immigrants that had come into the country over the centuries – some with the sword, some more peacefully. Safe behind their strongholds of rock, they had simply vanished into the mountain mists whenever they were hunted, and continued their ancient way of life undisturbed. Why would Yaruk be there unless he was accompanying his fugitive prince? No man who had tasted the comforts of civilisation would go there willingly.

Torna made his last camp in the foothills, and spent most of the night sleepless – sharpening his weapons.

Near dawn he fell asleep at last, but later wished he had not, for his dreams brought him no comfort. When the sun was up he woke with a start, filled with terror. Something he had just dreamed was so horrible that even he, who had brought fear and pain to so many others, was unmanned. But what it was he could not remember. And the very fact that, try as he would, he could not recall what had so frightened him was that which made him so uneasy now. He had been warned against something, but he did not know what. Torna was not an imaginative man, but now as he found himself walking through a deep, river-cut valley between high cliffs, he kept looking over his shoulder at every creak and flutter in a way he would have despised in other men.

The winter was coming on rapidly, snow already spreading down the slopes from the high peaks. From time to time he came upon hut settlements, but without exception all of these were deserted – though some with fires still smouldering and fresh meat left half eaten. He knew he was being watched from all sides and soon fear turned to anger.

'Come out, you bastards!' he yelled, shaking his spear. 'I know you're there!'

But it was only his own distorted voice that came back to him from the overhanging crags.

After several fruitless days and nights Torna realised that even under torture Yaruk's savage kinsmen had managed to outwit him. This was no less of a wild goose chase than the rest. He had been sent to his death, for Yaruk and Bladud were no more capable of finding succour in these savage mountains than he was.

He decided to retreat, but, caught up in fog and swirling

snowstorms, he soon lost his way. At the back of his mind, just out of reach, lurked that warning from his mysterious dream. Wrapped securely in fur as he was, he was still chilled to the bone. Shivering uncontrollably he withdrew into a cave and tried to light a fire. *I'll wait out the storm here*, he thought. *And as soon as it clears I'll go east. Sooner or later I'm bound to come out of these mountains.*

But even to light a fire seemed impossible. All the available wood was damp, soaked through as though it never stopped raining or snowing in this place. Irritably Torna threw the logs he had collected out into the storm. 'Useless!' he muttered. His hatred of Yaruk and Bladud, who had clearly led him into this trap, now knew no bounds. He would kill them both and the world would be well rid of them!

Something moved behind him and he swung round, gripping his sword. He could see nothing, not even how far the cave extended. Outside the wind was howling down the narrow gorge, bending strong trees almost double. Torna did not want to venture into that blizzard again.

'Man or beast!' he yelled. 'I'll have you. Come out and face me!'

Though he felt menacing eyes upon him, he could see nothing. What if . . . What if the watcher were neither man nor beast? Torna's courage almost failed him. Old tales he had disregarded began to come back to him vividly.

Nothing moved. The cave was uncannily silent and still – though outside the whole world seemed to be on the move, driven by the howling wind.

Torna could bear the suspense no longer, and he lunged blind into the darkness with his sword. He met no resistance, heard no scutter of retreating feet. Yet he knew invisible eyes were watching. He lunged again – lost his footing, and lost his sword. Screaming, he slipped and slithered and ended up jammed in a cleft in the rock, his leg trapped and in agony. Feverishly he tried to free his dagger from his belt and at last, sweating and trembling, held it in his hand. He still could see no one, hear no one, yet he knew there was someone there.

'Help me,' he ground out between clenched teeth. 'If you are human, help me. But if you are animal – come near me and you are dead!'

But no one came.

In struggling to free his leg, the pain was excruciating. He pushed and pulled at the rock that held him, but it would not budge. As surely as an animal caught by the innumerable traps he himself had set throughout his life, he remained fixed where he was. The light faded altogether. The chill set in even deeper. The long night of winter closed around him. He felt himself slipping into unconsciousness, and struggled fiercely to keep alert. If he fainted now, he would never survive. Muttering, shouting, snarling, cursing, even singing snatches of ribald songs, he fought to keep himself conscious. He dare not die! He had done terrible things in his life . . . Would he meet up with Keron? Would he meet up with all the others he had murdered and wronged? He had never thought much about an after-life in which he might be called to account, and he could not bear to think about it now! But the dread of facing something even worse than the dark and cold and pain of his present condition filled him with terror. If he lived . . . If he lived . . . With all his will he tried to bargain . . . He tried to make a deal . . . He tried to bribe . . .

'If I live . . .' he whispered hoarsely, 'I swear to do whatever you say . . . I swear to serve you for the rest of my days!' He had no idea to whom he was speaking, but visualised someone in his own image – strong, cruel, vengeful . . .

Suddenly he heard a noise. First a creaking, crumbling sound, and then a more definite cracking followed by a rumbling and a thundering. A huge rock split off from the back of the cave and came crashing down towards him. The whole place shook and reverberated. But the rock cleft holding Torna's leg shifted, and finally he was released. Choking on clouds of dust, Torna dragged himself towards the cave entrance.

At last he came out into the icy air. The storm had died down and everywhere looked peaceful in the snow.

But behind him . . . ? Torna shuddered. To whom had he just sworn allegiance?

Although Bladud recovered in time from the infected

wounds, he was considerably weakened by the fever and was beginning to despair of ever becoming well again. It seemed to him that he had lost everything and now he had even lost his hope of recovering his health. One bitter morning he turned his face to the wall and decided there was no point in even getting up. Outside in their pen the pigs snorted in their filth, waiting for the slops their minder usually put out for them when the snow was too deep for them to go snuffling in the forest. Inside the dark little hut, Alun the deer paced about, wondering when his master would open the door and let in the light. Bladud could hear these things, but paid them no attention. He could think of nothing but how sorry he felt for himself, and how he wished the boar had finished him off that fateful day.

At this nadir of his life, he could think of no other person who would be better off for his continuing to live. What was the point of survival on these terms? The irritating sores on his skin had begun to occupy his entire consciousness, to such an extent that he could no longer even escape into dreams. He was tortured flesh, and nothing more. He hated his body – rotting, disgusting, aching, itchy, festering as it was. He was no better than his pigs who did nothing but wake and sleep and eat – waiting for death. 'But in their death,' he muttered, 'at least *they* are useful to others.'

Alun began to nudge his shoulder with his soft nose. Bladud shrugged him off, but Alun persisted. Bladud turned round on him and shouted at him to leave him alone. Alun withdrew for a moment, large eyes hurt and shocked at Bladud's tone. Then, as Bladud rolled back to face the wall, he returned to nudge him.

Bladud sprang up, angry and cursing. 'You want the door open? I'll open the door!' he snarled, and flung back the rickety wooden slats so hard they almost shattered.

Outside the whole world was white and glistening. Blinding snow-light dazzled him. The bare branches of the trees were festooned with crystal. He had never seen such light! It blazed through his closed eyelids. It seemed to penetrate his very bones . . .

He staggered back a step or two into the dark, dank staleness of the hut, but the light followed him. He tried to

221

shut it out, but the door was so damaged from his rough treatment that it would not close. Alun stood daintily on the doorstep sniffing the cold, fresh air with delight. The light enclosed the animal in a halo of brilliance, so that he seemed to melt into it and disappear. There in his place stood a young woman shimmering with gold. Bladud blinked and stared, but almost immediately she was gone. The young deer turned his head and looked appealingly at his master.

'Oh, all right!' grumbled Bladud, and he pulled on his breeches, his boots and his sheepskin jacket. He plodded out, weak and dazed. He would just give Alun and his pigs their food and then . . . And then – what? He considered returning to bed and refusing ever to get up again. *If I eat nothing I will die*, he assured himself. But then he could feel the despair beginning to lift and no matter how he tried, he no longer wanted to give up his life. He groaned. Living was so much more difficult than he could ever have imagined when everything had been going well for him.

The pigs crowded to the wall of their sty snorting and grunting with excitement as he flung their winter feed into their trough. It seemed to him that Beauty looked at him with genuine love. Alun nuzzled his side, patiently waiting for his own food. Bladud stroked his soft head.

'Alun, my friend,' he whispered, 'I'm sorry.'

He heard a call, and Yarr was coming along the path from his cottage, holding a bowl of steaming porridge.

'My wife thought you were looking ill,' he said. They had indeed both been shocked to see how pale and hollow-eyed the young man looked.

Bladud cupped his hands around the hot bowl. He suddenly realised he was hungry – and he was glad to be alive.

Torna's source had not been lying when he said Yaruk had last been seen entering that wild and desolate region. For Yaruk too was looking for Bladud. It was not so much that Yaruk expected to find his friend there; but he remembered from a visit he made as a boy to these parts that there were men and women there who could scry across time and space. His intention was to enlist their help in locating the prince.

After a few false starts he found the route he remembered

222

from his youth. He recalled a particular lake which lay like a silver mirror held between the long green fingers of the Earth Goddess. In its magical surface he could see the high peaks reflected so clearly, so perfectly that he could believe another world lay beneath its surface, a world accurately corresponding in every detail to the world above, but differing in essence, in type of reality, in power.

Yaruk was tired. He had been walking and climbing non-stop all day. Finding a boulder on the pebble beach, he sat down facing the lake to drink in the beauty of it. He was content to sit and stare. Content to rest and dream.

How long he sat there he could not tell before he saw a sight he could not believe. It must have been late in the afternoon, for the sun was just disappearing behind the highest peak. As it did so, its light seemed to blaze up like a fire-diamond, and its reflection touched the centre of the lake with a point of light so intense that he involuntarily shut his eyes. When he opened them again he saw a series of circular ripples travelling out from the same spot, as though a fish had leapt. Yaruk marvelled at the extent of the expanding circles.

As the ripples reached the shore at his feet, he peered into the distance to see the fish that had caused such a wave. He saw not a fish but a young woman walking carefully and delicately on the shining surface of the lake, approaching him steadily. She was slender and ethereal, almost transparent. Her dress was gold. Her hair was gold, and flowed like a shining cloak around her body down to her knees. Her golden sandals did not even depress the water on which she trod.

At last she stood directly before him, but now she did not seem at all ethereal, but as solid as any woman of flesh and blood.

Yaruk became aware that his mouth was gaping open. He shut it with a snap.

'You are seeking . . . ?' she enquired softly, her voice like the gentlest and sweetest of melodies.

'I . . . I'm . . .' stammered Yaruk, flushing crimson. He tried to stand up, ashamed to sit in the presence of such a being. He stumbled as he rose and she smiled as though affectionately amused by his gaucheness. *Where was Bladud*

223

now? he thought desperately. *He* would know how to talk to such a person!

'Ah, Prince Bladud,' the lady said as if she had caught the name from his thoughts – although he had said no word.

He nodded vigorously, his mouth dry, his cheeks burning.

She looked suddenly dreamy, withdrawn. Half turned from him towards the lake, she gazed over its surface thoughtfully.

Yaruk waited, his heart pounding.

After what seemed a long time she turned back towards him, and smiled.

'Do not be concerned about Prince Bladud,' she said gently. 'He is not alone.'

'But where is he?'

She looked at him long and thoughtfully, as she had just looked towards the lake. As though she was sizing him up to see if she could trust him.

At last she replied. 'You have heard of the goddess Sul?' she asked.

He nodded. Of course! Why had he not thought of her? Bladud had consulted her oracle many years before in the West Country. He might well have gone there to seek her protection now.

The woman lifted her arms till her golden cloak flowed down like a waterfall of light. Yaruk blinked, dazzled. Then she was gone. The sun was gone. The shadows of the mountains fell dark and sombre on the lake. Its water no longer shone silver like a mirror.

He had once heard tell that Sul was the Sun Goddess herself. Surely the woman who had stood before him, was not . . . ?

Limping back into a more familiar and less forbidding landscape after his grim experience in the cave, Torna caught sight of Yaruk hurrying ahead of him along the road. Without hesitation he hurried after him, but keeping well out of sight.

224

16

The Healing

The winter had almost run its course, and though the frosts were still sometimes hard, light was coming earlier and staying later, and the first bulbs were beginning to press through the rich earth, when Bladud, venturing further afield and trying a new route for his pigs, discovered a strange phenomenon that reminded him both of the Oracle of Sul above the steaming crevice and the Cumaean Sibyl among the fumeroles. The land in this region was marshy, and that was why they had not come that way before. But this day the mists lifted early, the sun shone, and Bladud found himself driving his charges hard, almost without thinking. Later he wondered if it was not Alun who had led them to the place, for on that day the deer was more skittish than usual: he seemed to have caught the scent of something in the air that made him dart ahead, only occasionally looking back to make sure Bladud and those ungainly and lumbering animals were following.

From the hillside Bladud could see a flat area of marsh and reeds between a loop in the river. The sun was high and warm enough to have dispersed the river mist in the valley, yet here, in this marshy area, the mist still hung – or rather it rose like steam from a cauldron. While Bladud contemplated it thoughtfully, wondering how near he was to the Oracle of Sul, the pigs seemed to go crazy and rushed down the hillside to wallow with delight in the mud. Surprised at their sudden and unaccustomed turn of speed, the swineherd followed them down at a more leisurely pace. Alun had disappeared – but then he often did so, sometimes for hours at a time.

Bladud found that the mud was pleasantly warm, and he watched amused as his swine wallowed in it, squealing with delight. He had a hard time driving them home from the place when it came time to go, and he found himself promising them he would bring them back there.

He gave a wry smile as he walked, thinking of how he used to speak with kings and philosophers, and here he was glad to make conversation with swine.

Though Alun stayed away all day, he joined them again as they turned for home.

Bladud did not return to the marsh every day. Sometimes after a sleepless night he felt too tired and weak to venture so far afield, but as the weather improved and the pigs grew restless, he indulged them and took them back to what clearly seemed to them a form of paradise.

Then Yarr remarked one day that he had never seen the pigs look so healthy, and asked his swineherd how he had managed to rid them of the scurf and sores that usually blemished their skins. Bladud replied that he had done nothing special, but then began to think about it. After this he watched them closely, till he came to the conclusion that the only thing that had changed for them was their wallowing in the hot mud in the marsh. It was not long before another thought struck him.

The next time he could hardly wait to reach the place again. The first thing he did on arrival was to strip off his clothes and step into the marsh himself. He noticed that it had a pungent, unpleasant smell, and at first he was tentative about covering his open sores with such disgusting stuff. But there was no doubt the pigs who had formerly been afflicted with lesions were now clear and clean – and he was a desperate man. In the winter he had fallen into a kind of hibernation, a slowing down, a sluggishness of mind. But now that the spring was on the move, he felt his old restlessness returning.

Taking a deep breath he scooped up a handful of mud and packed it on to his leg over a place that was particularly painful and irritating. He found the result soothing, but when he came to peel it off later, the sores were still evident.

226

Alun found Bladud sitting on the earth, his head buried in his arms. Gently he nuzzled him, and the man-being flung his arms around the deer, tears flowing wetly on to his fur.

Next day, still suffering the bitterness of disappointment, the prince did not want to return to the marsh, but the pigs would not let themselves be led to any other place. With one accord, and with a disobedience never shown before, they made for the hot marshes. Bladud followed sullenly and sat on the hillside, brooding on his misfortunes. Suddenly he remembered the pigs had not come out of the mud magically cured that first day. They had wallowed many times before he and Yarr had noticed the change in them.

At once he was up and running. And this time covered himself from head to foot, shouting almost hysterical prayers and incantations to Sul, the Goddess of the Waters, the Golden Lady of the Sun, who each night plunged deep beneath the earth and who, no doubt, was responsible for the hot and healing waters that welled up from the depths.

The next day he behaved more soberly, and gradually, day by day, settled into a calm routine of covering himself with mud each morning, peeling it off dry each evening, and washing himself clean in the river before his return at dusk to Yarr's smallholding.

For a long time he noticed no change and was almost ready to give up hope when one day Yarr remarked that he too was looking better, and Bladud realised that he had slept through several nights without waking to scratch and toss and groan.

Hardly daring to hope, he returned to the marsh. The improvement began to be more and more noticeable each day. Gradually he was becoming whole and clean. Gradually his back straightened, his eyes brightened. Yarr and his wife rejoiced to see their swineherd looking so well, but wondered even more that such a noble looking man should be content to tend their pigs. They were not surprised, therefore, when one day he came to their cottage to ask if they could find someone else to work for them, since he felt it was now time to move on.

Bladud did not return to Trinovantum at once, but instead

227

turned towards the west, heading past the healing marshes and making for that region in which he had first seen the Oracle of Sul. His one sorrow was that Alun the deer had disappeared and could not be found.

He was not at all sure he wanted to return to his father's royal court. He was not sure he wanted to become High King. He was sure, however, that he wanted to show his gratitude for his miraculous recovery.

Would the Oracle of Sul know what had happened to him? Would she be expecting him? As he was about to enter the forest that hid her cave and the hot spring she presided over, he suddenly felt he was being watched. He spun round, and saw that he was indeed not alone. The same wild boar he had fought at the beginning of winter was there – and about to charge. The beast now possessed only one eye – but that eye was glaring at the enemy, and that eye was blazing with hatred.

Bladud gripped his knife in his hand and waited. This time he was not afraid as he had been the first time. This time the animal would find it had a worthy opponent.

Perhaps the beast sensed this, for it paused. For a long moment the two stared at each other, sizing each other up. The creature was huge, with long and vicious tusks. *Perhaps he will not attack*, Bladud hoped. The last time it had been aroused by a female and Bladud had merely got in the way. But there was something in the beast's one eye that seemed almost human. It looked as though it remembered Bladud. He could almost believe it had been deliberately hunting him.

And then the animal charged.

Bladud leapt aside in time, but the boar charged again.

Bladud did not want to fight, but the beast would not give up, so the man was forced to defend himself. Time and again he plunged with his knife, missed, and narrowly escaped the deadly tusks. Then the prince lost his footing and fell, helpless, the knife having fallen clear and out of reach. The monstrous beast rallied for its final charge. Frantically Bladud struggled to rise. Life had become very sweet, now that he felt well again, and he could not bear to give it up. He heard the approaching thunder and put his arms protectively over his face, half rising, half crouching, waiting for the inevitable.

But the impact did not come. There was a scream of agony, and the heavy sound of falling. He looked up to see the boar sprawled on the ground, one spear sticking from its head, another from its heart.

In astonishment Bladud turned to see who his saviour was. Yaruk was running towards him!

When Yaruk explained how he had seen Sul herself walking on the lake, and how it was she who had guided his steps towards the West Country, Bladud felt more certain than ever that it was she who was his benefactor.

The two friends approached her mysterious and sacred place together: Yaruk dreaming of the golden lady he had seen walking on the water, Bladud wondering how old the oracle would look now, having seemed such an ancient crone when last seen so many years before.

'She has always been associated with healing among my people,' Yaruk said when Bladud described the effect of the hot mud. 'She is known for healing and wisdom.'

'The waters that bring refreshment to the heart,' Bladud mused. 'The sun that brings light to the soul.' And then, after a long pause, he added: 'I am thinking of building a temple for her.'

'Maybe she doesn't need a temple.'

'Maybe she doesn't – but I do. I want to see my people healed of their wounds and their diseases, but if I show them marsh mud they will scoff. If there is a temple and an elaborate ritual, they will be more inclined to believe in her power.'

'Sul has never been confined in a temple. She has always walked free, appearing where and when she desires.'

'My temple will not limit her. Like a well, it will serve as a place where thirsty travellers may gather to refresh themselves.'

'You don't often see an owl in daylight,' Yaruk remarked as they made their way through the forest towards the hot spring of Sul. Bladud, who was walking ahead, turned at

229

once to join Yaruk's uneasy gaze upwards. He too was startled. An owl had watched him on his approach to the oracle's hide-out once before. An owl had sat on the shoulder of Athene. In the legends of Yaruk's people an owl was a bird to be feared, always associated with mysterious and dangerous forces. As the prince looked into its enormous eyes, he felt that time and space had slipped somehow, and for a moment he could not remember where he was, or where he was going. He could not even remember who he was. He could not remember if he was a stranger in a strange land where everything about him was questioned and questionable, and he had everything to defend and prove, or whether he was in his own land where everyone thought they knew everything about him, took everything for granted, and questioned nothing.

'What is the matter?' Yaruk stared at him in alarm. Bladud's expression was strange: as though his face was dissolving, and every moment different people were looking out through the windows of his eyes.

Yaruk watched for a while in growing dismay, then he seized his friend's shoulders and shook him.

'Prince Bladud!' he cried out again and again until he secured his attention. 'Prince Bladud . . .'

Suddenly the owl flew off with a flap and a flutter and Bladud looked at Yaruk with gradually dawning recognition.

'Yaruk?' he questioned as though he had not seen him for a long time.

'Yes. Yaruk!'

Bladud gazed around himself wonderingly.

'What happened to you?' Yaruk asked. 'You looked as though you'd . . . you'd . . .'

'What?'

'I don't know. You seemed to be . . . all sorts of people . . . strangers . . .'

Bladud shivered. 'I felt . . . I can't describe it . . . as though I *was* all sorts of people . . .'

'Well, you are Prince Bladud,' Yaruk said firmly. The experience had unnerved him. In all the changing, mysterious, inexplicable realms of being, if the 'self' was not a constant, what else was? For a moment he felt totally

230

insecure, but then Bladud, his friend of many years, the High King's favourite son, spoke out in a very ordinary voice to declare that he was ravenously hungry.

Yaruk laughed with relief, and produced from a pouch at his side the crumbling remains of some stale barley bread a farmer's wife had given to him the previous day.

When they reached the stones in the stream which were carved with significant spiralling signs, Yaruk began to grow very excited. He had heard about them when he was a child.

'These are the ciphers that open the door into the Otherworld,' he explained. 'The ancient tribes carved them long before my people came to this land.'

'If they were not carved by your own people, how do you know what they signify?'

'We didn't understand them at first, but our shamans worked on them, trying every possible combination, until finally the door opened. A story is told how a great priest-king was the one to decipher the code, and all his people gathered to watch him pass through the door.'

'These very stones? By this waterfall? This cave?'

'No. I don't think so. The place I heard described was on a vast open moor. There the stones were arranged in a circle, and the priest-king had worked out their sequence . . .'

'What happened when he went through the door?'

'It is said that he never came back. But generations later when even his great-grandson was old, a young stranger came walking into the royal court one day claiming to be that same priest-king. No one believed him and the people stoned him as a trouble-maker trying to usurp the throne from the rightful king. As he died, the young man cried out – but no one listened to him. Some later began to think that he might indeed have been the priest-king of the legend, and tried to recall exactly what he had said with his dying breath. Many versions of his words were set about. People were even put to death for reporting one version rather than another. Some believed he was a sorcerer, and had yelled out a curse on them all for what they did to him. Others believed he was a seer and a prophet giving them certainty of another world.'

'When I first came upon these signs years ago, I fingered

231

them,' Bladud said, indicating the carved boulders. 'I don't think I entered another world. I felt a bit strange, I admit, but what I experienced seemed very much of this world: hot steam, water, hard rock, narrow passage . . .'

'You obviously did not touch them in the correct sequence.'

Bladud gazed thoughtfully at the stones. He had returned from the hut of the oracle by a different route that did not involve the discomfort of crawling along a hot corridor and scratching himself on jagged rocks. He now had it in mind to try and rediscover that first route, and use it again. If what Yaruk said about the carvings was true he might be missing an important experience by taking the easier way.

'Do you know anything about the correct sequence?' he asked at last.

Yaruk shook his head. 'Some say that if you try it, and get the sequence wrong, something terrible will happen to you.'

'Dare we?' asked Bladud, his eyes shining.

Yaruk thought about this. He certainly would not try himself, but Bladud possessed the kind of mystic glamour, the kind of energy that came not just from generations of power-wielding ancestors, but from something deep within himself, something which caused him to experience visions and dreams more potent than those of the average man. If anyone was the true heir of that ancient priest-king who had unravelled the code to enter the Otherworld, it would be Bladud.

'It must be your decision,' Yaruk replied.

Bladud took up a position from which he could see all the carvings simultaneously. For a long, long time he stood silently staring at them.

The key will be in the mind – not in the stones, he thought. *The stones are only clues to stimulate the mind.*

Yaruk waited patiently.

Gradually the ciphers began to take shape in Bladud's inner vision. And when he shut his eyes, he could still see them as after-images of light. Carefully in his imagination his finger traced the grooves in each. As he began to trace the last one, that on the huge boulder just below the waterfall, the waterfall itself seemed to part like a shimmering silver curtain. In his imagination Bladud stepped back, startled, though Yaruk saw him make no movement. Emerging from behind the water came a woman of extraordinary radiance. His heart missed a beat. Was this Sul herself?

'Do you not recognise me, Bladud?' she asked. He stared at her. She was at once a stranger, a woman so beautiful he could hardly believe such could exist, yet at the same time she seemed to take on another more familiar form – that of Imogene. But even as he began to acknowledge her, the image dissolved into that of the Cumaean Sibyl – and then into the goddess Athene herself . . .

As the images changed and changed again, he could not be sure whether he was looking into the eyes of Alcestis or of Rheinid . . . or even the eyes of Aphrodite or of those two spirit-women who filled their cups from the same flask . . .

'Stop!' he cried at last. *Did nothing, no one, hold to its own identity any more?* 'I have come to offer my gratitude to the goddess Sul. It is she, and only she, I seek.'

'You may seek as much as you like,' the woman said sharply, having taken on the form of that old crone, the Oracle of Sul, 'but whom you find may not be whom you seek.'

'You are her oracle,' Bladud protested desperately, hoping she at least would hold her shape long enough for him to secure some answers. 'Sul has healed me of my disease. Will she now help me to reclaim my place as the High King's heir?'

'You once came to me as a young prince, full of assumptions about himself and about his future. I told you then you would become a great king because that is what you will be. But you assumed I meant a king in the worldly sense – as High King of these many petty kingdoms – the heir of Hudibras. But what if I had meant that you would be a great king among the swine? Did not your pigs look up to you? Did you not rule and order their lives the way a king orders the lives of his subjects? What if I had meant that you would have no kingdom but yourself, and that thus you rule over that kingdom which is the most difficult to rule of all – where all rebellions are within the mind, and the conflict of desires is within the heart?'

Bladud felt shock. So he might not become High King after all . . .

'What of your other prophecy?' he cried. 'You said I would fly like an eagle.'

Suddenly Yaruk pushed him hard, so he staggered and almost fell.

'Just as there are many kingdoms to rule, there are many ways to fly . . .' Her voice and her image were fading fast.

'Come back!' he cried, trying to hold on to the precious vision.

But she was gone. All the magic had vanished.

He turned to Yaruk furiously. 'Why . . .' But Yaruk pointed in horror to a spear embedded in the bank where Bladud had been standing a moment before. Within seconds another whistled past his ear as Yaruk pulled him to one side.

If Yaruk had not spotted Torna when he did, Bladud would now be dead.

'Come,' Yaruk urged, tugging at his arm. 'We must get away from here!'

Still half dazed from the recent vision, Bladud allowed himself to be drawn under cover. From there Yaruk let loose his own spear – and Torna withdrew.

Yaruk pleaded that they return to Trinovantum immediately.

'Torna would not be working for himself,' he insisted, as Bladud continued to protest that he could not leave, because he had almost figured out the sequence that would allow him through the door into the Otherworld. 'Forgive me, but I believe your brother Prince Liel wants to be sure you will never come back to challenge him. If you don't return now, you will *never* be High King.'

Bladud looked thoughtful.

'And what if I no longer want to be High King? What if I have found something else I would rather do?'

'You would desert all those who rely on you?' Yaruk cried, shocked. 'You would betray the trust of your father whose dearest wish has always been that you succeed him?'

'My brother . . .'

'Your brother will never make a good High King. You

234

know that and I know it. He will aim only to conquer more land, to extend his kingdom and his power by enslaving yet more people and ill-treating those already enslaved. My own people can stand only so much, till sooner or later they rebel, and then there will be bloodshed from one sea to the other. All that King Hudibras has worked for will be undone.'

'You exaggerate. Liel is not . . .'

'Why does he send Torna to murder his own brother?'

'You do not know that it was Liel.'

'Who else?'

Bladud fell silent. He sensed that Yaruk was right. Many people would suffer under Liel, though some young bloods of noble families would love him, for he would give them adventure and war, new land and rich booty. Yet still Bladud hesitated.

'I have been away too long. Liel will already be well in charge.'

He did not want to return to Trinovantum. He wanted to go through the door that he believed was for him already half open.

'If you go through that door now,' Yaruk cried, 'no one will listen when you tell them what you have seen. But if you become High King . . .'

'Perhaps it is not my destiny to rule *this* generation. You told me the priest-king returned after many generations had lived and died.'

'It is *this* generation that needs you!' Yaruk cried passionately. 'You have seen how we are oppressed in our own land! You have seen how it is only the strong hand of Hudibras that keeps the peace between the smaller kingdoms. But your father is now old. He cannot wait for you to chase dreams and shadows! He needs you now. Your people need you now!'

Bladud looked again towards the spirals, the circles, the ciphers. He gazed at the waterfall through which the shining lady had appeared. A kaleidoscope of images and words confused his mind. He felt pulled and pushed in every direction. He was surely already halfway through that magical door – and indeed had been for years. Otherwise how could so many weird and otherworldly things have happened

235

to him? If he pulled back now, when he felt he was so near, it might close itself to him forever . . . He might be shut completely out of those magical realms, and forced to live out his life like other people in an ordinary, limited, mundane world . . .

But Yaruk was right. People would certainly suffer under Liel.

For a long moment the two men stood in silence in the forest beside the stream, Yaruk watching the play of conflicting emotions in Bladud's eyes, sensing the struggle in his mind, knowing that if he pressed too hard he might alienate and lose his friend.

It is in your hands now, he thought, imagining the golden lady who had come to him walking over the lake. He remembered how her every step had set in motion a series of ripple-circles which, as they grew wider and wider, overlapped others, until the whole surface of the lake was an intricate pattern of interlocking circles, a geometric splendour, a template of the universe. Yaruk was startled that his memory of that moment contained so much more detail than he had noticed at the time. *She must be here*, he thought. *She must be here!*

'I will go back to Trinovantum,' Bladud said suddenly, decisively.

Relief showed in Yaruk's face.

'But I will return here when I am king and build a healing sanctuary and a shrine here, so that my people may benefit from Sul's grace just as I have done. I swear it by all the gods.'

And then, heavy of heart, he turned away from the waterfall and the mystery of Mysteries that lay there.

On the way back they kept out of sight as much as possible to avoid alerting Liel to Bladud's intentions until it was too late for him to do anything about them. The murderous Torna was on both their minds, though neither spoke of him.

It was on the second night of their secret journey that the assassin made his next move – and it was an owl that saved Bladud's life. Yaruk woke with a start as an owl hooted close by, just in time to see Torna stooping over the sleeping prince with dagger drawn.

Bladud himself woke a moment later to find the two men fighting. He leapt up at once and gave Yaruk a chance to recover his breath. Torna fought grimly, knowing that if he did not succeed this time, he himself was finished. Bladud found himself losing ground. Suddenly he lost his footing and landed flat on his back with Torna's blade inching inexorably towards his eyes. He remembered the wild boar he had fought and how he had aimed deliberately at its eyes. With all his strength Bladud forced the dagger away and brought his knee up in Torna's groin. The man loosened his grip and Yaruk was upon him at once.

'I don't want him killed,' Bladud ground out. 'Yaruk, hold back!'

Yaruk looked shocked, but did not loosen his grip on Torna's throat.

'We need him. We need him to denounce his master before the Council,' Bladud urged. 'He must be our prisoner. He must come with us to my father's court.'

Yaruk looked at Torna in the dirt, his face demonic with hate. His personal feelings for Torna almost got the better of him, and his hands around the man's windpipe squeezed tighter.

'Yaruk!' Bladud's voice was sharp and compelling.

Yaruk reduced the pressure a fraction, but Torna was still choking when Bladud bound his arms behind his back and hobbled his legs together like a beast's.

At first they travelled slowly, Yaruk dragging Torna by a rope tied around his waist. At the end of the second day they encountered a storm that brought them to a virtual standstill. They were now well out of the forests and travelling across exposed, gently rolling chalk downs, when a fierce wind sprang up, driving gigantic billowing black clouds before it to blot out almost all of what was left of the daylight. For a while they struggled on, bent almost double against the wind, but when the needle-sharp rain drove down, they decided to shelter as best they could. Luckily they found a derelict barn, but half its timbers were gone and the rest in danger of disintegrating in the wind.

Having tied Torna hastily to one of the wall struts, Yaruk

settled down close to Bladud for warmth. The night became wilder and stormier. Though all were exhausted, no one could sleep. Nearly every part in the old building flapped and slapped and creaked. The wind howled and screeched. The rain tore violently at the roofing thatch. At every moment they expected their temporary shelter to be ripped off the earth and blown away.

In the morning, when the storm had abated and daylight came, Bladud and Yaruk saw that their captive had escaped. Yaruk wanted to go after him at once, determined this time to kill him. But Bladud insisted they should waste no more time searching for him, but instead redouble their efforts to ensure that they reached Trinovantum before he did.

Yaruk stole horses and food from a nearby farm.

'You can recompense the farmer when you become king,' he said hastily, sensing Bladud's disapproval. 'And if you do not become king, you'll probably be dead,' he added under his breath. 'And you'll have to recompense him in your next life.'

But Torna had no intention of making for Trinovantum. His mission was to kill Bladud, and he was determined to achieve that. Under cover of darkness and the noise of the storm, Torna had painstakingly worked himself free from the rotten beam to which he had been tied. He staggered out of the barn and was met head-on by a wind that tore and ripped at him, driving rain into his eyes so that he was almost blinded. He cursed as he stumbled around in the pitch blackness of a moonless, starless night. He had not yet managed to free his hands, and without them to steady himself he could scarcely remain upright. More than once he fell to the ground, climbing to his feet again only with the greatest difficulty.

His hatred of his captors knew no bounds.

The first thing I will do, he thought bitterly, *I'll cut off Yaruk's arms! Let him feel what it is like to be so helpless! I'll kill them both slowly. I'll make them suffer.*

When he found a sharp-edged rock by dint of falling and cutting his leg on it, it gave him the implement he needed to saw through the cords that held him prisoner.

238

There was a sudden sickly glow of lightning, and in its pallid illumination he could swear he saw the tall dark figure of a man standing over him, staring down – too tall for either Bladud or Yaruk.

'Who is there?' he cried out hoarsely. When he opened his mouth the wind seemed to surge into his throat and freeze him to the very roots of his being. Was this the fell spirit he had sworn allegiance to after the rockfall in the cave?

Another brief glow – but this time he saw no one. He prised loose the sharp rock which had helped him cut the cords. He would waste no more time. This rock was as handy a weapon as any he would find. He set off back towards the barn.

Suddenly his foot slipped on a slide of mud and he felt himself falling . . .

Both Bladud and Yaruk fancied they heard the wind scream with a human voice during the small hours – but they did not think of Torna.

They rode the horses hard across country so as to avoid pursuit, but there was one diversion Bladud insisted on making in spite of Yaruk's urgent pleading that they press on. His destination was that same burial mound where he had first encountered the huge warrior figure holding the golden cup.

'I *have* to do this,' Bladud insisted, till Yaruk, responding to the passionate conviction in his voice, stood aside. He knew deep in his heart that it was a mistake to delay, but knowing the dangers and difficulties the prince would face once he arrived at Trinovantum, surely pity allowed this one indulgence.

Bladud did not let Yaruk accompany him up the hill towards the mound, and Yaruk, as superstitious as the rest of his people, was only too glad to wait below in the valley and keep a sharp look-out for trouble. It was puzzling that Torna had not made some further move, but perhaps he was already ahead of them, already on the last lap of his journey to bring warning to his master.

'I have to know,' Bladud whispered, kneeling on the

239

ancient burial mound, his hands pressed into the rich turf. 'I *have* to know who you are and why you come to me. And what it is you require of me.'

His heart ached with all that he desired to know – and that he feared he would never learn. Would he come now – the priest-king – the great warrior with the golden cup?

The leaves on the nearby trees rustled slightly in the breeze. But Bladud heard no one – saw no one.

He grew agitated, aware that Yaruk was waiting impatiently for his return, afraid that Torna would reach Trinovantum before them.

He is not here. He will not come, he thought. He felt deserted, alone, afraid. How quickly he had forgotten the spirit-help given to him in the past . . . How easily he dismissed potent and significant experiences as nothing more than imagination . . .

And without giving the place enough time to work its magic, he turned away from it, and ran down the hillside to where Yaruk was waiting with the horses.

'Come on,' he said brusquely. 'We have wasted enough time.'

If he had once looked back, he might have seen a figure on the mound watching him.

As they approached Trinovantum it became more and more difficult to avoid meeting other people on the way. Villages and farms clustered thick around the city, and all roads were busy with merchants and travellers. The unusual sight of two such ragged young men riding horses might have caused a few stares, but no one seemed to recognise them. Everyone went about their business as normal.

'Surely,' Yaruk said, 'if Torna has already arrived, we should have encountered some trouble by now.'

'Surely,' Bladud replied, relieved.

Though the guards at the gate routinely challenged them, they showed no more interest in them than in anyone else. Yaruk explained that they were delivering the horses to their masters within the city, and the guards did not question them further. They rode through the gate with well simulated calm.

But now, as they moved through the crowded streets, people began to turn and stare. Some even began to follow them, until it became impossible to pass unnoticed. A whisper started, swelling to a shout. 'Bladud! Prince Bladud is back. The Prince! The Prince!'

Bladud could no longer try to hide his identity. Yaruk insisted he pull off his ragged shirt to reveal his strong and healthy body.

'Let the people see that Bladud is back! Let them witness that Bladud is healed!' Yaruk shouted excitedly.

The hubbub soon reached the castle, and the High King's guards came out to investigate. Many of them knew Bladud well, and respected him. They formed an escort of honour, and cleared a path to the king's presence.

Bladud was shocked at how old and frail his father now looked. Had he himself been away so long? There was no sign of Liel or Rheinid – only smiling faces rejoicing at his return.

'Call the Council, father,' Bladud urged. 'I will not kiss you until they have pronounced me clean.'

'Come, my son,' the old man said, tears in his eyes. 'I need no Council to tell me what I can see with my own eyes.'

The father folded the son in his arms, and they both wept.

'Forgive me,' said Hudibras. 'I should never have turned my back on you.'

'You did what had to be done and I hold no grudge.'

Yaruk was embarrassed to find tears in his own eyes as he watched this scene. But where were Liel and Rheinid? He swallowed the lump in his throat and peered around carefully. But the king's chamber was full only of the king's closest companions, all of whom were also Bladud's supporters.

'Where is Prince Liel?' Yaruk asked one, at last.

'He rode out yesterday to attend to some trouble,' the man replied cheerfully, and then his face darkened and he looked at Yaruk. 'Prince Liel will not be pleased his brother has returned.' The eyes of the two men met significantly.

'Should we not make sure all loyal warriors are alerted?' Yaruk whispered.

The man nodded. 'Leave it to me,' he said, and slipped out of the room.

241

And so it was that when Liel stormed back at the head of a small army, having been given the news of Bladud's return, he was met and disarmed before he could enter the city.

Rheinid was close behind him, with Torna as her prisoner. She had been visiting her son at Urien's castle when men brought Torna in, both legs broken from the fall in the storm. She had set off immediately for Trinovantum, her devious mind already plotting and planning how to limit the damage her betrayal of Bladud, and her marriage to Liel, had done to her chances of ever becoming High Queen.

When she arrived back the High Council was already gathering to bear witness to Bladud's complete recovery and to reaffirm their original decision that he was the true heir of Hudibras. Liel at first had the sense to pretend that he willingly accepted his brother's return – though biding his time.

As Rheinid entered, she did so dramatically, in flowing robes of black and scarlet, her raven hair gleaming with gold. Behind her, slaves dragged a small cart containing the seated and bound figure of Torna. His eyes met those of Liel immediately, and the look that passed between them was not lost on Bladud and Yaruk.

Pretending outrage at her husband's murderous intent against a royal prince and her former husband, it seemed Rheinid had promised Torna his life and her protection if he would tell the Council exactly what Liel had ordered him to do. With broken legs he was helpless to consider any other plan, and had decided that in her now lay his best bet. It seemed to him that Liel, whatever was said or left unsaid, was finished as a power in the land. But Rheinid retained the aura of a survivor, a manipulator, a winner. Torna had often seen evidence of Bladud's unwillingness to punish and avenge, so he would not be surprised if Rheinid managed to win his forgiveness, and even a place back at the prince's side.

'My lord,' she began, sweeping up to the very dais where Hudibras and his two sons were seated: Bladud handsomely clad as royal prince once more, looking healthy and bronzed and confident, with his friend Yaruk behind him, reinstated to his former honoured position at court. 'My lord . . . my

242

father . . . I beg you listen to what this man will say. He brings evidence of a treachery that cannot be ignored.'

No one else saw the nod Liel gave, but the man it was intended for. Swiftly and silently, one of Liel's loyal followers drove a dagger into the prisoner's back and withdrew it just as silently. Torna slumped forward dead, without a sound. So swiftly and so efficiently did the execution take place that few even noticed it had occurred.

'My lady,' interrupted Liel in a voice at once smooth and full of menace. 'If it were possible for a dead man to speak, I am sure we would all be interested in what he might have to say.'

Rheinid spun round to see the body of Torna lolling out of its cart, blood already dripping on to the floor. She glared back at Liel, and saw in his eyes how easily her life too could be ended.

'What is this?' Hudibras demanded. 'What evil do you bring into our hall, woman? Have you not done enough harm already?'

For a moment she glanced from the corpse to Liel, and back again, a desperate decision to be made. And then she looked at Bladud, the golden prince who would soon be High King.

She began again, with a haughty emphasis, and clarity that all could hear.

'This fellow, sir, was employed by your son Liel to bring an end to his brother's life.'

There was a gasp, like wind through an autumn forest, presaging a storm.

Hudibras stared at Liel with an expression formidable with anger. 'Is this true?'

'Father, have you ever known Rheinid to tell the truth?' Liel answered at once, showing no sign of guilt. 'Have you ever known her be anything but treacherous?'

'This man could have proved the charge, and that is why Liel killed him,' Rheinid declared.

'How? How, lady? Was I not here before you all, in full sight? Did you hear me issue orders? Did my dagger leave my side?'

Bladud stepped forward.

243

'My lords, it is true this man Torna tried to kill me. But, as you see, he did not succeed – and he has paid dearly for it. Let it rest at that.'

His forgiving heart will be his undoing, Yaruk thought anxiously, and wondered if he should speak up.

'No!' cried Rheinid desperately. 'Liel ordered it. You all know Torna was a loyal servant of Liel's!'

'I sent out men to look for Bladud,' Liel said smoothly. 'But ask them, ask any one of them what orders I gave them! My only concern was to return my brother safe so that he would not spread infection among our people.'

'I cannot listen to such lies,' Rheinid cried. 'I denounce you, husband. I renounce our marriage. I demand divorce and accuse you of treason!'

Hudibras looked wearily towards Bladud.

'You will soon be High King, my son. What is your judgement on this? Whatever you decide, I and the Council will abide by.'

The stillness in the hall was palpable. Yaruk felt almost afraid to breathe in case the sound of it broke such an extraordinary silence. All eyes were fixed on Bladud.

He looked into the eyes of his brother, but Liel never flinched. Rheinid was not the only one who knew how to deceive.

Bladud sighed, and there was a wealth of sadness in the sound.

'If brother turns on brother in this dangerous world, what hope have we?' he said quietly. 'The land needs us both. Give me your hand.' And he reached out and shook Liel's sword hand in a gesture of faith and trust.

All who had been holding breath in suspense of the judgement now exhaled – and there was no more silence.

Hudibras slumped back in his seat and closed his eyes. For him that was the beginning of the end. It would not be long now before he turned his face to the wall and died.

But there was still Rheinid to deal with.

Bladud looked at her long and intently. Aye, she was so beautiful and passionate . . . He would never cease to desire her, but . . .

'Your petition for divorce is refused, lady. You have

chosen Prince Liel over me, and you will stay with him. No doubt he will forgive you – as I have already done.'

She was shocked. Stay with Liel after what she had tried to do to him? She met his cold, merciless eyes, knowing that she had gambled, and lost.

'As for myself,' Bladud now said, with a lift in his voice. 'I have chosen another bride. She is a princess from the royal line of my forefathers, and I will send for her to join me here at Trinovantum. I assure you she will be a worthy queen for you.'

Cheers went up as the crowd, bewildered by so many difficult emotions within the past hour, were relieved that the whole affair would have a happy ending.

Only Rheinid's eyes smouldered in frustration and rage.

17

Departure and Arrival

One day Bladud was called to the private chambers of
Hudibras. The great king had recently been in failing health
and increasingly left the business of governing the country in
Bladud's hands. This had not eased the tension between the
two brothers, but Bladud seemed determined to work with
Liel and overcome his enmity. While Liel pretended to co-
operativeness he did not feel, Yaruk, in the background,
studied his every move like a cat watching a mouse.

'How can you possibly trust him?' he would ask Bladud,
despairing of his friend's good sense.

'I don't,' Bladud replied simply. 'But I will not take the
throne over the dead body of my brother.'

'But you are giving him powers that one day he may use
against you!'

'He is more likely to do so if he has cause to hate
me.'

'He does have cause to hate you! He wants to become High
King and you stand in his way.'

'He wants power and riches. If he has those, he will not be
discontented.'

Yaruk threw up his hands. What more could he say?
Bladud seemed determined to leave everything at risk. But
Bladud was not the fool he might appear to Yaruk, for he had
many other loyal friends, and Liel was under constant
surveillance.

After her outburst in the Council, Rheinid had not
returned to her husband's bed, but had stormed out of the
court and set off immediately for Urien's rath and her son

Lear. If she could not be High Queen she was determined at least that her son would one day be High King. And when he was, she would be there at his side.

When Bladud reached his father's quarters, he found the antechamber full of whispering anxious people, all of whom fell instantly silent and bowed to the ground as the prince entered. A cold hand seemed to close over his heart. Was this it? Was this the moment that he had been expecting all his life? He still did not feel ready for it. Would he ever be ready?

The silent crowd parted as he walked through them.

'Has my brother been summoned?' he asked, turning just before the door into his father's bedchamber.

'No, my lord. The king asked to see you alone.'

'My brother must be informed.'

'Yes, my lord.'

Inside the bedchamber Bladud found his father deathly pale, wrapped in furs though it was a hot summer's day. Fergal stood at his side; no one else. On a brazier burned some concoction of herbs, scenting the air with its pungent but not unpleasant smell.

Bladud took his father's hands in his, and leaned down to kiss his forehead.

All his life, his father had been the main strength in a mighty land. His body had been firm and strong – a warrior's body; his mind quick and incisive – the mind of a true king. Bladud looked now at weak and shrivelled flesh, dull and yellowing eyes, and he shuddered inwardly at the touch of that flaccid, already half lifeless skin.

'Father . . .' he whispered, but he could not continue. Where *was* his father? This was certainly not he.

Fergal put a hand on his shoulder, and he could feel strength and energy flow into him from that touch.

'It is your son Bladud, my lord,' the Druid told the king.

'Aye . . .' whispered the dying man. 'Aye . . . my son.'

'You have two sons, father. And Liel is on his way.'

The eyes of Hudibras appeared to see him clearly for a moment – even to see into him.

'You were chosen . . .' he whispered in a voice so low that

248

leaves rustling on a forest floor would seem loud by comparison. 'You were sealed to a task from your very birth.' The whispering ceased. The old man closed his eyes.

'What do you mean? What task?'

'Fergal . . .' The voice made one last effort, and then faded away into a sigh, so sad, so lost, so lonely that tears came welling to Bladud's eyes.

'Father!' He put his hands on the old man's shoulders and tried to embrace him. But the king was gone. What was left in his son's hands seemed no more than old rags and bones. Bladud let him go and stood up, staring without comprehension at what now lay on the bed.

At that moment the door burst open and Liel rushed in.

'Father!' he shouted, running to the bed. He had left the door open behind him, and suddenly all the retainers of the old king who had been gathered in the antechamber came pushing into the room.

Bladud looked up, dazed.

'Why wasn't I called?' demanded Liel.

'You were sent for . . .'

'Too late! You've always tried to keep him from me!' Liel's face was furious, but Bladud could see the pain in his eyes. It was not the same pain he himself felt for the loss of a close relationship: rather it was the pain his brother felt for a relationship he had never experienced – nor now ever would.

Fergal took Bladud's arm, and gently but firmly pulled him away. Others closed in, noisily mourning, Liel the loudest of them all.

'You are High King now,' Fergal said quietly. 'You must act quickly to keep the transition of power peaceful and orderly. Your brother is almost out of control. Who knows what he will do?'

Bladud walked with him out through the now deserted antechamber and down the corridor. He felt as though he were sleep-walking, the burden of what he had just inherited gradually dawning on him. It was one thing to plan on becoming High King 'one day', but very different actually to feel the weight of it descend on his shoulders. Crowds were coming up to him, bowing, kneeling as he passed, speaking to him . . . He scarcely saw them, scarcely heard them . . .

How could he ever have wanted this? How could any man want this responsibility? He thought of Liel, and suddenly saw an escape. Let *him* have it! Crown, throne, power . . . the lot!

Fergal drew him into an empty room and shut the door.

'You must not think of giving up,' he said, looking deeply into Bladud's eyes.

'Fergal, I cannot . . . I cannot take this on.'

'You can. You must.'

'But I don't wish it!'

'You may not think so now, but consider the alternative.'

Bladud fell silent. Many things went through his mind, forcing their way through the darkness . . .

'What did my father mean?' he asked at last. 'Who chose me? Who sealed me to a task?'

'Your father had a vision at your birth. He never spoke of it to anyone but me.'

'He always struck me as so down-to-earth, so sceptical. I never thought him prone to visions!'

'Only the one. Perhaps that was why it impressed him so. It was the reason he was always so determined that you and not Liel should succeed him.'

'Tell me about it.'

'It seems he saw a tall man standing beside your mother's bed at your delivery. A man no one saw enter and no one knew.'

'How did he look, this man? What did he say?'

'He was dressed like some great king, but in clothes that today would be old-fashioned . . .' Fergal paused.

'Go on,' urged Bladud. He could hear running and shouting outside the door. The news of the death of Hudibras was spreading fast, and, as Fergal had warned, if he did not take control soon there would be danger of anarchy.

'He did not speak at all but offered your father a golden cup. Your father drew back and wouldn't accept it.'

Bladud's heart pounded. *The golden cup!*

'The stranger then leant over the bed and offered a drink to the child just emerged from his mother's womb. And the child drank!'

'*I* drank!'

'Yes.'

'And then what? What happened then?'

'Hudibras feared the man was a danger to the child, and lunged at him with his sword. But his sword passed right through him, and he disappeared.'

'And?'

'That was all. Hudibras never set eyes on him again. He never saw any kind of vision ever again. But he felt that you had been marked in some way by the gods. He watched you grow, and anything you did that was unusual, he believed it was because you had drunk from that cup. He seemed to believe that when you became ruler, that ancient king would return to be at your side and guide you.'

'Fergal,' Bladud whispered. 'I do believe it will be so.'

Outside the room the level of noise had risen alarmingly.

'Come,' Fergal said. 'We can delay no longer.'

Bladud took a deep breath. He now knew he was not alone. He could face the challenge.

The coronation of a High King had not been seen in the Pretanic Isles for many years. Bladud had already sent for Alcestis, but he was advised by Fergal that it would be unwise to delay until her arrival. For the ceremony he chose mid-summer's day: the day when the sun would stand at its highest and most powerful, and when all the spirit-beings associated with the sun would be at hand to give the new High King their blessing.

From the most remote parts of his kingdom, all the sub-kings, their families and their companions converged on Trinovantum. Every road seemed full of travellers. Buskers and merchants and camp followers swelled the crowds of nobles and warriors, of priests and bards and musicians. Cattle were driven along in lowing herds to provide meat for the feast, while carts loaded with vegetables, fruit, milk, wheat and cheese lumbered through the throngs. The drama of the prince who was once a leper and who had been imprisoned but had escaped and returned magically healed to take his rightful place on the throne of his father, was already

251

the subject of story and song, from the grand orations of the court bards down to the ribald songs of the soldiers; from the romantic dreams of young girls, to the prophetic tales of wise old women.

Liel watched these preparations with bitterness, but he was helpless to halt their progress, for Bladud had isolated him from his most loyal followers, and one by one his supporters had been dispersed into the remotest parts of the country, so that they could find no easy way to unite in a dangerous liaison against the new king. Bladud's popularity with the common people was now so high, and he so generous with his largesse, that it would be an unwise man who made any move against him.

Lear was summoned back to court in the company of his mother. Liel then, playing the role of husband who had been wronged but was magnanimous enough to forgive – forgiveness being the fashion under Bladud's example – even took her back into his house. Their mutual greeting was public and intentionally well witnessed. Tongues wagged. Whispers circulated, for it looked as though they were reconciled.

'Perhaps,' Yaruk murmured, 'having now been deprived of all his supporters, he feels that having Rheinid as an ally is better than no ally at all.'

Standing at his father's side, Prince Lear watched the coronation ceremony with sullen disinterest. It seemed to go on forever, with various dignitaries making long speeches. Queues of noblemen filed past, knelt down, laid their swords at Bladud's feet, and vowed to him undying love and eternal loyalty. With each he lifted the sword and handed it back to its owner, then the herald would announce what gifts the High King was bestowing on his vassal, listing in detail the gold, the horses, the cattle, the land. As each nobleman moved away, another took his place. Lear yawned loudly more than once, and Rheinid, excluded from the royal dais, standing to one side with other noble wives, gave him many a reproving glare.

After the endless formalities were about to liven up with feasting and drinking and singing and dancing, Rheinid tried to persuade Lear to leave and go to bed. He pouted and dug in his heels. To his surprise he was rescued by, of all people, his father!

'He will stay here with me,' Bladud said firmly. 'On this night of all nights I want my son beside me.'

'He is only a child,' she protested.

'He is my son,' Bladud replied.

She shrugged and turned her back on them and walked away. Hours later, when the novelty had worn off, and Lear was sick of the endless tearing of meats, the greasy hands and faces, the drunken shouting and out-of-tune singing, the lurching and falling and vomiting, he began to wonder if his small victory had been worth it. The whole thing had become almost as boring as the earlier rituals. Bladud tried to keep the wine away from him, but when he was not looking the boy sipped from whatever goblet he could reach until in the end he saw the night out asleep under the table.

The autumn came, then the winter, but there was no sign of Alcestis. Bladud began to fret. Every ship's captain was questioned on arrival, but there was still no news. The High King had sent off to Greece a party of six young nobles, seasoned warriors, and absolutely trustworthy, to escort her, but, as he knew only too well, the journey was long and dangerous and anything could happen. He now wished desperately that he had undertaken the journey himself, but if he had done so he would not have had a kingdom to come back to. He knew very well how the country would disintegrate into separate fragments if Liel was left in charge, many sub-kings preferring to break away from the centre rather than swear loyalty to a man they could not respect. Others, greedy for land, would take advantage of the shift in power to grab territory from their neighbours. No, King Hudibras had established stability with great effort over many years, and he had trusted Bladud to maintain it. No matter how he longed to return to Greece, Bladud knew where his responsibility now lay.

Rheinid watched, amused, as he became more and more morose, going often to the hilltop and the White Mound to gaze out over the river curving away towards the sea, waiting for his foreign princess to arrive. She knew how to take advantage of the situation, becoming gentler and sweeter by the day, causing no trouble, treating her slaves well where it showed, dressing in the most cunningly seductive clothes when she knew she would encounter him, accompanying Lear time and again when the boy was summoned to the presence of his father, appearing always as the conscientious and concerned mother training a prince for his future role as king.

For a long time Bladud resisted, well aware of her game, but one night when wind and storm howled outside the wooden city and Rheinid came to him with some pretence of anxiety about their son, and stood there beside the fire with the flame-light flickering on her skin, his old desire for her was so aroused that he succumbed, and they lay on the fur rugs before the hearth making love all night. Would Alcestis ever come? He doubted it now. But Rheinid was here, and though in many ways he distrusted her, still her touch could always make him forget everything else.

As the storm died eventually and the dawn light began to creep over the grey city, he lay propped on his elbow, running the tips of his fingers over her body. *Once more*, he thought. *Just once more*. Guilt was mixed with his desire – a potent and almost irresistible combination. *If Alcestis doesn't come* . . .

Rheinid, smiling, drew away from him. *Let that woman come*, she was thinking. *She will never take my place!*

He tried to hold her but she slipped from his grasp . . . drawing on her robe and floating out of the room and away into the darkness.

He lay a long time beside the cold embers, beginning to shiver as even the memory of her body heat deserted him.

'Fool!' he cried suddenly, leaping to his feet, unbelievably angry with himself. How could he expect to rule a whole kingdom if he could not even govern his own body! How could he hope to honour the trust placed in him, not only by his father, but by Beings beyond this mortal world . . .

Later that day he went once more to the White Mound. The wind had dropped and the rain had ceased, but everything lay wet and sodden. He recalled his dreams when

254

he had first returned: the building of a proper city with stone-paved streets and stone dwellings . . . A city planned and orderly. Not like this jumble, this mess, this *warren* that had grown up almost by accident . . . He stood on his hill and thought about what he would do. Whether Alcestis came or not, he must change this land – change it radically . . .

But Alcestis did come to Britain. She came in the spring with the birds and the blossom and the sunlight. Rheinid by this time was no longer in Trinovantum. The ruler of a goodly sized kingdom in the north had died without heir, and to save the squabbling that would inevitably have taken place among the lesser nobles to seize what they could, and to give his discontented brother some occupation sufficient to keep him out of mischief, Bladud had installed Liel as king there, with Rheinid as his queen. Lear remained at Trinovantum.

Since that one stormy night in the heart of winter, Bladud had avoided seeing Rheinid alone and in private. That had not been easy, for he had to do battle with his own desire for her as much as with her determination to win him back. It should have been a great relief when she left the city, yet he watched her go with painful regret. Messengers had already brought news that Alcestis was on her way, and he knew that it was too late now to change matters. He tried to remember what he had felt for her in those golden, carefree days in Greece, but that time seemed now as insubstantial as a dream. He tried to summon the vision of Imogene at the White Mound, as he had done in his youth, but he had not felt her presence there for a long while. Whenever he tried to conjure up in his mind an image of the beautiful swan lady, the dark-haired raven beauty of Rheinid intruded and pushed it aside. One night he dreamed of a contest between a swan and a raven, horrified by the shrill screams and shrieks and the savage violence of the two great birds fighting to the death. For at the end the swan lay dying, while the raven, croaking in triumph, winged its way up into the sky, drops of its blood falling on Bladud's upturned face. He woke shivering. Was this some prophetic dream, or just induced by his own anxious and confused feelings?

Lear stood beside him as the ship bearing the Greek

255

princess sailed into the harbour. The boy could see the white figure of a woman standing beside the helmsman. His father had already told him this was to be his new mother. He had received the news impassively; mothers seemed to come and go easily, and so did fathers. He was alternately fussed over or ignored by them: when he could win some attention for himself he did, but that never seemed to last. This new mother doubtless would be no different.

As she stepped ashore he could see admiration on every face. She was tall and very slender, taller than Rheinid. Her hair shone like gold, and was bound up on top of her head. Her white dress fell around her in loose and graceful folds, a cloak of white fur flung casually back from her shoulders. In spite of himself Lear was impressed. Bladud had been teaching him how to greet his 'new mother' in her own language, and he stepped forward now at a sharp nudge from his father, and spoke the alien words in his clear and piping voice. Everyone laughed and clapped as she, the vision of beauty, stooped and kissed his cheek and responded with something in her own language that he could not understand but which made him think of warm and wonderful things.

Bladud was stunned: all the old feelings came rushing back. The eeriness of her likeness to Imogene – her beauty so unlike that of the women of his own country, her elegance, her grace, her poise . . . He felt gauche and awkward as he stepped forward to mutter his own greeting. She met his eyes with a clear sea-green gaze. As he took her hands, he noticed that she wore the ring he had sent her with his messengers, tied round with a little golden cord to make it fit her slender finger. He did not trust himself to kiss her lips in front of all those staring, gaping people gathered close around. It was with some relief that he noticed the men standing behind her.

'Hermias!' he cried. 'And Diomede!' His old friends were here. Though Hermias was bent double with age and the strains of the long journey, his face lit up with pleasure to see his former companion again. Diomede, pomaded and ornamented in outrageously luxurious garments, gazed around with obvious distaste at so many unwashed 'barbarians'.

'My dear prince,' he said, 'we never thought we'd make it!

And now we are here, I'm not sure I'm glad of it.' Then he laughed and hugged his friend nevertheless.

Alcestis won the hearts of the people at once through her calm and assured beauty, and within a short time she set herself the task of learning their language. Even Lear started to behave better as she lavished on him the love she could not give a child of her own. For the first time in his life, he felt almost secure and happy. On hearing his complaint that he found Fergal too dry and strict a teacher, she persuaded Bladud to let him study with another, younger tutor.

Following Bladud's request, Hermias had chosen four scientist-philosophers to accompany him on the journey from Greece, and with them Bladud planned to set up the country's first academy in the Greek style. But first he ordered a stone temple dedicated to Apollo to be built on the outskirts of the city, not only to fulfil his own vow, but to make his wife feel more at home.

Stone-cutting was not a skill that came easily to the Celts. They had always been a people on the move, content with houses of timber and thatch, or makeshift shelters of reed. But Yaruk's kinsmen had race memories of the old days when huge stone monuments had been erected, and the idea of a stone temple appealed to them. They did not care to whom the temple was raised, for all gods were much the same to them, but several of the Celts began to murmur against the importance of alien gods and alien ways, so that on the day the temple was dedicated many prominent nobles boycotted the proceedings.

Bladud was not worried. He knew these new ways and new ideas would meet with opposition. He had promised Apollo to spread his influence to these northern lands, and he was happy he now had the opportunity.

After the temple was built, he started implementing his plan to improve Trinovantum itself. He spoke most eloquently in public to inform his people of his purpose, and many seemed to like his ideas. But once work started on clearing whole areas of shacks inhabited for generations in order to make way for wide, paved roads and more durable houses then the protests began.

Bladud found it easy to talk to Alcestis. Her ideas on ruling the kingdom were similar to his own, and, unlike Rheinid, she was receptive when he spoke about his encounters with beings of the Otherworld.

Her likeness to Imogene still haunted him, till one day, unable any longer to contain his curiosity, he suggested they visit the White Mound together secretly at dawn.

As they stood beside the ancient mound Bladud told her about all the strange things that had happened to him there. He showed her the exact place where he had removed the piece of crystal he had subsequently placed on the grave of his ancestress. He told her about the ring the raven had snatched from his finger, and how he had found it again so far away in Imogene's family tomb – the same ring he had sent with his messengers, the same ring she now wore on her finger. The stone was jet carved with a strange device: three spirals interlinked. He had never made the connection before, but suddenly he saw how it corresponded to the cipher carved on the boulder beneath the waterfall of Sul. His mother had left him this ring when she died. It was not beautiful; its only value for him, up to now, was that it had been hers. He had once learned from Hudibras that it had been given to the queen by her old nurse. Questioned further as to why a woman of the local tribes should possess a gold ring of such evident value, Hudibras had recalled some story that the nurse had inherited it from her grandparents, who in turn had found it in a stream somewhere in the West Country.

Bladud grew excited as the implications of the ring began to dawn on him.

'Take it off,' he urged. 'Perhaps it will help us now.'

He untied the golden thread with shaking hands, and withdrew the band of gold from her slender finger. He stared hard at the faint carving of the three interlinked spirals, and was amazed that he had owned it all this time and never really *noticed* it. He held the ring up high to study it more clearly, and the first rays of the rising sun caught the gold.

And then he began to have a strange sensation, as though he was poised in the centre of a Silence, in the centre of a spaceless Space, a timeless Time . . .

Imogene and the priest-king were now standing before them, holding hands just as he and Alcestis were holding hands, the priest-king holding up a ring identical to the one in Bladud's palm. Bladud had the eerie feeling he was looking at a mirror image of himself and Alcestis. The symbol of the three interlocking spirals seemed to project into the air before them, appearing huge and all-embracing. *The three worlds are separate yet linked*, Bladud thought, *the strength of each is available to each.*

As the two figures began to fade, Imogene reached out a hand towards Alcestis, and the princess stepped towards her. But before they could touch the spirit-image disappeared. Bladud turned to Alcestis. There were tears shining on her cheeks.

'Just before I left home my adoptive father told me that he was my real father – and that my real mother, his secret lover, came from the line of Pandrasus.'

Bladud stared at her. So Imogene *was* her ancestor after all. And he had been sent to Greece by Imogene to find the true and probably last remaining descendant of her line in her native land.

Bladud felt himself suddenly at the centre of a rich and complex pattern of relationships – within the body and out of the body – time and space having no relevance.

Finding the reaction to his rebuilding of Trinovantum more hostile than he expected, Bladud decided to proceed more slowly, more gradually, on that project. Instead he turned his attention to the building of the academy for the Greek philosophers Hermias had brought with him. He chose a site well to the north of Trinovantum where there was fertile soil and easy access by river. There he constructed a town of sturdy timber and stone, with a central building large enough to house his men of learning. It even had a colonnade in the Greek style, but this proved of little advantage here because of the difference in climate. For much of the year the driving rain and wind made the open walkway unusable. Even in the summer months the students would rather stroll and discuss in the warmth of the sun out among the trees than in the chilly shade. Seeing how this was, Bladud redesigned the building and ran the colonnade around the four sides of an internal courtyard, so that his students and their mentors were protected from the wind and the worst of the rain. These 'cloisters' were found ideal for quiet discussion and meditation. The courtyard itself was filled with light and richly planted with shrubs and trees, watered by fountains, so that the inspiration of nature was always at hand, while its most disturbing aspects were kept at bay.

The four Greek scholars had been learning the local language while these buildings were constructed, and were eager to start their work of instruction among the barbarians. But Bladud had the sense to see that what was right for the Greeks might not immediately be right for his own very different people. So he persuaded Fergal and some other Druids to come and work alongside the Greeks in the academy.

Yaruk the woodcarver, being very much involved in the decoration of the building, was able to report back many incidents that might have been amusing if they were not so disappointing for Bladud. The two groups of wise men clearly did not take to each other. Their methods of expanding the minds of their students were totally opposed. The Greeks aimed to clarify everything – to leave no mystery. Everything must be examined, analysed, measured, categorised . . . Their method was principally question and answer, the students constantly prodded to provide rational answers, their answers in turn questioned, until they either broke down and withdrew them, or managed to uphold them under the gimlet scrutiny of their masters.

The Druids, on the other hand, taught by means of a series of stories and metaphors: leading the students through a labyrinth of ancient myths and legends that were complex, mysterious, enigmatic, ambiguous, paradoxical. As the layer upon layer of rich, imaginative material built up in the students' minds, they reached a state of consciousness where suddenly the stories came alive and were experienced in such vivid form that a burst of illumination helped them to understand things never understood before.

As Yaruk observed, the Greeks seemed to approach knowledge directly, while the Druids approached it obliquely.

Yet both methods seemed effective for different types of knowledge.

'Both have value,' Bladud mused. 'And the one without the other is perhaps not enough.' He was pleased then that he had thought to put them both together, believing that this combination might give his people great benefit.

But he had reckoned without the imperfections of human nature. The welfare of the students was soon forgotten as these two schools of thought battled it out between themselves, each despising the other and convinced that their own way was the only way.

It came to something of a climax one day after the Greeks challenged the Druids to a demonstration of their skills. The Druids accepted and the stage was set. Bladud and Alcestis were invited to witness and judge the encounter. The students gathered eagerly, arguing among themselves.

Both Greek and Druid prepared to calculate the precise moment of a lunar eclipse which both agreed was imminent, the Greeks using mathematics, while the Druids drew on their ancient lore, in which millennia of observation of the heavens were incorporated into a calendar of festivals and rituals, each marked in legend by tales of dramatic change, eerie appearance of figures from other worlds, prophecies and premonitions . . .

On the night when both sides believed the eclipse was due – the Greeks before midnight, the Druids just before dawn – all gathered in an open meadow and prepared to wait. The moon was full and silver-white, in appearance no different from many another night. Bladud and Alcestis, warmly clad in fur, sat on comfortable chairs with a few distinguished guests. The students lolled about or sat cross-legged on the grass. Their teachers huddled in two separate groups, refusing to fraternise.

Time passed and nothing happened. More time elapsed while water clocks marked and measured its passing.

At last came the exact moment the Greeks had calculated. As a shadow began to cross the silver face, a cheer went up from their supporters.

Gradually the silver changed colour, and, like a great bronze ball, the moon rolled silently across the sky. Its light dimmed, a myriad stars appeared that had been outshone and invisible moments before. Bladud gazed upwards in awe at the magnificent beauty of it: the spectacular, wonderful drama of light and dark, good and evil, known and unknown. He felt clearly the presence of gigantic forces shaping the world and the worlds beyond. He was afraid . . . He was elated . . . He was exhilarated . . .

When it was all over he had to confess himself impressed by the Greeks' predictive mathematics, but maintained that as he was experiencing the eclipse, it was the ancient myths and legends that had made the event for him such a powerful and wonderful experience. 'Science can give us the literal bones of knowledge,' he declared 'but the living flesh of it comes with imagination, metaphor and symbol. That the earth's shadow will cover the moon at certain predictable times is important to know. But that, when it does so, it opens up our minds to visions and experiences beyond the rational and ordinary is equally important! The one type of knowledge without the other is not enough. So I declare there is no winner and no loser in this contest. You have shown me the importance of balance, and I want you to respect each other. Each student should spend equal time with the Greek and the Celtic knowledge. Each student should learn myth and music and poetry, as well as mathematics and the art of reasoning.'

And then he declared three days' holiday to celebrate before classes recommenced, which brought a mighty cheer from the students.

He and Alcestis walked away from the field hand in hand. Their own union worked so well that he did not see why others should not find similar felicity in the interplay of differing cultures.

18

Baddon

Bladud's next big project was to build the temple, and a healing sanctuary dedicated to Sul, in the West Country. All this he supervised himself. First he established a town on a flat-topped hill overlooking the winding river, the very place where he had passed the night before his first encounter with the oracle – that night of potent and significant visions, and a magnificent experience of stars. It was necessary to flatten the hilltop further, using earth and rock removed from the summit to build up ramparts around the circumference.

This town became known as Baddon.

In the valley below he then drained the marshes, and started to build the healing sanctuary around the outflow of hot waters. Even before its completion people came flocking to it, crowding into the valley, filling with noise and confusion a place that had once been a peaceful haven suitable for silent communion with the goddess.

Before he allowed the work to begin Bladud had tried to warn the oracle of his intentions. But he had found her hut deserted, and there was no trace of her nearby.

Then one day she suddenly appeared – but not as he remembered her. The crowds buzzing around the waters looked up startled, to see a huge apparition hovering above them. It was the gigantic but almost transparent form of an ancient, wizened crone – white hair floating out like fine spider web around her, her eyes burning with rage. Behind her loomed the shadowy form of a wolf with fangs bared.

Suddenly the apparition raised her arms on either side of

her like the wings of a huge hunting-owl. People ducked instinctively as she flew low above them, casting a deep chill on their hearts.

'Goddess Sul!' Bladud cried aloud, 'if I have offended you by raising buildings in your forest and diverting your waters from their natural course – only tell me and I will withdraw.'

The wolf leaped – and Bladud stood still, awaiting his fate.

But just before the fearsome yellow teeth sunk into his flesh, the creature disintegrated into dust which fell slowly, silently through the air, caught in the beams of sunlight.

'Goddess,' the High King said in a clear and steady voice, 'in this sanctuary my people will benefit from your grace. I vow the temple here will be used to your perpetual honour.'

It was later the same day that Yaruk found the discarded body of the oracle while walking through the forest. It was nothing more than skin and bone and old rags, but the smell of death was still strong. So this was the great and fearsome Oracle of Sul he had wanted – yet not wanted – to see all his life? As a child he had listened with shining eyes to stories of her wise sayings. He had shivered and shuddered at tales of her anger. He had imagined her to be immortal. Was she already dead when that dreadful vision had appeared to them?

He looked over his shoulder. He had the feeling a thousand eyes were watching him – the tiny eyes of insects, the bead-black eyes of birds, the quick and darting eyes of deer and squirrels, badgers and weasels . . . Even the trees were watching him . . . He wondered if a new oracle had already been chosen. She was so ancient, it seemed she had always been there, and that she always would be.

With the countless eyes still on him, Yaruk stood up and retraced his steps towards the new sanctuary. Behind him the forest, which had been so silent while he contemplated the death of the oracle, burst into noisy life. Birds sang, insects creaked and whistled and buzzed, leaves rustled, twigs cracked . . .

Bladud followed him back at once. He stood looking down at her thoughtfully. Nature was already moving in to devour the corpse. He and Yaruk gathered wood and they built a funeral pyre on the flat rock beside her hut. On this same stone she had many times built her own fires, to stare into the flames, communing with the spirits.

They carried the desiccated body and laid it on the piled wood. They lit the kindling and then watched reverently as the flames licked around the pathetic shell of what had once been a strong and formidable being.

They began to pray for her soul, for her spirit, for her safety on the journey that has no end . . .

The blaze flared up, the smoke plumed thickly, billowing out to engulf all around it. Bladud and Yaruk stepped back, choking. As a spark caught on the thatch, the oracle's hut roared up in flames until nothing was left but charred wood and bone – and the sacred crevice still steaming from water at the centre of the earth. Tiny fragments of ash mounted high above the forest, then slowly settled on branches and leaves and earth.

Appearing suddenly, as though from nowhere, came a young girl. She wore a fresh green dress held in at the waist by a long trailing strand of ivy. Her red-gold hair, hanging almost to her knees, was bound around her forehead with a circlet of flowers, slightly tilted to one side at a rakish angle.

'So this is the place?' she said cheerfully.

Yaruk and Bladud stared dumbly.

She ignored them and wandered about, as though sizing things up.

'You'll have to build a new hut,' she said at last. 'I think I'll have it here.' She pointed.

Then she picked up an earthenware bowl that was lying unbroken on the ground, and stared closely at three interlinking spirals carved on its surface.

'This will be my scrying bowl,' she said at last, holding it up for them to see.

Bladud stepped forward to greet her. It was indeed the tradition that the land must never be without an oracle: so as one died, another must take her place. This was Sul's place, and this girl must be Sul's choice.

About this time Alcestis was journeying from Trinovantum

to see how Bladud's dream was progressing. After she had admired the town rapidly taking shape on the hill, and the small complex of buildings grouped around the healing waters, Bladud suggested they leave the crowds behind and go off, just the two of them, to ride into the country beyond.

'You know nothing of the West Country,' he explained. 'Yet it is one of the most beautiful regions of my kingdom.'

And so they set off to explore – not as king and queen would, but as a young couple eager to be alone together.

As they climbed a ridge of hills to the south-west, they came upon a round knoll standing out above the rest. Its summit was bare apart from a single stone monolith.

Bladud and Alcestis left their horses at the bottom of the knoll and climbed the rest on foot. From the top they could see the whole land spread out to every distant horizon – hills and valleys, forests and fields, villages and wild places – and a distant gleam of the sea with the hint of hills even beyond that fading into blue mist . . . And on other ridges they now saw similar small round hills – the sacred places of the goddess Sul.

A breeze tossed Alcestis's golden hair about, and Bladud put his arm around her shoulders.

'This is not Greece, my love,' he said, 'yet my country has its own beauty.'

She smiled and nodded, nestling against him as she gazed around at a gentler landscape than any she had been accustomed to in her own land. This day, in this place, she felt no homesickness. She was content.

And then Bladud put out his hand to touch the standing stone. 'Yaruk's people claim that these stones mark the entrances to Other Worlds,' he said dreamily.

Alcestis felt suddenly alarmed. 'Don't!' she cried, trying to draw his hand away.

But she was already too late. Though he still stood beside her, the arm draped around her shoulders was now as heavy as that of a dead man. And when she peered into his face she saw that he was gazing into the far distance – a distance beyond any she could see.

Bladud found himself walking down an avenue of standing stones, towards that huge stone circle he had visited once before. The two young women were there again, waiting for him and smiling. This time they did not offer him anything to drink, but each took him by one hand and pulled him forward. He found himself watching a vast circle dance: the throbbing of a drum marked the rhythm, echoing his heartbeat. Three lines of dancers spiralled to the centre, then outwards again. Three snaking lines came together and then parted. Three columns of people passed through each other like smoke.

At first he was delighted to witness such a beautiful scene. But as the pace became faster, the drums louder, the women on either side of him began to urge him to join the dance, their pressure on his arms increasing until he could scarcely withstand it. Though he exerted all his strength to resist, he could not break free.

I am dead weight being pulled asunder by two opposite forces, he thought. He remembered the three interlinked spirals on Sul's rock. If one were removed, the power of the whole would be lost. By his resistance, he realised, he was destroying the balance of the triple spiral. If he worked with these two forces, instead of against them, much could be achieved. He believed the number three had a kind of magical significance. Again and again and yet again different groups of three came to mind: sun, moon, earth . . . father, mother, child . . . past, present, future . . . beginning, middle, end . . . birth, life, death . . . body, soul, spirit . . . idea, word, understanding . . .

He found he was no longer resisting the pressure from the two women, but had joined with them willingly in the mighty cosmic dance. Then suddenly he was aware again of Alcestis on the windy hilltop.

She felt his return by a lightening of the burden of his arm across her shoulders. She turned to smile into his eyes.

'I love you,' she said simply.

Ah – to hear those words and to know that they are true!

After this experience they did not ride back to Baddon, but on, further, to the south-west. When the sun began to set they had gone too far to return home, so chose to stay overnight with an old man who lived in an isolated cabin beside a stream. He must have been surprised that two such elegant people should thus come to his humble home, but kept his counsel and asked no questions.

All afternoon the clouds had been gathering and now, with nightfall, heavy rain set in.

Alcestis curled up in the old man's bed, but Bladud and his host sat by the hearth fire talking deep into the night.

After a while Bladud noticed how the fire never seemed to die down, yet the old man never seemed to put on new logs. In fact he could see no logs at all in the place, only a pile of strange black stones in the corner. He peered more closely into the flames.

'Are you burning *stone*?' he asked incredulously.

The old man smiled and nodded.

'Stone?' Bladud repeated.

'Yes. But not just any stone.' He stood up and fetched a piece of the stuff for Bladud to examine. It was shining black, but not too hard. Bladud easily broke a fragment off.

'This burns?'

'Yes,' the man said. 'And it burns for much longer than wood.'

'Where did you find it?'

'There is a lot of it around here,' he replied. 'I can show you in the morning.'

Bladud felt tremendously excited. He had planned that there would be a fire burning always in his Temple of Sul – as a symbol of her connection with the sun. What if he had now found a stone that could burn forever?

In the morning, at first light, even before Alcestis awoke, Bladud insisted on being shown the source of the black stones.

And so it was that Sul had everlasting fire. And Bladud's reputation as a necromancer grew.

19

The Raven and the Swan

When Bladud and Alcestis returned to Trinovantum they found Rheinid there. The meeting of these two women in Bladud's life could not be postponed any longer.

Alcestis was with some other women, wives of Bladud's close companions, when the conversation that had been bubbling along in such a lively fashion suddenly came to a stop, and an air of nervous anticipation entered the room. She turned to see who had caused such an effect and came face to face with Rheinid for the first time. But for the expressions on the faces of the others she might not have guessed who this woman was, for she had understood that Rheinid was far away.

Rheinid was the sort of woman who, on entering a room, inevitably caused a stir. It was as though the very air became vibrant in her presence. She strode forward now as though at the head of an entourage, though, in fact, she was alone. She was dressed in rich purples, black and gold, while by contrast the High Queen seemed pale and almost insignificant in a simple gown of primrose yellow and ivory white.

'I come looking for Queen Alcestis,' Rheinid announced imperiously, staring straight past the queen to one of the other women. There was no one present but knew this was intended as a deliberate insult, for Rheinid must have realised that the tall, golden-haired stranger was Bladud's wife.

The woman she addressed was put in an awkward position. Should she point towards the queen? Should she introduce them formally?

Rheinid surveyed the group haughtily. She could not miss that everyone else was now looking at the fair stranger – waiting for her reaction.

Alcestis stepped forward with dignity. 'I am the queen,' she said quietly. 'And who are you?'

The women sucked in their breath. This was going to prove interesting.

Rheinid did not immediately reply, but stared with black, blazing eyes into the cool blue-green of her rival's. Her lips tightened slightly. So the lady was not to be so easily outfaced?

'I am the mother of Prince Lear,' she said at last, 'who is heir to the High King.'

'Welcome to our court, Queen Rheinid,' Alcestis said graciously. 'Have you seen the prince?'

'Not yet. I believe he is off on some hunting expedition, though I sent word that I was coming.'

'My husband and I have ourselves only just returned to Trinovantum. Prince Lear will be recalled at once, of course. Will you be staying long with us?'

Rheinid flushed. By now she had the impression that Alcestis was altogether untroubled by her presence, while she herself was rapidly becoming flustered and angry. And she sensed that the women watching this confrontation were siding with the imposter, waiting for Rheinid to be humiliated.

'I will stay as long as my son wishes,' she replied, keeping control with difficulty.

'I will have guest quarters made ready for you.'

'I have my own quarters,' Rheinid said haughtily, 'and I have already ordered them to be prepared.'

'Then, if you will excuse me, I have other matters that I must attend to. My friends here will see that you are comfortable. Will you join us for dinner this evening?'

Rheinid glared. How could this woman who looked so mild and spoke so fair make her feel so *reduced*?

She bowed with mock exaggeration as Alcestis glided regally out of the room.

Having carefully avoided her since his return, the first time

270

Bladud encountered Rheinid was that night in the great hall. As all gathered for the evening banquet, a certain undercurrent of anticipation was running through the guests. Word was quickly spread and all were on tenterhooks to see how these three would conduct themselves.

Rheinid did not have many friends left at court, since most had accompanied her to her northern kingdom. But there were few there that night who did not remember her, or the events leading up to her marriage and her divorce. Alcestis had quickly won all hearts, and Rheinid had antagonised many, but it had to be admitted a certain spark had gone from court life since Rheinid and Liel had departed. There was less to cause shock, to gossip about, to fear or avoid.

That night Rheinid was so late in arriving that many feared the show they were awaiting would not now happen. But she came at last, sweeping into the hall at just the moment when anticipation was on the point of becoming painful.

She looked magnificent in crimson, her hair brushed out like a cape and falling from a tall and shining crown of gold and precious stones. Without intending to honour her, they all rose to their feet. The movement started with those sitting at the back who could not see her properly; and it spread like wind through corn until only those at the high table remained seated.

Bladud leant back in his chair, one of his elbows on its arm, his chin resting in his hand. He noticed her the moment she came through the door and his eyes did not leave her as she walked triumphantly around the hall greeting everyone as though they were old and dear friends. He made no effort to straighten up from his relaxed pose, though Alcestis beside him could feel the agitation he was so carefully concealing. Diomede, on his other side, could not hold back an exclamation of admiration.

'What a beauty! What a woman!' For the first time since arriving in this barbarian land, he now saw a woman to rival those of Greece – indeed, she outshone any woman he had ever seen. As he watched the fire and force of her, the grace and power, it crossed his mind that Bladud must be crazy to have given her up.

271

Alcestis also watched her progress quietly.

Reaching her place at last, Rheinid stood before the king, her eyes sparkling with exhilaration at the reception she had just enjoyed. Alcestis noted her full red lips, her golden skin, her fine eyebrows and neat nose. She noted the splendid jewellery, every piece of which Bladud must have given her. For the first time since leaving Greece Alcestis felt insecure in the love of her husband. The dark and sensual power of this woman, the way she was gazing down at Bladud, brought images crowding to the mind of Alcestis that she wished she could dismiss. Try as she would, she could not banish the thought of how this man and this woman had formerly made love together, and it was clear that there remained the memory of that in both their hearts.

It was Diomede who at last broke the tension.

'My lord,' he said cheerfully. 'This lady and I have not yet met . . .'

'Ah, but, Diomede,' she said quietly before Bladud could reply, 'I know well who you are.' She turned her shining gaze on the handsome Greek. 'Your reputation is spoken of even in my poor and distant country.' Her deprecation was ironic, for the kingdom Liel ruled was by no means poor, but one of the largest and richest of all the sub-kingdoms.

Diomede laughed. 'What reputation, my lady? I protest I *have* no reputation in this . . .' He paused just in time, before he insulted his host. 'In this country.'

'You are too modest. A handsome foreigner? The ladies are all aflutter!'

'And you, my lady? Do you find me as you expected, or are you disappointed?'

As Diomede continued to flirt outrageously, Alcestis could have hugged her countryman for helping them through this difficult encounter, though a twinge of jealousy accompanied her relief. Was there *no* man who would not fall at her rival's feet?

'Ah,' Rheinid said lightly laughing, 'if I told you that, you would become insufferable.'

Bladud had now straightened up. He turned to Alcestis and suggested she give the signal for the feast to begin. As Alcestis was about to raise her hand to catch the eye of the overseer, Rheinid beat her to it by calling out in a loud and commanding voice, as though she were still the mistress of the house.

'Why are we waiting, Janu? Bring on the food. And what of the music? Where is the music?'

Alcestis flushed and Bladud frowned, but Janu, flustered and flattered that the former queen should remember his name, gave a signal for the servants to bring in the platters, and for the musicians to start their playing.

'My lord,' Rheinid said at last now speaking directly to Bladud, though everything said so far had been intended for his ears, 'your queen is pale. Does our climate not agree with her?'

Bladud was angry, as Rheinid well knew he would be. Her audience, watching every movement, listening to every word, waited for the storm to break.

'Lady, ask the queen herself. Only she is able to answer your question.'

'My husband's climate suits me well,' Alcestis said coolly, laying her hand on his arm, with no sign that she was discomforted. 'My husband's country suits me well. My husband's people suit me well. Indeed I am most happy here.'

A discreet but enthusiastic cheer went up in the hall. The queen had scored.

'You are lucky then,' Rheinid said. 'The climate in the north is too cold for me. I miss the milder winters here.'

'You speak of mild winters!' Diomede interrupted. 'To me this mildness you mention is an intolerable chill. I cannot endure it, and before another winter comes I will be on my way home – back to the sun.'

'And yet your countrywoman says our winters suit her?'

'She has more than I to keep her warm, lady,' Diomede replied.

Alcestis smiled. 'This is my home now,' she intervened. 'And I will never leave it no matter how inclement the weather.'

In truth she had more than once longed to return to her own country, but seeing now how eager Rheinid was to retrieve her lost love, Alcestis was equally determined not to leave the way clear for her. *But if*, she thought, *Bladud shows any sign of going back to Rheinid – any sign at all! – I will accompany Diomede back to Greece.*

And so the evening wore on, with animosity, sometimes veiled and sometimes not, between the two queens, and elaborate but light-hearted flirting between Rheinid and Diomede. Bladud said very little, and so studiously avoided gazing too long at his former wife that Alcestis wondered if this very evasion indicated that he could not trust his feelings for her.

That night the love-making of Bladud and Alcestis seemed less satisfactory than usual. They did not speak of Rheinid, or the incidents of the evening, but her presence intruded nevertheless. At last they gave up and turned away from each other, both lying awake long into the night, separate and sad.

The next day Prince Lear returned to court, which provided something else for observers to watch. Entering a room where both his mother and Alcestis were present, he walked straight up to his stepmother and hugged her affectionately, before turning to his own mother with a polite but distant greeting. It was at this moment that some of the shrewder among those watching Rheinid's expression began to fear for the life of the High Queen.

Lear had grown considerably since Rheinid had last seen him, and not only in height. He was an athletic youngster, tough and well developed, and a passionate hunter. He was good to look at, but not to know, being morose and moody and changeable so that what friends he had, and they were few and often very temporary, never knew quite where they stood with him. If his father or anyone tried to guide him in one direction, it was certain he would take the other. Strangely the only one with a calming influence on him was Alcestis. For some reason he trusted her.

No one would have blamed her if she had found him too much of a handful and sent him back to his mother, but she seemed to take pleasure in his company and often the two could be seen walking and talking together, even laughing, which was rare for him.

'Mother,' he said now, looking at Rheinid. 'What brings you here?'

'You, my son.'

'I, mother?' he said mockingly. 'After all this time?'

Rheinid bit her lip. Her instinct was to slap his face, but she was being well watched, and besides he was too big now to slap. He was tall enough to stand on a level with Alcestis's shoulder.

'It was through no wish of mine that I stayed away,' she said.

'Nor invited me to visit your kingdom?'

'Your father wanted you here, my son. If you want to take issue on the subject, speak to the king about it.'

He shrugged. 'The king is rarely here himself. He would not have missed me.'

'The prince has much to learn as heir to such a great kingdom,' Alcestis said quickly. 'His tutors could not spare him. But I'm sure a visit can be arranged soon, if it is your wish.'

Rheinid's eyes seemed to snap. How dare her rival throw her crumbs from her rich table?

After a few weeks of Rheinid's constant nagging to be allowed to take Lear home with her, Bladud finally agreed that his son could visit his mother's kingdom.

'For a year, but no more,' he said. 'A year from this day you must return.'

Lear scowled. 'And if I don't want to go at all?'

'You'll go,' Bladud said sharply. He was finding Rheinid's continual presence a strain, never knowing what she might do or say next. If he let her have Lear, perhaps she would depart at once.

'Your tutors will go with you,' he added, 'for your studies must not be interrupted.'

'You think you have hunted here!' Rheinid said to Lear, seeing his reluctance. 'You have never seen forests as thick or mountains as high as are found in my country. The beasts are bigger and fiercer than any you have yet encountered. But perhaps you are still too young . . .'

275

Lear, of course, took her bait at once. 'I can hunt as well as any man, mother. As you will see!'

And so it was arranged, and she got her wish. Rheinid made preparations to leave immediately, anxious to get away before Bladud could change his mind. Lear grew excited at the thought of the journey ahead and a new land to explore, and for a time seemed almost happy. He had no illusions about his mother and father: as usual he was but a gaming piece between them. But to test out his hunting skills in that mountainous land would provide a real challenge.

20

'Scar-face'

The house for the new oracle rose more slowly than it should, partly because Yaruk took such care, and partly because the young girl was not satisfied with a simple wooden hut such as her predecessor had used.

His interest in her was becoming intense, but she would not tell him her name, or anything else about herself. Guess and probe as he might, he could elicit nothing.

'An oracle cannot be known by name like any other woman,' she said. 'If the people are given a name, they will have no respect for the office of the oracle. And if they know her family origin, they would not hesitate to question her pronouncements.'

'So the oracle is just an ordinary woman, like anyone else, who is pretending to be something she is not?'

'No, Yaruk,' she replied. 'An oracle is an ordinary woman, yes, but one who becomes extraordinary by reason of her office.'

'And how is it decided *which* ordinary woman shall become extraordinary?'

She smiled enigmatically, but did not reply. Then she changed the subject by drawing his attention to the pile of reeds that still waited to be lashed to her roof.

Later, when the work of the day was finished, and the two sat eating an evening meal, Yaruk asked if she could tell him about *his* future.

She stared at him thoughtfully for a long time. Did he imagine a shadow of sadness cross her face?

'An oracle cannot be expected to satisfy idle curiosity,' she said at last.

'Do you avoid answering because you see something evil in my future, or because you just don't know?'

'When you question me, sincerely believing me to be a true oracle, then I will answer. But that time has not yet arrived,' she replied quietly.

For a time there was a silence between them, Yaruk alarmed by her sudden seriousness. What *had* she seen in his future?

The next evening, after the day's work, they again sat together beside her hearth fire. Laughing over certain incidents of the day, he felt bold enough to put his arm around her. She drew back at once.

But later, when they rose to make their separate ways to bed, he held her in his arms and kissed her. At first she leant into the kiss, and he could feel her longing was equal to his own for her. But within seconds, she pulled away from him.

'No. Yaruk, no!' she cried. 'This cannot be! You *know* it cannot be!'

'Why not?' he groaned. 'It is not too late!' Though he knew an oracle must be a virgin, surely this young woman was not yet fully committed? Surely she had not yet made her final vows to Sul?

'It *is* too late. You must leave. *Now!* This moment.' She pushed him roughly away.

He stood – trembling – breathing hard.

'You love me, lady, as I love you. Why would the goddess of this place have put us together, if our love was not meant to be?'

'She arranges many things – but it is not for us to know her motives.'

'Would her motives be simply to torment us? To destroy us?'

'Perhaps simply to test us.'

'Why?'

'To see if we are ready for higher things.'

Yaruk's face grew dark with anger. 'She plays with us!' he said bitterly.

The young girl looked alarmed. 'Not "play", Yaruk. She does not play with us.'

'If I move a piece on a gaming board to challenge another, is that not "playing"?'

'The game may seem an analogy, but an analogy is not reality.'

'You play with words as she plays with us. I have no patience with games. Life is too short.'

'Short indeed,' the young oracle said sadly, her eyes filling with tears.

He turned and strode away from her, frightened, angry, frustrated. That night he lay rolled up in his blanket under the shelter of the small reed lean-to he had made for himself, but could not sleep.

It must have been nearly dawn when he noticed a shadowy figure standing beside him, looking down, faint light outlining her shape. When he reached up, she came in to his arms. Now there was no hesitation, no drawing back, no ambiguity about her feelings. They made love there on the soft bed of forest leaves, as though there was no tomorrow. Yaruk had never known such love-making, though he was no virgin. Time and again his body rose to her – unbelievably. It was as though he was fed from that ancient cauldron of regeneration he had heard about in bardic tales, and he felt no weariness . . .

At last they drew apart, and he, turning on his side, looked away from her. There, in an early ray of sunlight, he saw her standing in the forest, watching him, a gentle-eyed deer close against her side, her hand resting on its head.

Startled, he turned to look at the woman lying beside him.

As he stared, she began to fade, as though she was made of river mist . . .

'No!' he shouted, leaping, naked, to his feet. 'Yet another game!'

He rushed across to the woman standing with the deer. Seizing her shoulders, he shook her violently.

'Yaruk! Yaruk!' she cried. 'Let me go! Why are you doing this?'

'I have made love to you! We made love! Deny it if you can!'

'You must have dreamed it.'

'That was no dream. It was real!'

He had released her now, but he was still confronting her with anger.

'Real?' she said quietly – and then looked over his shoulder.

He turned quickly – following her gaze. There was an image of her, beautiful as sunlight, walking away into the forest, a young deer at her side. And yet here she was still in front of him!

He stared from one figure to the other and could not tell which one was real and which one was not.

'I will not stay to serve you, Sul,' he shouted, his voice full of pain. 'I will not play your cruel games!' And then to the girl beside him he said: 'Lady, I have given all my love to you, but shadows and dreams are not enough!'

With this he walked away, collected his belongings, and left the forest clearing without a backward glance. What if she was still standing there? He did not turn. *Let her long for me as I long for her*, he thought. *Let her find it impossible to serve her mistress.*

When Yaruk arrived back at Trinovantum, Bladud questioned him about the new oracle. Yaruk was noncommittal. It was only after persistence that Bladud managed to learn what had happened.

'That pleases me,' he said, 'though I am sorry for you, my friend. It means this girl has the makings of a true oracle, and that Alun has found a safe haven.' For he could not doubt this was the same deer whose life he had saved, and who had subsequently saved his own life.

At the end of the year Lear did not return. When questioned by messengers, Rheinid claimed the boy was happy with her, and did not want to leave her court.

'I will leave him there a while longer, then we will go and fetch him back,' the king told Alcestis.

The queen dreaded visiting Rheinid in her lair, but she agreed Lear should be with his father, and to achieve this, she would suffer whatever was necessary.

So another winter passed . . .

The academy had settled down at last, and the students were beginning to benefit from its unusual combination of Greek and Celtic teaching. Fergal was enjoying himself so much he showed no inclination to return to court.

Yaruk stayed in Trinovantum, undertaking carving commissions and training young apprentices in his craft. Bladud could not help worrying about him, for the spirit seemed to have gone out of him, and it was clear his work was deteriorating.

There were reports from the West Country that Baddon was flourishing and merchants were making a good living out of the many pilgrims who came to Sul's sacred complex to plunge into the hot, healing waters.

In the latter part of spring Bladud announced to his court that he was going north, Alcestis to accompany him on the journey with many companions and servants.

The column of horses and heavily laden carts made good progress on the roads that had been improved on Bladud's orders, and as they at last approached the mountainous region where Liel had his stronghold, messengers rode ahead from Bladud's column, and were met by heralds riding out to greet them.

Alcestis might have enjoyed the long journey through all the different regions of her husband's land, amid trees light and silken green and clouds of blossom and butterflies, had it not been for the feeling of foreboding that troubled her. Since this visit had been first mooted she had felt uneasy, hating the thought of meeting Rheinid again – and this time on the woman's own territory. But if she did not accompany Bladud, she would leave him exposed to Rheinid's wiles on his own.

'Hudibras had made sure to visit every one of his sub-kingdoms as frequently as possible,' Bladud explained before they set out. 'That was how he kept such control. His vassals knew that he was not relying only on his network of spies and messengers to keep him informed. He knew precisely what was going on in their lands. I have left Liel alone too long, and that is dangerous.'

281

'Promise me, then, that we will take a well armed body of men with us, led by a man with the intelligence to watch for signs of trouble and act before it is too late.'

To this he agreed readily.

Alcestis would have liked to extract another promise from her husband, but had the sense not to press it.

If the Greek princess had originally thought the southern countries 'uncivilised', she was astonished at the barbaric splendour of Liel's court. And beyond Liel's northern boundaries lay other lands, that had never fallen under the sway of the Trojan dynasty or any Celtic overlord, peopled by savage and hostile tribes. From time to time their raiding parties came whooping down from the mountains to pillage and terrorise these borderlands. There was a continual sense of imminent conflict about Liel's court.

Liel's kingdom contained a higher proportion of Yaruk's native people than was found in the south, and Liel had not been slow to exploit them. His palace was a huge and magnificent construction, his every whim catered for by a host of slaves. Bladud was instantly reminded of Keron, Rheinid's father, who had also lived in great luxury while his people were miserable and poor. Alcestis was quick to notice too and all the more appreciated what her husband had done for his own people in the south. He might not think he had improved their lot as much as he would wish, but their lives were infinitely better than those of the people she saw around her now.

Diomede had not after all returned to Greece when the winter came, but lingered on, complaining, and swearing that he would be on his way at the very next opportunity. He too had accompanied them on this journey, no doubt with a view to seeing the beautiful Rheinid again. He had never ceased to sing her praises, even to Alcestis, and the queen had a shrewd idea that Rheinid had favoured him with a night of sensual pleasure during her last visit to Trinovantum. Diomede certainly hinted as much, and Alcestis noted with sorrow how badly her husband reacted to these hints, and how strained his friendship with Diomede was becoming.

As they were ushered into the great hall, Diomede

whispered to Bladud: 'Everything here seems so much bigger and better than yours at Trinovantum. Look at that throne! You would think he was High King and you the vassal.'

Liel indeed was surrounded by all the trappings and panoply of a High King, and he even remained seated on his throne, with Rheinid beside him in equal magnificence, watching the slow and dignified approach of his brother without rising.

At last Liel and Rheinid rose and stepped down to greet their guests. Liel gave only a short, peremptory bow, while Rheinid made a mockery of the whole event by bowing to the ground and staying there until Bladud himself stooped down to lift her up.

So it begins already! Alcestis thought. But she calmly and graciously ignored the obeisance and, while the northern queen was down, she stepped up and seated herself on the empty throne.

After a moment's hesitation, Liel offered his throne to Bladud. It was the custom, after all, that the visiting High King should take precedence in everything over the local monarch. Before he took his place Bladud embraced his brother. Liel responded without warmth.

There was a disturbance at the entrance as the young Prince Lear came bustling in. He still wore his hunting clothes, somewhat mud-bespattered, and was complaining loudly that he had not been informed of the arrival. The face of Alcestis lit up when she saw him, and it was to her he went first, kneeling at her feet and kissing her hand with affection. He had grown taller since they had last seen him, and his body looked leaner and harder from the vigorous life he had enjoyed in Liel's mountain kingdom. Indeed he seemed healthier and happier than ever before.

'Are you not going to greet your father, Lear?' Rheinid asked sharply but with a certain amount of satisfaction.

Lear turned to his father. There was a similarity in their looks, though Lear had inherited his mother's dark hair and eyes, even the same arrogant lift to his chin. The youth looked at the man, and the man looked at the youth, and they both were silent, as if sizing each other up.

'The agreement was for just one year, Lear,' Bladud said at

last. 'What have you been doing that was so absorbing that you lost track of time?'

'There is a mountain bear, sir, greater than any other, and so fierce it has become a legend. I have sworn to bring it down, and I cannot leave until I do.'

Bladud turned to Liel. Knowing that Lear was his only son, was it possible that Liel had deliberately encouraged Lear to take such dangerous risks? If Lear were killed, Liel himself might well become the next High King on Bladud's death.

'We miss you, Lear,' Alcestis intervened softly. 'Will you not return with us, and let the poor beast keep his mountain kingdom?'

'You don't understand,' Lear said passionately. 'He has killed men, and he has defied every hunter in the land. It is a matter of honour . . .'

'You are becoming a stranger to our people,' Bladud said. 'They might not welcome you as High King when it is your time.'

'That time is long off, father,' Lear said. 'There will be many years for your people to grow sick of my face!'

'The boy is obsessed,' Rheinid said. 'No one will ever get any sense out of him until he has slain the creature.'

'I am surprised, Rheinid,' said Alcestis, 'that you encourage your son in this dangerous pursuit.'

'I don't encourage him, but . . .'

'But he has to prove he is a man, if he wants to rule a kingdom as vast as . . . yours.' Liel paused momentarily before the last word, as though he would like to have said 'mine'.

'There are many better ways to prove he is a man than by killing some animal,' Alcestis argued.

But Bladud was remembering the one-eyed boar, and his feeling that it had been chosen by Fate as his adversary. Perhaps this mountain bear was similarly chosen for Lear.

'We will go out together, son, and I will see you bring this legend quickly to an end.'

'I hunt on my own, father! I don't go out to perform for the pleasure of an audience!'

Bladud bit back something he would like to have said.

284

I hunt too, he thought, *and I hunt bigger game than any mountain bear.*

The matter was temporarily dropped as Rheinid clapped her hands, and slaves entered bearing food and drink. Behind them came dancers, jugglers and acrobats for their entertainment.

A few days after their arrival, Rheinid intercepted Lear as he was leaving the presence of Alcestis. She told him she had a favour to ask of him.

'A favour, mother?' Although Lear had stayed in the north with Rheinid and Liel, it was because he liked the country and its challenges rather than because he particularly wanted to stay with his mother and his stepfather. He felt freer here than he did in Trinovantum. Although there were tutors, he could easily give them the slip. His mother showed him no affection, and he showed her none back. They rarely spoke. But now she must want something badly, since she invited him into her luxurious quarters and set before him his favourite delicacies. She enquired how his studies were going and did not probe when he gave only a non-committal reply. He soon raised the subject that interested him most, the mountain bear he called 'Scar-face'. She showed unexpected interest in where the beast had last been seen; what methods Lear used to track him; what weapons might bring him down. Lear was pleasantly surprised to find her at last showing some interest in his life.

When the material of this discussion ran dry, she still did not show her usual impatience to be rid of him, but turned the conversation to other matters. To Alcestis.

'You are fond of your stepmother, Lear?' she asked almost sweetly.

Lear looked at her sharply. It sounded like a simple question, no hidden trick or barb, but he was suspicious nevertheless.

'Yes,' he answered, cautiously.

'I am glad of it,' she said, and there was no trace of sarcasm in her voice.

He looked at her, puzzled, knowing very well how hard she had been trying to make his stepmother's visit a misery.

'I've been thinking, my son, I have been unfair to her. I'm sure that even at your age it's possible to understand I would feel a certain resentment . . .'

'I don't see why,' he said. 'It was you who went off and married Uncle Liel and abandoned my father when he was so ill.'

'It wasn't quite like that,' she said quietly. 'You could not be expected to understand the full story. However, I admit I did resent Queen Alcestis at first. But now . . .'

'Now?' He raised his eyebrows. He had noticed no recent softening of her resentment.

'Now I would like to make a gesture to show your father and your stepmother that I have accepted the situation – and to make amends for my former hostility.'

Lear was amazed. She sounded so genuinely contrite.

'But I need your help in this, Lear.'

'How can I help?'

'I have in mind a jewelled gift as a token of apology.'

He looked at her in puzzlement. He had no jewels whilst she possessed countless numbers.

'For this I will need a lock of hair – a lock belonging to the one who has been wronged.'

'You mean Alcestis?'

'Indeed.'

He still did not see how he could help her.

'Since you are so close to your stepmother,' Rheinid continued smoothly, 'perhaps you could ask for a lock of her hair, and that would seem quite natural – whereas if I asked her, she would be surprised and suspicious. Would you do this for me? You are the only one I can ask.'

When he thought about it, it seemed innocent enough. A lock of that beautiful golden hair?

'Just that? Nothing more?'

'Nothing more, my dear. But be careful not to tell her it is intended for me.' She paused, watching him closely. 'If you do this for me,' she added, 'I will ask your father to give you your grandfather's spear; the spear of Hudibras, feared throughout the world. Such a spear would certainly help you to bring down Scar-face.'

286

Lear's eyes gleamed. He had long coveted that spear. 'I will ask Alcestis for a lock of her hair,' he said at once.

Rheinid smiled, and drew a deep breath. Now all she had to do was wait.

Yaruk had meanwhile set off for the West Country, determined on one last attempt to win the oracle away from her calling. He had become obsessed with her. *I can't go on living like this*, he brooded. It was clear the skill that had always been such a joy to him was now deserting him. As day after day passed, he found he was delegating more and more to his apprentices.

He found the oracle standing at the door of her hut, as though waiting for him. She greeted him with grave and gentle affection as he stood there awkwardly. All his dreams of sweeping her up in his arms and carrying her off seemed ridiculous now. She had changed in some subtle way since he had last seen her.

'I have been worried about you,' she said suddenly. 'I felt your pain. Your loneliness.'

'It is in your power to cure that.'

'I wish it were,' she said sadly.

'Has nothing changed?'

'Nothing.'

'My love for you has not changed. It will never change.'

She sighed and shook her head.

'If you knew how I was feeling despite all that distance,' Yaruk insisted, 'surely that means our love is meant to be?'

'It means only that I am an oracle, so time and distance mean nothing to me.'

'It means you love me.'

She did not deny it, and he saw the truth in her eyes. He stepped nearer.

'There is a reason I am glad you have come,' she said, drawing back. 'I've had a premonition of danger.'

'For me?'

'No. For your mistress, Queen Alcestis.'

'She and the king are away in the north, visiting his brother Liel. I would not be surprised if they are in danger, but

Bladud knows the risks and has taken precautions against them.'

'What precautions?'

'Soldiers. Weapons. Spies.'

'Those will not help the queen.'

Yaruk looked worried. 'It would take too long for me to reach them, even if I set off now. Is there nothing we can do?'

'I have been sending her thought-messages,' she replied. 'Usually that would suffice for a woman so close to the Otherworld as is your queen. But someone else is blocking them. Someone is cutting her off from all possible help.'

'Rheinid hates her. She would certainly mean her harm.'

'Does Rheinid practise black necromancy?'

Yaruk drew a sharp breath. If Rheinid had indeed mastered such arts, they were all in trouble.

'Come with me,' the oracle urged. 'You have been close to Bladud all your life, so perhaps together we can reach him since we cannot reach the queen.'

Yaruk followed her, for the moment putting aside all personal feelings in his concern to help his friend.

The hut he had left half finished had now been completed by others, and they had built a separate sanctuary for the steam-hole, with walls of woven reed for privacy, but open to the sky. Yaruk noticed Alun quietly grazing nearby. The deer looked up as he passed, and Yaruk felt sure he was recognised.

They entered the sacred place together, then she indicated where Yaruk should sit. Opening a wooden box, the oracle carefully took out a series of round, river-worn pebbles. Each had a sign carved on it, similar to those marking the huge boulders in the stream below. She placed them carefully around the steam-hole, to form a precise pattern, then sat down cross-legged on a platform of stone also carved with the same three spirals.

Her preparations complete, she gazed across at Yaruk, her eyes distant and misty as though he had become a stranger.

'You must think of King Bladud now. Think hard. Remember all you can about him: every detail however small. You need a vivid, living picture of him in your mind. You must not let your thoughts stray from him at all.'

'Should I think warning thoughts?'

'Just imagine him. Remember him. I need the link through you . . .'

She shut her eyes. The steam rising up around her made her seem insubstantial. Yaruk tried hard not to think about her. He shut his eyes and thought about Bladud. He thought of that time Bladud had rescued him from Torna. He thought of the time he had rescued Bladud from the wild boar. Without his meaning them to be, his thoughts were all of dangerous times, times of near disaster and near death. *Perhaps this is good*, he thought, *for it is warning against danger we must project.*

He thought until his head ached, and he longed to stop concentrating. Then he heard her moving and he opened his eyes. She was now standing up, looking straight at him.

'Do you think he heard us?'

'I can't be sure. If he is busy with worldly affairs and there are people around him demanding his attention, he will not hear us no matter how hard we call. Come,' she added, and took his hand and led him outside.

Still half dazed from the intensity of the experience, he was easily led. She sat him down inside her hut and gave him herb tea to drink. She was talking now like any ordinary woman, and the awe he had felt for her at first gradually faded, and his desire for her returned.

As it grew late, the sun set. The first stars came out. He talked and talked. He poured his life out and laid it at her feet. She seemed to understand everything.

At last it was completely dark in the room, but neither had risen to light the lamp. Neither wanted to move, lest the spell of their togetherness be broken. But the moment at last came when silence fell between them – and that silence had a power to draw them together.

In the darkness he found her. And in the darkness she did not draw back.

This time their love-making relied on no magical cauldron of regeneration. He made love to his own capacity, and she to hers. When they had finished, they lay curled on the furs of her bed and drifted into sleep together.

When he woke dawn sunlight was pouring into the room, and he was alone.

'*No!*' he thought. '*Please let it not have been a dream! Let it not have been yet another trick!*'

He pulled his clothes on and staggered out of the dim chamber into the blazing sunlight. He wanted to call out her name, but he did not know it. He stood waiting for her, not sure what to do. Perhaps she had gone to fetch water? He ran down to the stream. Perhaps to fetch wood for the fire? He searched the nearby forest. But there was no sign of her or her deer. He went to the Temple of Sul, but she was not there. He asked people who were visiting the healing sanctuary, but they had not seen her.

He hurried back to her house; perhaps he would find her there after all.

But when he entered the hut it was empty. He could smell the dried herbs hanging from the rafters. He could see the bed just as he had left it.

He stared at everything in the place again and again as though he hoped to find some clue. And then he swung round eagerly as a shadow fell across the floor.

An old woman stood in the doorway, a stern, strong old woman with knotted brown skin, and her hair in a tight bun on the top of her head.

'Where is the oracle?' he asked her.

'I am the oracle,' she replied.

'No. No. The young one. The one that was here before?'

'I know nothing of any young one. I am the Oracle of Sul.'

'No!' he shouted. 'You are not! There was another. She was here . . .'

He stopped. *I made love to her!* he thought. And an oracle needs to be a virgin. Suddenly his heart lifted. If she was no longer a virgin, she could no longer be the oracle. She would be free to marry him!

'I know you are the oracle now,' he said. 'Forgive me. But there was one here before you. Where did she go?'

'I have been here ever since the old one died. You and your king burned her body and scattered the ashes.'

He stared at her in horror. There was *nothing* about this

290

hag that had any resemblance to his love. It could not, it absolutely could not be the same woman.

Another game of the goddess!

In a rage he stormed from the hut and, with a howl like an animal in pain, he snatched up a rock and hurled it at the neat wall of the sanctuary, smashing it down. Then he rushed into the enclosure and threw her box of precious stones into the steam-hole . . .

Once Lear had acquired a lock of Alcestis's hair, he gave half of it to his mother and put the other half in a small deerskin pouch, next to his heart, believing it would somehow protect him against all harm from the mountain bear.

Slightly disturbed that the youth had requested it with such a glow of adoration in his eyes, Alcestis informed Bladud, and the king began to wonder if the close relationship between Alcestis and Lear was becoming too intense for the boy's own good. He decided to speak with his son.

'She told you?' was Lear's first shocked reaction. 'Why did she do that? It was a private matter between us.' It appeared to him that she had betrayed a trust, and somehow sullied their relationship. She was the only one in the world he truly loved, and who he had thought truly loved him, and here she was laughing at him behind his back and telling everyone their secrets.

When Bladud saw the flush of outrage on his son's face, he instantly regretted that he had spoken. He remembered how precious had been his own secret relationship with the spirit of Imogene on the White Mound, and how Rheinid's mockery had destroyed so much between them. Recently Lear had seemed less hostile towards his father. Now it seemed Bladud had undone everything.

'She told me only out of her affection for you, my son.'

But Lear refused to be mollified and tore the pouch off his neck, flinging it in on the floor at Bladud's feet. Then he stormed out of the room.

'Lear!' Bladud called after him, but the boy was gone.

At this moment Rheinid entered. 'What did you say to him? I've never seen him so upset,' she said in surprise.

'It was nothing,' Bladud growled.

'You really don't seem able to handle your son,' Rheinid continued with some satisfaction. 'Are you sure you want him back?'

'I haven't seen you do any better,' snapped Bladud.

Rheinid smiled comfortably. 'I didn't come to quarrel,' she said mildly. 'I came to ask if you would reconsider your decision about leaving us so soon. Could I persuade you to stay longer? For Lear's sake,' she added, as he glanced at her suspiciously.

Bladud frowned. Increasingly moments of intense, inexplicable anxiety were troubling him. Were they premonitions of danger? He wanted to depart for home, but not without his son, and after this upset it might prove more difficult than ever to persuade Lear to come willingly.

'I haven't decided on the day,' he said grudgingly. 'But we cannot stay much longer.'

Rheinid started to withdraw. At the door she turned. 'If you wish to win Lear's heart,' she said casually, 'if you *really* want to win Lear's heart, let him have the spear of Hudibras. I know he covets it.'

And then she left.

For the rest of that day Lear could not be found, though Bladud looked and enquired everywhere for him. Alcestis was upset when she heard what had happened and now wished she had revealed nothing to Bladud.

Late that same afternoon, Rheinid came to Alcestis to tell her that Lear had been seen sulking in a grove nearby. 'I don't know what your husband said to him,' she said slyly, 'but Lear seems very upset.'

It was not long after this that Rheinid watched the queen hurrying towards the grove, a thin cloak over her shoulders, her heart no doubt anxious for the boy who had put his trust in her.

When at last she found the place Rheinid had described so precisely to her, the sun was low and flickered disturbingly in her eyes through the twigs and leaves. She called out to Lear, wondering where he was, hoping he had not moved on. A sound above among the rocks of a steep knoll caused her to turn, a smile of relief already on her lips. Surely this was Lear?

With horror she found herself staring into the hostile eyes of a huge bear, a deep scar down its left cheek.

She screamed and took a quick backward step. She lost her footing and fell. In that instant the beast was on her.

Her screams brought Bladud running. He too had gone out looking for Lear, and was not far from the grove when he heard her. In his hand he held the spear of Hudibras.

Not since the Olympic Games had he run so fast. Yet he was still too late. When he came upon the scene Alcestis lay limp on the ground, the beast still towering above her.

With silent fury, Bladud flung the spear straight to its heart. It did not even attempt to escape the deadly blade.

Another shout, and suddenly Lear appeared, standing on the knoll to gaze down on the scene below. He too had a spear in his hand for he had tracked his enemy to this same grove, and intended to make an end of him this day or die in the attempt. He saw the bleeding figure of Alcestis. He saw the bear dead with his grandfather's spear deep in his heart. He saw his father desperately trying to tug the carcase off his wife. All seemed frozen, as though time had ceased.

What he did not see was his own mother Rheinid going back to her chamber in the palace, bolting the door and pulling out a chest from under her bed. Carefully she unlocked it and lifted out a crudely carved wooden bear – a scar on its left cheek corresponding precisely with the scar on the face of the killer bear. In its fangs and wound around its claws were strands of golden hair.

Rheinid stared at it thoughtfully. Then she placed the straw on which the effigy had rested in a stone bowl and set it alight. On top of this pyre she placed the wooden image itself. For a long while she stood watching it burn, until there was nothing left to show what had been there.

21

The Flight of the Eagle King

Bladud insisted on taking the body of Alcestis back to Trinovantum for burial.

Their progress was slow, for whenever they passed an inhabited area, the local people wanted to pay tribute to their dead queen. Wherever they halted, Bladud sat silently on his horse, his face pale and set, as his people filed weeping past the coffin of oak and lead.

On the third day a flight of white swans joined them, travelling south, just as they travelled south – sometimes vanishing, sometimes reappearing. Bladud began to watch and wait for them each day, taking comfort in their presence, remembering the swans of Greece that had played a part in his betrothal to Alcestis, and the swan on the gold chain that had been on the foundling girl King Lysander had accepted as his own daughter.

She has not left me, he told himself. Her spirit-presence is here with me . . . It will always be with me.

But, oh, the pain of not being able to hold her in his arms again: not being able to touch her, smell her, kiss her! He believed in the other worlds. Had he not seen and spoken with the denizens of them? But their reality was not the comfortable and familiar reality of the physical world. Their beauty was not the beauty of the material world. He was shocked that he felt so lost without Alcestis, even knowing that she still existed. But those other realities, no matter how magnificent, seemed so insubstantial, so mysterious, so enigmatic . . . Impressions and hints of them came and went, but nothing could be known for sure, nothing understood in full.

★ ★ ★

Lear did not accompany his father south. Believing that it was his own fault that Alcestis had been killed, because it was he who had driven the beast closer and closer towards the palace, he fled into the forests and could not be found. Now it was his turn to become the hunted, when trackers and dogs were sent after him to fetch him home. But as cunning as he had been as hunter, so was he now as quarry. Deeper and deeper into the forest he penetrated, higher and higher into the mountains, until he was no longer even in his stepfather's kingdom, but in some dangerous unknown country of the northern savages.

One night on the verge of dropping off to sleep in a cave, he suddenly had the strangest feeling that he was no longer Lear, Prince of Britain, but Scar-face, the mountain bear himself. He was immediately aware only of scents and sounds and images. His memories were shadowy impressions involving fear and hate and relentless pursuit. His feelings were bitter as he felt himself more and more isolated from everyone and everything he had ever known.

The days and nights slid by but Lear lost track of them. Forced to hunt for his food, sometimes he was so hungry he ate raw meat like an animal.

At last Bladud's men gave up the chase, driven back not only by almost unscaleable mountains and dense forests, but by dread of the unknown beings that lurked in those unfamiliar regions.

Lear's first intimation of change was an eerie sensation that he was being watched. His father's men had been easy to avoid; he could hear and see them on his trail. Now he noticed a total quiet. No longer did birds rise shrieking from the path. No longer did twigs crack. A shadow passed over him, and, looking up, he saw a giant eagle, slowly, silently, circling . . .

He felt afraid. He sensed presences nearby, yet no matter how cunningly he doubled back or took up positions of vantage, he neither saw nor heard anyone. It was as though they were somehow hidden *in* the silence.

One day he could bear the tension no longer and decided to

return to what he knew. His resentment of his father who had robbed him of honour by killing the beast he had vowed to destroy, his bitterness at the death of the only person whose love for him seemed unequivocal . . . all now took second place to this feeling of unease that grew stronger in him every moment.

But he had come a long way into this alien country and it would not be easy to find his way back again.

Had he noticed that particular lake before? He stared at the mirror image of mountains on its still, dark surface. The place seemed so remote that he would not be surprised if no other human being had ever come this way or seen this sight before.

He back-tracked through the forest, but soon found he had lost any landmarks noticed earlier. Surrounded on every side by mountains and forests, he could tell only by the position of the sun the direction in which he was travelling. And on cloudy days – of which there were many – he lost even this guidance.

One morning, after a fitful and dream-haunted sleep, he woke to find himself surrounded by men, heavily armed with broad-bladed bronze spears, their naked bodies covered all over with weird and intricate designs in indigo blue, their beards long and bushy, their eyes piercingly hostile.

It was soon made clear, by much prodding and brandishing of spears, that they wanted him to follow them.

They travelled fast, jogging through the forest, barely slowing for steep slopes. All Lear's weapons had been stripped from him while he slept, even the dagger which had been closely bound to his body. And he had felt nothing! He tried to speak with them, but soon it was clear they had no common language.

At noon the leader called a halt. Exhausted, Lear fell to his knees beside a stream, and scooped some water thankfully over his head. Though ice cold and brackish, it served to refresh him a little.

At nightfall they arrived at their destination. The last part of the journey had been lit by the flickering light of torches, the forest shadows running beside them as silent as wolves.

297

Now they had come to a cluster of turf-covered huts in a clearing. Instantly they were surrounded by a curious crowd pointing and staring at Lear. Not all were naked, but all were covered with tattoos. Some of the faces thrust close to his were more elaborately patterned than any mask. One man was noticeable above the others from the magnificent bearskin cloak flung over his shoulders. Lear assumed he must be the leader of this tribe of savages.

He was roughly flung at the man's feet. Rising again, with difficulty but determination, he met the fierce black eyes of the chief.

'I am Lear,' he proclaimed. 'Prince Lear. Heir to the High King Bladud. Grandson of Hudibras.' He paused but the eyes stared back into his steadily, uncomprehendingly. Was it possible that in this part of the world his father and his grandfather were not known, and so it meant nothing that he was heir to a vast kingdom?

The chief spoke a few words in a deep, guttural voice, then two men seized Lear by the arms and pushed and pulled him away towards one of the huts, where his head was roughly thrust down to avoid the low lintel. Inside a fire burned at the centre, with a grid on which strips of meat were grilling. The smell of it made him aware that he was faint with hunger. The air around was thick with smoke and his eyes smarted.

His captors pushed him to the floor and a woman handed him meat to eat. He wolfed it down and looked up for more. Eyeing him with curiosity but no friendliness, she gave him another piece, drawing her hand back quickly as though feeding an animal who might bite her. After this he was given some strong and bitter liquid in a wooden bowl. Its potency combined with his weariness to almost instantly put him to sleep.

Lear woke with a start in the stuffy, dim room. Unsure where he was he stared around in disbelief. Bear skins hung from the rafters, bear skulls were stacked on high shelves. A feeble beam of light entered through the open doorway, colouring everything that was not blackened by smoke a pale and lifeless grey. Finding that he was not bound or constrained in any way, he rose and hurried to the door. He stared out at the surrounding village. How could he escape these people? Would he ever find his way back through those endless, trackless forests and over the mountains beyond?

A cold drizzle was falling. As though through a veil, he watched the inhabitants hurrying backwards and forwards. There seemed an urgency about their activities, as though they were preparing for some important event.

Suddenly the chief appeared, flanked by two smaller men. Instantly people stopped what they were doing and gathered at the village centre, most carrying heavy bundles on their backs, waiting expectantly for their leader to speak. His words were greeted with much stamping of feet and banging of spears on the ground. Soon after this they all moved off into the forest, the chief leading, followed by some men carrying tall standards surmounted by bear skulls, strips of fur dangling and flapping below them. Behind these came the warriors armed with a forest of spears, and finally the rest an untidy throng laden with baskets and bundles and children. Lear found himself jostled along at the rear of the procession.

All day they walked, and came at last to a settlement whose huts were much bigger and better constructed than those in the village they had left behind.

Clearly this must be some kind of festival, for more and more groups kept arriving from every direction, each carrying standards which represented some different animal or bird.

One by one these standards were thrust into the ground to form concentric circles around a huge carved stone. As Lear peered at the carvings, he observed that many kinds of creature were depicted there, but pride of place was given to a giant eagle under a zig-zag sign resembling a jagged flash of lightning. As each group added its standard to the growing circle, the people watching bowed to the ground. All the while a naked shaman danced and chanted, hurling fine white ash in the air and scattering it over the sacred stone.

Lear was escorted towards the largest, most impressive building and pushed inside. There he came face to face with a magnificent old man with a long flowing white beard and hair like white silk which fell from a golden crown that Hudibras himself would have been proud to wear. A cloak of eagle feathers hung back from his shoulders to reveal that every inch of his naked skin was covered with intricate indigo blue designs. All around him were gathered what appeared to be the chiefs and sub-kings of his kingdom, for all were heavily bejewelled and painted.

Then one stepped forward, much younger than the rest. To Lear's astonishment he spoke in the prince's own language.

'What is your name and lineage?' he asked sternly. 'Where have you come from? Why have you come to our land?'

'Lear is my name,' he began eagerly, and started to list his titles and the names and titles of his father and his grandfather.

The young man eventually raised his hand to stop the flow. 'That is enough,' he said. 'Your father is known to me.'

He turned to the white-haired man and addressed him in his own language. Lear could see that the old king was pleased with what he heard. The young man then moved forward and took Lear's hands in his own.

'I was captured and made a slave in your country once,' he said. 'And your father set me free. *My* father is grateful.'

Lear had heard of the time when Bladud had set many slaves free after Rheinid's cruel treatment of them. So this man had once been a slave! What right had he now to act so mighty! He drew his hands away.

'I demand to be released so I can return to my own country,' he said coldly.

The young man looked taken aback. Had he expected respect and friendship from the son of Bladud?

'You are not our prisoner, sir, and you are free to go,' he replied with dignity. He could now see in Lear's eyes something he had often seen in Rheinid's.

Lear stood up straight now, like the royal warrior he was. No man who had once been a slave would humiliate him. He was ashamed at the way he had allowed himself to be treated by these people. He had been exhausted but he was recovered now, and he would show these savages who he was!

'Tell your father to provide me with an escort back to my own country, or he will pay for the indignities that have been done to me!'

The northern prince examined Lear closely. He saw the flush of youthful arrogance, the eyes that glared but did not see.

'I myself will be your guide, Prince Lear,' he said. 'But we are now about to celebrate our festival, so the return to your own country will have to wait until after that.' His voice was polite but firm.

Lear glowered, but the prince had turned away from him to speak to his father. Lear stepped forward impulsively, angry that any slave should turn his back on him, but instantly guards seized him by the arms. He struggled and swore, but to no avail. The prince did not look at him, but walked calmly away.

'Come back!' Lear yelled, but it was as though no one could hear him, no one could see him.

From that moment on everyone went about their business as though he was not there. No matter how he raged no one could understand his words and no one tried to.

Weary at last he slumped down on the stump of a tree, watching with sullen and resentful eyes the rites now being performed around the sacred stone. Group after group, each dressed in the skins of its own totem animal, or the feathers of its totem bird, performed an elaborate dance around the central inscribed stone. The ritual seemed endless, and Lear found himself drifting off to sleep. Then came the horror of his dream – a dream in which he found himself bound fast to the stone itself, the navel of the world, while around him circled a mêlée of shrieking, hostile savages, animals and birds, all demanding his blood. Then up in front of him, its eyes red with hatred and lust for vengeance, reared Scar-face himself, his grandfather's spear still in its heart, with blood gushing from the wound. Was there no one he could turn to for help?

Lear woke screaming as the giant bear's claws lashed out to rip at his face. Through swirling dust and smoke he could still see the wild dance of the northern tribes: boars and wolves and bears . . . deer and badgers . . . eagles and curlews and hawks. He could no longer tell if they were men or animal. All were part of the same frenzy, the same violent passion . . .

301

Then out of this vortex of energy rose the king dressed like an eagle, his white hair streaming out around him, the cloak of feathers billowing from his arms.

From the crowd a cry went up – a cry so strange that Lear's blood ran cold.

'He is flying!' he whispered. 'He is *flying*!'

All motion amid the crowd had ceased. All sound had died with that one last cry. Every eye was turned upwards. Every eye watched their king rise above them. Every heart was beating with his, feeling the air, feeling the earth slide away . . .

Lear did not see him descend again – perhaps he had glanced sideways at the crowd. When he looked back, the king was back on earth again standing beside the symbol-stone. The crowd was flat on the ground surrounding him, faces down, honouring him.

Lear could hardly wait to leave the place. The nights became stranger than the days, so after a while he was not sure what was dream and what was reality. Had he really seen the king fly? Had he seen the chieftains in their totem skins transform into the animals they represented? Had he lain awake at night and seen the sky become a moving, rippling curtain of lights and colours? He was not sure.

As the visiting tribes at last began to disperse, Lear confronted the white-haired king and demanded that he too be allowed to return to his home. The king stared silently at his angry face so long that the youth began to feel uneasy. He turned enquiringly to the young prince Pellor.

'My father wonders why you address him in that tone of voice. Did we not promise I would take you home once the festival was over?'

'The festival has finished.'

'And tomorrow we will be on our way.'

'How could I know he would keep his word?'

The look Pellor directed at Lear left him in no doubt what he thought. Lear flushed. The insolence of these people!

At first the journey was so slow and Lear so impatient that he even suspected Pellor was deliberately leading him around

302

in circles, with no intention of taking him back to his own land. But gradually, as they struggled up steep and rocky mountains, and slid down slopes covered deep in fallen leaves, as they camped beside streams that bubbled and sang all night, and walked beside silver-blue lakes reflecting magnificent cloud-scapes, even Lear began to relax, no longer taking note of how many times day turned into night and night into day.

At first they walked in silence, Lear still morose and resentful. But after a while he found the need to talk, so one night, as they warmed themselves beside their small fire, he began to tell Pellor about Scar-face, the bear.

To his surprise Pellor seemed to recognise the beast.

'And your father killed him?' he asked in awe.

Lear frowned. That tone of respect should rightfully have been for him.

'I had cornered him. Another moment and the spear that slew him would have been mine.'

'It is said that was no ordinary bear.'

'I know it. None has ever proved fiercer or more difficult to track.'

'It is even said that he was no bear at all, but once a chief of the Bear tribe. But he showed such arrogant disrespect for his people that one year during the dance of the animals he became a bear and stayed thus. That scar on his face was a wound the chief himself had suffered as a man.'

Lear stared at him in disbelief. 'When was that supposed to have happened?'

'Many years ago. The man-bear then ran off into the forest and never returned. But the stories of hunters who have seen him are told around many a hearth fire in these mountains. It is believed that the creature enjoyed a kind of immortality which was becoming wearisome to it. The chief now longed for release and respite from the role he was forced to play, so deliberately sought dangerous conflict in which he might be killed – but the bear's cunning survival instinct still kept him alive. Frustration and anger at his endless punishment made the creature cantankerous and violent beyond the norm of either man or bear. It was believed that whoever caused his death at last would earn the gratitude of the man but the

303

vengeance of the bear. He would be rewarded in some splendid and mysterious way, but the reward would be his undoing in the end. If I were you, I would not regret that it was not you yourself who brought him down.'

Lear kept silent, thinking about his father – thinking about the death of Alcestis.

Lear was surprised at how sorry he felt in the end to take his leave of Pellor. For some time after their parting he stood watching the youth's figure grow smaller and smaller as the path wound away into the hills. A feeling that had often troubled his young life now manifested again. Loneliness. If only the man had not belonged to such an uncouth tribe, he was thinking. If only he had not been an ex-slave . . . perhaps he could have made a good friend. He even thought of running after him, but instead turned sadly and made his way towards Liel's fort.

He was soon spotted, and for the last part of the journey he was accompanied by some of Liel's outriders and warriors.

Rheinid was thus prepared for his arrival, and showed no surprise. She greeted him with angry accusations of wasting everyone's time by disappearing for so long.

'And your father would have appreciated your presence at your stepmother's funeral,' she added coldly.

As Lear looked at her, the exhilaration of those last few days journeying through the mountains with Pellor was fading fast.

'My father gave up looking for me.'

'It was soon clear you did not want to be found. We knew you would return when you felt like it.'

No one asked him about his adventures. No one seemed interested in what he had witnessed or endured.

Liel strode in, showing no pleasure at Lear's return, though he seemed elated about something.

'My men have caught a spy,' he announced to Rheinid. 'They're bringing him.'

There was a scuffle at the door, and suddenly a man, heavily bound, was shoved in to the room and flung at Rheinid's feet.

'No!' Lear cried. 'This is no spy. It is Pellor, my – guide!'

He nearly said 'friend', but stopped himself. How different he looked now grovelling on the floor, no longer the tall, noble prince he had been among his own people.

Liel gestured the guards to stand back, but no one moved to help the prisoner to his feet.

'Your guide?' he asked, surprised.

'Yes. When I was lost in the mountains, his people found me and . . . and he brought me back here. His father is the High King of the northern tribes.'

'So what was he doing skulking in my hills?'

'I expect he was trying to avoid what has just happened here!'

Liel looked hard at his young stepson. 'You would vouch for him?'

Pellor's eyes met those of Lear. He had no illusions about that young man's character. Would he remember those last few days when they had become close, or would he remember that earlier time when he had so evidently resented and despised his captors?

Lear hesitated. Normally he never expected favours, and he never gave any. But perhaps he had learned something of how it felt to be bound at the mercy of an alien people.

He stepped forward and helped Pellor to his feet, then untied his ropes. 'I will vouch for him,' he said.

Pellor rubbed his wrists, where the bindings had bitten deep.

'It seems we are in your debt,' Rheinid said, but Pellor did not miss the edge to her voice. He wished he was far away from here. He was crazy to have ventured into their territory.

'We shall prepare a feast of welcome for our son – and you must be an honoured guest.'

'I thank you, my lady. But I would prefer to return to my own people without delay.'

'Nonsense!' Liel argued. 'We have shown you discourtesy, and now insist on making it up to you.'

'Take him away,' Rheinid gestured to Lear. 'Dress him in your finest garments. Then bring him back looking like a prince, and not a *slave*.' Only Rheinid could put such subtle venom into the word while smiling so pleasantly.

Still trying to protest, Pellor was led away.

Once the two youths were safely out of earshot, Rheinid and Liel looked at each other significantly.

'What do you think, lady?' Liel asked, but it seemed he already knew the answer.

'Just what we've been waiting for.' She smiled.

'I wonder what his father will concede to get him back safe?'

She laughed. 'The gods have dropped a gift into our lap. We'll not be slow to make the most of it!'

'And what about Lear? He seems to like the creature.'

'Lear has been away from his father's court too long. He will soon be on his way south.'

Liel clasped her in his arms and kissed her. This woman thought of everything!

22

Fall of the Sky-stone

Bladud watched Diomede's departure with mixed feelings. The man had become an irritation lately, criticising everything Bladud was trying to do, insisting that he would never be able to establish Greek order among 'these barbarians'. No matter how often Bladud protested that he was not trying to impose 'Greek' ways Diomede continued to mock. When he finally packed up his belongings, Bladud was relieved. Those early days in Greece had been made easier for him by Diomede's friendship, but Diomede seemed to have changed since he had come to Britain. He had lost his glamour. Nothing seemed to please him, and on more than one occasion Bladud felt ashamed of the arrogant way his guest treated other people.

As the ship pulled away from the shore, Bladud stood watching. He was glad to see Diomede go, but with him went another link with Greece, that country that still stirred his imagination, though now his memories of it were painfully tinged with sorrow. Diomede he associated with his youth, with adventure, with pleasure and success. It was as though that side of him was leaving forever as the big ship sailed away.

Hermias however had chosen to stay on, too old now to risk the journey, and seeing how listless Bladud had grown since the death of Alcestis, he endeavoured to stimulate his friend's old obsession with the possibility of flight. Hermias had been secretly evolving a plan for wings of fine leather stretched across light hollow reeds, and his eagerness to try out the device at last rekindled Bladud's enthusiasm.

307

Even Yaruk, who since his return from Baddon had seemed as morose as Bladud himself, became interested. 'My people have legends about men flying,' he said. 'It is said that one king actually won a battle with an army of flying men.'

Bladud set some men to finding a certain kind of reed, tall and strong, yet pliable and light, and others to scraping skins until they were almost fine as woven cloth. When all these materials were ready and prepared, arrangements were made for them to leave the city secretly. There would be no limelight for this project until it was guaranteed success.

They had chosen to make the first attempt from a low and grassy ridge in a remote and isolated area. The wings were assembled with difficulty, and only after many setbacks were they finally ready to test out.

Bladud insisted that he himself should carry out the first test, despite the protests of both Yaruk and Hermias.

'And if you are killed?' Yaruk demanded.

'And if I sent someone else, and he was killed?' Bladud countered.

'But he would not be a king, with all the land resting on his shoulders. Let *me* go, my lord.'

'No one is going to die,' Bladud said firmly.

One fresh and beautiful dawn they put the finishing touches to the wings and strapped them to the king's arms. Yaruk and Hermias, and the few others privileged to work on the project, watched anxiously.

For the first time since the death of Alcestis Bladud felt exhilarated and excited. Taking a deep breath, he began to run forwards, extending his arms to their limits till he could feel the frames and the leather pulling on them, heavy despite all efforts to make them light. He ran until he reached the edge of the ridge, then with a supreme effort launched himself up into the air, threshing his arms. His friends saw him lift, and they held their breaths. But almost immediately he began to fall in a tangle of ripping leather and snapping reed.

Yaruk was the first to reach him, and found him scratched and bruised, but not seriously hurt. Hermias soon came puffing up to join them. 'I know what was wrong,' he cried. 'Those wings aren't big enough to bear your body weight. We'll have to extend them beyond the length of your arms.'

Bladud began laughing as Yaruk helped extricate him from the broken mess.

'Right, old man.' Yaruk grinned. 'Just make the wings longer, and launch him from a higher hill!'

But Bladud was not prepared to give up, and began to agree with Hermias. 'I must go back to court now,' he said, 'or there'll be questions. But I'll return when you think the new wings are ready.' He stared hard at Yaruk. 'And you, my friend,' he added, 'stay on the ground!'

Yaruk nodded ruefully.

'Don't worry,' Hermias said. 'I'll see that he does.'

Meanwhile Rheinid and Liel were stirring up a hornet's nest in the north.

They had managed for several days to keep up the charade that Prince Pellor was their honoured guest, but the young man was becoming increasingly suspicious. After several attempts to take his leave were skilfully blocked, he ventured to voice these suspicions to Lear. The prince assured him they were unfounded.

Pellor insisted. 'My father is a very old man, and I had not intended to leave him for so long. Perhaps you'll accompany me to the border? That way we will not have to part so soon.'

Lear readily agreed, not realising how yet again he was being used.

When he informed Rheinid she appeared unconcerned and showered Pellor with costly gifts to take to his father.

But as they were about to set off, a group of warriors joined them. 'To protect you from robbers,' Rheinid explained.

Pellor protested that he needed no such protection, but the queen insisted, and Lear played into her hands by unthinkingly agreeing.

On the border, as Rheinid had arranged, Lear parted from Pellor and turned south at once for the long journey to Trinovantum.

In the foothills, that no-man's-land that lay between the northern and the southern tribes, Pellor was again ambushed, and dragged back a prisoner to Rheinid's fort – a useful pawn in a dangerous game.

As he lay in his cage, bound and heavily guarded, his father, the Eagle King, waited in vain for Pellor's return, and Liel's whole kingdom prepared for war. There was a new vigour to Liel's step, a sparkle to his eye. He was sick of minor raids and skirmishes. This time he would win or lose a great kingdom. He would be the man who would reduce the alien north to subjection. With that land and its people under his control, his brother's domain would seem insignificant.

He and Rheinid knew well that they could never defeat the northern tribes on their own ground, in the mountains. Pellor, the crown prince to their High King, would lure the enemy out on to terrain where they would be much more vulnerable. Nor would they have their usual advantage of surprise, for every man in Liel's kingdom would be armed and ready for them. Ditches were dug, traps were set; the pace of the preparations was feverish. Liel seemed tireless as he and his captains rode up and down the border country day and night, giving his orders, terrifying his people with warnings of the huge invasion about to take place. All were led to believe that the hostilities would be initiated from the north.

Slaves were sent to carry taunting messages to the Eagle King. They did not return, nor did Liel expect them.

Men familiar with mountain territory were given a special assignment. They were not to be drawn into the battles in the foothills, but were to bide their time in hiding. Then when the main forces were seriously engaged, they were to slip around behind into the mountains and wreak what havoc they could among the villages there. One well trained group was instructed to seek out the Eagle King's eyrie and take possession. Lear's answers to Rheinid's questions about his experiences among the northern tribes were now proving invaluable.

As time went by and still his son did not return, the Eagle King sensed what had happened without being told. He had held misgivings about Pellor's expedition, but his gratitude to Bladud had meant that no other action seemed honourable.

Then men came with Liel's message: that Pellor would be

dead by next new moon if the Eagle King did not submit his
territory and his people. His worst fears were confirmed. As
word went out, fighting men from every tribe began to
converge on the High King's rath. Beacons were lit on the
mountain tops, and the long, mournful howl of the war-horn
echoed among the cliffs and kranses.

The new moon was fast approaching and the Eagle King had
not enough time to muster the army he needed. Although he
was High King, the tribal chiefs were fiercely independent,
and if he wanted their support he must persuade them that it
was in their interests. Much valuable time was wasted on
words, but at last most realised there was more at stake here
than the life of just one prince. Then they were on the move.

It was on the day of the new moon itself that Liel's
outriders brought news of the enemy's approach. Like a
black cloud, the warriors of the Eagle King moved across the
land. In hiding and in silence, Liel's warriors waited for
them.

In their castle stronghold Liel and Rheinid smiled at each
other and raised their fine silver wine cups. It had been a
gamble, and as day after day stretched out in waiting they had
often wondered if all their effort would come to nothing.

Pellor in his cage knew nothing of what was happening,
but could guess. He saw by the agitation of the guards that
something had changed. More men were assigned to watch
him, all heavily armed.

Suddenly there was a stir among them and Rheinid swept
in. Standing in front of him, she gazed at him through the
bars with undisguised satisfaction.

'Your father is coming to fetch you.' She smiled.

He glared at her with simmering hatred in his eyes. 'Am I
to meet him in this condition?' He indicated the filth he had
been forced to live in since his capture. His hair was lank and
matted, his clothes in rags, his skin caked with dirt.

Rheinid stared at him, remembering the proud and
handsome young man she had entertained the night of his
arrival.

'Your father will no doubt be glad to get you back in
whatever condition,' she said, and then, after a moment's

311

pause, she added: 'Besides, you people live like animals, I believe, and worship animals, so surely it is fitting that you look like one!' She turned with a laugh and left him.

In his frustration, Pellor clutched the bars until his knuckles went white.

The Eagle King called a halt, sensing a trap. But many of his warriors, scenting battle and rich booty, and believing the despised southerners to be both inferior and unprepared, went whooping into the attack, as though this was no more than a border raid of the type they had carried out hundreds of times before.

Then from every side, as though out of the earth itself, Liel's men arose, wave after wave, and behind them came phalanxes of women, shooting stones from catapults, their children ready to load them as fast as they were discharged.

Finding themselves outnumbered and surrounded, the northern tribes fought savagely for survival, and such was their prowess that some did manage at last to break free and return to the Eagle tribe which had not rushed blindly in. Now the old king hurriedly supervised the regrouping and led them out of range.

'We can never defeat them if we do as they expect us to,' he declared, standing before them, tall and strong, an old man given youth by the power of his anger. 'There is only one way for us, and that is the way of our ancestors.'

He called all the chiefs to him, all the old men, all the priests and shamans. As Liel's men slaughtered all they could catch of the northern tribes, and began to celebrate their spectacularly easy victory, something was brewing that would be recalled down through the ages in legends, and would be sung about by bards for generations.

In the dark of an almost moonless night, Liel's warriors felt able to relax, gathering strength for a dawn offensive that would carry them triumphantly into the northerners' own territory. Even the guards around Pellor's cage relaxed until only one man remained awake and sober at his post, staring into the dark. He heard an owl hoot, but took no notice.

In his cage Pellor lifted his head to listen. He heard the sound repeated. Alert now, he peered through the dying glow of the fire towards his guards. No one moved. He cupped his hands to his mouth and answered the owl's call. No one looked round. There was silence, and then the answer came from some trees to his left.

As quiet as a cat, a figure crept through the darkness, and approached the cage. Pellor took the knife that was slipped into his hand, and under cover of drunken singing from some of the guards, and the snores of others, he and his rescuer worked at the locks.

Just past midnight, a sudden wind sprang up.

Those on watch along Liel's northern border sounded the alarm.

Liel and Rheinid awoke to find the night sky was red. Every hill, every field, every forest was ablaze with fire driven south by a raging gale. Above the roar and crackle of the approaching flames, they could hear high and eerie sounds of ululating, howling, screeching.

Horrified, they stared from their battlements and watched thousands of animals leaping, running, galloping, towards them ahead of the flames – thundering, lowing, growling, screaming. Above their heads sped flights of birds . . .

Liel could see at once that the castle lay directly in the path of the conflagration and of the stampede it had caused.

Where had that violent wind come from? There had been scarce a breeze when they had retired to bed. But there was no time to wonder now the why and the wherefore . . . All around, people were on the move, gathering what possessions they could and fleeing from the flames. Some villages were already totally consumed; others were imminently threatened.

Liel assumed their castle would be safe so high on its hill, but the air was full of flying sparks and the thatch on the servants' quarters caught easily. He despatched men at once to fight the blaze, while Rheinid ordered her maids to pack up her treasures, despite their pleas to be allowed to flee with the rest.

From the battlements Rheinid could see they were now an island in a sea of flame: the hillside beneath swarmed with struggling figures scrambling desperately to reach the

313

relative safety of the castle. As shadow fell on her she looked up. The sky above was dark with birds. She glanced across at Liel who was standing on the castle's highest point gazing out across the devastation. She called his name in alarm as she saw, hovering above him, a giant eagle with a wing-span greater than she would have believed possible. In the light of the surrounding fire she saw its talons gleam like iron, its beak flash like a dagger.

'Liel! Liel!' she shrieked – but too late. He looked up only in time to see it fall upon him. When Rheinid reached him, her husband had been ripped to pieces.

As suddenly as they had come, the birds were gone. Servants and warriors rushed towards them, but stopped and stared in horror at the bleeding corpse of their king. The wind had dropped and, below the hilltop castle, the fires were already dying down.

When morning arrived, from horizon to horizon the land lay desolate, smouldering and black.

When Bladud heard this news from the north, and of the events preceding it, his sorrow at his brother's death was marred by fury that Liel and Rheinid had thus jeopardised all possibility of peaceful coexistence with the northern tribes. There was other bad news too. He had begun to put Yaruk's people in certain positions of responsibility, but the Celtic nobles objected and were causing trouble. It seemed that everything he tried to do, every dream he tried to follow, was coming to nothing. As he sat in his great chair, High King of a mighty kingdom, he felt like a child hopelessly building a dam against the sea.

Suddenly Bladud made a decision. It was not sensible. It was not safe. He announced that he was going north himself. Those who heard his decision assumed he was taking an army to avenge his brother's death, but this was not at all what he had in mind. He took Yaruk along with him, but otherwise no more than his usual complement of servants and guards. The rest watched him go in disbelief. What was his plan? Was he intending to gather an army on the way? Many were angry that they were to be left out of what might prove to be the greatest battle of their lifetime.

'Let me come with you, father,' pleaded Lear. 'I have been right into the heart of their territory, so can lead you better than any man.'

Bladud gazed at his son at that moment as though seeing him for the first time. He had heard the story of Lear's capture by the Bear tribe and his subsequent release by the Eagle King. He could see now the boy had entered young manhood. He could see many things he had not seen before. But he needed Lear kept safe, since he was risking his own life.

'You'll stay here,' he said firmly. And that, to his shame, was all he said. Lear watched him depart as he had watched him so many times before – not understanding either his motives or his feelings.

After that one night of extraordinary devastation, the northern tribes withdrew, their own forces severely depleted by the battles of the day before, and their Eagle King now a sick man.

When Bladud arrived at Rheinid's castle, her crippled kingdom was already beginning to revive, and there was much talk of vengeance. He had driven himself hard on the way north, knowing that he must act swiftly if he was to do anything to avert a long and dangerous war.

'You're insane!' Rheinid exploded as she heard his plans. 'You'll be killed before you get anywhere near him.'

'I may be captured, certainly,' Bladud said calmly.

'So you'll give them a hostage even more valuable than the one we took?'

'I do not ask you to rescue me or ransom me. I am offering my own life for the life of his son so that this terrible blood feud may stop before it destroys us all.'

Rheinid's dark eyes flashed. 'You are not dealing with men with our code of honour.' She paused as Bladud raised his eyebrows quizzically. 'You will throw away your life,' she continued defiantly, 'and it will make no difference.'

'I'll not be throwing away my life,' he said quietly. 'I will be offering it. And if what I've heard from Pellor about his father is true, he will respect that.'

'You gamble for high stakes, my lord.'

315

'It will not be the first time,' he said, almost under his breath.

She turned her back on him impatiently. 'Do what you will,' she snapped. 'It's nothing to me!'

The first day of their incursion into the territory of the northern tribes passed without incident. Bladud and Yaruk sensed that they were constantly being watched, but none made a move against them. On the second day they found stray corpses picked clean by birds. Evidently Liel's secret force had got no further than this.

On the third night they were seized.

Bladud had taken Yaruk along because he could speak a little of the local language; for his grandmother had belonged to the Eagle tribe before being captured as a young girl. She had lived and died in the south, but Yaruk still remembered those long dark nights of childhood when he could not sleep and she would sit rocking him in her arms, crooning her old tribal songs and telling him the stories of her distant people.

His knowledge of part of an Eagle prayer now saved their lives, and, once their captors were prepared to listen, he delivered a halting speech. At first there seemed uncertainty as to what should be done with the prisoners, but the men were sufficiently intrigued by Yaruk's words to decide to keep them alive until they could show them to the High King.

Several days passed as the two were dragged and pushed, uncomfortably bound, over rough country. It was clear they were not being taken directly to the king, but were threading a labyrinth through the mountains, perhaps to confuse them so that they could never find their way out again. Or perhaps their captors wanted to show off their prize to as many straggling communities as they could.

At last, weary, bruised and aching, they came to the castle of the Eagle King. There, to their astonishment, they found Pellor, who they imagined had perished in his cage during the blaze. He was seated on a great throne, his father's jewelled and feathered crown set firmly on his head.

Recognising Bladud at once in spite of his dirty rags and

haggard face, he commanded his men to release the pair, greeting them with warmth for old times' sake, though also with a certain reservation given the present tension between their two nations.

Bladud enquired about Pellor's father.

'My father is dead,' Pellor said quietly. There was no accusation in his voice, though it was his belief that the tremendous effort the aged king had made to defeat Liel had hastened his death.

'My sorrow links with your sorrow, my friend. I wish I could have met him face to face, to speak the words that are in my heart.'

'He hears them, friend. He knows that treachery was not of your making.'

'Nevertheless, I have come to offer recompense. Whatever you think fit, I will pay it, even to my own life, if it will ensure peace between our two peoples.'

'I do not require your life, lord Bladud. But there is one thing would seal the peace between us, and would satisfy my people's desire for vengeance.'

'What is that, lord Pellor?'

'This is not the time to speak of it. I must first consult with the Elders. But now we need to attend to my father's journey.'

That night Bladud slept well, but in his dreams he seemed to be searching and searching for something. When he was at last about to find it, and reached out a hand to grasp it, instead he hesitated and withdrew. It was as though he knew what it was, yet he did not want to know.

In the morning while they dressed in the new clothes provided, Yaruk asked him what he thought Pellor might demand of them in settlement. Bladud shook his head. There was no way of knowing.

As with the festival that Lear had witnessed, the tribesmen came from far and wide to attend the funeral of the great Eagle King. He had reigned over them for more than half a century, and very few could remember a time when he was not with them. As they filed past the wooden platform on which the body lay, his weapons and the symbols of his magic

317

power carefully arranged around him, and his long white hair spread out on either side of his head, it was with anger and with sorrow as well as reverence that they raised their arms in the farewell salute. Bladud, standing behind the new High King, was in no doubt as to the bitterness in their hearts. These tribes would not let Liel's treachery go unpunished. That they had not made their attack already must only have been because they needed first to pay homage to their dead king.

Bladud gazed at the lined and noble face, the stern calm that had settled on it in death. He regretted not having known this man in life. Everyone who had witnessed the holocaust was convinced that storm of fire and wind had been raised by magic – the magic of this man. Lear had told him he had seen the old king fly. Bladud could have wept with frustration at his death, and he was again consumed with anger at the arrogance and stupidity of Liel and Rheinid.

All day the people had been paying their respects. Now evening and darkness were beginning to fall. Warriors formed a circle around the bier, and the people fell back.

Pellor touched Bladud's arm. 'If there is something you wish to say to my father,' he told him quietly, 'say it now, for he leaves us this night.'

Bladud eyed the guarding warriors, but Pellor gave a signal that he should be allowed through.

Close beside the bier, Bladud's heart was so full of things he wanted to say that he could say almost nothing.

'You know what is in my heart,' he whispered at last. 'Listen for my sorrow, my regret, my admiration . . .' He suddenly felt the presence of the old man very strongly. 'Listen for my yearning to know what you knew . . .'

The colour of the sky was deepening, the stars beginning to show. Bladud seemed to stand at the centre of that same profound silence he had encountered previously on the threshold of the Otherworld. His deepest senses became alert – as if something momentous was about to happen.

Suddenly there came a gasp from those encircling him, and his attention was drawn back to the present world. Dazed, he looked around to see them all gazing upwards, pointing at the

318

sky. There, a shower of stars was falling to earth, one much brighter than the rest, as if streaking directly towards them. As it came blazing downwards, singing its weird, high song, all the warriors turned and fled. Pellor and Yaruk withdrew a few steps, but stood their ground, straining to see where the star would fall.

As Bladud stood unmoving beside the bier, he sensed that he was intimately linked to this event. He was not afraid.

The sky-traveller fell to earth exactly where destiny dictated it should. The body of the Eagle King erupted in a roar of flame.

Now at last Bladud fell back, his physical body unable to endure the heat, his eyes blinded by the light. He staggered and fell.

Yaruk rushed forward to draw him back to safety. 'Bladud! My king!' he called in alarm.

'I will fly,' Bladud murmured. 'I know it. I will fly.'

At first light on the day following this extraordinary event, Yaruk crept from the chamber he and Bladud shared and secretly returned to the place where the funerary rites had been performed, before anyone else was stirring. The night had passed in rhythmic drumming, dancing and chanting around the burned-out bier, the final act being the scattering of the ashes in every direction.

Yaruk was in search of one thing only. He knew his chances of finding it were small, and he could scarcely believe that Pellor's men had not already removed it, but he had not been able to sleep for wondering about it. Having heard a solid thud as the sky-traveller hit the earth before the roar of the flames distracted them all, he believed that there was a good chance that somewhere in that place there was the remains of a fallen star.

Luckily the excesses of the night had taken their toll, and all others slept soundly. Some had fallen where they were, and were snoring noisily on the open ground. Yaruk picked his way carefully between them, aware that if his intentions became known he might well be shown no mercy. But he had seen his friend, the king, at that moment the star had fallen. He had seen the light of inspiration in his face. Yaruk felt

319

convinced this sky-traveller had been sent not to the dead king, but to Bladud – and it was Bladud who must take it away and make use of it.

Reaching the burned-out area of the funeral pyre, Yaruk stopped to look around. There was no one else about, but the first flocks of birds were on the wing, high in the sky. As quietly as he could he poked about in the charred remains. All the loose ash had been dispersed and in some places the bare, scorched earth was revealed. He knelt down and explored feverishly. He heard a dog bark in the distance. Soon the servants would be awake.

At last he found a hole, a pit, a deep incision in the earth. Digging like a dog, he drew it out, the small hard metallic ball of rock that had travelled far across the universe and landed at the feet of his king. Seeing someone emerge from one of the houses, yawning and stretching, Yaruk hastily scraped earth back over the hole as best he could, and covered the spot with pieces of charred wood. He walked away, fast but casually, not back towards the homesteads where at every moment more people were appearing, but into the forest nearby. From there he would emerge innocently later, and return to Bladud. Meanwhile he kept the precious object hidden. He would bring it out only when the time was right.

During the days that followed Bladud and Yaruk waited patiently while the new Eagle King consulted the elders of his tribe, and the chiefs and wise men of all the other tribes who had attended the funeral. During this time the pair were treated politely, but distantly, by all they encountered. It seemed no one knew quite what to make of their presence there. They were southerners, and therefore enemies, yet their king treated them like honoured guests. Realising the strangeness of their position, they kept close together and out of everybody's way.

One by one the tribes departed, each man placing a stone on the great king's last resting place, so that a huge cairn would rise to mark the place for millennia to come. When the last tribesman had left, Pellor summoned Bladud and Yaruk to his presence. There he sat in full regalia on his great throne, with the elders of the Eagle tribe ranged on either

320

side of him. Their faces without exception seemed hard and serious. Yaruk's heart sank as he looked into Pellor's eyes.

'My lord Bladud,' said the Eagle King in a stern and formal voice. 'My chiefs and my Council have come to a decision about the price for peace between our kingdoms.' He paused as Bladud and Yaruk stood waiting. 'I have told them that you have offered your own life to secure this peace.'

Again he paused. The silence was almost unbearable as they waited. Yaruk began to sweat, feeling the sky-stone ice cold and yet burning in the pouch against his thigh. Could it be used to bargain for his friend's life?

But Pellor continued. 'I have informed them that you cannot be held to blame for what happened. I have told them what kind of man you are. My father himself respected you. All of us saw a star fall as you and he were in communion. We take that as a sign that you, as well as he, are the chosen of the gods.'

Though Yaruk was trembling, Bladud stood still as rock, his eyes never leaving the face of Pellor.

'Therefore it is not *your* life we demand in exchange for peace, but the life of one who will never let us exist at peace so long as she lives. We demand the life of Rheinid the queen.'

As it was said Bladud turned white. He swayed as though he might fall. Yaruk put out a hand to steady him.

'And if I do not grant you the life of Queen Rheinid?' Bladud spoke at last, his voice deep and low.

'Then there can be no peace between our lands. There will be no rest for us until we have destroyed her, and her kingdom, and all those who support her. Even you, my friend.'

'Why will you not take *my* life? I offer it freely.'

'We do not require your life, my lord.'

'But as High King I am responsible for the actions of my brother and his wife. I should pay the blood-price.'

'It has been decided. We have sworn to all the tribes that we will give them the life of Rheinid.'

'It is not yours to give,' Bladud declared bitterly.

'No. But it is *yours*,' Pellor replied.

Yaruk could sense the anger building up in Bladud. He took his arm. 'Come, my lord, let us go from this place.'

321

He brooded about the sky-traveller. No doubt the Eagle King believed that potent, magical object still lay buried somewhere under the cairn with his father. If Yaruk were to produce it now . . . Then he told himself he would do so only if Bladud's life was at stake. But for Rheinid he would venture nothing.

'Come,' he urged again. The faces of Pellor's Council were implacable. What they had demanded seemed to them more than fair. 'My lord, hurry.' He tugged at Bladud's arm, and Bladud came away at last.

Within the hour they had set out, and were on their way back towards Rheinid's kingdom with a party of Pellor's warriors to show them the way. Bladud had not spoken a word since his last protest in the council chamber. His face was so closed and set that not even Yaruk could read his thoughts.

Arriving at Rheinid's castle, Bladud greeted her coldly, but almost immediately summoned those men who had ridden with him from Trinovantum. Yaruk listened with interest as he despatched each of them on errands, one after the other. Rheinid's nearest royal neighbour was two days' ride away. It was to him Bladud sent the deputation including his highest ranking companions. Their destination was the court of a sub-king called Arrak, an iron-fisted man in his fifties, whom Bladud respected. He was a hard man who enjoyed fighting, but he was not known for cunning or deceit or wanton cruelty. In fact Arrak was an old-fashioned warrior of the type Hudibras admired and trusted: slow to rouse to battle, but once roused stopping for nothing until he had achieved victory.

Meanwhile, unaware of the death sentence that hung over her head, Rheinid entertained them lavishly. It was extraordinary how quickly she had gathered together her luxuries again. Within the castle it almost seemed that no catastrophe had occurred. Outside, in the countryside, farmers were ploughing their fields again and the villagers were rebuilding houses. Those who had escaped the conflagration because they lived far from the border were now encouraged to move closer by the offer of rich rewards.

322

Rheinid wanted as many people as she could find to fill the depleted border lands, for many people meant many warriors, and she was determined the Eagle King should not escape unpunished for having devastated her country.

She could not find out what had occurred up north, but Bladud seemed tired and drawn, and would hardly speak to her. She turned her attention to Yaruk instead, trying to get him drunk enough to lower his guard, but he held firm.

When Arrak finally arrived with his great entourage of warriors, she demanded to know what was going on. 'I do not begrudge my hospitality,' she cried, 'but it is usual for the hostess to decide on her guests!'

'Unusual times call for unusual measures, lady,' Bladud replied. 'King Arrak himself does not know why I have insisted on his presence here, but soon all will be clear. I'd be grateful, lady, if you would call the nobles of your court together. There is something I must announce.'

Rheinid was furious. 'Would it not be courteous to consult with me before you make any announcements at *my* court?'

'In this case, no, lady. The matter is too grave.'

'Call them yourself then, sir.' She flounced haughtily out of the room.

Bladud watched her go, his face stern and troubled.

The nobles were summoned, King Arrak and his entourage were ushered in and seated. Rheinid was also invited to join them but she refused. Yaruk wondered if she had got wind of Pellor's demand and had fled. But only Bladud and he himself knew what had been decided by the Eagle tribe, and neither had breathed a word of it to anyone.

Though Rheinid did not deign to come into the hall, she had her spies there. So within moments of Bladud's speech, Rheinid in her chamber was informed of his intentions.

'What?' she screamed. 'Arrak to take over my kingdom!'

'Yes, my lady,' her informant confirmed nervously. 'And you are now to return to Trinovantum.'

Yaruk had listened attentively to Bladud's words as he warned of yet further trouble with the northern tribes following on the actions of Rheinid and Liel. Bladud insisted that he wanted only peace between them, and that no one swearing allegiance to him should initiate any hostility with the followers of the Eagle King.

'But if those tribes themselves invade this territory, I want a strong force here to resist them and keep our frontier safe. King Arrak is the right man to hold this vital position.'

He has decided not to surrender her to Pellor, Yaruk thought. *He will risk other lives to keep her safe!*

A door swung open and Rheinid stormed into the room. 'What is this?' she demanded, eyes flashing. 'What is this, lord Bladud? I am told you are giving my kingdom away!'

'Not *your* kingdom, lady. Mine. I have given it in trust to a man who will not stir up unnecessary wars. A man who will not betray his friends.'

Her mounting rage seemed to form a vortex into which all their lives might soon be drawn. 'I cannot accept this,' she replied fiercely. 'I will fight you in every way I can.'

Bladud shrugged. 'I expected no less of you, Rheinid. But your husband the king is dead, and Arrak is now lord of this land. Instruct your women to prepare for the long journey. We'll leave in the morning at first light.'

She glared back at him for one long moment, and no basilisk could have shot a deadlier glance. At that moment Yaruk realised that Bladud had made a terrible mistake in keeping her alive.

Then Rheinid turned on her heel, and strode from the room.

324

23

The Winged Man

It was in Baddon that Yaruk finally gave Bladud the sky-stone. The responsibility of holding it had been weighing heavily on him, and on more than one occasion he had woken in the night feeling that the ghost of the old Eagle King was standing beside him in his darkened chamber.

The journey from the northern frontier back to Trinovantum had been hurried and exhausting. Rheinid and Bladud scarcely spoke to each other, but she was constantly under surveillance in case she decided to double back and cause trouble in what was now Arrak's kingdom. Yaruk waited for the right time to deliver the precious object, but the proper moment never seemed to come. Bladud continued morose and short-tempered, and Yaruk was never conveniently alone with him.

Back in the royal city there seemed even less opportunity. After his long absence there were many urgent matters Bladud had to deal with, and each day and night seemed busier than the last. More than a month had elapsed since their return when Bladud announced he intended heading west to Baddon. With his painful memories of the oracle, Yaruk had no great wish to accompany him, but he believed that the journey might present an opportunity for him to reveal to the king what he had hitherto kept hidden.

As soon as they reached the lush green hills of the West Country, Yaruk could sense the tension in Bladud disappearing. *Soon*, he told himself, *soon will be the right time*. It was as though his friend had previously been tied up in knots, and now one by one they were loosening. Yet still Yaruk hesitated.

One night he dreamed an eagle descended on him, and snatched away the sky-stone in its talons. He woke in a sweat and searched it out at once. It still lay safe in his pouch, where he had left it.

The following day Bladud set off to visit the Temple of Sul and the healing sanctuary he had caused to be built around the hot waters. Yaruk accompanied him unwillingly, dreading an encounter with the oracle, yet sensing that this might also be a good opportunity to unburden himself of his secret.

The place had been totally transformed since Bladud had first arrived to consult the oracle so many years earlier. Sturdy wooden buildings in the valley beside the river housed the many pilgrims who now came for healing, and around the issue of waters itself, a circular sanctuary had been built: tall columns of oak holding up a roof of thatched river reeds. Shafts of light descended from high open windows to the mysterious, steamy atmosphere within. Priestesses emerged and disappeared, gliding in and out of the light, as they tended the sick, the crippled, the insane.

It was in the Temple of Sul, also circular, to which the stone of three spirals had been moved, that Yaruk could hold back no longer. As Bladud knelt in silent meditation before the goddess, Yaruk at last produced the sky-traveller and placed it on the sacred stone as though on an altar.

When Bladud opened his eyes he looked at it in astonishment. 'Yaruk,' he whispered, 'what is this?'

His heart thumping, Yaruk told him. Would Bladud be angry that he had stolen it from the Eagle King?

Slowly Bladud reached out both hands and raised the stone above his head.

'I have been seeking this,' he said quietly, lowering his arms. 'In dream after dream since it fell that night, I have been searching the earth for it. And I thought I would never find it.'

'It is yours.'

'No, it is not mine. But I will hold it in trust.'

Bladud examined the stone long and carefully. It was small

326

enough to fit neatly into the palm of his hand, but within it he saw a vision of the mighty cosmos: the vast and beautiful reaches where the stars dance; the limitless spaces of darkness where dreams form, awaiting birth.

'I will fly,' he whispered. '*Now* I will be able to fly.'

Yaruk wanted to ask what he meant, but Bladud's attention was so intensely focused on the stone that he knew he should keep silent.

It was as though the sky-stone restored Bladud to all the strength and enthusiasm which had deserted him on the death of Alcestis.

Though Hermias had been left behind in Trinovantum, Bladud at once started constructing a new set of wings without him. This time he did not attempt to attach them to his arms, but instead built a kind of frame with light but sturdy reeds, and then over the frame he fitted great sheets of leather carefully stitched. 'This way,' he told Yaruk, 'I'll be able to jump free if I feel my flight going wrong. Also it will provide a much larger wingspan, for they won't be limited by the size of my body.'

It was not easy to keep such an ambitious project secret, so Bladud established his workshop and workmen a little away from Baddon, and did not encourage curious onlookers.

Among the ordinary people rumours were quick to spread. 'King Bladud has gone crazy. He believes he can fly like a bird!' 'King Bladud has been given the power of flight by the goddess Sul!' 'King Bladud intends to challenge the gods – it will come to no good.'

This time he felt he dare not fail, for expectation was high and no king could afford to look a fool.

But the first attempts all ended in failure. Time and again the winged frame tipped clumsily, and ended up a wreckage of broken reed and pierced leather. Each time, luckily, Bladud managed to leap free. Though badly bruised, he would not give up, nor would he allow anyone else to undertake the risk. The leather was scraped finer and finer; various combinations of pliable willow wands and thin, rigid reeds were tested; different sizes and shapes of frame constructed.

327

Almost in despair, he sat one night on the hilltop alone, the wreckage of his latest attempt still lying on the slope below him. There was a full moon and the world was silent, shadows and pools of light creating a very different landscape from that which the sun shone on by day. In the distance, down in the valley, he could see a fiery glow: the sacred perpetual flame of the Temple of Sul. Had she been playing games with him? The eagle? The promised flight? Had she meant something else altogether. For oracles often spoke in riddles, and that man was surely a fool who lived his life slavishly by their pronouncements.

He clasped the sky-stone, turning it over and over in his hand, wondering about the Eagle King. How had he managed to fly. Was he borne up by nothing more than the magical power of his will? If anyone had the will to fly, surely he, Bladud, did? But the Eagle King was a man to whom the gods sent fire from heaven. What kind of mortal was that? A man who strides between the worlds with confidence; a man who believes in this world *and* in the next; who works with the other realms yet keeps his own strength and his own integrity. No slave, but a free man.

I will fly, Bladud thought – and then aloud, with conviction, he shouted: 'I *will* fly.'

On the next attempt he finally succeeded. It was not a long flight, but the frame held firm and he glided from the hilltop to the level ground below without mishap. During this flight he kept the sky-stone with him.

From then on it was just a matter of refinement and adjustment of wings and frame. Hermias had arrived from Trinovantum. He had spent much time studying birds gliding on air currents, so had many valuable suggestions to make. On his advice Bladud chose the precise time of day carefully, then monitored the flow of air around and above the hill before he ventured out. The wings lifted and this time he glided much further. Yaruk and the rest ran along the ground beneath, cheering as he did so. On the hill, Hermias stood weeping for joy.

Day by day further flights were attempted, more success achieved. When the people of Baddon heard about it, soon

328

the valley was crowded with people staring upwards, astonished at the winged man passing overhead.

Floating in the air, Bladud looked down at the field below, the people running and staring and waving. He saw a pattern to everything. *If only men could fly*, he thought, *they would be much less limited, less concerned with the petty and the mean, and more with the grand, with the wider issues. They would then see that what seemed so great at the moment was only a minimal part of a much greater scheme of things.*

The king's return to Trinovantum became a procession of triumph, as people poured in along the route from all over the country to see the winged man. On the way he gave several further demonstrations, each producing a sensation. Many of the old prophesied dire consequences for attempting something so unnatural to man; many of the young rushed off to construct wings of their own. After the third youngster had been killed in his attempt to emulate, Bladud was forced to declare a ban. Only he, the High King, was permitted to fly. By sending him the sky-stone the gods had given him a sign.

But all his pleasure in his success was soon overshadowed by news that a savage war had erupted in the north.

Rheinid soon confronted him. 'By taking me away,' she declared, 'you left my kingdom weak and vulnerable. Arrak does not know these people as I do!'

It was all Bladud could do not to blurt out to her what Pellor had demanded as the price of peace. He turned from her impatiently, and strode away. She looked after him bitterly. He seemed to go from strength to strength no matter what she did to diminish him. Now he could even *fly*, and all the country was at his feet!

Soon after their return to court, aged Hermias died. When Bladud was called to his bedside one dim and rainy afternoon, he found him frail as an autumn leaf, holding to life only by a thread.

There was a flicker of light in his eyes as he saw the king, and the old man struggled to raise his head. Bladud knelt on one knee beside him, and clasped both his hands in his own.

'Don't move, my friend,' he said softly. 'There's no need to move.'

'I wanted to tell you . . .' His voice trailed away, his breath coming hard.

'What is it, Hermias? Rest a while, and then tell me.'

Yaruk was standing behind Bladud and he now leant forward to catch the faint and faltering voice, feeling as sad as Bladud to see the old man go.

'I saw the queen last night,' the dry voice whispered.

Bladud leaned closer, puzzled. 'Alcestis?'

Hermias nodded almost imperceptibly. 'She wanted me to warn you . . .'

'Against what, Hermias? Against what?'

'You must not continue your attempts to fly . . .'

Bladud was shocked. All his life had led towards this glorious achievement. Now that he had arrived, must he turn back again? His only regret was that Alcestis herself was not present to share in his triumph.

'He is rambling,' Yaruk whispered, seeing Bladud's stunned expression. And then he turned to Hermias. 'What makes you think it was the queen who spoke to you?' He could see Hermias slipping away, and his anxiety to know what was really said was as great as the king's.

'A swan . . .' the old man murmured. 'A swan.' And on that last word his breath ceased altogether. Hermias the Greek was gone.

For a long, long moment Bladud stared down at the discarded shell in disbelief. Then he seemed to grasp the implication of what had just passed between them. He stood up and shouted, 'Hermias! Hermias!'

Yaruk took his arm. 'He has gone, my lord. He cannot answer you.'

Bladud turned on him furiously. 'If Alcestis can speak to him then he can speak to me!'

'He was dying! He was already between the worlds.' Yaruk could see the pain in Bladud's face: the frustration, the anger, the sorrow, the bewilderment. 'Come,' he said gently. 'It is time for the priests. If Hermias is going to speak to you again, it will not be from this place.'

★ ★ ★

330

Bladud could not forget Hermias's last words. After a sleepless night he went straight to the White Mound, hoping there he might meet Alcestis just as he had met with Imogene in his youth. But the place seemed to have lost its magic – or perhaps he had lost his capacity to respond to it. No spirit came to speak with him.

Disappointed, he returned to the city. There he found messengers from the north who brought news that Arrak's war with Pellor was not going well. The northern tribes were rampaging far and wide into neighbouring kingdoms, and would soon threaten regions that had never been raided by them before.

Bladud grimly retired to his private chambers, and would see no one.

Then, after two days, he sent for Yaruk.

'My lord?'

'I must ask you to go north again, Yaruk,' he said. 'I want you to return to Pellor.'

'Am I to offer him what he asked for?'

'No.'

'Then why am I to go?'

'You are to tell him I possess the sky-stone. You are to tell him I believe the gods sent it as a special token that our two kingdoms should work together. You are to tell him it has great power, and whoever possesses it holds more than *this* world can offer. You are to tell him I will give it to him in exchange for peace between us. Persuade him, Yaruk, that it is worth more than vengeance.'

Yaruk nodded slowly, 'I will do my best, lord. Shall I take the stone with me?'

'No. The first step in making peace is always trust. As soon as he withdraws from our territory I will send it to him. Besides,' he added thoughtfully, 'I need it one more time.'

Yaruk's expression was questioning.

'Rheinid has challenged me to make a public flight from the roof of the Temple of Apollo, to be witnessed by the whole city.'

'Is that wise? Are the air currents right?'

331

'It will not be easy. But she challenged me in front of the Council to make the flight so that the people may see how a man can fly, and also that the Greek gods have the power I claim for them.'

'How so?'

'She declares that if Apollo supports me in undertaking this flight from his temple roof, then my people will cease their opposition to the foreign god and he will take his place in their hearts with the ancient gods of our race. A great deal is at stake here, Yaruk. I must have the power of the sky-stone for this flight. After that, I will give it up.'

'Should I not delay my journey then?' Yaruk asked anxiously. 'Should I not be here to assist you?'

'Your journey is urgent, my friend. People are dying even as we speak.'

'What of the warning you received from Hermias?'

'Rheinid has made her challenge too widely known. Would you have me fail in the sight of my people because of the ramblings of a dying man?'

Yaruk fell silent, his heart full of misgiving. It even crossed his mind to seize Rheinid and deliver her himself to Pellor. But it was clear that Bladud believed a lot was riding on his success in meeting her challenge. It was imperative she should be present to see him win.

If Pellor will not accept the substitute, Yaruk told himself darkly, *then we will see. North she shall go, whether Bladud sanctions it or not!*

No hill in Trinovantum could compare with the hills of the West Country, but the Temple of Apollo was built on top of the highest there was. Not having the beautiful white marble of Greece, it could not compare with the grandeur and grace of those on which Bladud had modelled it, but it was nevertheless an impressive building. The foundations were of stone, but the tall columns and the high roof were constructed of oak. Built on the outskirts it still towered over the city, and was a landmark for miles around.

Rheinid had ensured that the flight would take place at the festival of Lughnasa so that the maximum number of influential people could be there to witness it. She chose

Lughnasa for another reason as well: Lugh was the Celtic god Bladud associated with light, as Apollo was for him the Greek equivalent. Bladud seemed to see no difference except in the names, but she made capital out of the differences she discerned between them, as if setting the two gods at variance with one another – to such an extent that the coming event was seen as a confrontation and contest between them. In vain Bladud tried to dispel this impression, but the excitement had mounted too far for that. It was as though all the pent-up dissatisfaction at his Greek innovations was coming to a head, and win or lose rode on that one flight.

Before dawn one day not long before this great test, Rheinid entered Bladud's private chamber. He woke to find himself enclosed in her arms, her body warm against his. Still half asleep he began to rouse to her, but then, as he woke fully, he pulled away angrily, leaping out of bed.

'You have done too much mischief to me, woman. Do you think to mend it by this means?'

'It is you who have done mischief to me, lord. Yet I love you still.'

He turned away from her, pulling on his clothes. 'I think there has been much wrong done between us, Rheinid, since the time we first met,' he said with a sigh. 'And for my part I regret it.'

'Come back to me, husband. Let us forget what is past.'

He turned and gazed at her lying naked on his bed, raised on one elbow, her long dark hair flowing over his pillow.

'I am not your husband now, Rheinid,' he replied grimly. 'Nor ever more will be. It is best you accept that now.'

Once again he turned away from her, and this time left the room.

She watched him go, then all her melting softness of a moment before disappeared. Picking up a tall Greek vase that stood beside his bed, she flung it with all her force against the wall, where it smashed into a myriad pieces.

Yaruk's heart sank as he entered the gorge. Dark clouds pressed down upon the high rocks, snuffing out the light. Would he get through it before the storm broke? Should he delay until it had passed? He had already taken longer than

333

he intended, dodging and hiding from both contesting armies while trying to make all speed over difficult terrain. At the back of his mind he kept thinking of Bladud, about to stake so much on his flight from Apollo's temple. He longed to be back in Trinovantum, but first he must speak with Pellor. First he must pass through these gates of hell!

Then his horse shied and would go no further.

'You too, my friend?' Yaruk murmured. 'I don't blame you. But this is the only way through that will give me the speed I need.' The horse trembled and snorted, pawing the ground. It was as though it sensed something even more terrifying than the storm that was brewing.

At last Yaruk was forced to dismount. Beyond this gorge there would be mountains. Perhaps it was best for him to leave the beast here and continue on foot. He was exhausted. Since he had first approached the border lands, he had scarcely rested, but the devastation he witnessed everywhere lent his mission urgency.

Releasing his steed with many a soft and comforting word, he set off walking alongside the stream that rushed over the rocks down into the valley as though itself fleeing from the mysterious fell force Yaruk and his animal feared. There was the trace of a track beside the water, which Yaruk followed. But after a while even this petered out, and he was left to pick his way gingerly over boulders. He was well down into the gorge when the first thunderclap reverberated along the narrow cleft. Yaruk looked anxiously up into the black and swirling mass of cloud which bore down on him. He must make it to higher ground. The water was already beginning to rise, and from a distance, he could hear the roar and grinding of rocks as the swollen river gouged a wider channel for itself further up. And then he was almost blinded as the rain enveloped him, beating down with such force that he could scarcely progress against it. He scrambled up the rock to one side as best he could, slipping and slithering as the pockets of sodden topsoil slid away from him. But at last he reached relative safety on a ledge. Below him the swollen river hurtled, thrusting aside everything in its path. Yaruk was now glad he had not tried to bring the horse, as he crept under a shallow overhang out of the main deluge of the rain.

As the thunder rumbled on, it seemed the whole mountain was muttering and grumbling. He could almost believe it was on the move, as he cowered against its side.

What if he did not find his way through to Pellor? What if he lost his life here, now, before he could deliver Bladud's message? Would the war continue till Bladud was forced to come north with his own warriors? Yaruk's thoughts about Rheinid were very bitter.

Meanwhile, in Trinovantum, Rheinid was weaving her own plot.

Lear found his mother often at his side, and he had never known her so attentive to him. He could not guess that she had played a part in the death of Alcestis, and he was touched that she seemed conscious of how deeply he mourned his stepmother. Rheinid claimed to understand his grief so well – for was she not in mourning for her husband? Lear forgot that he had never seen much sign of affection between the two of them, and tried to comfort her as she tried to comfort him.

She began to work on others too. She turned her charm on Fergal, now an old and disillusioned man, who saw much of the Druids' ancient power usurped by this new breed of priests influenced by Bladud's Greek academy. It did not take much to fuel his resentment and to make him dread a successful flight from the Temple of Apollo.

'How the old ways are changing,' she sighed to him. 'Soon there will be nothing left of the old gods. I do not trust this Apollo. The dark forces that beset us are rough and dangerous and powerful. What will become of us with only this effete foreign god to defend us? We need the mighty spirit of Lugh. We need a wild and shining warrior.'

Fergal listened to her, and became more morose by the day.

As the members of the Council gathered in the city to witness Bladud's flight, she worried aloud about what would happen should the High King perish, Prince Lear being too young to rule in his place. Beneath her anxious concern, she covertly canvassed support for the idea of herself becoming regent in such a dire eventuality.

Caught up in his preparations for the crucial day, Bladud noticed nothing of all this. On the evening before his flight, he went to the Temple of Apollo. From the rear of the building he could just see the edge of the great golden disc of the sun while most of the land was already in shadow. Its rays fanned out, touching high spots here and there, a river, a grove of trees – giving ordinary objects a magical significance. Bladud thought of Lugh and of Sul; in his mind, along with Apollo, these made a trinity of light. He found it sad that his people demanded one or the other – that they insisted on limiting such a great force to an image and a name.

Once clear of this earth, he thought, *we can perceive things as they truly are. But on this earth, sadly, we see things only as we want to see them.*

Entering the darkening temple, he quickly dismissed all the priests. On the eve of this greatest challenge of his life he wanted no human company to distract him.

The statue of Apollo, rough-hewn by local artists, bore very little resemblance to those beautiful statues of the god he had seen in Greece. It was positioned in the circular sanctuary so that the dawn light of the summer solstice would fall directly upon it. Now it should have been in shadow, but as Bladud turned his attention to it, it seemed to blaze out with sudden glory.

Startled, Bladud stood staring at it.

From the haze of light that enclosed the statue, figures began to emerge, stepping out from it as though through a door. One by one they came until they formed a circle around the king. He recognized at once the two beautiful young women he had encountered in the stone circle. For the first time he knew one to be Imogene, and one Alcestis. But now their images glimmered in and out of each other until they became one image – and that image offered him directly a single crystal flask.

More figures then emerged: stern Athene herself and her far-seeing owl; Aphrodite the seducer of Anchises, and Hermes with the winged sandals and the mocking eyes that had seen too much of human folly. Boars and bears and wolves with human eyes . . . ravens, swans and eagles with human heads . . . He saw the disembodied heads of Bran and of his own ancestors floating in light . . . The temple was soon crowded with extraordinary beings, all gazing back expectantly towards the statue in its cocoon of light. There was a pause and then, stepping elegantly through the haze, came Sul herself, trailing a cloak of fire, accompanied by the warrior king Lugh of the shining shield, holding up the very golden cup Bladud had been offered before. And on her other side, was Apollo himself – son of the sun.

The three stood before Bladud, and he sank down to his knees overwhelmed by their beauty and their power. Behind them, in light too bright to look upon, he sensed there were other beings, but he had no means of perceiving them.

Suddenly Sul spoke out, her voice reverberating like deep, sweet music around the chamber. 'Bladud son of Hudibras,' she said. 'Trust us.'

'Bladud, royal king of kings,' Lugh said now in a voice like distant thunder. 'Keep faith.'

'Bladud, victor of victories.' Apollo's voice sounded like water in the mountains. 'Trust yourself.'

In Bladud's hand was the sky-stone.

He held it up to them, and for a moment it seemed to blaze again as it had blazed that night of the Eagle King's funeral. For a moment it blinded him, and he shut his eyes, and was dazzled by the after-image of all that strange and powerful glory. He was filled with confidence and strength.

When he opened his eyes again he found himself all alone in the dim chamber of the temple. Slowly he rose to his feet, staring into the shadows . . . wondering . . .

Then Bladud climbed up to the roof of the temple, where his wings were laid ready for the morning. He placed the sky-stone in the little leather pouch bound to the nose of the strange contraption, then he took a deep breath of the cool night air. He would trust them. He would keep faith. He believed the sky-stone was the pledge.

In the war camp of Pellor a prisoner was dragged forward and flung at the feet of the young Eagle King.

'This spy claims to have a message for you!' sneered his captor.

Pellor looked down at the bedraggled figure. His men had

not been gentle with him, for his clothes were torn, his lips swollen and bleeding, his body bruised and cut. At a gesture from the king, the guards hauled the prisoner roughly to his feet, and supported him as he staggered and almost fell.

'Yaruk,' Pellor said gravely. 'What brings you here?'

'My lord, a message from my king.' Yaruk uttered the words with difficulty. Pellor stared at him thoughtfully, then turned to the woman at his side.

'Dress his wounds. Clean him up. Give him rest and food. And only then bring him back before me.'

'My lord . . .'

'Later, Yaruk. You're in no fit state to talk.'

Knowing he was right, Yaruk allowed himself to be helped out and lodged in one of the makeshift wooden shacks. He did not think he slept, but it was already midnight when he suddenly woke to find the flame of a lamp shining directly into his eyes. Behind the light could be seen the dim shape of a tall figure.

He heard Pellor's voice as though it were part of his dream. 'It is time to talk, my friend,' he was saying.

Yaruk floundered out of sleep and raised himself painfully on one elbow, still blinking at the light. Pellor stooped and helped him to stand upright.

'Speak quickly, Yaruk. We may not have long alone. What does your king say?'

How to begin? 'My king sends you greetings . . .'

'Yes. Yes. But what is his message?'

'He begs you to understand why he could not execute the mother of his own son.' Yaruk could not see Pellor's face, but he suspected it had not relaxed.

'And . . . ?'

'But he offers in exchange . . .' Here Yaruk almost choked. The moment had come for him to admit the sacrilege he had committed. Suddenly what had seemed so right at that time, seemed now unforgivable. His throat constricted. He could say nothing.

'What? He offers me what?' Pellor urged impatiently.

Yaruk at last found the courage to utter the words. 'The sky-stone that fell at the funeral of your father . . .'

Pellor started. 'The sky-stone?'

'The sign. The message from the gods. Given to Bladud while he communed with your father.'

'Given to Bladud?' repeated Pellor in astonishment.

'I saw it fall. I knew it was meant for Bladud. Your father was dead. Bladud was alive . . .'

Neither had noticed the figure that had entered the room and now stood silently in the shadows. It was an aged shaman who had served the previous Eagle King loyally all his life. At these words he strode suddenly forward. In the flickering lamplight Yaruk saw the man's face distorted by rage.

'You!' he screamed. '*You* robbed my master of his right of passage! It was you who did this deed!'

And before Pellor could grasp what was happening the shaman lunged forward, driving a dagger through the heart of Yaruk. The stricken man fell forward with a gasp, and in his falling the flamelight seemed to be sucked into a vortex of darkness. In his falling he saw the oracle, who was no longer an oracle because of him. He saw the war that now would not end because he had failed . . .

Pellor looked down at the crumpled body, and the pool of blood that was rapidly spreading across the floor.

'Search him!' yelled the shaman. 'Search him for the stone!'

Others came rushing into the chamber and, without knowing for what reason, they turned the body over and searched it thoroughly. They found nothing, for there was nothing to find.

Rheinid heard of the sky-stone. She did not know quite what it signified, but her spies had told her Bladud kept this ordinary-looking object always about him. He was often seen turning it over and over in his hand, staring at it thoughtfully.

'He'll never fly without it,' she was informed. 'He keeps it close to his body at most times, but when he flies he binds it to the wings.'

So on the night before his flight she climbed to the roof of the temple where his wings were waiting for the morning flight, and searched the strange ungainly construction of reed and leather. She could not believe that such a

339

contraption could fly, though witnesses had sworn to her that it was possible.

Eventually she found Bladud's secret pouch and withdrew the sky-stone. It was dull, heavy, metallic, and looked like nothing much. She would have understood a precious jewel. A jewelled talisman was something not unusual for a king to cherish. She had brought with her another stone of roughly the same size and shape. This she put into the leather pouch instead and lashed it back to the wings where it had been fixed before. Then she left.

Returning to her private chamber, she there examined the sky-stone more closely. There *was* something about it. She began to feel strange. She began to feel small and inadequate and depressed. It was diminishing her. It was somehow telling her she would never win, never succeed, never take Bladud back, or sit on the throne of the High Queen. Her son would never love her. Her powers as witch-woman would fade. She threw the cursed stone across the room in disgust. But it still seemed to mock her – to deride her.

Pulling on her cloak, she picked it up again and rushed from the chamber. She made her way up to the ramparts of the castle, and from there she flung the sky-stone as far as her strength would allow. She watched it spinning through the night, leaving a trail of disturbance in the air behind, until it fell into darkness and was lost.

Triumphantly she returned to her bed, satisfied with the night's work, sleeping well and dreamlessly.

Even before sunrise the town awoke and thousands of people crowded out round the Temple of Apollo. Bladud and his wings were ready on the roof. His attendants were making their last checks and their last adjustments. He glanced at the leather pouch. He was happy that the gods would be with him on this most dangerous of all his flights. Through the sky-stone he felt linked to the great Eagle King who had held the secret of a different kind of flight. 'Together,' he whispered, 'together we will free men from the earth . . .' Birds were high above him – winging towards the sun . . .

As the huge blood-red orb rose slowly above the horizon, Bladud stood poised, holding firmly to the fragile framework of leather and reed. The lightest breezes fluttered the leaves on the trees far below him. It was almost time. He wished Yaruk was with him. He wished Hermias could see him. How proud Alcestis would be . . .

The moment when the sun first fully appeared would be the signal. There would be a short run – much shorter than ever before – and then he would leap.

He gazed down at the sea of faces gazing up. There was not a sound; all chatter and laughter had died away. Everyone was waiting. He could even see Rheinid and Lear standing together, slightly apart from the others.

'My lord, the sun is rising,' someone murmured at his elbow.

The time had come.

He began to run. He could hear his feet pounding, his heart thudding. He could see the gigantic ball of the sun rising . . . rising . . .

He leaped.

The air caught his wings and he soared. He could feel the glory of it, the wonder of it. He could hear the gasp of his people as they gazed up at the winged man, the man who was showing them that there was no end to their potential. The air currents carried him out into a long slow circle above their staring faces. He felt he could do anything, achieve anything. Beneath him the earth unfolded her glowing robes, rich in a hundred shades of green. He saw the curving hills, the silver belt of the river . . . His heart sang for the beauty that dazzled and danced all around him – the gold and crimson of the sky giving way to silver-green and eggshell blue . . .

Glancing back at the leather pouch, he murmured a prayer of gratitude to the gods. But the binding had worked loose and the pouch was opening. The stone was easing out. Bladud made a quick movement to reach it before it fell. In doing so he managed only to destabilise the wings, and the whole structure began to rock and shudder. He started to fall, and as he fell he became even more awkwardly entangled . . .

Horrified, the people down below watched the winged man flounder in the air. What was he doing? He seemed to be trying to catch something . . . Then a strut snapped as he

341

made one last clumsy movement. They screamed and ran for safety as they saw him hurtle to the earth.

Rheinid stood transfixed. Lear ran forward as if to try and catch his father. He cried out in a voice charged with genuine and desperate love.

Too late.

When the young prince arrived at the spot, men were already hauling the mess of broken reed and tattered leather off the bleeding, broken body of King Bladud.

'Is he dead?' someone murmured.

No one replied. The terrible silence confirmed their worst fears. Lear flung himself on his knees, lifting his father in his arms, sobbing. Rheinid stood behind him, looking down, her face white as ash.

For Bladud a door opened and he passed through, the three spirals swirling in a mist of brilliant light around him. Figures dimly seen ahead of him became stronger . . . Figures dimly seen behind him . . . faded . . .

Notes

The story of King Bladud is considered legend rather than history, as is also the story of the coming to Britain of the Trojans from whom he is reputed to have descended. But it is a persistent legend and one that, like the story of King Arthur and that of Robin Hood, might well contain some historical truth. '. . . archaeological evidence suggests that trade routes between the Mediterranean world and Britain were established from a significantly early date. So that there seems no difficulty in believing that a group of people escaping from the fall of Troy (wherever and whenever that event occurred) might indeed have sailed to these shores and established a colony here.' John Matthews: *The Aquarian Guide to Legendary London*.

But whatever may be the claims to historical truth, it certainly has mythic truth, which is perhaps the more valuable of the two, for myth deals with the different levels in the human psyche and with our often difficult and painful approach towards a higher consciousness.

I have drawn the substance of my novel from various sources, the chief being a book first published privately in 1919, and then reprinted in a public edition in 1973. It is called *Bladud of Bath*, by Howard C. Levis FSA, and is a collection of all the known references to King Bladud throughout the ages. Where there were gaps in this information I have largely filled them with imaginative material based on Celtic and Greek legends and myths, so that the whole may give a picture not only of this famous king of ancient Britain, but also of someone we

The Ancestry of Bladud

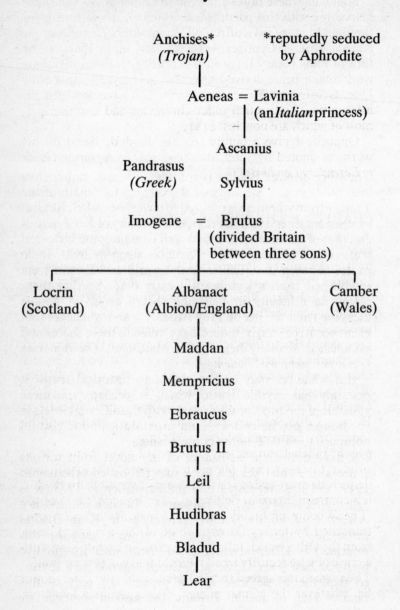

Anchises*   *reputedly seduced
(Trojan)   by Aphrodite

Aeneas = Lavinia
(an *Italian* princess)

Ascanius

Pandrasus
(Greek)   Sylvius

Imogene = Brutus
(divided Britain
between three sons)

Locrin   Albanact   Camber
(Scotland)   (Albion/England)   (Wales)

Maddan

Mempricius

Ebraucus

Brutus II

Leil

Hudibras

Bladud

Lear

can recognise as an archetype of our own deepest humanity.

Following these notes I list the principal books that have helped me with this particular research. A major source for the Bladud story is Geoffrey of Monmouth's *Histories of the Kings of Britain*. Geoffrey was a scholarly monk living at the time of King Henry II (twelfth century AD). From this same work Shakespeare derived several of his plays, notably *King Lear*. Geoffrey of Monmouth claimed to have obtained his information from much older chronicles and manuscripts, most of which are now lost to us.

Opposite I give a family tree for Bladud, based on his work, as quoted by John Matthews in *The Aquarian Guide to Legendary London*.

CHAPTER 1: THE GAME OF FIDCHELL

page 2: Trinovantum, or New Troy, was the name given by the legendary Trojans to the city we now know as London.

Rath: hill fort. This was a feature of the Iron Age in Britain, when raids and warfare were common. Peasants lived and worked on the land, but when conflict threatened they would flee to the shelter of their overlord's hilltop fort. Surrounding ridges and earthworks gave it extra height and security, and within the fort would be a village or small town of permanent residents surrounding the great house of the overlord. Examples of British hill forts: Maiden Castle in Dorset, Little Solsbury near Bath. Keron's rath would be somewhere between London and Bath.

page 8: Fidchell: an ancient Celtic board-game thought to be similar to chess, and played for stakes. The foolish and dangerous open-ended stake that leads to trouble for Bladud is a common theme in Celtic and other legends, for example 'The Wooing of Étaín' (see *Early Irish Myths and Sagas*, translated by Jeffrey Gantz), where Midir, a magical being from the Otherworld, lulls Echu Airem, an earthly king, into a sense of false security by allowing him to win several games. Then, when it is agreed that in the last game the stake should be 'whatever the winner names', Midir claims a kiss from

Echu's wife Étaín. In spite of all the court being present to witness the kiss, as soon as Midir has his arms around Étaín, he transforms them both into swans and Echu watches in frustration as they fly away, linked by a golden chain.

Another example of an open-ended promise leading to trouble occurs at the wedding feast of Pwyll and Rhiannon in the *Mabinogion*.

CHAPTER 2: JOURNEY BETWEEN THE WORLDS

page 11: Stories of haunted burial mounds are not uncommon. In an article on Taliesin published in *Y Cymmrodor*, vol. xxviii (1918), quoted in *Bladud of Bath* (p. 15), Professor J. Morris Jones refers to a cairn called Bryn yr Ellyllon, which stood at Mold: 'It was believed to be haunted; a spectre clad in gold armour had been seen to enter it. That this story was current before the mound was opened is a fact beyond dispute. In 1832 the cairn was explored. Three hundred cartloads of stones were removed, and beneath them was a skeleton laid at full length, wearing a corslet of beautiful wrought gold, which had been placed on a lining of bronze.'

The idea of the dead warrior from a burial mound presenting Bladud with a drink from a golden cup is based on a story I once heard about the Rillington gold cup now in the British Museum. It seems that several people reported meeting the ghost of an ancient warrior who offered them a drink from a golden cup. In every case they fled in terror. But when the burial mound associated with the haunting was excavated, a golden cup was found inside.

page 14: The magical drink that opens communications with the Otherworld is a common theme in ancient myth and legend. Example: in the *Mabinogion* Keridwen concocts a magical brew in a cauldron designed to give her son spectacular knowledge and wisdom. Three drops splash on to the finger of the boy who is stirring the cauldron; he licks them off and becomes the possessor of great insight and wisdom. From ordinary village boy he passes through a series of transformations and trials, to be reborn at last as the mighty seer and poet Taliesin.

John Matthews, in *Taliesin: Shamanism and the Bardic Mysteries in Britain and Ireland*, writes: 'In another poem, "The Chair of Taliesin", he gives some, if not all, of the ingredients of a sacred drink (akin to that of Eleusis) which was imbibed by all who underwent the rigorous ceremony resulting in a series of visions. In Taliesin's case, this took the form of transformation into bird, beast and fish.'

page 15: I was thinking here of the great avenue and stone circles at Avebury, Wiltshire, England, which were already several millennia old by the time of Bladud.

page 18: We have an example of the entrance to the Otherworld being through the ancient standing stones in 'The Story of the Wasting Sickness of Cú Chulaind' (*Early Irish Myths and Sagas*, translated by Jeffrey Gantz, p. 157): 'Cú Chulaind walked on until he sat down with his back against a stone . . . sleep overcame him. While sleeping he saw two women approach: one wore a green cloak and the other a crimson cloak folded five times, and the one in green smiled at him and began to beat him with a horsewhip. The other woman then came and smiled also and struck him in the same fashion . . .'

This leads, after many ramifications of the story, to Cú Chulaind entering the Otherworld through the doorway to the east, 'where were three trees of brilliant crystal' (p. 168). There he wins the love of one of the Otherworld sisters, Fand, which results in conflict with his flesh-and-blood wife, Emer.

The theme of identical women of the Otherworld presenting a challenge of choice appears in many legends. For example: 'Undine's Kymric Sisters', quoted by John Rhys: *Celtic Folklore: Welsh and Manx* Vol. 1 (pp. 2–11). Here a herdboy falls in love with a beautiful woman who emerges from a lake. He finally wins her consent to marriage, but her father confronts him with two identical women and demands that he choose which is the one he fell in love with.

In the story of Midir and Étaín, 'The Wooing of Étaín' (*Early Irish Myths and Sagas*), when Echu goes to the Otherworld to reclaim his wife Étaín from Midir, he is confronted by fifty women identical to Étaín. He has to choose, and he uses the way she pours liquid from a flask as the means to identify her.

'The Celtic religion was one of the first to evolve a doctrine of immortality. The druids taught that death is only a changing place, and that life goes on with all its forms and goods in another world, a world of the dead which gives up living souls. Therefore, a constant exchange of souls takes place between the two worlds; death in this world brings a soul to the other and death in the other world brings a soul to this world.' Peter Berresford Ellis: *Celtic Inheritance* pp. 10, 11. 'Death (to these) is but the centre of a long life.' Lucan c. 39–65 AD, regarding the Celts.

CHAPTER 3: THE ORACLE OF SUL

page 24: The ancient world relied a great deal on divination as a means of communicating with both ancestors and the Otherworld, and oracles played an important role, too. In *The Waters of the Gap* (p. 35) R. J. Stewart points out that 'prophecy is based upon the belief that the divine powers controlled the flow of energies from the Otherworld and could give information, instruction and actual pre-vision of what was going to happen next . . .' Therefore, places where the divine powers could be contacted would often be associated with oracles, for example at Delphi and Dodona in Greece, Cumae in Italy, and Bath in England. There is a strong tradition of there having been a pre-Roman oracle at Bath.

In ancient times the role of the oracle was often indistinguishable from that of the shaman. Geoffrey Ashe, in his book *The Ancient Wisdom*, writes: 'It is worth while to grasp what a shaman is. Though correctly described as medicine-man and visionary, he is neither a mere purveyor of superstition nor a mere holy lunatic. His initiation and training are rigorous . . . The vocation and the techniques are not confined to males. There are shamanesses as well as shamans. Both have psychic gifts that set them apart. They are certainly mediums of a sort. They are at least able to convince others, and themselves, that they can leave the body and voyage astrally through space, or even travel physically without normal locomotion. A shaman may look barbaric in his ritual gear, representing an animal or bird; he may not suggest a sage exactly; yet he is credible as heir to a heritage of value . . .'

Even before the Romans arrived, the great natural hot spring at Bath 'was revered by the local Iron Age population. They associated it with a native deity called Sul who was probably a god of healing. At this stage the main centre of the population lay 7 km away within the defences of the hillfort at Little Solsbury.' The Romans built a temple to Sulis Minerva – 'a conflation of the pre-Roman deity Sulis and the nearest Roman equivalent, Minerva, the goddess of wisdom and healing'. Barry Cunliffe: *A Guide to the Roman Baths and the Roman Museum.*

page 32: The hot waters of Bath issue from deep fissures and cracks in the rock in the earth's interior.

page 34: Bladud pursues the oracle, but he cannot catch up with her until he humbles himself and asks outright for her help, just as Prince Pwyll in the *Mabinogion* (Pwyll Lord of Dyved) sends servants after Rhiannon, the beautiful young woman in gold he sees riding by; but none can catch up with her, though she appears to be riding slowly. He is forced to pursue her himself at last, but she will not stop even then, until he drops his arrogance and pleads with her.

page 35: Wolves 'are often familiars of the primitive gods of the dead'. In Celtic myth 'a wolf swallows the sun . . . at night' (J. C. Cooper: *An Illustrated Encyclopaedia of Traditional Symbols*).

page 36: The eagle is a solar symbol. 'Thought to be able to fly up to the sun and gaze unwaveringly upon it and to identify with it, the eagle represents the spiritual principle in man which is able to soar heavenwards' (J. C. Cooper as above).

CHAPTER 4: THE WHITE MOUND AND THE ISLAND OF THORNS

page 39: 'Each part of the year was preceded by a great

religious festival commemorating some cult legend. The festival was accompanied by feasting and merry-making, by fairs and marketing, games and sport, and by solemn religious observances . . .' (Anne Ross: *The Pagan Celts*, p. 11). The four great festivals of the Celts were: *Samhain*: 31 October, our Hallowe'en or All Saints, which marks the moment when the gates open between the worlds and the souls of the dead may walk freely on the earth again; *Imbolg*: 1 February, sacred to the goddess Brigit/Brigantia, the female trinity of Britain; *Beltain*: 1 May, the threshold of summer, representing fertility; *Lughnasa*: 1 August, associated with 'the shining one', 'the many-skilled', Lugh, a god of wisdom and light. Lugh is sometimes called 'the stranger from across the sea' which suggests he was not native to Britain. (See *The Celtic Realms* by Myles Dillon and Nora Chadwick, p. 199.)

page 40: The river Thames was called, in ancient times, the Tain – according to E. O. Gordon, *Prehistoric London*, p. 10.

The White Mound, or White Hill, is the ancient name for a great burial mound in prehistoric London. It is traditionally thought to have been where the Tower of London stands now, or possibly St Paul's. There is a powerful story from the *Mabinogion* that the severed head of the great Welsh hero-god Bran was buried there. See 'Branwen Daughter of Llyr' in Jeffrey Gantz: *The Mabinogion*. 'Bran commanded them to cut off his head when he was severely wounded in the battle with Ireland. "Take my head," he said, "and carry it to the White Hill in London." There it was to remain as a source of prophecy and protection for the ages to come.' I have described the burial mound as being covered with white quartz because it was a custom of the very ancient pre-Celtic peoples to do this, for example at New Grange in Ireland. Ravens were associated with Bran, and it is interesting that even today there are ravens at the Tower of London, their wings clipped so that they cannot fly away, the superstition being that as long as they remain there, England will not fall to an enemy. E. O. Gordon in *Prehistoric London* (p. 101) writes: 'We heard about the Bryn Gwyn, or White Mound, as the burial place of Brutus and Imogene in about 1100 BC according to the generally accepted chronology.'

Brutus the Trojan. 'Brutus, son of Sylvius, grandson of Aeneas the Trojan, killed his father while hunting, was expelled from Italy, and settled in Greece. Here the scattered Trojans to the number of seven thousand, besides women and children, placed themselves under his command; and led by him they defeated the Grecian king, Pendrasu (Pandrasus). Pendrasu gave Brutus his daughter (Ignoge/Imogene) to wife and provided 324 ships, laden with all kind of provisions, in which ships the Trojans sailed away to seek their fortunes. An oracle of Diana directed them to an island in the Western Sea, beyond Gaul . . .' (Percy Russell: *The Good Town of Totnes*). The tradition is that Brutus, after many battles and adventures, finally arrived at Totnes in Devon and founded his ruling dynasty, of which Bladud was part.

page 56: Thorn Island, Thorney, was probably where the present Westminster now stands, according to E. O. Gordon, *Prehistoric London*, p. 3. And p. 10: 'About two miles west of the Port of London on Thorney Island was a second Druidic circle, with a College and Sanctuary, where now stands Westminster Abbey . . .' 'One of the cluster of islets in this the shallowest and widest part of the great waterway . . .' The earliest historical account about the circle on Thorney is in connection with the British King Lleuwer Mawr in the second century AD. 'On the site of the Druidic circle Lucius, the Latinised name of the British king, erected a church' (p. 115).

Britain is dotted with the remnants of ancient mazes or labyrinths traditionally called 'Troy towns'. A recent revival of interest in them has brought about the restoration of many. A small journal called *Caerdroia* (Troy Castle), written and published by Jeff and Deb Saward, monitors everything to do with them. No one knows precisely their origins, but the tradition is that they came to Britain with Brutus and his Trojans, the Trojans in their turn having descended from the Minoans in Crete (according to Virgil) who were famous for their labyrinth (Virgil: *The Aeneid*, Book V, p. 144). Fleeing from Troy, Aeneas's father suggests they go to Crete, to Mount Ida, 'the cradle of our race'. 'From Crete came our mighty ancestor, Teucrus.' They settle there for a while but

leave because of plague. There is a magnificent and interesting description of a labyrinthine Trojan game or dance in Book V of *The Aeneid*. (See also *Prehistoric London*.)
page 58: Deer are often Otherworld messengers in Celtic myth. 'One May evening the Lord of Kilmersdon was riding back over Mendip, full of care, for there was a pestilence among his people, when before him through the forest sped the fairy hind. It led him on for more than a mile, and then it vanished, and with it went all his fears and heaviness' (quoted in Kaledon Naddair's book: *Keltic Folk and Faerie Tales*, p. 122).

CHAPTER 5: THE CAULDRON AND THE WHEEL

page 67: The story 'Bricriu's Feast' in *Early Irish Myths and Sagas* (Jeffrey Gantz) tells of a series of famous and bloody battles started over no greater matter than who should be given the 'champion's portion' of meat at the feast.
page 68: The cauldron. See the story 'Branwen Daughter of Llyr' in the *Mabinogion*. In compensation for his brother's insult to the Irish king Bran offers him a magic cauldron 'the property of which is this: take a man who has been slain today and throw him into it, and tomorrow he will fight as well as ever, only he will not be able to speak.' This same cauldron was used against Bran and his men later and was only destroyed by Bran's brother, who had started the trouble in the first place. He sacrificed himself by leaping into it alive and destroying it from the inside.
page 70: Cattle raids were common in Celtic society. Example: 'The Cattle Raid of Froech' (*Early Irish Myths and Sagas*); 'The War for the Bull of Cuailgne (Lady Gregory: *Cuchulain of Muirthemne*).
page 79: A challenge at a feast by a magical stranger is by no means uncommon in Celtic myth. Example: The story of Sir Gawain and the Green Knight (translated by Brian Stone). Here a stranger rides in to Arthur's court and challenges the knights to cut off his head. The catch is that whoever succeeds must present his own neck for a similar blow a year later. The stranger, a being from the Otherworld, can put his

head back on – but the mortal cannot. The same challenge is presented to Cuchulain in an Irish legend. Only he out of all the heroes present has the courage to meet Uath mac Imomain (Terror, son of Great Fear) a year later and allow the three blows that might kill him.

The man who brings the challenge to Bladud appears to be a wildman of the woods. We can still find carvings of this important and potent archetype in our medieval churches. A good book on the subject is: *Green Man: The Archetype of Our Oneness with the Earth* by William Anderson. He is essentially the spirit of wild, untamed nature sent to remind us of our roots in the earth. That this challenger rolls a sun-wheel reminds us also of our roots in the spiritual world. Remember Christ went into the wilderness from time to time. John the Baptist was a 'wildman'. Geoffrey of Monmouth describes a period in Merlin's life when he lived as a wildman of the woods (*Vita Merlini*). Hermits living in mountains or caves have always been thought to be significantly spiritual – though they may look dirty and uncouth.

page 81: The wheel. 'Solar power, the sun revolving in the heavens . . . The wheel is an attribute of all sun gods (and goddesses) and their earthly delegates as sun kings . . . the cycle of life; birth and renewal . . . In Greece the solar wheel depicts the sun chariot of Helios/Apollo . . . the Eye of Zeus . . .' (J. C. Cooper: *Illustrated Encyclopaedia of Traditional Symbols*). Frank Delaney, in *The Celts*, suggests that the circle we see on the Celtic Christian cross is referring back to the sun-wheel of Lugh (p. 103).

CHAPTER 6: CONFRONTATION

Bladud's ancestor Brutus helped Trojan slaves escape to the forests and then sent the Greek king Pandrasus a letter to try to explain to him why he should not hold them. See Geoffrey of Monmouth: *The History of the Kings of Britain* (p. 56): 'Brutus, the leader of those who survived the fall of Troy, sends his greeting to King Pandrasus. The people sprung from the illustrious line of Dardanus have withdrawn to the hidden depths of the forests, for they have found it intolerable that they should be treated in your kingdom otherwise than as the purity of their noble blood demands. They have preferred to keep themselves alive on flesh and herbs, as though they were wild beasts, and have their liberty, rather than remain under the yoke of your slavery, even if pampered there by every kind of wealth. If, in the pride of your power, this offends you, then you should not count it against them. Rather you should pardon them, for it is the natural aim of everyone in captivity to strive to return to his former dignity. Be moved to pity for them, and deign to bestow upon them their lost liberty . . .' (translation by Lewis Thorpe).

CHAPTER 7: THE TALKING HEADS

page 89: The Druids, or Celtic priests, on the whole used sacred oak groves for their religious rites. The stone circles so many people associate with them these days were already more than a thousand years old before the Celts came to Britain.

Crystal lenses have been found from ancient times and there is a strong possibility that 'sacred fire' was lit in this way from the sun's concentrated rays.

page 90: Passing through fire for purification is an age-old initiatory custom. That it is possible to walk on fire in certain transcendent states is well attested in modern times by witnesses of Hindu rituals.

Fire was an important part of the great Druid festivals. In the *Journal of the Research into Lost Knowledge Society* (*R.I.L.K.O.*) No. 40, Spring/Summer 1992, Eileen Goodchild concludes, after reading *The Firewalk of Ancient Ireland* by R. A. S. MacAlister, 'that a ritual firewalk was carried out by adepts in honour of the sun goddess . . .'

page 92: Shape-changing is a feature of ancient Celtic shamanism. Example: When Keridwen pursues Gwion, first he changes into a hare and she pursues him as a hound, then he changes into a fish and she pursues him as an otter. He becomes a bird and she pursues him as a hawk. Finally he becomes a grain of wheat on a threshing floor and she becomes a hen and pecks him up. Nine months later he is reborn as the great and magical poet Taliesin. See Taliesin in the *Mabinogion*, as translated by Lady Charlotte Guest (p. 264).

In *Keltic Folk and Faerie Tales*, Kaledon Naddair mentions that the name 'Blaidd' means wolf, and occurs in several personal names including 'Bleiddudd' (which is another spelling for the name Bladud). 'The wolf stands beside the Keltic god Kernunos on the Gundestrop cauldron. Odin is accompanied by wise wolves in Scandinavian lore; in Greece the Lykomanean Zeus had a winter wolf-form, and his son Apollo (the young Sun God) was born from the Wolf Goddess Leto' (Naddair, p. 125).

page 94: Very little is known about the actual rituals of the Celts. We get most of our information from the Romans who conquered them centuries later than the time of Bladud. Pliny writes: 'They call the mistletoe by a name meaning the all-healing. Having made preparation for sacrifice . . . they bring thither two white bulls, whose horns are bound then for the first time. Clad in a white robe, the priest ascends the tree and cuts the mistletoe with a golden sickle, and it is received by others in a white cloak. Then they kill the victims, praying that God will render this gift of his propitious to those to whom he has granted it' (quoted by Anne Ross in *The Pagan Celts*, p. 113).

page 94, 95: The severed human head. 'The Celts like many other barbarian peoples hunted human heads. We know this from the skulls found in Celtic hill-forts . . . These severed heads would serve as trophies testifying to the military prowess of their owners; and, at the same time, the powers, believed to be in the human head, would act protectively and keep evil from the fortress or the home, while ensuring positive good luck and success.' Then: 'The Celts believed that the human head was the seat of the soul, the essence of being . . . It could remain alive after the death of the body; it could avert evil and convey prophetic information; it could move and act and speak and sing; it could tell tales and entertain; it presided over the Otherworld feast' (Anne Ross: *The Pagan Celts*, pp. 121, 122).

See the story of Bran in the *Mabinogion* where, in the story of 'Branwen Daughter of Llyr', Bran's head went on talking and prophesying for eighty years and was finally buried in the White Mound at Trinovantum (London).

page 99: Britain was often called the White Island, or the Island of the Mighty, or Albion, in the ancient stories. The Greeks called it the Pretanic Isles. But Bladud, looking back, would have seen the famous white chalk cliffs of the southern coast and would no doubt at this moment have thought of it as the White Island.

CHAPTER 8: LEAVING HOME

page 104: The ancient Celts had a special regard for trinity, and the mystical number of three-times-three permeates Celtic mythology and art. Diogenes Laertius (c. 3/2 century BC) specifically mentions that the druids taught in the form of triads – sentences of three phrases – and held the number three to be mystical. It is perhaps due to this pre-Christian Celtic tradition of the trinity that the Holy Trinity of the Christians 'achieved a prominent position in Celtic symbolism.' (Peter Berresford Ellis: *Celtic Inheritance*, pp. 15, 16).

page 105: Massallia – the city that is now called Marseilles. It was founded by the Phoenicians well before Bladud's time.

CHAPTER 9: THE SIBYL OF CUMAE

page 107: Cumae is on the coast of Italy, very near Naples. The cave of the famous sibyl and the ruins of the temples can still be visited today. At the time of Bladud this area was a Greek colony, part of Magna Graecia. (I am aware that no one spoke of Britain, Greece or Italy in those days, for there was no sense of nationhood as we know it. I have used these terms for convenience.)

page 111: 'In the fifth century the Sibyl of Cumae, a priestess of Apollo, offered to sell King Tarquin nine books of prophecy. Twice the King refused, finding the price too high. Each time the priestess tossed three books into the fire

356

and doubled the price of those remaining. Tarquin finally bought the last three which were preserved in the Temple of the Capitol, and called the Sibylline Books. They contained instructions for gaining the favours of foreign gods, Greek and Oriental' (*Larousse Mythology*, p. 233).

The story of the handful of sand and the sibyl's great age can be found in Virgil's *Aeneid* and Thomas Bulfinch's *The Golden Age of Myth and Legend*.

page 112: 'In her cave she was accustomed to inscribe on leaves gathered from the trees the names and fates of individuals . . . But if perchance at the opening of the door the wind rushed in and dispersed the leaves the sibyl gave no aid to restoring them again, and the oracle was irreparably lost' (Thomas Bulfinch: *The Golden Age of Myth and Legend*, p. 336).

page 116: After the Trojan war, many Trojans fled and became scattered about the Mediterranean. Virgil's *Aeneid* describes the journeys and adventures of Aeneas, his love and desertion of Dido of Carthage, his journey to the Underworld with the Sibyl of Cumae, his founding of mighty Rome. The story of the golden bough and the journey of Aeneas to the Underworld from which I have derived Bladud's similar journey is to be found in *Aeneid* Book VI (translated by W. F. Jackson Knight, first pub. Penguin 1956).

page 126: The story of Persephone and Hades can be found in the *Larousse Mythology*, p. 175. Persephone (also known as Kore) was the daughter of Demeter who represented in Greek myth the fertility of the earth. One day the young Persephone was gathering flowers in a field when the earth opened and the Lord of the Underworld, Hades, appeared, seized her and dragged her down to his kingdom. Mourning her daughter, Demeter blasted the earth with her suffering. In order to save the earth, Zeus sent Hermes down to the Underworld to plead for the return of Persephone. Hades pretended to comply, but meanwhile tempted her to eat a few pomegranate seeds. 'Now this fruit was a symbol of marriage and the effect of eating it was to render the union of man and wife indissoluble.' Persephone was therefore bound to Hades and could not return to her mother. A compromise was eventually worked out whereby Persephone spent a third of the year with Hades (our winter), and two-thirds with her mother (our spring and summer).

CHAPTER 10: IMOGENE AND ATHENE

page 131: Athene was said to have sprung fully armed from the head of her father Zeus. She was the stern defender of Athens, but also a goddess of intelligence. She took the Greek side in the famous war with Troy described by Homer in the *Iliad*. When the Romans adapted the Greek pantheon of gods and goddesses, their Minerva was thought to be the nearest equivalent to Athene. When the Romans established themselves at Bath, England c. AD43–AD410, they found an already existing temple and healing sanctuary dedicated to the ancient British goddess Sul. They equated Sul with Minerva. We can still see the remnants of their temple to Sulis-Minerva at Bath.

For a description of the Panathenaic Festival Bladud witnessed see *Larousse Mythology* p. 117, and the magnificent frieze depicting it taken from the Acropolis in Athens and currently in the British Museum (the Elgin Marbles).

page 131: 'The oldest name under which classical authors commonly refer to the British Isles is the Pretanic Islands, a name probably derived from a Celtic root (see *The Celtic Realms*, p. 36).

Rhyton: tall ceremonial vase for ritual use.

page 135: The prince comes from the country Thessaly. In *The Penguin Atlas of Ancient History* (p. 48) there is mention of the 'Thessalian League'. The Bible refers to Paul's letters to the Thessalonians. There is a city in Macedonia called Thessaloniki from which the Pauline word is derived.

CHAPTER 11: DELPHI

page 143: Delphi was originally the sacred place of the earth goddess Gaia before Apollo made it his own. The myth goes that Apollo fought and defeated the mighty Python that lurked in these regions and founded his sanctuary in a sacred grove. 'The place was deserted and Apollo was wondering where he would find priests for his new cult, when he perceived in the distance on the dark sea a ship manned by some Cretans. Immediately assuming the form of a dolphin, he sped after the ship and leapt on to the deck . . .' He brought the ship to the shores of Crissa, resumed his own form, and told the Cretans they would remain in that place and become his priests. The name Delphi is derived from the word dolphin. The Oracle of Delphi, the Pythoness, drew people from all over the world and made many very famous pronouncements. It became a tremendously important cult centre and is still today a centre of tourist pilgrimage (*Larousse Mythology* p. 123).

page 148: A great deal has been discovered about the dolphin lately; it is recognised that the animals are very intelligent and often friendly towards humans. In ancient Greek art we find depictions of humans riding on dolphins. Recently a friendly dolphin became famous off the coast of Ireland and many people have swum with him. Extraordinary healings are reported to have taken place after such contact. Dr Horace Dobbs is doing a research project using wild dolphins to treat the clinically depressed.

CHAPTER 12: THE TOMB

page 161: There is a good description of ancient Greek wedding tradition in *Life in Greece in Ancient Times* by Paul Werner (trans. by David Macrae, pub. Minerva, Geneve 1978/81) p. 9: 'in the Greek mind, each dead person was a god, and was capable of using his power, for good or evil, depending on the degree of respect or disdain which his kin showed for him.' And '. . . a stranger entering the family had to be initiated into the forms of domestic worship and be presented to the family ancestors.' Our tradition of the white wedding dress with veil, and the tradition of carrying the bride over the threshold, derive from the ancient Greeks.

CHAPTER 13: THE OLYMPIC GAMES

page 175: In the scene within the Temple of Athene I was thinking of holographs that, when divided, yield a complete image repeated, rather than half an image. I was also thinking of the story of the Sorcerer's Apprentice.

page 177: For this chapter I consulted a very readable and interesting account, *The Ancient Olympic Games* by Judith Swadding (British Museum Publications, 1980/1987). When I visited Olympia in the Peloponnese I was struck by the number of wild tortoises there.

The first Games were held in 776 BC so the event would have been already established by the time of Bladud's visit, which I envisage sometime between 700 and 500 BC. I was interested to read that our phrase 'to start from scratch' comes from the scratch mark from which the runners at Olympia commenced their race.

page 178: Aphrodite, the beautiful goddess of love, saw the Trojan Anchises on the slopes of Mount Ida and desired him. She disguised herself as a mortal woman and made love to him. Afterwards she revealed herself in her full splendour as the goddess and told him they would have a son who would be called Aeneas. It is this father, Anchises, whom Aeneas seeks in the Underworld with the Sibyl of Cumae. As Aeneas is the ancestor of Bladud, the implication is that Bladud has something of Aphrodite in his veins as well. Because of this love for Anchises, Aphrodite supports the Trojans in the war against Greece. As Athene supports the Greeks, and is much more of a warrior, Aphrodite's assistance does not in fact win the war for her protégés. See *Larousse Mythology* p. 148.

CHAPTER 14: RETURN TO TRINOVANTUM

page 181: Divorce was possible in Celtic lands, but it was also possible to take a secondary wife (see Myles Dillon & Nora Chadwick: *The Celtic Realms*, p. 132).

page 190: 'The practice of placing one's children in the care of foster-parents was a normal feature of Irish society. Sometimes children were fostered for love, but usually a fosterage-fee was paid . . .' And: 'The time of fosterage ended for boys at seventeen, for girls at fourteen, and they returned home. But the tie of fosterage remained close: there was an obligation on the part of the children to support their foster-parents in old age, and those who had been fostered together were bound in close companionship. The tragic climax of Táin Bó Cualnge is Cú Chulainn's fight with his foster-brother' (*The Celtic Realms*, p. 133). Lady Gregory tells the story of the Bull of Cuailgne in *Cuchulain of Muirthemne* (pub. Colin Smythe 1902/1984).

page 191: 'No man who was physically blemished was eligible for kingship' (*The Celtic Realms*, p. 126).

page 199: The tree and the magical fountain/spring/well at its roots is highly charged with spiritual significance in Celtic myth. See 'The Lady and the Fountain' in the *Mabinogion*. See also the well and the golden bowl in the story of 'Manawydan Son of Llŷr (in the *Mabinogion*). Jeffrey Gantz in the introduction to his translation of the *Mabinogion* quotes from the story 'Peredur Son of Evrawg': 'On the bank of the river he saw a tall tree: from roots to crown one half was aflame and the other green with leaves.' 'Of all the strange and supernatural images in the *Mabinogion*,' Gantz writes, 'none captures the essence of the tale so concisely as does this vertically halved tree, the green leaves symbolising the rich and concrete beauty of the mortal world, the flames symbolising the flickering, shadowy uncertainty of the Otherworld.'

Prophetic and revelatory dreams are important in Celtic myths. See 'The Dream of Òengus' (Jeffrey Gantz: *Early Irish Myths and Sagas*).

CHAPTER 15: THE SWINEHERD

page 206: Ogham writing: ancient British and Irish alphabet of 'twenty characters', each letter named after a plant or a tree. Appears to us as a series of groups of dots and strokes.

page 211: For the story of Bladud as a swineherd I here quote extensively from the book *Bladud of Bath* by Howard C. Levis, pp. 90, 91, which in turn quotes 'The History and Memoirs of the Bath: containing . . . An Account of King

Bladud, said to be the first Founder of the Baths . . . By Robert Pierce, M.D. near Sixty Years Physician in Bath. London: Printed for Henry Hammond Bookseller in Bath. M.DCC.XIII' of which 'The Conclusion' is signed 'Rob. Pierce', and is dated 'Bath, March 25th, 1697'.

'Bladud, eldest Son of Lud-Hudibras (then King of Britain and eighth from Brute), having spent eleven years at Athens in the Study of the Liberal Arts and Sciences . . . came home a Leper . . . and for that reason (was) shut up, that he might not infect others. He, impatient of his confinement, chose rather a mean Liberty than a Royal Restraint, and contrived his Escape in Disguise, and went very remote from his Father's Court, and into an untravell'd part of the Country . . . He was entertain'd in Service at Swainswicke (a small Village, two Miles from this City (Bath). His Business . . . was to take Care of the Pigs, which he was to drive from place to place, for their Advantage in Feeding upon Beech-masts, Acorns, and Haws . . . He thus driving his Swine from place to place, observ'd some of the Herd, in very cold Weather, to go down from the Side of the Hill into an Alder-moor, and thence to return, cover'd with black Mud . . .

'He . . . made observation: that whereas those filthy Creatures, by their foul Feeding, and nasty Lying, are subject to Scabs, and foul Scurfs, and Eruptions on their Skin, some of his Herd that were so, after a while, became whole and smooth, by their often wallowing in this Mud.

'Upon this he considers with himself, why he should not receive the same Benefit by the same Means; he trys it, and succeeded in it; and when he found himself cured of his Leprosie, declares who he was.'

page 214: 'The boar was one of the most powerful animals for the Kelts . . . One of the mightiest magical boars in the Gaelic traditions is Tork Forbartach, and in a Fenian Tale it is said: "The description of that huge boar was enough to cause mortal terror, for he was blue-black, with rough bristles . . . grey, horrible, without ears, without tail, without testicles and his teeth standing out long and horrid outside its big head . . . and it raised the mane of its back on high so that a plump wild apple would have stuck on each of its rough bristles"' (Kaledon Naddair: *Keltic Folk and Faerie Tales*, p. 120).

In Irish tales Diarmuid was hunted to death by one Beinn Gulbain (see Lady Gregory: *Gods and Fighting Men*). In the *Mabinogion* King Arthur himself joined in the hunt for the fearsome Twrch Trwyth (see Jeffrey Gantz: the story of 'How Culhwch won Olwen'). Yet sows were often the indicators of the presence of the Great Mother. It was a sow that led Gwydyon to find his adopted son Llew Llaw Gyffes as a wounded eagle in a tree in the story of 'Math Son of Mathonwy'.

page 217: The wild mountainous regions of North Wales where indigenous tribes continued to exist independently long after the rest of the country was overrun by invaders from the Continent.

page 223: There are many Celtic myths about mortals seeing beautiful women emerging from and walking on the surface of a lake. Example: Undine's Kymric Sisters (see John Rhys: *Celtic Folklore: Welsh and Manx*, vol. 1, pp. 2–11). Many times young and golden women, a visible form of the sun goddess, inspire love and bring help to someone, on a spiritual journey. Example: 'The Countess and the Fountain' in the *Mabinogion*.

CHAPTER 16: THE HEALING

page 238: The Celts believed so strongly in reincarnation, it was not uncommon to expect to pay back debts in some future life.

CHAPTER 17: DEPARTURE AND ARRIVAL

page 259: 'While still a youth, Bladud the great, 10th king of Britain spent much time at Athens in Greece in order to make a careful study of philosophy. On the death of his father Ruthudibras he returned home after several years of study, bringing with him teachers of the four principal sciences that for the future his kingdom might enjoy the advantage of their instructions. According to Merlin he founded a school of literature for these men at Stamford that they might there teach the liberal arts, and to it they drew a considerable audience . . .' (quoted by Levis in *Bladud of Bath* from John Bale's *Chronicle*, 1548).

In *Stamford Myths and Legends* by Martin Smith (pub. Paul Watkins) we read: 'King Bladud, the Trojan King of ancient Albion (or Britain) and the father of King Lear, founded the first university in the world at Stamford (Lincolnshire). The event was first recorded by the venerable sixth-century wizard, Merlin of Caledonia, the "British Apollo", and was elaborated by later writers. After attending the famous schools in Athens, Bladud – who was a descendant of Aeneas of the Trojan Wars – returned to Albion with many wise and learned teachers to establish a place of learning. On the banks of the Welland they found the sylvan setting appropriate for such an illustrious academic institution . . . Athenian style temples and halls were built by the Welland . . . The university was later occupied by the Druids . . . and closed down by Pope Gregory through Augustine of Canterbury in 605 AD because the students were "engaged in heretical practices, particularly Pelagianism – a belief which denied original sin and promoted free will."'

This story is also mentioned by John Higgins in the *First Parte of the Mirour for Magistrates*, 1575, and by Michael Drayton in *Poly-Olbion*, Song viii, 1622. Also by John Hardyng: *Chronicle*, c. 1465.

page 261: Many ancient civilisations, including the Greeks, had water-clocks. The passing of time was measured by the regulated dripping of water from one container to another.

page 262: Note that the ancients knew many things that were later forgotten or denied by medieval scholars. Example: Anaxagoras the Greek, who lived before Socrates, knew that the moon's light was derived from the sun and that eclipses of the moon were due to its being screened by the earth. He taught that the heavenly bodies were red-hot stones – not gods – and that the true god was an abstract force, not in human form (Richard Olson: *Science Deified and Science Defied*, p. 79, Univ. of California Press 1982). Aristarchus of Samos knew the earth went round the sun – yet more than a millennium later people were being burned at the stake for suggesting this 'heresy'.

CHAPTER 18: BADDON

page 263: Little Solsbury Hill near Batheaston (near Bath) was an Iron Age hill-fort. Hard evidence dates it back to 300 BC, but there is no reason to believe that it was not occupied before then. It seems possible to me that Bladud built his town there.

Caervaddon is an ancient name for Bath. Baddon is the Welsh name (see Howard C. Levis: *Bladud of Bath*, p. 13). On other pages of Levis's book, other ancient names are given for Bath: p. 29 Kaerbadus (castle of Badus); p. 30 Blade; p. 33 Caerbadu; p. 34 Caerbadon.

page 268: Geoffrey of Monmouth writes (*The History of the Kings of Britain*, Penguin, p. 80): 'Hudibras's son Bladud finally succeeded him and ruled the kingdom for twenty years. It was he who built the town of Kaerbadum, which is now called Bath, and who constructed the hot baths there which are so suited to the needs of mortal men. He chose the goddess Minerva as the tutelary deity of the baths. In her temple he lit fires which never went out and which never fell away into ash, for the moment that they began to die down they were turned into balls of stone.' As there are coalmines at Radstock not twenty miles from Bath, I can't help thinking Bladud must have discovered the use of coal.

CHAPTER 20: 'SCAR-FACE'

page 279: In the case of the young woman who appears to Yaruk in two places at once, I was thinking of the phenomenon of the Doppelgänger. 'The novelist John Cowper Powys could, seemingly, target his Doppelgänger at will and appeared before his friend Theodore Dreiser at a specified time in New York one evening in the 1920s' (this incident is quoted in an article on the phenomenon of the psychic double by Paul Newman in *Prediction*, April 1992). There have been many well attested sightings of the contemporary Indian 'holy man' Sai Baba appearing in more than one place at once. A friend of mine in hospital in Jordon saw him beside her bed when he was in fact still in India.

Everyone agreed that her recovery from the accident that broke her spine was miraculous.

Another widely discussed psychic phenomenon is the experience of being made love to by an incubus or a succubus. Stan Gooch deals with this most interestingly in his book *Creatures from Inner Space* (Rider, London, 1984).

page 284: 'The bear is in legend King of all the Animals of the North . . . The Kaledonian bear was also a shamanistic guise for the early Pictish Myrddin (Merlin) as a Wildman Prophet . . . The proud North European warriors often invoked their tribal and personal animal totems before going into battle. This would sometimes involve them dressing in bear skins and turning ber-serk and fighting furiously . . . As bear-cult sites . . . have been discovered throughout Keltic lands, it is not surprising that people still encounter spectral/phantom bears (e.g. on Shipworth Common, and in the Jewel Chamber in London, etc.) for they will still come through from the Otherworlds . . .' (Kaledon Naddair: *Keltic Folk and Faerie Tales*, p. 124).

'To survey the role of bears in religion, ancient and not so ancient, is to catch glimpses of a very strong magic . . . immensely formidable and not-quite-animal . . .' (Geoffrey Ashe: *Ancient Wisdom*, p. 147).

CHAPTER 21: THE FLIGHT OF THE EAGLE KING

page 299: 'What is a totem beast? It is an animal emblematic of a tribe or person which has its reality and draws its power from the Otherworld. A tribe might acquire a totem by virtue of a famous ancestor's exploits or through some inherent affinity with a beast. Such a totem would appear as a standard in battle and play an important role in the tribal mysteries . . . In the *Mabinogion* . . . the totem beast is an Otherworldly helper whose resonance is with the ancestral source of wisdom: the adoption of such a totem is a powerful link with the Otherworld, conveying not only the virtues and qualities of that beast to the person under its aegis but also contact with ancestral levels. The totem beast is not to be confused with an animal of the same species which can be hunted or eaten for food; it is a beast of the Platonic realms, having archetypal reality' (Caitlin Matthews: *Mabon and the Mysteries of Britain*, p. 131).

page 302: The Druid Mog Ruith 'is accredited with being a powerful sorcerer, and with the ability of causing a tempest or creating a cloud by a mere breath. In the story of "The Siege of Druim Damhghaire" he wears . . . a bird-dress, which is described in the following terms: "Mog Ruith's skin of the hornless, dun-coloured bull was brought to him then, and his speckled bird-dress with its winged flying, and his druidic gear besides. And he rose up, in company with the fire, into the air and the heavens"' (Anne Ross: *The Pagan Celts*, pp. 114, 115).

page 303: In her interesting analysis of the story of 'Culhwch and Olwen' from the *Mabinogion* in her book *Mabon and the Mysteries of Britain*, Caitlin Matthew writes (p. 101): 'Arthur sends Gwrhyr, who knows the speech of beasts, to parley with the swine; he learns that the boar was once a king, the son of Prince Taredd, condemned to boar shape for his sins. This legend has a direct parallel in Irish tradition where a druid, Cian Mac Cainte, bewitched his pupils into beasts of the chase and would hunt them himself, in the form of a hound. The Children of Turenn struck him with his own magic wand and turned him into a black pig, whence the *Clad na Muice* or Black Pig's Dike in Northern Ireland – the great defensive earthwork which can be seen today – which was thrown up by the fury of Cian the druid in his rampage across Ireland, until he plunged into the sea off Donegal – where the dike ends.'

CHAPTER 22: FALL OF THE SKY-STONE

page 308: For the story of a battle won by flying men see my novel: *Guardians of the Tall Stones* (Arrow 1986).

CHAPTER 23: THE WINGED MAN

page 342: 'Bladud was a most ingenious man who encouraged

necromancy throughout the kingdom of Britain. He pressed on with his experiments and finally constructed a pair of wings for himself and tried to fly through the upper air. He came down on top of the Temple of Apollo in the town of Trinovantum and was dashed into countless fragments. After Bladud had met his fate in this way, his son Leir was raised to the kingship. Leir ruled the country for sixty years' (Geoffrey of Monmouth: *The History of the Kings of Britain* II xx, Penguin edition, p. 81). For the story of Lear (Leir) in his later years see Shakespeare's play *King Lear*.

Book List

Anderson, William: *Green Man: The Archetype of our Oneness with the Earth*. HarperCollins, 1990

Ashe, Geoffrey: *The Ancient Wisdom: A Quest for the Source of Mystic Knowledge*. Macmillan, 1977

Bulfinch, Thomas: *The Golden Age of Myth and Legend*. Harrap, 1917

Campbell, Joseph: *The Masks of God: Occidental Mythology*. Penguin, 1982

Chadwick, Nora: *The Celts*. Penguin, 1971

Chant, Joy: *The High Kings: Arthur's Celtic Ancestors*. Allen & Unwin, 1983

Cooper, J. C.: *An Illustrated Encyclopaedia of Traditional Symbols*. Thames & Hudson, 1978

Cunliffe, B.: *Iron Age Communities in Britain: An Account of England, Scotland and Wales from the 7th Century BC until the Roman Conquest*. Routledge, 1974

Cunliffe, B.: *The Roman Baths*. Bath Archaeological Trust, 1978

Delaney, Frank: *The Celts*. Guild Publishing, 1986

Dillon, Myles and Nora Chadwick: *The Celtic Realms*. Cardinal, 1973

Dillon, Myles: *Irish Sagas*. Mercian Press, Dublin, 1968

Eliade, Mircea: *Shamanism: Archaic Techniques of Ecstasy*. Princeton, 1964

Ellis, Peter Berresford: *Celtic Inheritance*. Muller, 1985

Gantz, Jeffrey: *Early Irish Myths and Sagas*. Penguin, 1981

Gantz, Jeffrey: *The Mabinogion*. Penguin, 1976

Geoffrey of Monmouth: *The History of the Kings of Britain* (translated by Lewis Thorpe). Penguin, 1966

Gordon, E. O.: *Prehistoric London: Its Mounds and Circles*. Covenant, 1946

Gregory, Lady: *Cuchulain of Muirthemne*. Colin Smythe, 1970

Gregory, Lady: *Gods and Fighting Men*. Colin Smythe, 1970

Guest, Lady Charlotte: *The Mabinogion*. J. M. Dent, 1906

Hogg, A. H. A.: *A Guide to the Hill-Forts of Britain*. Paladin, 1975

Larousse Encyclopaedia of Mythology. Hamlyn, 1960

Levis, Howard C.: *Bladud of Bath*. West Country Edition, Bath, 1973

Mackenzie, Donald A.: *The World's Heritage of Epical, Heroic and Romantic Literature*, in 2 volumes. Gresham, 1918

Matthews, Caitlin: *Mabon and the Mysteries of Britain: An Exploration of the Mabinogion*. Arkana, 1987

Matthews, John: *A Celtic Reader: Selections from Celtic Legend, Scholarship and Story*. Aquarian Press, 1991

Matthews, John and Chesca Potter: *The Aquarian Guide to Legendary London*. Aquarian Press, 1990

Matthews, Caitlin and John: *The Western Way: A Practical Guide to the Western Mystery Tradition*, in 2 volumes. Arkana, 1985

Matthews, John: *Taliesin: Shamanism and the Bardic Mysteries in Britain and Ireland*. Aquarian Press, 1991

Naddair, Kaledon: *Keltic Folk and Faerie Tales: Their Hidden Meaning Explored*. Rider, 1987

R.I.L.K.O. Journal (Research into Lost Knowledge). Orpington, Kent

Rhys, John: *Celtic Folklore: Welsh and Manx*, in 2 volumes. Republished Wildwood House, 1980

Rolleston, T. W.: *Myths and Legends of the Celtic Race*. Harrap, 1911

Ross, Anne: *The Pagan Celts*. Batsford, 1970

Russell, Percy: *The Good Town of Totnes*. Devonshire Association for the Advancement of Science, Literature & Art, Exeter, 1964

Smith, Martin: *Stamford Myths and Legends*. Paul Watkins, Lincolnshire, 1991

Stewart, R. J.: *The Waters of the Gap: Magic, Mythology and the Celtic Heritage*. Arcania, Ashgrove Press, Bath, 1989

Stewart, R. J. and John Matthews: *Legendary Britain: An Illustrated Journey*. Blandford, 1989

Stone, Brian: Translation of *Sir Gawain and the Green Knight*. Penguin, 1959

Swadding, Judith: *The Ancient Olympic Games*. British Museum Publications, 1980

Werner, Paul: *Life in Greece in Ancient Times* (translated by David Macrae). Minerva, Geneva, 1978

Wentz, W. Y. Evans: *The Fairy-Faith in Celtic Countries*. Colin Smythe, 1977

Whitehouse, David and Ruth: *Archaeological Atlas of the World*. Thames & Hudson, 1975